PENGUIN BOOKS
ENRIQUE THE BLACK

Danny Jalil majored in Multimedia Arts and studied Creative Writing and Screenwriting at LaSalle-SIA College of the Arts, during which time he wrote numerous short stories and film scripts.

His short film comedy *Spun* was nominated for the merit prize at the National University of Singapore Student's Union (NUSSU) Inter-Tertiary Video Festival.

He has also written movie reviews and conducted interviews for *First Magazine* and has had his works published in *Singapore's Greatest Comics* (Nice One Entertainment) and *ACTOR* (A Commitment To Our Roots).

His novel *The Machine Boy* was a winner of NAC's Beyond Words: Young and Younger Award and published by *Straits Times Press* and he has also written the graphic novel *Lieutenant Adnan* and *The Last Regiment*, illustrated by artist Zaki Ragman, published by Asiapac Books.

Enrique the Black

Danny Jalil

PENGUIN BOOKS
An imprint of Penguin Random House

PENGUIN BOOKS

USA | Canada | UK | Ireland | Australia
New Zealand | India | South Africa | China | Southeast Asia

Penguin Books is part of the Penguin Random House group of companies
whose addresses can be found at global.penguinrandomhouse.com

Published by Penguin Random House SEA Pte Ltd
9, Changi South Street 3, Level 08-01,
Singapore 486361

First published in Penguin Books by Penguin Random House SEA 2021

Copyright © Danny Jalil 2021

ISBN 9789814954051

Typeset in Adobe Garamond Pro by Manipal Technologies Limited, Manipal

www.penguin.sg

Foreword

It all started innocently enough with a book.

I stumbled on this book called *Malay Weddings Don't Cost $50*, by Hidayah Amin, at a book store. Tongue-in-cheek, it detailed a lot of fun stuff about Malay culture.

Flipping to the end was a segment on Malay heroes, you know, the usual Hang Tuah and the lot. And then there was the picture of the guy who was allegedly the first Malay man to circumnavigate the globe. This intrigued me.

What further intrigued me, was his name. Enrique. The. Black. Enrique the Black? Cool! That sounded mysterious, and I wanted to find out more about him, and discovered he was enslaved by the Portuguese during the capture of Malacca in the year 1511, and was under the care of the explorer Ferdinand Magellan, and was Magellan's loyal slave and interpreter. Magellan himself was a kind master, a man Enrique respected.

Some things, you don't find. Some things, and some ideas, they find you, they consume you, until you have no choice but to fight back and consume them. Ideas are shapeless things, and the creative's job of course, is to give form.

It was less than a month later that I decided to give Enrique form, in my own way, through the filter of my personal zeitgeist, through my own creative lens.

In that month when I was casually researching Enrique, I found out he was already given prior form in the Malay epic novel *Panglima Awang*, published in 1957. That was the name given to Enrique by

Harun Aminurrashid, the novel's author. Enrique's true name, is however, lost in the annals of history.

So I searched and found the novel in the library. I got the English translation, and read the book. In the author's bio, I found out Mr Harun lived in Telok Kurau, in the eastern side of Singapore. I lived in Kembangan, a neighbourhood only twenty minutes away.

There was already a commonality there, we were neighbours, separated by half a century. Reading the novel, I had this distinct feeling that Mr Harun too was a product of the zeitgeist of his times.

Panglima Awang read like a classic black and white P. Ramlee movie, painting people in shades of absolute black and purest white. The Portuguese were VILLAINS, and the oppressed people of Malacca were HEROES loyal to their Sultan, though he was still a corrupt man.

Panglima meant warrior, and Awang meant young fellow, according to Mr Harun's own intro. But just as Mr Harun was affected by the cultural influences of his time, perhaps I too am a product of mine.

My heroes and villains live in the grey, where no hero is absolute, and no villain is without a redeeming quality, and this is how I shall choose to write my rendition of Enrique the Black.

Perhaps there was a subliminal agenda with Mr Harun. He was living in a Singapore that was still part of the Federated Malay States, and Malay pride was at an all-time high. Many a time in his novel does he paint the heroes, the Malays, Awang himself, with such a heroic light that it seemed rather one-sided and sadly a tad unrealistic in current times.

Awang fights and wins, loves and never loses his lovers. His is the wise, brave, magnificent, handsome Awang, a hero of multiple adjectives. I hope not to do that. I hope all the heroes and villains and everybody else is evenly represented.

But in order to make narrative interesting, I have decided to represent the story not exactly according to history. If I were to be a slave to history, I would have just written a non-fiction book. But no, I am in the business of making exciting stories, and in order to make this story go through the paces, I shall be taking many liberties with facts and figures, but endeavour to make the emotions truthful.

My spirit of the times includes such movies as *Gladiator*, *The Last Samurai*, *Apocalypto*, the TV *series Shogun*, *Marco Polo*, shows that take place in history, but are not rooted in pure historical fact.

So, what does indeed happen to the first Malay man to circle the world? We may never know, but not knowing is part of the fun.

The Author
April 2020

Prologue
May, 1521

Enrique walked along the shore with Rajah Charles, his head low, constantly bowing to hear what the old ruler was saying. They stopped and the Rajah looked up at the young man, then averted his gaze to the wide sea.

'If I could cry an ocean for him, I would,' Rajah Charles said, thinking about Magellan.

'All the seas cannot contain my tears,' Enrique told him. He wondered how long it would be before they would look for him. The expedition seemed to have done exploring, they were in a nothing place in a nothing land with nothing left to invigorate their spirits.

'I appreciate these stories you have been telling me, Enrique. About your fleet's journey here. But you have told me nothing about yourself. How did a boy from Malacca come to be with the Spanish?'

Enrique sighed and took a deep breath. The breeze grew colder, and he reckoned it dried the tears forming in his eyes.

'I was just a boy when they took me,' he began.

PART ONE

1511 A.D.

(GAROTO)

1

The hammer struck the curve of the blade again.

His father raised the hot blade, its glowing iron embers carving deep canyons of shadow upon his face.

The boy flinched, taking a step back, only to realize he was on his knees. He tried to be brave, consoling himself with the knowledge that his father and therefore the wavy blade, also known as the keris, was a distance from him.

In one swift motion his father bridged the distance between him and the blade. Now the boy did not flinch or attempt to move.

'Making the blade is a skill that will take time, son, but I will teach you to master this art.' His father motioned his hand in waves, in sync with the curves of the blade before he placed the keris in a tray of water. The blade fizzled, steam rising off its curves, hissing as though it were glad to be relieved of its heat.

'The keris is alive, can you hear that? The water sets it free,' the boy's father raised the keris out of the tray, traces of warm water cascading down his arm.

His father's panjak rested his shaping hammer on the ground. The sun began to set, and in the approaching dark the glow of iron in the kiln was a second sun.

The boy stood up, regarding the materials with a studiousness that made his father beam with pride. He placed the supit aside. The keris was still raw and crude, but now had its basic form.

'Making a keris, it's like raising a child,' his father placed a hand on his shoulder. 'If the blade is stubborn, you beat it until it takes shape.'

The boy shrugged, knowing full well what his father meant.

The next day his father and the panjak continued making the keris, refining the blade's curves into something more than just crude metal. The curves had beauty and shape, but that was not what fascinated the boy.

He observed his father using various acids and tools to weaken the centre of the blade in order to carve the intricate shapes that people liked to see.

As the day wore on into the evening, the boy looked over his father's hunched shoulder, smiling. He looked at the shapes and patterns that began to form within the keris. He held out a piece of paper and compared what was drawn on the paper to the patterns within the keris, fascinated his father's patterns were the same as the ones on the paper that he drew.

'You didn't even look,' the boy said in surprise, proud that his father was following his work.

'I don't have to,' his father said, wiping the sweat off his forehead with the back of his wrist, fingers clenching into a fist save for the index finger that pointed to his temple, 'It's all in here. Soon, when you get older, you won't need to draw on that paper anymore.'

'Straight into the keris itself?' the boy wondered.

'Straight into the enemy's heart,' his father said, half-kidding. 'When you stab an enemy in the heart, you have to make sure he stays dead. You will see his eyes, wide and wondering why this is happening, then you'll see the air leave his lungs. When you're that close to him, you will feel his body stiffening, you might feel his last sputtering breaths on your face, but never withdraw the keris until you know he is dead,' his father's hand pulled out the keris from the body of an imaginary assailant.

'The world is full of people who are out to get you. We live in a world of cutthroats and invaders from other lands. You are a boy, but after I blink, you will become a man. Soon too, it will be dark. Go home, help your mother, learn to be a man.'

'Meaning I got to learn how to cook?' the boy wondered, 'but that's usually a woman's thing.'

'It's a skill, much like learning how to make a keris. Preparing a meal is truly the higher art. Making a keris pleases just the maker and the wielder. Making dinner, pleases an entire family,' his father told him.

This confused the boy, but he nodded as though he understood. It began to sink in as he turned and dashed off to his house, and to his mother.

His house was filled with the laughter of children. Jali was six and Suri was four. He heard them as he came around back to the outdoor kitchen and saw his mother kneeling while making a fire. Remembering what his father had said, he offered his help.

'It's fine, but thank you so much,' his mother thanked him, making him feel guilty as he saw her struggling to strike the flint, and he wondered if he could make himself useful.

The laughter of the children got his attention, serving as a reminder that he was the eldest. Soon your time will come children, he thought.

The sky grew darker as each minute passed, just as his father had promised. The siblings ran chasing each other just outside the front porch. The warm air grew colder, a gentle breeze tickling and cooling their faces.

'Jali! Suri'' he called his younger siblings. 'Get inside, it's getting dark.'

'Just a little longer?' Suri pleaded.

'See this,' he showed Suri his clenched fist.

Suri humphed, then sulked into the house, crestfallen.

'Yeah, back in the house,' Jali jeered at her.

'You too, little brother,' Jali felt a hand rubbing his thick head of hair.

Jali looked up, bared his teeth to hiss, but his older brother's stare did not waver. Jali relented, walking into the house the same way Suri did.

'Where is your father?' their mother asked her eldest.

'He told me to come first. He should be coming soon. He says he's going to teach me how to make a keris.'

'And then when are you going to be an apprentice to me here?' his mother wondered.

'I did ask for help,' he told his mother, one brow raised higher than the other.

His father came home to the sight of him throwing half a dozen marinated mackerels into the wok.

'So you're heeding my advice,' he beamed proudly, stroking his thick mustache.

'Yes,' he told his father, wincing and almost leaping away as the fish reacted to the heated wok. He took his bearings, glad that his mother was still around in the kitchen. He had this nagging feeling that she might leave him to do the rest of the cooking, his father's presence making more than half that doubt come true.

'Aren't you staying here? Help me out?' he implored his father.

'I've done more than my fair share in the kitchen when I was your age,' his father told him.

This left him only the mackerel to contend with. His hands were still greasy with marinade. He wiped them with a dishrag and felt some relief when he felt a woman sidle past him, taking a wooden ladle and stirring the fish as he watched. He smiled, glad that his mother was there to guide him.

Inside the house, Jali and Suri were doing their part, running around and pulling from one end to the other a white cloth, a placemat the length of the living room, across the floor. Their father came in with the plates and set them down, admonishing the kids, grabbing them by the shoulders and telling them to sit on either side of him.

They began their dinner by passing around the washing pot, dripping the water over their right hands while the bowl below collected the waste. They ate with those hands, and even Jali and Suri were quiet when they got down to the business of eating, their attention focused on the intricate work of pulling apart the fish with their fingers without taking the bones along with them, careful not swallow any stray fish bones as they chewed the rice.

Jali and his older brother had the same penchant for spicy food, adding sambal to their rice, but Suri did not, keeping the rice in her plate clean save for the fried fish and vegetables.

Suri was a picky eater, smacking her lips to discern each ingredient, wincing before she swallowed her food. She chewed pensively, looked up at nowhere as she formulated a thought. She mumbled a 'Hmmm' then carried on eating.

He watched as his parents and siblings ate, content that the fruits of his labour were being enjoyed. On that night, he understood the pride a mother and father felt when their children appreciated their hard work. The same pride that his father felt when a keris was completed, a job that took months of hard work.

As the night wore on, the children helped roll out the floor mats, while his father swept the floor. His mother put Jali and Suri to sleep, while his father took a walk outside the house, lighting up a tobacco pipe.

He did not feel tired or sleepy, excited still by the pleasant rush of reward still coursing through him. The musky scent of burning tobacco enticed him to stand up and find his father through the window. It was a decision that he thought a man might make. Though he had not yet attempted to steal that pipe, he had a plan in mind.

2

The ground shook and there was panic in the air. There were no stars in the sky, and the sand along the beach ran red with blood while the waves along the shore licked wounds that did not stop bleeding.

Sleeping villagers awakened as they noticed an inferno growing brighter and hotter, and deep within the forest leaves cracked and warped and turned to ash.

Among those sleeping villagers was the keris maker's family. The boy's father woke along with his wife. He heard the two young ones Jali and Suri crying. His wife leapt off the floor mat where she slept, feet stamping against floorboards to hold them, while the boy's father called out to him.

'Keep your head away from the window,' the boy's father pulled him away, placing both hands on his shoulders.

The boy nodded when his father placed a finger to his lips, to keep quiet. The family said nothing and remained silent as the shore around them fell under the bombardment of explosions louder than thunder.

This was a buildup of events that took years, and no one knew better of these burdens than Sultan Mahmud Shah of Malacca, who knew the invaders and exactly what they wanted. His mind raced, questions and thoughts wrestling for a chance to take centre stage. *Was I the one that caused the downfall of my own kingdom? What if I had done things differently? Why did I listen to the Goans who served in my court? Take control of yourself,* he decided, rushing to change from his night clothes into something more regal.

Even in the face of imminent failure and defeat, a Sultan must look the part. Half his mind was a blank, the other a cascading fall of thoughts flooding the empty places in his skull. The rituals of dressing calmed him, he even took a quick second to admire the silk caressing his body, running his fingers along the shirt's golden trimmings.

Sultan Mahmud Shah sucked air between his teeth, undid his clothes then got dressed again, his arms folding over themselves repeatedly as though he were split a thousand ways and was trying to contain himself.

When he collected as much of himself as he could, he hugged his body to make sure he wouldn't lose himself again, and began mumbling the way wealthy men who always wanted more but were never satisfied were wont to do, by excessive swearing.

He spat expletives hoping the wind would carry it to the Portuguese by the shore. A curse word for himself, a dozen for the Portuguese invaders, and stray vulgarities dribbling off his tongue for his wife to see.

He looked out the window, his mind reeling further back in time to two years ago, when meeting and discussing business with these foreign Portuguese seemed more pleasant and beneficial. A voice pulled him into the moment.

'What are you going to do?'

Sultan Mahmud Shah regarded this woman with degrees of awe, respect, and an unhealthy amount of fear. He wished tonight's circumstances were different, where she was lying between the sheets wearing nothing else, but tonight's occasion caused her to be fully dressed.

Fatimah had been dressed before he was. Sultan Mahmud regarded her for a moment, her slim figure, the dress she wore flattering her shape, and it made him mad with lust. The round sweetness of her cheeks had been replaced with an angular firmness, hardened by running affairs of the state.

Mahmud wanted to be taken back to a time when he was courting any one of his wives. He missed that mad thrill of the chase, falling in love, though in Mahmud's case courtship and winning a girl over was in fact willing a girl to him.

Tonight, Sultan Mahmud Shah saw things in perspective. He did not know it yet, but his days were far from ending. Tonight, all seemed lost and he was powerless, in need of his fourth wife to put him back together.

He tidied up his clothes, rushed past her, acting as though he still had some semblance of royalty. His subjects listened to him only in passing, but of recent note they had begun listening to Fatimah, perhaps from sympathy for her situation, one of a woman being forced to marry the Sultan. He had won her over in his own way.

While Mahmud barked orders, Fatimah was the one that considered the weight of his words against the repercussions his orders might have. Only she was daring enough to decline a decree he might mete out, able to justify her own counter-decisions, and it was this ability that scared Mahmud out of his room tonight, more than the impending end of his kingdom. He hoped she did not override him when he commanded his men. He found his Bendahara in the throne room and asked for a status report.

'Forgive me my lord, but our men are falling and the flanks are breaking as we speak,' the Bendehara told Mahmud.

'Send more then!'

'That would not be wise,' Fatimah said, cutting through his childish shriek like a needle piercing the underside of a fingernail.

Mahmud felt his heart race, felt it being squeezed, his breath rasping, gasping. She was doing it again. Scrambling to regain control of his own authority, he asked, 'Why would you say that?'

Fatimah sighed the same way someone might try explaining something obvious to an unreasonable, oblivious child. 'We are simply running out of men, and the Portuguese are angry we captured their men the last time.'

'Diogo Lopes de Sequiera, he was hurting the Tamil Muslims in Goa. I had to extend some measure of justice to them,' Mahmud gritted.

'And blood begets blood,' Fatimah lamented, exhaling her last breath of hope.

'And what would you have me do? Make me wait until we are all dead before we fight back?' Mahmud spat out each word, enunciating each syllable.

Fatimah remained silent, sighing as she walked away from the room.

Once she was gone, the Bendehara took a moment to let his Sultan calm down. He stroked his uncombed mustache, trying best as he could to realign its thick stray strands. 'There are still the cannons that we stole from the Portuguese that first time they invaded,' he told the Sultan.

Mahmud raised his eyebrows. He may have been a number of negative things, but he did have the ability of foresight. His mind began to drift off into the future, that of hundreds of years hence, imagining the perceptions of those future people, and of how they would perceive him. He ruminated and concluded that they would think of him as a great king, flaws and all.

If they did not see his perfection, they might then see the greatness and ingenuity of the Malaccan people, and the skill it took for them to win the battle against the Portuguese.

He did not need the luxury of a second thought. 'Ready those cannons,' he instructed his Bendahara.

In villages around the shore, all of them saw the same thing, a sea of fire under the moonlight. Some swear that night was a full moon, other claimed it was a crescent moon, surrounded by a smattering of dim stars.

There was a general consensus that there was panic in the air, children awoke from their beds, while parents looked on in worry. Palace guards were alerted while those that were trained to operate a cannon went straight to the cannon Mahmud was dying to fire.

Mahmud was riding high on the idea of victory against Diogo Lopes de Sequiera from two years ago, but he had not yet made much against the new Portuguese commander from Goa. Alfonso de Albuquerque had sailed from that Indian city which he captured in less than a day from its Tamil-Muslim ruler Adul Shah, more than six months ago.

Alfonso had captured the city without permission from any of his official superiors. His captains had disagreed with this capture of Goa, and half a world away his Portuguese King Manuel was furious as he had only ordered that Alfonso capture Malacca, the Yemeni city of Aden and the Persian kingdom of Hormuz.

Alfonso added Goa to that list, and in a very short time in the future the capture of Goa would prove to be a prosperous endeavour, soon surpassing their current most prosperous city of Calicut, Kerala, in profit and trade.

Alfonso was adamant when he captured Goa that the Mohammedan population were to be put to the sword. Although this prejudice and cruelty would discredit him slightly, the killing of the Muslim population was more a political move as he needed the help of the Hindus, who were resentful of the Muslims for taking over their city a decade ago.

Alfonso felt his propensity for violence was justified. Portugal's imperial ambitions lied in places like the Iberian Peninsula and North Africa, making his work in India heavily underfunded. He compensated with heavy firepower and cold-blooded cruelty, the likes of which had yet been seen in India at this time, to show the Portuguese were to be feared and respected.

Many began to call him 'The Terrible', as he destroyed every grave stone and left no Islamic structure standing. Alfonso knew he would have to make himself loved and feared in India for there to be a modicum of respect.

The side effect of his violence though was the threat of peace, as he reaffirmed Goa was not to be sacked, that no harm would come to its people under the penalty of death.

The captains' logs on the ships would all say today was July the 25th in the year of their lord, 1511. Alfonso did not listen to the advice of his captains who did not agree with the attack against Malacca, on account of de Sequeira's failure two years ago. His failure gave Alfonso the opportunity for this conquest, and he convinced himself that he was the one who captured Goa, same as he would be the man who would capture Malacca.

What outsiders did not know was that Malacca had always been an advanced nation, having had the best ships, but the misplaced loyalty of men who would die for their Sultan, men who would betray their own friends for his love. It was this undying loyalty that propelled these men to load the cannons.

Alfonso Albuquerque pierced his boots in the grey sand, fingers twisted in the tangle of his beard, realizing he had not a proper shave or a good facial trim since he left Goa.

Behind him was the constant bustle of eighteen ships and the murmur of 1,200 men within those ships. He sensed each ship as they docked, the scurry and pattering of thousands of boots crushing against the sand, killing tiny crabs and turtle eggs not yet born, desecrating nature as a precursor to their desecration of other people.

They called themselves mankind, but men have been anything but kind to one another. Alfonso pondered this as the ships pointed their large and hand-held cannons toward the city, while at the same time pondering on the nature of man, of peace, and he accepted that his nature was to be a constant bringer of sorrow for his kingdom.

Peace, he decided, was an illusion tempered by the whims of kings and conquerors, the waiting period between one war and the next. How long had the people of Malacca known peace before Alfonso's kind came along? How long had the people of Goa? Peace was temporary and war was eternal.

Alfonso smiled at this thought as he led the men forward while cannons fired inward, the sounds of their explosions so loud the earth shattered beneath them, thunder without the relief of rain, only the burden of fire, and the sense that an end was near.

The Bendahara inspected his men as they prepared their retaliation. The soldiers were young, barely in the throes of puberty. There was a heavy burden in his heart, a burden he reckoned the Sultan was unaware of. He reckoned his Sultan's passionate behaviour was a way of struggling to grasp on to a life that had left him long ago. People claimed to have loved him, but what did the people know, except the fairy tale that perpetuated that the Sultan was the greatest ruler that ever lived.

He wondered if this was what the young soldiers felt. The Bendahara can't help but think of these soldiers as boys as he saw them haul the cannons in teams on wooden carts towed by oxen while they avoided cannon fire. In the distance, he saw explosions as bodies twisted away, necks snapping from shoulders, waists twisting at obtuse angles as they broke away from their spines.

'Fight on, soldiers!' he yelled to these boys, riding on horseback, the animal itself a product of trade between the kingdoms that the Portuguese had already overthrown. From his horse the Bendahara screamed orders until his voice turned raspy and sore. They were holding their ground for now. The Bendehara pulled the reins of his steed and wondered where was his damned Sultan?

'Hurry up, why don't you!' Mahmud yelled to a whipping boy, pulling out as fast as he could a telescope, stolen from the first successful victory against the Portuguese two years ago. He loved this marvel for its ability to see long distances farther than the eye ever could see. With it he peered into the battle, wondered who was winning, unable to discern who and what was happening in the dark. He could only see the motion of flames and torches, but his eyes adjusted to the dim light, and he saw a pair of torches that were dominant in their movements. He saw those torches among all others most clearly. Two horses, one ridden by the Bendahara, the other, by a woman.

Her.

She would be his undoing, and not the invading Portuguese, unraveling him one string at a time until he was naked of his power. She knew he would be angry if he knew of her work here on the shore, but she also knew if she did nothing tonight they would have no home tomorrow.

She barked orders at the soldiers, her boys, to keep the invaders firmly planted in the sand, observing that Portuguese armour, though protective, was weighing them down. She made a gamble that they did not have as many shells or explosives as they let on, giving her soldiers an order that made her overshadow the Bendahara.

'Do not do this for your Sultan or for me! Do this for your families! Fight on, for without this fight there is no tomorrow!' she inspired them with this speech, and some of the soldiers swore they saw her glow, but some would have said that was just the torch fire shining on her face at the right angle.

The soldiers hailed on, a thousand voices as one large, continuous voice that ran barefoot in hundreds of pairs, agile feet that have sunk and played in these sands since childhood. They knew these beaches, where to tread, where to avoid, the sand enveloping and recognizing these feet and sometimes springing these soldiers off the ground, they were feathers armed with nothing more than rusted wavy blades, a total symbiosis of man and nature.

The Portuguese in their heavy armour felt only their boots sinking as they ran forward, the shore disagreeing with them, and with each passing, sinking step the barefooted soldiers loomed closer to the Portuguese until rusted blades clang against steel armour.

Fatimah heard the clash of two thousand men against each other in unison, a rumble of passing thunder, the random clangs of metal against metal, a cacophony of screams, a blue shore turned blood red.

If this ended well, she would certainly make him pay. She wondered what good had he done for this kingdom.

On these shores, she imagined what might happen in the morning as her eyes scanned the shoreline to find the leader of these invaders as he screamed orders in a language she did not understand. What other languages she knew, Arabic with its guttural tones, Chinese with its melodic but simultaneously staccato rhythms, were different than this accent she was listening to now, an accent she found grating.

Whoever mastered this foreign language would be a boon to those around him, this much she figured, and she also considered the impatience with which her husband Mahmud Shah handled the previous times the Portuguese came to these shores years ago.

Back then there were no translators to interpret each other's languages, relying on simple sign language and hand gestures they made to one another.

Fatimah did not remember much of this previous time. Time dulled the pain of all memories and wounds. Time had also dulled the anger she felt when Mahmud killed her first husband, and their in-laws, including her first husband's father, the previous Bendehara, just because she refused to take his hand in marriage.

After intense deliberation she only agreed if Mahmud promised her a child to ascend the throne when the time came. As Fatimah saw the man giving out the orders to his own men, she pondered what was she here for? Was it for the future child she was not yet carrying? Was it for the future of Malacca? Was she telling the truth to her soldiers when she said she was doing this for her people, whom she loved more than the Sultan?

These thoughts flashed before her sudden epiphany. 'Do not let them leave the shoreline!' she ordered her soldiers.

Her soldiers split into two units, with one unit running to the shoreline when a senior officer advised them the Portuguese had no advantage when their boots were still halfway in the water.

'We have to stop them before they come any further,' the senior officer agreed with what Fatimah instructed.

The first unit held bows and arrows that were drawn taut for a quick second before they fired, they were not accurate as that was not their purpose. Hundreds of arrows shot high and arced downwards into the water and dotted the shoreline with poisoned arrow tips that pierced kneecaps and thighs and boots and feet. Hundreds of Portuguese soldiers fell and created an effective bottleneck that gave signal for the second unit to come express themselves at the forefront.

Their favourite mode of expression was explosive, lighting the fuses and firing spheres of fire that lit the night sky and crashed into the Portuguese ships, the sea beginning its slow swallow of the burning ships into its belly.

Alfonso resigned himself to fate. He had not yet had the chance to dock all the ships and his men. In the heat of this moment there was only the nagging in his head of all the naysayers that told him not to attack Malacca. Hating himself for this, he spun around and contemplated if he should order his men to retreat. But he was a man defined by his unyielding determination, by his need to make things better than they were, especially if the thing he needed to make better was himself. He was fuelled by the anger of his mistakes, and the need to prove his peers wrong. He would capture Malacca, just not the way he had initially planned.

3

Back when the Portuguese first came in 1509, Sultan Mahmud Shah captured nineteen Portuguese soldiers who were now locked behind steel bars at the rear end of the palace.

Even from where they were, the prisoners could still hear the battle that was raging by the shores. They felt the cannon fire rumble beneath them, but the rumble had a consistency to it, a marching pattern that became a gallop, then the trumpeting of victory.

There were more rumbles, turning into something stronger, trumpeting that melodically laid them one atop another, with cries of men yelling for victory soon joining them.

The Portuguese prisoners leaned their faces against the gaps of their iron bars, eyes crossed to the side. They saw the giant beasts running out the palace.

Riding on these elephants were the mahouts, but they were no ordinary herders, but also trained soldiers, some of whom were Malay but the for the most part these riders and the elephants were Indian.

The fact these elephants were even here was a sign of Malacca's wealth, a major part of which attracted the Portuguese to Malacca in the first place.

Its houses, or villages, were wood, attap and dead leaves, and even the palaces were made of wood, though the wood in the royal palace was made of a higher quality, timber as opposed to teak, but wood would prove to be the Sultanate's biggest weakness. Each year the architects and builders had to attend a meeting to assess the damage caused by rain and weather, patching up holes, gathering new teak, filing and planking new planks, exterminating termites by smoking them out. Tonight, Fatimah was finding weaknesses, gathering intelligence, filling up their flanks, and exterminating pests that were gnawing at the foundations of their kingdom.

Men stomped on termites with the soles of sandals while men were to be stomped by elephant hooves. Mahmud did not want to be outdone by his wife. The elephants were all his idea, a show of ostentation, continuing their stomping march toward the shore, their rumbling march against the ground proved to be so loud the villagers heard it as they shoved against one another trying to rush back to their homes, some trampling over children and old women. Others though were not as brash and picked up these old women and children off the ground.

When they heard the elephants roaring, they turned cautiously. In a melee, such as this, civilians were never sure who were the enemy and who were their saviours. Those out on the sandy streets shuffled home and if they were close enough, they peeked out to see the elephants trumpeting their entrance along the shore.

Good, many of them thought, though the relief they felt was tinged with suspicion, as Sultan Mahmud Shah's rule was one of temperament.

The boy's father looked on and could barely see in the distance the inferno along the shore, knowing that for the moment the villagers were safe in their own homes, as the battle now was with the Sultan and Portuguese troops and had not yet spilled over to the villages. He leaned against the wooden wall, taking deep breaths. He could discern the salty air of sweat in the air, of his children and wife panting, laying low on the floor. He dimmed the oil lamp beside where he stood, breathing in its thick, acrid odour.

'It's either we bow to one dictator or another one,' he lamented to his wife.

'Are we going to die, Aba,' Jali and Suri wondered.

The boy held his siblings close, one in the crook of each arm. All three sobbed together while their mother stroked their hair. Their father began looking for something sharp to defend them with.

Alfonso Albuquerque rubbed his callused fingers against the scruff of his greying beard. Even among the noise of battle he could still hear the creak of bows pulled taut, he could feel the desperation of their anticipation.

'How are the cannons coming along!' he demanded more than he asked.

One of his 1,200 men, whose name he doesn't bother to recall shot back a confident, 'Ready on your command, Sir', as he lit the fuse, a very short fuse that soon volleyed a cannonball out into a grey sky.

An elephant looked up and trumpeted its discontent as it saw that cannonball rising and rising, for a brief second even eclipsing the moon, descending back to the world in a sphere of fire. It may as well have been a comet, furious and impatient, landing in a loud bang, scattering debris mixed with water, mud, sand and brick.

The elephant made a squeak of despair that rose to a squeal of pain ending with a sigh of resignation. Its hind legs, once firmly planted in the sand, were pushed a couple inches backward, forelegs raised in defeat, its tough leather hide now exposed raw flesh that stung and burned, and its rider fared no better.

He was knocked off his harness as he tried to grab at the reins, but he might as well have been grasping at straws, both arms desperate for purchase. He landed hard on his buttocks, pain cushioned by sand, though this was only a temporary respite as his elephant tipped backward into the rider's path, falling on the rider, not even noticing there was someone beneath it as the rider's bones cracked and his breath came in short rasps, the air escaping his punctured lungs in all the wrong directions. The interval between one gasp the next grew shorter until he could not notice his breathing at all when he gave out his final breath.

But this rider's death was to be a footnote that would be buried in the sand. Some riders looked for a brief moment at the fallen beast and rider, shedding no tears though they knew they should, but this was not a time and place for emotions. The only emotion to be had on this battle fought at the crack of dawn, a well-trained emotion, was the single-mindedness to complete the mission at hand.

So they rode on wiser, dodging cannon fire, their minds two steps ahead in an ever-changing battle.

While his wife rode on a healthy steed, Mahmud rode on one dressed in a leather hide. He sat back on a throne built on the animal's back while a mahout lashed the side of the elephant to make it lumber forward.

Mahmud ordered the mahout to stop the beast, preferring to stay aside and avoid cannon fire. He did not think or care where Fatimah might be, for his eyes were elsewhere and his mind was far away, knowing finally that if he does nothing his kingdom would be nothing as well.

He leaned forward in his high elephant throne, his body slanted to keep himself balanced. He thought about what his advisors told him before he came riding with his cavalry, that his cannons would soon run out of ammunition.

Alfonso was not surprised by the sight of these elephants. He had already seen these beasts in many battles in Goa. 'Fucking Indians', Alfonso said as he saw the elephant cavalry, not caring that they were Malays.

The Indians in Malacca were not too pleased with what the Portuguese in Goa were doing to their kind, and had told Mahmud many times in these last few years about the mistreatment of the Tamil Muslims there. The Tamil Muslims were mostly traders and merchants, upset by what their fellow countrymen reported when they came to Malacca, stories of others of Alfonso's ilk hanging Muslim captives, chopping off their hands and heads and feet, and even burning a ship full of Muslim pilgrims.

In the distance they cheered on as they heard the elephants riding and blaring their trunks, and if one got closer to an elephant, they might have then noticed its scent, hides washed every other day and smelling of burnt leather.

As the Tamil Muslims cheered on, the elephants' mahouts whipped and goaded their steeds with sharpened hooks that cut into and pulled the elephant's ears, and if one could see the beasts' eyes, they would know that beasts could also cry.

The Portuguese troops saw the whole cavalry of hairy leather hides and realized they might stink like beasts themselves, their sweat permeating beneath their armour in this humid weather, sweat baking in steel armour lined with cloth, sweat rolling down their thighs.

They wanted to stand their ground, but their bravado was brief, as the sight of this army of roaring beasts made them shake in the sand.

Above them cannon balls streaked overhead, landing too far away now, a sign this was done without proper authority. Alfonso rushed out of his own ship, his hirsute countenance like fire in the dying moonlight. 'Who gave the order to fire!'

This dispersion pleased Mahmud. It gave him enough confidence to motion forward. His mahout nodded, whipping and goading the elephant to move on ahead as Mahmud rocked gently in his elaborate howdah, moving ahead toward victory, while Alfonso marched on in anger.

Both leaders motioned toward each other as their respective troops moved aside to make way for the leaders' might, their presence alone could move troops the way the moon moved the tides.

Alfonso looked up while Mahmud looked down at him. What they lacked now was an interpreter, though their faces were clear with their respective intents, and their respective refusals.

Mahmud's mahout pointed his goad at Alfonso, a gesture that irked and inflamed the Portuguese commander. A younger version of Alfonso would have chosen to draw out his flintlock, but the wiser and more battle-hardened version of himself that was standing here now knew the power of patience and diplomacy, knew the cost of reckless rage, and knew he had to refrain, instead holding his ground by focusing his intense stare at Mahmud and his mahout.

Fatimah's steed galloped close to the Sultan's elephant. She pulled the reins to hold her horse back.

The elephant cavalry slowed down their movements, and the music of victory played its beat across the river bank, the marching drum of giant leathery hooves making their slow stomp along the ground, the silent choir of soldiers lowering their weapons, the twang of arrows withdrawn and bowstrings plucked loose like guitars.

Alfonso was aware of this music, the music of a winning party. He raised his hand and ordered his troops to move back to their ships, and the chorus of soldiers began to rise, a cheerful chorus bridged by the cheers of villagers as well.

As dawn broke, the ships pushed back from the bank of the Malacca river to the deeper water, boat anchors pulled by crews with rapid succession, their skin breaking off their palms, callused hands that have been hurt and blistered more times than they can count.

The sun rose to pierce away the last remnants of night, searing the cool dark with its encroaching heat. Across the waters of the Malacca river the ships retreated, all except a smaller boat that awaited its commander.

Alfonso took two steps forward, without an escort, to regard Tun Fatimah and Sultan Mahmud Shah. Alfonso bowed with his eyes keeping watching of Mahmud and Fatimah. '*Em seguida, na proxima vez,*' he told them. Next time, then.

In one of the boats a decorated soldier named Ferdinand Magellan watched as his commander recede into a tinier version of himself, as the ship he was in pulled away into the sea. Magellan had already been around the Straits of Malacca for the past two years, first escorting the Portuguese fidalgo Diogo Lopes de Sequiera in the first Portuguese embassy to Malacca, along with his cousin Francisco Serrano. So much had happened since then. Sequeira had left in failure, while Francisco Serrano had gone further south to the Moluccas Islands, a place filled with spices, as he had told Magellan in a letter.

Magellan turned away, knowing his commander would come soon. Now it was time for *retiro,* but soon the time for return would come.

The day after the foiled attack, people assumed they could resume their lives as if the battle were just a figment on the tail end of a bad dream, one you might forget when you awoke, but the aftermaths of such battles proved otherwise. At dawn the villagers were greeted with the stench of gunpowder lingering in the air, of burnt flesh and dried blood. Some people could still hear moaning, of soldiers barely men faintly groaning and wishing to die, while those truly dead were carried and brought out from the streets.

The boy walked along the trading posts near the river and saw craters instead of sand and silt. He did not know men could cause such damage, but the most brutal thing he knew was the power of the keris especially of the ones his father made. Blades pierced clean, but then again, cannon fire caused holes in the earth.

That thought made him shudder. He searched for his father, but did not see him. He recalled hearing the cannons fire, and contemplated the meaning of the passage of time: how could something seem to have happened so long ago yet happened just so recently?

He finally heard his father call out his name. He turned and tried to find his father among the bustle of people. Sometimes when he traversed among the trading posts he was reminded of a larger world. When he was alone, this was the sweet spot when his father was away that he enjoyed himself most. This was when he took his time to listen to the people from the larger world. The Arabs, the Indians, the Chinese, he would take the time to distinguish their accents and their words of trade, secretly mouthing out the words, speaking to himself, mumbling just audibly enough that he could hear it back to himself.

Today, talk was rife about the battle last night. He didn't know the exact words in their conversations, dialogues in a multitude of languages that filled his ears. He enjoyed hearing them speak, though today most of the words he could catch did not bear good tidings.

His father called him again, and he turned and found his father holding an elongated box tucked under his arm. 'I thought I'd lost you.'

'You know where to find me,' he told his father.

As they walked past the people, he mumbled excuse me more than once, though not only in his native Malay, but in Chinese, Arabic and Tamil as well.

'You're getting pretty good,' his father told him.

'Yeah, something like that,' he mumbled, still trying to figure out what the traders were saying, trying to link those words against his own language, taking mental notes as he walked along with his father.

Sometimes as he walked along anywhere he forgot what his purpose was, especially if it involved walking along with his father. He forgot, especially when he was this deep into listening. These young ears were still learning, and this boy loved to learn. He snapped back to his true purpose this afternoon when he saw the box his father was holding tighter and tighter as he kept on walking.

The afternoon heat made him sweat and he realized he had been walking for hours, having left the house at dawn, and now the sun was high and full, baking then melting him.

'Are we there yet?'

'A little while more,' his father said.

'You told me that at dawn.'

Both of them stood motionless and felt their sweat dribbling down to their brows but did nothing to wipe it off. The world around them went by. Time moved onward and they counted to three before they wiped the sweat off their brows, laughing among themselves as they wiped their sweat on their pants. After this they kept on walking but with an extra spring in their steps.

'So how long before we reach the palace?' he asked his father again, this time a little more chirpily.

'Any minute now,' his father told him.

That minute came soon enough, and they were now standing before the gates of the palace. His father showed the palace guards the wooden chest and explained what he and his son were here for.

The guards contemplated and looked at each other. There was a long moment before both of them nodded, allowing father and son to enter the palace.

They were led into another section of the palace by another palace hand, a young man just a few years older than the boy. Along the way into the palace the boy noticed that the grounds were clean, like they were swept twice a day, and there was no sand as he walked. He didn't have this luxury in his own village, always having sand in his slippers, but not here. Here his feet and toes were sand-free.

He looked ahead and was astonished by the majesty of the mahogany palace. He felt a hand on his shoulder and for a moment thought it was the hand of someone royal, maybe even the Sultan himself? But it was just his father. This was not the first time he had come here. They walked up the steps and entered the palace proper, shaded from the sun.

The palace was cool inside and the centre was carpeted. Tall wooden columns held the ceiling in place while wooden and iron partitions separated the palace in a proper fashion, nothing like the curtains in his own house.

Although he was indoors he felt there was more air within the walls of the palace than there was outside, and it made him wonder if nature loved royalty more than normal people.

They were led into another room where the Bendahara himself greeted them. His father bowed and began the formal salutations. 'Forgive me my lord, I apologize a thousand times over. I am but a humble servant come to seek your master and bestow upon him a weapon made by my own hands.'

Not knowing what to do, the boy bowed even lower, head cocked to the side to see what his father would do next.

'Rise,' the Bendahara commanded.

His father rose and the son followed. His feet stumbled, the back of one foot hitting the heel of the other, though he quickly found purchase and balance.

'You have honoured the Sultan with your presence. Now wait here,' the Bendahara left the room, and it were as though he took some of the air in the room with him. The boy coughed as if he felt the air sucked out of his lungs.

The solid oak doors seemed to implode as the Bendahara closed them, and the cool air the boy thought was all-pervasive within the palace walls, burned to an immeasurable degree. Did royals also have mystic powers privy only to them?

'What are we waiting for, Pa?'

'Well if you are lucky, you might meet someone higher than the Bendahara,' his father hinted coyly, regarding the chest and thought of the hard work he put into it, having made the chest as well as what lay inside it. His restrained pride hid inside a cave, cowering from the sunlight, afraid that the sun might singe his wounds.

They heard the door creak open. This was the first time the boy saw the grace and might of royalty, realizing that royalty was not something that needed overt magic to move mountains. The magic was just in a royal's presence alone, the power to move people by the gesture of parted lips, an utterance that could move one man or kill thousands with a single command, or with the twitch of a finger to make one submit to you.

The boy had yet to decipher the language for that, but he was much willing to learn. The doors opened and there was one man on each side of the door, keeping the handles apart.

When the royal entered, the boy turned to his father quickly, imploring what to do next. The anticipation was palpable, and he swore the air that seemed trapped and inhibited now rushed in a cool breeze, a type that soothed not only the skin but the soul. The boy next noticed a fragrance that made him wonder if maybe it was a pretty handmaiden, a proposition he knew he wouldn't have minded.

But what walked through the door was something more. He perhaps half-expected the Sultan but then again, she was just as grand. It was Sultanah Tun Fatimah after all. Word had spread through the kingdom that she was the first one on the scene when the Portuguese had invaded via the Malacca River, and that her esteem had risen to higher regards since then.

His father bowed and got to one knee, and the boy followed suit. 'Forgive me your highness, for your humble servant seeks your forgiveness a thousand times over.'

'Rise, my humble servant,' Fatimah said.

His father and he rose with their heads still bowed low. She implored them to face her, and they raised their heads to meet with her stern eyes. Beneath the facade of those eyes lay something deeper, that of a woman that has felt pain and lived to endure it.

There was something motherly in her that attracted the boy, or at the very least she felt like a favourite aunt, her presence made him feel at ease.

'I believe you have something for the Sultan? I would like to apologize for his absence, he is away on urgent matters,' Fatimah explained for Mahmud's absence, though she sometimes wondered why as she blinked rapidly, trying her best not to keep her eyes shut. If she had but a moment's privacy, she would close her eyes tight and fight the urge to let her tears stream. She had done this on so rare an occasion she could count them on her fingers. Her relationship with her own tears was a complicated one in which she had no answers. Why she would cry at the oddest times without even warning herself? At such moments she reckoned it was an accumulation of sadness and grief at the lot life had dealt her, collecting like darkening clouds before the rain.

As it were, she had guests, and faked a smile of which she had much practice. She took a controlled breath, one that none of the guests barely noticed, and before the moment got more awkward than she had imagined in her head, she implored the keris maker to show what he had made.

'Yes, your Highness,' and the boy's father led her to the table where the chest awaited. 'Crafted this myself,' he added, keeping mystery as to what he had crafted, a pride only wounded tigers knew. Fatimah's grace beckoned and the tiger knew it was safe to come out of hiding.

Walking beside Fatimah was the Bendehara, who was also curious about what lay inside the chest.

The chest opened smoothly without a creak. Fatimah tried to hold back a smile when she saw it. The father reached inside the chest and showed his handiwork to Fatimah. She accepted it with both hands carefully, remarking the grace of the patterned sheath.

'May I?' she asked the craftsman. She caressed the handle and pulled it barely an inch off its sheath.

The father, the craftsman, felt a certain satisfaction in giving her royal highness permission. He felt a certain kind of power.

Fatimah pulled out the keris slowly, admiring every line that he carved within it. The boy beamed quietly to himself, knowing some of those lines were his ideas. Fatimah found each wave and curve of the blade perfect by human measure. 'The Sultan would be most displeased,' she said curtly as she sheathed the keris with a sharp snap.

The room was silent as they waited for her next word. She knew she had their attention. 'He would be disappointed by this weapon's perfection. The beauty of this weapon, this piece of art made by your hands, so beautiful it would make him wallow in a well of infinite sadness. It is like a beauty he cannot have, a beauty he is not worthy of wielding.' As her mind very briefly wandered into a private place, imagining the things she could do against her husband with this keris, her eyes began to drip tears that rolled down the curve of her cheeks. 'And I am saddened he is not here to see for himself this keris at this very moment, the moment where the morning light glints along the weapon's curves.'

There was a single, solitary clap that echoed along the ceiling, bouncing along the walls, snaking its way past pillars and worming into everyone's ears. That clap was followed by another, then a continuous succession of claps that told the people in the room that the walls belonged to him.

'No better words were said about what lies deep within my soul. Your Highness, you truly know the meandering paths that lead to my dark heart,' Mahmud said as he walked into the room.

'My Lord,' the Bendahara said as he rushed to his Sultan, ready to ask those in the room to get back to some form of attention, but Mahmud told his prime minister to remain calm, that such formalities were not necessary right now.

Fatimah walked to the chest and kept the keris. She closed it and searched for Mahmud's eyes as he walked toward her to open the chest again, feeling the work of the master craftsman in his hand.

He unsheathed the keris and inspected every inch of the blade, holding it high to let it catch the light, turning its handle so the light split and shone across the entire room.

'This blade,' Mahmud paused for effect, 'captures the light of the kingdom!' He sheathed the blade and closed the chest. Mahmud turned to the boy, a tectonic smile shifting across his lips. 'It shines for the future generations of this kingdom. Are you learning what your father teaches you? Will you be a blade maker like him?'

The boy gulped. 'Yes, my lord. I am still a novice, but I am always willing to learn.'

Mahmud gave a loud laugh, satisfied with the boy's answer. 'Your father's keris brings light to the kingdom. But would you like to see what darkness the light casts out?'

'Y-Yes, my Lord. I would very much like to see that,' the boy replied cautiously.

Mahmud stroked his chin, the corners of his lips filled with cat-like glee. 'Prepare our guests for a visit to the prison!'

'This is the dark underbelly of what we are,' Mahmud said aloud, but to no one in particular. Everyone around him looked on in fascination at the surroundings of the prison. Even the men who opened the doors for Mahmud did not often come here.

This prison was not built underground like a European prison, as this was built at the back end of the palace, partitioned by another set of walls. It was walls within walls shaded by the mercy of unkempt palm trees. Here one got the feeling that light came in less often, shielded by the palm leaves, some believed that that sun avoided this part of the palace, having shone most of its grace in the front portions of the palace, the place which demanded the most light.

The cages that held the prisoners were iron bars that had rusted with the excruciating march of time. The boy noticed the stink of these men, daring not to look directly into the cages.

'Criminals, all of them, each with a varying degree of offence. Some are just thieves, some are murderers and some,' Mahmud stopped to revel in this next bit, 'are spoils of war,' he told the boy as he spread out a hand as if presenting to his audience a grand prize layered in sweat and stink, and wrapped in iron bars.

The prisoners leapt at the bars of their cells, sputtering words that the Sultan's audience did not understand, but from what the boy heard and could figure out from their vicious inflections, he could tell they weren't nice words.

The prison guards emerged from the walls with the ghostly quality of smoke and shoved their spears into the gaps of the cages to keep the prisoners back in.

'These *puta*,' Mahmud declared proudly, making sure the prisoners heard that second word, 'are the prisoners we captured two years ago, back during their first attempt to invade us.'

'Portuguese,' the boy mumbled beneath his own breath.

'Yes, yes they are,' Mahmud agreed with the boy. 'Portuguese pigs, all of them. The tried to invade us time and time again, but we are the victors every single time.'

The boy pondered this as he looked into the depths of the cell. The floor was dirty and filled with dried coconut leaves used as a makeshift carpet and perhaps a mattress. The prisoners blended in with the dried leaves, shrivelled husks of their former selves, with their beards grown long and unkempt, their hair dry and filled with lice, touching their shoulders, straggly and spread out in all directions.

The prisoners gained a brief burst of energy and leapt again at the bars, landing their hands with a thunderous smack and they screamed obscenities to the Sultan in Portuguese.

The guards held their spears and told them to stay back, the other palace hands flinched, but Fatimah, who had been silent on this tour of the prison, saw the boy bravely motion forward to try capture their dialogue.

He took a hard look as he searched their faces, a map of lines and scars and scribbles, each face leading to a different destination, telling a different story. He counted nineteen men, all with their tan taken out of them, a loss of colour that signified their loss of freedom. Basking and walking in the sun, the boy began to realize, was a sign of being able to walk without anyone leashing or reining you in. None of these prisoners had this luxury anymore.

In the boy's mind there was a cacophony of sound, a room full of random noises that he could discern when he kept his mind calm. He could notice them once he quieted the noises, compartmentalized the sounds and then used it as a weapon he could fire upon at will. The prisoner's language was still a scurrying rat trying to break free from his mind, so he caught it, and the rat looked into his mind's eye and gave him a word he could use.

The boy took another step forward and greeted them with a simple, '*Ola.*'

The prisoners became silent. Mahmud and Fatimah both were cautious but nevertheless impressed by the boy's natural prowess for language.

The prisoners then broke their silence, by laughing. They laughed so hard, it was a mystery to the boy as to why they were doing so, and hands held tight on iron bars began to loosen while some of the prisoners fell back and rolled their emaciated, dirty bodies on the floor, rolling in the rustle of dried coconut leaves.

One of them stood up and said, '*Onde você conseguiu esse garoto?*'

The others joined in the revelry and screamed the words 'garoto!' over and over again.

The palace guards, who were barely a decade older than the boy looked at one another, shook their heads in disapproval.

Show off, the guards seemed to say with their furrowed eyebrows. The boy's father however, beamed with pride, eyes scanning the room to see if this pride was shared with the others around him as he shuffled his stance. He even caught himself chuckling at how ridiculously, ecstatically odd he felt.

The boy placed his hand over chest lightly to ask, *'Garoto? Saya Garoto?'* mixing his own Malay with Portuguese with those two words, inferring the question, 'Boy? I am boy?'

'Yes! Where did you get this garoto?' They repeated over and over again.

The laughter was short-lived, cut short when the guards rushed to the iron bars, though the others in the back carried on laughing, the laughter dying out in gasping whispers. They had not laughed or experienced a happy emotion for a very long time.

Once the prisoners quieted down, they paused to look at each other. All of them had the same look of agreement, that there was something special about this boy, especially the boy's tongue. At this moment, even their captor Sultan Mahmud agreed.

Mahmud placed a hand on the boy's shoulder. He addressed the keris maker, 'Well, maybe your son might have a future in the palace as a man of words.'

Over the next few weeks the boy was allowed to enter the palace grounds to talk to the prisoners. This was gold to him, to be able to learn a language directly from the source.

He came to the prisoners bearing loaves of bread, a loaf for a lesson, or perhaps, *'Um pedaco de pao para uma licao,'* if his translation proved correct. Each day he spent three hours with them, until noon, with each minute being a treasure for him. In return he taught them some Malay as well, but felt guilty for upgrading their fluency in his own language. The Sultan did not tell him to teach them, though he was allowed to learn from them, all this in the hopes that the boy might some day be their interpreter.

A week into his informal Portuguese lessons, he wondered if he had given them his name, because he remembered most of theirs.

Once they started calling him Garoto it kind of stuck. Boy was his name, but he remembered Abilio, Abel, Bernardo, and all the rest of them.

By the second week he had some fluency in Portuguese, and he brought fruits as well as stale bread. The court hands had only given Garoto bananas whose skins were on the verge of turning black, and when the prisoners peeled away the skins, the bananas though yellow on the inside, were soft and melted in their hands.

'These are delicious, Garoto, thank you,' they would say to him.

'*Obrigado*,' he told them in return, smiling.

By the third week, he had full conversations with them, and he began to wonder about many things, about what they were, where they came from, why they were here, why they were captured, and what the recent failed invasion meant for the people of Malacca.

Garoto listened as they explained their world to him, and what the other side entailed, what it took to cross here by sea, the years it took to get them here. They had sailed from Portugal, down to the lands of the Moors, to the land of pyramids, past China, then India. They told the tales of the attack on Goa, and finally their voyage here, to Malacca.

He absorbed all their stories, wondering how far this relationship with the prisoners might last. Was he amusement for them? Or was it the opposite? Perhaps he was nothing but a thief of language, stealing their words right in front of them, stealing their knowledge of the outside world. He entertained the possibility they were telling lies about the lands they visited, but the lands the prisoners spoke of had corresponding peoples that traded at the trading posts and docks where he walked along with his father.

Malacca was the centre of trade in this side of the world, or at least as far as the Malay empire was concerned. He saw the Chinese and the Arabs and the Indians, and learnt some of their words via aural osmosis, showed off those foreign words to the prisoners, amusing them, but he was proud, happy he could show off what he had learned.

'Thing is, Garoto, this will not be the end,' one of the prisoners, Bernardo, said to the boy as he motioned toward the bars while the boy did likewise, though he flinched when he noticed Bernardo's ancient stink, a stench that had a life separate from Bernardo's body. But the boy kept on listening. 'It's only a matter of time before Albuquerque comes again. Just like in Goa, he tries and tries until he gets what he wants. And what he wants, is Malacca.'

'Is it true what the prisoners say?' the boy asked his father during dinner. His mother was working her way through the kitchen, busying herself so that she did not have to hear their conversation. They were all having dinner earlier these days, for fear that the invaders might be coming.

Jali and Suri were playing five stones inside the house at their father's suggestion to keep them occupied while the elders occupied themselves with worry.

His father smoked a pipe in front of him, and he regarded his son, almost twelve, almost a young man, and pondered where did all the time go? His son was straddling the points between boyhood and man, and his next words he weighed carefully: was he to address his answer to the boy, or the man that was coming out of his shell?

'They are not wrong,' his father told him as he exhaled a cloud of smoke, deciding at last that perhaps the boy and the man were both going to hear this. He inhaled from his pipe again, 'Each night these days when the sun sets your mother and I worry. We have bad dreams about what might happen, that one fine night, when we are sound asleep, they might attack again. Would we die asleep or will we be wide awake with nowhere to run?'

The boy paced down the porch steps and tried to understand what his father told him. He himself couldn't recall any nightmares, but his dreams were with filled with conversations in other languages, and he almost felt guilty for not having the nightmares his parents had.

The kitchen began to glow a bright amber as his mother meandered past an oil lamp as she made her way out the kitchen.

'Don't try to worry too much, son, because worry only leads to more worry. I know you are thinking about all of us, especially Jali and Suri. But they have the three of us to protect them, don't they? And if the Portuguese come again, so be it. We will survive.' She placed her hand where her son's shoulder met his neck and held it there, leaning down to kiss his forehead while her son stared into the forest and imagined the river and the shore turning red with the blood of a thousand soldiers.

Crickets cricked around him and the wind rustled against the leaves in the trees. The air was thick and grey, bearing the weight of an invisible fire that filled their lungs, infesting them like a black cancer.

'Not if they kill all of us first,' the boy lamented.

4

The second time Alfonso Albuquerque came, it was with stealth and not bravado or cannons to signal his entry. Now it was a game of spy against spy, his lookouts against the men that guarded the shores of Malacca.

While the boy was learning their language, they were doing a different sort of learning. Spread throughout the smaller islands that dotted Malacca were Portuguese spies who were learning the ins and outs of boats that entered the river and the docks and the beaches, determining the schedule of these ships; these spies were the vessels and veins that connected Albuquerque's mind.

Mahmud meanwhile had begun to prepare his city with heavier artillery fortifications, planting palisades and arming them with guns along the river banks, many of which he planted himself, driven by the haunting visions of his city on fire, visions that kept him awake at night. Some nights he would wake up in cold sweat, searching his bed for Fatimah, but she was not beside him. She had taken to sleeping in the guest rooms.

This frustrated him to no end, but he had little say in the matter. He had a city to defend, but his grip on the city felt to him like he was grasping a clump of sand where the grains seeped out between his fingers, each second the grains would dribble until he was only grasping at crumbs from a very poor table.

Those grains that were left were the people who did not have the city's best interests at heart, people who cared more about the value in their pocket books than the value of the citizens.

These merchants were transient in nature, though they were in many ways the lifeblood of the city, flowing, ebbing, bleeding with gold and silver and silk and riches.

Merchants also played both sides, merchants such as Utimuti Rajah, who gifted both sides with separate gifts. To Alfonso Albuquerque he had given a gift made of sandalwood, but he also sent his people to help Sultan Mahmud build new palisades and barricades. Duplicity was a condition more common among those with riches to trade, and is it any wonder why currencies had two sides, a head and a tail? Toss it enough times, and both sides would equally prevail.

Around the city life seemed to go on, the boy's father had plans to make another keris, his siblings continued running around the house, while his mother motioned around their home a specter of her old self, and the boy couldn't help but feel responsible that what he had said had drained the spirit out of her.

His father noticed the change in her, but said nothing as he continued making another keris, hammering away any signs of sadness with a mallet, each strike tinging him with the regret that he could have done more. He was not among the men that built the palisades or any of these fortifications, feeling guilty that all he could make were not walls but little curved blades.

The boy, Garoto, hid in the forest in the early mornings before the sun baked his skin, climbing a tree and nestling himself in the crook where branch met tree, and losing himself in his own thoughts. His thoughts were mostly in Malay, but sometimes he felt other languages described better his true feelings.

Chinese and Portuguese, he decided, had far more colourful ways to describe anger and frustration, and those languages danced in his head for a very long time, long enough for him to feel the sun rising above him and heating his body.

Once it got too hot, even the shade of trees did not save him. He slid down and landed on both feet and realized something he had not before. The distance between height and ground was now lesser. He reckoned he was growing taller.

Back on solid ground he was then faced with an epiphany.

He turned and dashed out the forest, toward the Istana, the king's palace.

In less than an hour he was at the prison, body matted in sweat, panting as he began to probe Abilio, more than Abilio was comfortable with.

'What more you want of me, boy? You are no spy or inquisitor to your country. What, you think you can talk in our language and now we're friends, huh? That we share secrets? Say I tell you, say who dies?' Abilio asked.

The boy paused. He still needed time to process the words. What lingered in his mind was that last question, and he told Abilio, 'No, Señor, say you tell me, its who dies first? Is it you for being a traitor, or me for knowing too much already?'

Abilio leaned into the bars of the cell, baring his blackened teeth that looked as though they had not been cleaned for a thousand days. The gruesome sight of bad teeth was half-covered by the messy sight of the beard curtaining his lips, and what the boy felt was not fear, but disgust, brought on by the whiff of Abilio's stench. 'You will get nothing from me here today, garoto. And who cares if I die first? I am already a dead man.'

The boy bowed his head as he turned away, his idealized motives having lost out to the cruel reality these prisoners were not his friends, and they would not tell him what he wanted to know. This sojourn to the prison had only sunken his spirits into an endless abyss in which he could only find his dark reflection staring back at him. *You could have done better if you knew how to talk to them*, his abysmal doppelgänger told him.

He walked out the Istana hungry and longing for home food. He walked with his head down. In the Gregorian calendar it was the 8th of August in the year 1511, and the sun would set soon, and he prepared himself to be admonished by his parents for staying out too late.

Darkness rolled into the sky, black waves rolling over the sun as if eating it whole until all light was swallowed from the world. Just as the boy stepped out the palace, he felt something bright burn in the sky, and knew it was not the sun. He looked up gazing at a comet made of iron and gunpowder descending into the city.

He gasped and felt his heart drop. There was then the sound that shook him to his core, an explosion that was to be the first of many. He had to find his family, the thought that it couldn't have been so soon, drowned out his other thoughts.

Soldiers rushed past him while he stood still to let them. Soon he felt an emptiness in the palace, like all life had left, save for a cancer within it. He knew the prisoners were laughing in their cells now, and they were right, so damned right it hurt as they laughed.

The boy was angry and worried, his heart beating in his ears. He ran toward his home, his slippers ground and twisted away from his feet as he gained great distance from those things, choosing not to pick them up, his bare feet cutting against sand and rocks. He was sweating and crying and got his shirt caught in a low hanging branch.

He paid it no mind as the shirt ripped and hung, billowing in the chill of the forest, serving as a torn flag and marker that he was here. He ran with arms bleeding, drops of blood trickling in his wake. He had to find his family, cursing himself for staying out so late.

His father wondered too where his son was, torch in hand as he stepped down the porch, and felt a hand grab his shoulder. 'What?'

'The little ones, don't you forget them,' she told her husband.

'They're all precious, love, even if we had a hundred children each one of them would be just as precious,' he ran deeper into the forest, hoping to find his eldest son.

His bravado though, was cut short by another explosion.

That explosion engulfed the forest, knocking the boy out cold. He was soon found by armoured Portuguese soldiers, his nostrils rousing him to wakefulness by their stench borne of tropical weather and fermented sweat boiling beneath their armour.

The boy struggled, screaming and pulling his way out their arms and elbows. His father thought he heard his son somewhere in the forest, but it was now too late.

Malacca had fallen.

All around them there was fire. Alfonso Albuquerque came this time with more strategy than the previous time, when he came about the invasion the way a younger man might have fought, more rage than strategy. He took his failure hard and twisted this shame into victory. Whenever he looked in a mirror, he was staring into the face of failure. He was getting older, and the divide between youthful bravado and middle age was a line all men across time had to contend and struggle with.

'Take this into account, Ferdinand,' he addressed his best soldier, Ferdinand Magellan, liking to call his best ones by name, and others, by rank. 'My mistake the last time was that I was too brash. too much like a street fighter leaping into the fray before I studied the opponent. This time around, I studied them, found and exploited their weaknesses and caught them off guard. Some people can't keep their mouths shut. People close to the Sultan leaked the secrets I needed to conquer the city, he explained. 'Do you have children, in any port, Ferdinand?'

'Just one. Out of wedlock,' Magellan said this softly.

Alfonso nodded and grunted. 'When he grows up, teach him not to be so brash as I was,' Alfonso said.

Both of them walked along the sand that lined the shore, and Alfonso smiled as he heard the world around them explode and burn.

'I'll keep that in mind, Sir,' Ferdinand told Alfonso, searching his commander's eyes for some faint kind of approval.

Both of them heard a boy getting caught, squealing, struggling to escape.

'Spoils of war,' Alfonso remarked of the boy.

The boy struggled, though there was nothing he could do, held at odd angles that kept him from turning around or sneak an escape from under them. They held him tight, with one soldier tucking his arm beneath the boy's armpit, folding the arm inward.

'Shut your mouth, boy!' this soldier said, unable to stand the boy's screams.

The boy's father ran into the darkening forest, with each step his son's voice seemed louder than the cannons that were firing across the entire city. He called out for his son, exiting the denseness of the forest to find his son being held by Portuguese soldiers.

'Let him go,' his father seethed through gritted teeth.

'We are laying claim to him,' the soldier said, tightening his grip around the boy, words the father did not understand but knew the context just the same.

'Just let my son go,' the boy's father implored.

The boy then heard the unsheathing of a musket. 'Don't Pa, don't come any closer,' the boy pleaded.

His father walked faster forward, unsheathing a keris from his back. He threatened and pointed the keris at them again, 'Let. My. Boy. Go.'

Magellan and Alfonso jogged right in the middle of this. Ferdinand Magellan stood steady, while the older Alfonso panted to catch his breath. As he steadied himself, he began to lose patience with the scene. 'Don't waste time,' he told the soldiers.

The boy's father took a determined step forward, though his determination was overpowered by something even stronger than will.

The unsheathed musket discharged its fire, but the randomness of it grazed his father's shoulder, but his father continued toward the soldiers, and his son could only look on in horror as another shot fired, this time with truer aim, into his father's chest. His father fell face forward and the keris he held dropped and slid toward Magellan.

The face of the soldier who fired upon the boy's father was pale, though his pallor soon blushed again when he noticed how well his shot landed. He looked at another one of the soldiers, tried to contain his excitement, though more than a few chuckles escaped his cheeky grin.

The boy, little garoto, was now silenced, body shaking and tears filling his eyes as he held back from crying. He was the eldest brother, and the onus was imperative upon him to always be the better person and give in to his siblings, to be the steward of the house when his father was not around. Now his father was gone, and all the lessons inculcated to him by parents came flooding toward him. His parents spoke always in future tense, saying *'When your father is gone, you'll be the man of the house.'* The boy did not expect this until his father was an old man. His father wasn't that old. But he was gone.

He held himself from tears because he was under the sometimes-false allusion that real men didn't cry. But with each passing second, it seemed less and less of a truth.

His body shook. His head felt not part of his body. His mother cried, but there was an inner strength he knew he could not deny. Upon this realization, he shook, and let the tears pour out his eyes, followed by breathless sobs.

Alfonso said nothing as the boy cried. He had seen so many families cry over the bodies of loved ones that his mind was at a permanent remove from death's palpable grief. 'The boy is all yours, Ferdinand. Spoils of war,' Alfonso nudged him.

Magellan looked at the boy, and did not see a child for the taking, but a child robbed of his father, and felt pity for the boy.

'Come son,' Magellan tried to appeal to the boy. 'Let him go,' he implored to the soldiers.

The soldiers looked at each before nodding in agreement. Magellan was right.

The boy did not run away, instead crawling to his father's body. He cradled his father, and his screams turned to sobs, and for Magellan it was the saddest sound in the world.

Some of the other soldiers took pity on the boy, one even took a step forward as though consoling a little brother, but another held him back, shook his head to punctuate the fact he had rules and decorum to comply to.

Magellan knelt beside the boy, placing a hand on his shoulder, and felt the boy's shoulders trembling. 'Let's go,' he told him in his native Malay.

The boy's trembling calmed before his muscles tensed and he became still. It was this stone silence as though the boy had hardened to actual rock that frightened Magellan.

The sobbing grew into a tiny grunt, and his stillness seemed to stop time itself. The boy regarded his surroundings. The soldiers flanked him in a loose circle. He gauged how far he was from them; at how much time and how much strength he would need. If he were calmer, or a trained soldier, he would have had the benefit of patience, but anger clouded him, it was the fuel and the catalyst of all his actions today. He even gauged the distance between his hands, and the wavy blade on the ground. If he moved fast enough, maybe, just maybe . . .

The boy's stone hard muscles sprung forward, leaping to his grab his father's keris off the ground, and with it he slashed at the soldiers, screaming repeatedly, 'You killed my father!' His screams were long notes of dissonant anger, but his shrieking was so loud the Magellan almost burst his eardrums.

The soldier with the musket aimed again. Magellan looked at the soldier, then at the boy, came to realize the kid was grasping at straws. There was something about this boy that brought out pity in Magellan. What that something was, he couldn't fathom, but he knew he couldn't let the soldier shoot a child.

Magellan, used to fighting adults, found it strange to tackle a child, but he found the best angle to tackle this garoto, grabbing him and at the same time screaming for the soldier to put the musket down. He twisted the keris away and another soldier held the boy's hands to his back. He tried to scream now, but he could only cough out spit. He had lost his voice.

If I can't shoot him, at least I can do this to him, the musketeer thought, stepping forward and smacking the butt of his musket against the boy's face.

The boy lost consciousness. The keris fell and Magellan took it in his hand, and brought it closer for inspection. 'Remarkable,' Magellan said softly. He admired its craftsmanship, its hilt, its wavy blade. He looked around the ground and found the keris' wooden sheath, golden patterns carved intricately into it. A thought crept into Magellan. *We have lost a great craftsman.* He placed the keris into the sheath and looked at the boy's head hung low and loose. He sighed as he clutched the keris to his breast.

'Bring the boy to the ship,' Magellan instructed the soldiers.

While the boy lay unconscious in the ship, Magellan ordered the soldiers to bury the boy's father. Magellan himself held the shovel, and laid the last scoops of soil onto the gravesite. He stood up to say a prayer, but then he heard the rustle of footsteps. He turned, and the soldiers drew their muskets, pointing them at the intruders.

Magellan saw a woman with a young boy and little girl, all of them sobbing, all of them looking at Magellan's belt, at the keris sheathed with it. The wife knew her husband's handiwork.

In broken Malay he implored to her to, 'Go. Son safe. Before mind they change go, beg you, please.'

Holding back the tears in their eyes, they looked at the mound of soil that held their father, her husband. The woman noticed no tombstone, only a pair of foreigner's boots stepped over the earth that enveloped her husband's body. She lamented the tragedy that he was not given a gravestone to mark his site, and that he was not given a proper Muslim funeral, with the appropriate prayers and processions. She would remember this spot. If the passing of time permitted, she would come here again and complete his funeral. She wiped her tears, and held Jali and Suri in each hand. She only wished she had another pair of arms to hold her eldest boy. Her eyes darted for a second to find him, crestfallen her eldest son was nowhere in sight. For that brief second she wondered if this Portuguese man was telling the truth.

'Go!' Magellan told them again, his tone this time harsher. Perhaps she could trust him. There was a truth to his eyes, a conviction. It would have to do. She hoped her eldest would join him, but she turned Jali and Suri around and began moving. Unlike her son, she did nothing to hold back her tears. She wanted to scream, not exactly in sadness but in frustration. She held that back. She would need some modicum of decorum for the children she had with her now.

They left, disappearing into the forest, specters that would haunt Magellan's memories in years to come. Magellan sighed as the soldiers put their muskets down, one of them muttering, 'I would have shot them.'

Magellan swung the shovel at that soldier's face, and there was an audible crack of bone. 'I would have shot you, fool! Get out of my sight, all of you.'

The soldiers left Magellan alone. Magellan pulled up that soldier and he muttered something low enough that Magellan couldn't hear. He heard exactly what the swear was but chose to ignore it for now. He focused his energies to say the final lines of his prayer. He knelt down, palms clasped together, whispering a prayer. As a man who had seen many battles death was no stranger to him, but today, something in him had changed. Could it have been because the people he saw being killed were soldiers, young men who were prepared to die in battle, but with the death of this boy's father it solidified the connections people have? A boy would always have a father, but to have taken it from him, and right in front of him wrenched Ferdinand Magellan more than he cared to admit.

A tear rolled down the corner of his eye. He turned to make sure no one saw this tear. For a ruthless Portuguese army, this was unacceptable. He knew he shouldn't have to cry, but deep inside he knew he had to let it all out.

He asked the boy's father to forgive him, and promised he would take care of the boy. Magellan's chest felt as though a hand went into his body and crushed his heart. There was an actual pain in his heart, sharp and unrelenting in its deliverance. Drool ran down his nostrils and the corners of his mouth. He coughed and his lips bubbled and he eked out one grunting sob and his body rolled head first onto the soil.

Once he had calmed himself, he rose back to his feet, and walked away for good. He knew he would never come to this grave ever again. Now, he had a boy to console.

When the soldiers stormed the Royal palace, Mahmud was nowhere to be found. His absence mirrored that of his kingdom, a city on fire, where many had fled and the first to go were the traders and merchants, while the locals fought and died. Those born on Malaccan soil were the ones who had the most to lose, while expatriates had the choice to flee.

Mahmud and his entourage were already at the harbour. His men were loading crates and sacks of clothes and amenities into various ships and boats. They had plans to move elsewhere. Mahmud could smell the thickness of the fire even from here. He made sure Fatimah went into his ship first. The Bendahara held his hand on the Sultan's shoulder. 'It's all that we could do. Malacca is gone now, your highness.'

As the dock hands unmoored the ship Mahmud stood alone at the bow, looking at the inferno that once was his city. His advisors at least had enough foresight to plan ahead years in advance. There had been many meetings over the years of contingency plans, and of how to rebuild if his kingdom had fallen, though Mahmud never expected it to happen in his lifetime.

Sultan Mahmud lowered his head and sighed, lamenting not of his people suffering, but regretting that he had lost his seat of power. After a long moment he raised his head, only to find his wife on deck. He wondered if it was fate that brought her here? As much as he hated to admit this, he knew she was the kind of strength his new kingdom would need.

The wind whipped Fatimah's hair. She clenched her fist, her upper teeth bit her lower lip so hard until it bled. She knew this wasn't fair, after all she had done and been through. She heard Mahmud stepping onto the deck, coming onboard with the Bendehara. She chose not to look at him, but most of her anger was not directed at him. She felt angry at herself, for not doing more.

The ships unmoored quickly, and at the very least, the wind was in their favour. They left Malacca to burn as their ships headed for Johore, a journey south that was weeks away. There, Mahmud wanted to establish a new sultanate, and perhaps, a fresh start.

With the leaders of the Malaccan kingdom gone, its invaders stayed behind. Alfonso stayed for many months until January 1512 when he departed for Cochin. During this time he oversaw the construction of a great fort in Malacca which he named *A Famosa,* or the Great Fort. He also began to dispatch ships to the Spice Islands of the Moluccas up north, an inspiration that would fill Magellan's head almost a decade later when Magellan himself would embark on his own arduous journey there.

While all this was happening, a boy opened his eyes in a dark room and felt the floor beneath him rock sideways. He moved his arms and felt something heavy hold them back. Shackles. Will this be his life now? An endless transfer from one set of shackles to the next? He had been here for weeks. His sore cheeks began to throb. He reckoned he had a black eye, but can't remember where he got it from.

His body shook and all he could think of was finding his family. He needed to hold someone, he thought. He hadn't even spoken to anyone about his father's death, and had no time to process the fact his father was gone, to make sense of the notion his father would never walk this earth again. He didn't know much, but he knew with all honesty he missed his father.

At times he would think the shadows around him were his father, telling him how to behave and sometimes he imagined it was his mother telling him how to calm himself. He sucked in his snot, and the spit bubbling around his mouth. There was no way he could've wiped it off with his shackles restraining him. He heard footsteps and his eyes searched for the brightest part of the ship's cargo hold. A door creaked open, and he waited for whoever it was to come to him.

Those footsteps approached while his eyes adjusted to the dark. A tall amorphous shape formed into something solid in his vision. The man who tried to stop the soldiers from killing his father. The boy struggled and dashed forward but the shackles held him back. 'Let me go!' he kept saying, struggling, the chains rattling along with him. He soon stopped, realizing the futility of his struggle. He crumpled to the floor and sobbed.

Magellan approached the boy, knelt down beside him, and placed a hand on his shoulder. 'There, there. You're with me now. Your mother and siblings are safe. I told them to leave before it got worse. We have orders from the Governor Albuquerque to return to Portugal.'

'My mother's safe,' he said more as statement than query.

'Yes,' Magellan said. He held the boy's shoulder and the boy slumped. He had not felt this much kindness in a long while, a brief lifetime ago. The boy recalled how this man had tried to save his father and him, though he knew these shackles were an even harsher truth than this Portuguese man's kindness.

The boy sighed, and knew no matter how kind this man was, he would only extend his kindness as far as it suited his needs. He would probably never be free to run to a hill to see the sun setting by himself ever again.

This was what kept the boy sobbing, and Magellan embraced the boy, much to the boy's own chagrin, as their ship sailed into the night, on its way back to Portugal, where this little garoto would gain a new name, and a new life.

Interlude

Valladolid, Spain, September 1522

'So tell me, Señor Pigafetta, you claimed the slave was the one that survived?'

'Yes,' the chronicler said simply as he replied to Maximillian Transylvanus, who sat at the table facing him in the Spanish court at Valladolid. Antonio Pigafetta tried to say that one word with a sense of false gravitas, because the truth was, he has had all the gravity taken out of him.

After being one of the few survivors of the massacre at Rajah Charles' dinner, all that time ago, months that teetered on the edge of eternity, Pigafetta did not wish to talk further of the long gone past, a past that is, was, half a world away. When he first left for his journey with Ferdinand Magellan, he thought he was thin, but upon arriving back in Spain, his emaciation was obvious. Bones protruding where he didn't know bones were hidden. Cheekbones sunken in like a ship at the bottom of a deep dark ocean, his own countenance made darker by the shadows his protruding bones cast.

Though his stomach yearned for food, his mouth couldn't take anything much in. Gone was his appetite now. His cravings for tasty things had gone away, and he wondered if they would ever come back.

Even eating the bland things had lost its appeal. There was just no taste in his tongue at all, and even his passion for travel, for learning new things was gone. His body was in Spain, but his mind was still half a world away, still searching for himself as if his past was still catching up to him, in the ghost of a ship with the skeleton crew that made its way back here.

He wondered what had happened to Enrique, and wondered if the interpreter was ever at home here in Europe, or if he was ever at home anywhere. Pigafetta wondered what it must have been like for a boy to be taken away from his family in a siege and taken halfway around the world. He could imagine it at its most base facts, but figured he can't imagine the emotions that made up the heart of such an ordeal.

Pigafetta shifted in his chair. It was a large chair too large for someone of his social stature, though he reckoned this kind of chair was the lowest of its kind in this palace of the highest regard. And it was made even larger by his emaciation.

'And these savages, what did they do to you?' Transylvanus asked again.

PART TWO

1511-1518 A.D.

(A NEW NAME)

5

If the boy had known what had happened in Malacca after he and the Sultan left the city, he would have felt a sickness that had no cure. He would have been endlessly worried about his mother and siblings.

In the weeks that followed, Portuguese agents took note of the places where the Arab inhabitants resided. Many of these Arabs were either traders or merchants, some were missionaries that taught religious classes, none of them were men trained for war. Many of them had suspected the Portuguese might do something, based on their attack against the Tamil Muslims back in Goa. Though they wished it, the missionaries were not trained to fight, and could only cast spears of suspicion. They were afraid if they fought back, they would only gain an ignominious death.

The armoured Portuguese soldiers traversed the docks and streets in the first few days, silver helmets glinting in tropical sunshine, brandishing swords and muskets, their presence at this point just a show of intimidation, and surveillance. They were also finding out where the Arabs lived.

When the second week of their occupation began, they began raids on these houses after sunset, burning the Arabs' homes and killing them in their sleep. Some who had the chance to escape as far as the front door were only nabbed and thrown out on the streets where they were bayoneted.

If the Arabs had to plead, they had no one to plead to. Their Sultan and his people had left them.

After culling out the Arabs the Portuguese began to kill the locals, moving now into the forests where the villages were, burning down houses, torching mosques, firing muskets into the backs of helpless men while women and children watched.

Not many were lucky enough to escape but among those who did were a little boy and girl and their mother, who were miles out into the sea. The mother knew once her son was taken and her husband murdered there was no reason to stay. They had left quietly on the first few days of the Arab killings, and as the waves motioned her children into a lullaby, the mother could feel her city dying. She knew because she was dying on the inside too.

Before dying, the Arabs at least knew these killings had nothing to do with religious fervour, but it was all about money, about monopoly. Alfonso knew this as he planned these killings. He had to break the Arab trade monopoly in spices in this region. If Malacca was nothing, if the Arabs were reduced to nothing, then the Portuguese could make something of this vacuum.

The boy sat down in his bunk and felt the waves beneath him gently rock the boat. As far as days out at sea went, this was a gentle day. He had been months out at sea, and the clothes they had given him fit for the most part, albeit a tad loose. He reckoned there were no children on board boats such as this. He thought that soon he would grow into his clothes. He grazed his fingers across his chin and lips and felt hair bristling there. The gaps between the hairs were still far apart and the bristles were still soft rather than coarse, but soon enough shaving his face was going to be inevitable.

He felt puberty creeping within him in the darkness of the bunk, a place so devoid of light there was no way to tell if it was day or night. The time of day was determined by the bunk's temperature, warm in midday, with the bustle of work in the mornings, cold and quiet at night, but once the men in the ship decided he was a healthy, able-bodied member of this ship, they began to use him for menial things like wiping walls and mopping below deck. As the weeks passed he graduated to more mature things, things such as throwing shit over the decks, a job he was sure the sailors had enjoyed relinquishing to him as they laughed at their mulatto garoto and his shitty job.

Once the sun set he was allowed to go below deck, walking past the bunk of the man he was supposed to now call Master, though he didn't always hear the others call him that. To the others he was just a soldier. But to him he was to be the man he was supposed to lay his servitude to. In all fairness, he knew that Magellan didn't treat him as badly as the other sailors.

On many a night he would walk past his Master Magellan's bunk, but was afraid to enter, with a fathomless sense of fear sinking his courage. This went on for days, until he swam out of this sea of fear.

What caught his eye each time he peeked into the bunk was that bookshelf, a tall, dark, mysterious monolith containing mysteries that beckoned his curiosity. But the problem the boy always had when peeking into the bunk were the admonishments of any of the sailors who always screamed at him, in some form or another the words, 'What the hell are you doing here, bloody kid? Out of the way,' which always sent him scooting away from his master's bunk and into the mess deck lined with hundreds of hammocks, and he was given the ostensible privacy of but one hammock for sleeping amongst the sailors.

Each night as he closed his eyes he always dreamt of fire, hazy, smog-filled visions that dispersed into clarity, visions of his Malacca burning, of his village on fire and being caught by someone in the Portuguese armour he was now intimately familiar with, especially in his mind, but even in dreams he could smell the stink of armour, of men he reckoned hardly showered or cleaned and washed their attire.

Now he was in a boat full of them, soldiers and sailors and scum of the earth. The bunk was large enough to fill a few hundred men, and though they still called him garoto, or more precisely, Garoto, he was now no longer regarded as a boy, he was breaking free of this boyish shell and would soon break out as a man. So they had captured him, but he was also a thief, capturing their language, stealing a word here, and a phrase there, stashing enough in the vault of his young mind to eventually withdraw whole sentences, and in time entire paragraphs, and due to his good ear he began to hear himself being referred to as *Quase Um Homem,* almost a man, or even shorter, Quasi. Almost. Semi.

Part of a boy growing to be like a man was to act tough. The words he had learnt from the Portuguese prisoners in Malacca he began to use liberally in this ship, words like *puta, cadela, merda, cagar, chupa-rola* and *enrabar;* whore, bitch, shit, cocksucker and ass fucker and perhaps his favourite, *cona da tua mae,* though he didn't wish to do dastardly things like that to his mother.

The soldiers and sailors found this mostly charming, this mulatto garoto who tried to swear, and when they patted him on his growing head he would sometimes blurt out '*punheteiro!'* or more explicitly, 'wanker!' and they laughed at and on very rare occasions, with him.

When they slept in the mess decks, even cocooned in their hammocks they were rowdy with mirth, genuine or otherwise, and once they slept they were purring with snores and various other sounds the human body could make from either ends of the orifices, burps, farts, grunts, sneezes, coughs and snorts.

When he awoke from his nightmares he leaned up and observed the people around him. This calmed him, their various noises while asleep, and the rocking of the ship beneath the waves that gently caressed it. He made it a point to mumble to himself, in low tones of the words that he knew in Portuguese, and before he ended, words in Malay, lest he forget his native tongue being around others that didn't speak it.

And if he were still awake after that he recited phrases he heard from the men in the ship, but not just the swear words that he knew by heart. He recited words and sometimes whole conversations, confirming with himself the validity of those pronunciations when he heard them speaking those phrases the next day. He knew enough at least for now to talk about shipping terms, about explaining his whereabouts in the ship, about bows and sterns and sails and even wind direction.

And if his master was not too busy, Master Magellan himself would instruct him in speaking Portuguese. '*Meu nome é,*' he practiced in front of Magellan, who nodded, smiled, proud of his little slave, patting the *garoto* on his head, and sometimes the shoulder, trusting the boy enough to run some errands, simple things like fetching boots to scrub and polish them, and later lifting and pulling things such as anchors or pulleys, knowing full well his slave would get laughed at.

'Let them laugh at him,' Magellan thought, thinking the ridicule and the constant jabbing from the crew would build character, his theory proven when he saw the little garoto grow up before his eyes in the weeks ahead, the hard work making the boy's shoulders grow wider. The boy also spoke full sentences of Portuguese now.

On his part, the boy gave Ferdinand Magellan further lessons in Malay, but older people didn't pick up languages as fast as he could. Magellan's Malay was broken while the boy's Portuguese grew more fluent with each passing day, and it came to the point where the boy just gave up teaching his master.

One day, the boy was finally treated to the thing he had been wanting to see for all these weeks. Magellan invited him into his bunk. At first the boy was unsure, doubting, wondering if this was some cruel joke that the others would screw him for, but after a moment of convincing by Magellan, he entered the room.

'Come here,' Magellan guided the boy to the bookshelf, and pulled out one of the many books on display, leather-bound and large, onto the table just beside it. As Magellan opened the book the boy could smell the leather, it had aged well and reminded him of cows; the book's pages, kept moist in the dankness of the ship, reminded him of trees after the rain.

It was the captain's log, and apart from lists and charts there were thoughts he wished to pry into once he learned to read them. In one of the pages, almost dead centre in the book, was a map of the known world, spread across two pages. The boy did not yet know what the drawings meant.

'The world is right here, most of what we know, at least. We are here,' Magellan pointed at the map. 'And we are going to my homeland, Portugal.'

The boy nodded, fascinated by the cartography lines drawn on the map, before he glanced at his master's beard. It reminded him of Alfonso Albuquerque but decades younger. He reckoned his master might even be younger than his own father was, guessing that his master was no more than in his mid-thirties, the tangle and mess of that beard seemed to take the same shape as the map he saw before him.

The boy said the name of his master's country over and over again, breaking down its component syllables, *port, you, gall,* and even further still, dragging out the letters; *pour, tee, yew, gaaall,* before making sense of it whole. Portugal. This would be the new world in which he would lay the rest of his life in eternal servitude to this one man, wondering if he would die soon, for he couldn't bear the thought of being a slave to the same man all his life, couldn't bear the idea of bending over to take and polish boots and clean scum with a disheveled rag until he was in his eighties, with grey hair and a hunch from all that bending down. No, he had to make himself more useful, but how?

He kept that thought buried, and looked at the map in the logbook. Buried, but not deep enough that he would forget later.

Time waved forward, and after making pit stops for supplies, the ship finally arrived in Portugal, a land as alien to him as dry land to fish.

'This is Lisbon,' Magellan told him, and even he was in awe of his own city. Lisbon had changed in the seven years he had been gone, the port now filled with masts flying the flags of every nation in Europe. To his eyes these flags were just a dream, rainbow colours that would fade to black when he awoke.

When he left Lisbon was a quiet provincial city, but King Manuel's daring sailors had brought back riches that had turned Lisbon into a bustling port, and made the king rich. As Magellan walked along the port he had to be careful not to bump against other people's shoulders. They numbered in the thousands, meandering through buildings that were not erect when Magellan left.

All he could overhear was talk of the conquest of the Indies. He wished to escape the crowd as soon as possible.

They took a carriage to a well-tended house out in the country, away from the bustle of the port from which they arrived, and Magellan breathed in the fresh cool air, glad he was away from the port's madness.

He saw this new world transition from sea port to city, and what a city it was, filled with brick walls and cobblestone streets that rose with the stench of horse manure as those beasts of burden galloped and liberally deposited their green manure, with people having to avoid and walk around that, people littering the streets all dressed in clothes similar to what Magellan and the crew had worn, their similarity anchored and kept him calm while he rode their carriage to his master's house, a house so different in design to his own.

His own home was made of wood and had a porch raised a foot above the ground to prevent flooding. The autumn air seemed to grow colder by the day, and he had felt it since the week before he arrived here in Lisbon, the air grew colder still when he reached the countryside.

'This is my home,' Magellan told the boy. 'It was my parents' home, and when they died, I inherited this place.'

The boy stepped off the carriage and attempted to lift their luggage, but their driver and a lady dashed past him and together lifted the luggage while the boy stood doing nothing.

Magellan thanked the lady while placing a hand on the boy's shoulder. 'Next time,' he told his slave, 'next time you can help her. But today, you are free from these heavy burdens. Your last day before tomorrow. Tomorrow, you shall follow me.'

Not knowing what to do next, the boy ran his fingers across his longish hair, which had not been cut these last few months.

'Go ahead, Garoto,' Magellan implored him. 'But if you do not come back by sundown, you will regret it when we find you.'

The boy nodded and ran into the field and breathed in the air, sniffling because the air was colder than the air he was used to. The autumn leaves here were bright emerald, the birds were singing a song he did not recognise. He reckoned even the birds sang in Portuguese.

Nothing in this field felt normal to him, nothing was normal except for this feeling inside him. For the first time in months he felt like himself, being away from everyone else around him, he would remind himself to thank his new master for allowing him this temporary freedom.

He stopped running for the first time in what felt like hours, panting ever so slightly to catch his breath. When he was done it was almost sundown, and those hours of limitless freedom came crashing down on him. The sun set in his heart, and he knew now how temporary this freedom was. He thought it cruel now for his master to have him feel this abandon only for it to be taken away from him. He felt it was better that Magellan never allowed him this time in the field.

He did not want to be found alone out here, and as the sun sank behind him into the horizon, he turned to face the long shadow the sun cast and followed it to his new house.

He opened the back door of the kitchen, panting and looking around to see if anyone was looking for him, when his eyes stumbled upon a vision in a blue dress that addressed him. 'You must be the new boy.'

He looked up and took a deep breath, not knowing what to do. Did he even remember how to speak? Her mere presence took the breath out of him, took his words and left nothing but a void in his mind. Only one word seemed to linger as if he were falling off a cliff and that word was his only purchase.

'Yes,' he said the word, and the void was filled.

'I'm Ferdinand's sister,' she told him.

'I see,' the boy spoke those words quick and confident, finally able to catch his breath.

'Isabel,' she said slowly, purring out her name.

The corners of the boy's lips curled into a devilish smile. She was older than him but younger than his mother, and younger than

Magellan. But the smile was taken away when he heard his master call him, his tone showing no sign of his sister's sweetness. His tone was harsh, it reverberated with the rockiness of a ship against a storm at sea.

He sunk his neck within his shoulders when he saw his master, though Magellan did not address him.

'Isabel,' he called out to his sister. They held each other in a long embrace, each second for each day they were apart. They composed themselves, dusted off the other's shoulders and gave the other a longing smile.

Magellan placed a hand on his slave's shoulder. 'I see you have met this little garoto.'

'Yes, we have met. He seems a fine boy,' Isabel addressed them both.

The boy nodded very slowly. The hand around his shoulder may as well have been a noose around his neck.

'Fine and strong,' Magellan remarked. He patted the boy on his shoulder and told him, 'Please, kindly, carry my sister's things inside the house.'

Magellan lifted his arm away, as if unlocking the boy, who waited for a second gesture while he stared at Isabel's bags. They were hard, and made of fine leather. There was no instruction left to be given, he realized. Before his master laid a hand on his shoulder again, he grabbed the bags, lifting and staggering under their' weight.

Once inside the house he placed the bags and took a few short, panting gasps, and was more tired than he would admit to himself.

Isabel patted the boy on his head, remarking how long the boy's hair had grown. 'Have you no barbers on your ship?'

'We should cut it then,' Magellan figured.

'No, keep it. It hides his features well. We will keep you within these walls, garoto, and keep you safe. Provided you work for us. Is that agreeable?'

'Si, Señorita,' he nodded, eyes marked on his new masters.

What Magellan's sister did not tell his new slave was that there was not much confinement in the house. There were daily chores, the literal shit work he had been relegated to at the outhouse, he swore who just left by their stenches alone, and he sadly began to realize even beautiful people stank just as bad as the ugly people on boats. He had to clean the shit out of the boat that took him to Lisbon, and now he had to clean the stools of his new masters. He reckoned this shit also belonged Isabel, as lovely as she was, she still produced the same shit as everyone else.

There were other helpers, who lived in the house, while the boy lived in a little barn where he slept alone in the hay. He had come to terms with the idea he was lesser than the helpers. Many of them were women, though some were teenagers on the verge of being men. Their skin was fairer than his, and though there was no outright animosity, they did make a great deal of keeping their distance. Which gave the boy the impression they were suspicious of him, and that in spite of their lowly station, still thought they were better than him.

For many weeks he did not see his master, who was always away. This made him feel even more alone. Apart from humble passing glances with Isabel, he rarely spoke to anyone else. Isabel though kind, had seemed to have faded from him, their initial kind encounter dissolving like sand in a river. She would be concerned with the boy, sometimes sneaking in food in his barn, rolls of bread and cheese wrapped in cloth before he slept at night. He appreciated at least that, and wondered if she didn't see him because she did not want to be associated with a slave boy, or that she was afraid people might say things of her if she did?

The last woman to shower him with kindness was his mother, and he wondered how she was now. He missed all the little things he had, things he never knew he would never have again, things like seeing his father make a keris, or helping his mother in the kitchen, and wrestling with his siblings in the house.

His master Magellan had said nothing more of his mother, but he was glad she and Jalil and Suri were not killed. Yet.

That thought saddened him even more, and it made him feel truly alone.

Then on a Sunday, a day when he thought he was resigned to be alone forever, he was approached by his master. 'Get up,' his master told him at the crack of dawn. They took a carriage to a local church where they met a priest. The boy was brought inside the church, and he noted how large and opulent it was. Once, he had walked inside a mosque and felt its holy power. Today, he was in another holy place and felt the same power. While in the mosque they knelt and prostrated, in the church there were benches and booths and altars and paintings and candles. He wondered how they prayed with all these distractions.

'Today is the first day of your new life. You shall be born anew, cleansed of all your past sins,' Magellan explained to him.

They stood at the baptistry where Magellan stood behind the boy while the priest chanted his prayers in Latin. The boy observed the motions of the priest, waited impatiently for what was to come next.

'And now, in the name of the Father, Son, and Holy Spirit,' the priest said, 'you are cleansed of all sin.'

Magellan took the boy closer to the baptistry, a wooden pole elevated to a height just as tall as the boy was. He placed his hand behind the boy's head. 'Stay calm,' he told the boy.

The boy made a guess as to what would happen next. Magellan submerged the boy's head in the water, and he took a deep breath before his head was dunked in. A second later his head emerged, and he gasped for air.

'Now my son, you are born anew,' the priest said. 'What name shall you give him?'

'Enrique,' Magellan decided.

The boy took a deep breath. 'Enrique,' the boy acknowledged. '*Meu nome é Enrique,*' the boy said his name again, casting that word on his tongue the way blacksmiths forged iron.

Enrique spent the rest of the week getting used to his new name and the presence of his new master. He was now used to his master in the house, the last few weeks of his absence now made up for it.

His master spent his days in the house mostly in his office, drawing up plans.

Now that his master was in the house, he spent less time outside of it. Magellan was kind enough to invite Enrique in his office to explain what was going on.

'There was a man,' he told Enrique, 'who explored the world and found strange new lands. His name was Christopher Columbus, and he had always been one of my heroes. I wish to one day continue Columbus' work, though I had no idea how to begin, or where to go. Then I received these letters,' he showed Enrique the table, stacks of rolls that threatened to fall off the table, 'letters from Francisco Serrano, who wrote to me of the riches of the Moluccas Spice Islands. These letters have inspired me for a long time now, and my mind is clear. Soon we might be able to set sail to these spice islands.'

Enrique nodded. He had no idea what Magellan was talking about. He got the gist of traveling to strange new lands, but that was as far as he understood. Then one day, Magellan brought with him some new clothes for Enrique to wear.

'Come my boy, we are going to see the king,' Magellan told him.

He was not used to dressing up for royalty. When he met Sultan Mahmud, he was dressed in nothing but slacks and slippers. This time he was dressed in a set of clothes very different from his old Malay village outfit. Now he was dressed in long sleeves, leather belt, vest, things to keep the cold at bay, save for this pair of tights he was pulling on. Tight, and not really comfortable.

To top things off Magellan gave Enrique a slave hat. A hat for him to hate, Enrique thought. Well, better to look a fool than to clean shit off ships, he reckoned. As best he could, he tried recalling the name of this king he was about to meet. The King of Portugal. He vaguely remembered that name, a name that had more than once been spoken on the ship that brought him here, uttered by sailors and soldiers.

Manuel.

I am going to see King Manuel, of Portugal, Enrique told himself.

On days when he got to do things like these it seemed like his master was pampering him, and he wondered if there might be a *balasan*, or a *'retribuicao' in* Portuguese.

If truth be told he was digging at straws, scraping at the bottoms of barrels. His master might have been stern to his subordinates, but not that much to him. He reckoned that perhaps it was because he was a boy, and maybe when he became a man he might get the whipping he deserved. Today, he felt as though he were a prince from some faraway land, of which half were true. Stolen from a faraway land to be dressed in strange robes.

This feeling of being some pretender prince was brought further into reality when the carriage arrived. The horses looked more groomed that usual, though he wondered if it was just his imagination. In the carriage he wondered what the King of Portugal looked like, and if he was still too crude to see the likes of kings and queens.

'Why are we here to see the King, exactly, Master Magellan?' Enrique asked.

Magellan stroked his beard. It looked neater today, and Enrique wondered if his master had trimmed it.

'I have a proposal to bring forth to the king. I want you to be mindful. Do not say anything needless, and do not say anything unless you are spoken to. Understand?'

Enrique nodded.

When they entered the court, it was a discreet affair. Enrique kept silent as they were brought into the throne room. He wished he could raise his voice when he saw the women of the court, young maidens he reckoned were barely a few years older than him, and he wished he were grown up now, so that he might have a chance to talk to them. He remembered his master's warnings, and maintained his silence.

'Greetings and salutations, your most esteemed Majesty, I am glad that we have finally met. I am, of course, Commander Ferdinand Magellan, and this is my slave, Enrique,' Magellan began, bowing

before the King. Enrique followed his master's lead, though he felt
his master was laying the introduction a little thick.

The older King Manuel had a smile that was practiced. The
corners of his lips rose but his eyes stayed firm, unmoving, forming
the caricature of a smile. 'Yes, Magellan. Your letters were exciting,
and precise, full of well, how do I say this? Fantasy.'

Enrique rose slowly, searching both his master's and the King's
eyes. His master's eyes trembled, and his lips curved maliciously
down toward his neck. 'I am sure your Majesty has read my letter
thoroughly. I mean no disrespect, your Majesty, but do you not
think that Portugal needs to find a new route to the Spice Islands?
The Spanish are already making some leads there. I can vouch from
the letters of my esteemed colleague Francisco Serrano that the Spice
Islands of the Moluccas are full of rich spices. If we sail westward
instead of east, we can bypass the Spanish trade routes and—'

'No one has sailed in the opposite direction, Ferdinand. No one
perhaps, except for a madman like you,' King Manuel cut him short.

'Only if you would allow me then perhaps this madman would
do well to serve his king,' Magellan stood high with his chest
displayed proudly.

'Your way westward would cost the kingdom too much money,
and it is too dangerous,' King Manuel told Magellan, making his
point the way an arrow strikes prey.

Magellan snapped, his arms exploding into motions of fury,
'What Portugal lacks is imagination, and an adventuring spirit!
You have already told Alfonso Albuquerque not to invade Goa and
Malacca and by not listening to you he has conquered both cities!'
He pointed an arrow-like finger to his slave. 'This here, my reward
from the spoils of war, a decent boy from Malacca.' He sighed. 'At
least consider it, your Majesty.'

Enrique dared not move, he barely understood yet what his
master was asking for. This was not the master who held him as he
cried when he was in shackles. This was a man filled with ambition
and zeal. He almost didn't recognize his master.

'My decision is final,' King Manuel told Magellan. He seemed bitter from the mention of Alfonso Albuquerque. He gritted his teeth. 'We however, have a mission for you in Azemmour. A mission to quell a Moor uprising.'

A Moor uprising? Magellan sucked a deep breath through his nostrils, his eyes burned as he clenched his jaw and he shot daggers at his King. It occurred to Enrique why his master was seething. His master wanted to prove himself. He was a soldier but he wanted to be so much more than his current station in life had to offer.

Enrique could not yet understand the talk of trade routes and spices and sailing over the other side of the world, but he understood that Magellan wished to be seen on equal terms with King Manuel, but the King could only see him as a lesser being. Enrique could still not fathom the gravity of what King Manuel had asked of his master.

'Very well then, my most gracious and very wise king. It shall be done. Come, Enrique.' Magellan pulled Enrique out of the King's sight the way a harpoon dug into and pulled at a whale.

6

At first it was dressing up for a king. Now he was dressed for battle. What he was told was that some kind of disagreement had occurred with the governor of Azemmour, Morocco, Moulay Zayam, who had refused to pay tribute to King Manuel, and had prepared an army to defend himself. This act of defiance left King Manuel no choice but to send a fleet to that city on the 15th of August in the year 1513.

So here he was, a slave brought to a battle where he was to serve as a soldier. Ferdinand Magellan was the master of him, but he was beginning to learn that there was always a bigger fish. His master was just a subordinate to King Manuel, and on this voyage to Morocco, his master was subordinate to Dom Jaime, the Duke of Braganza.

The two weeks on the ship to Morocco gave Enrique plenty of time to listen to their conversations, and he tried as best he could to stay in his place. He served only his master, and to his master's credit, Magellan defended Enrique when others in the ship asked the boy to do chores for them. 'He's with me,' Magellan told whoever asked him to run any silly errand.

One day, Dom Jaime found Enrique hauling empty buckets up and down the deck stairs, and glanced at him. 'Did you know how I became the Duke of Braganza, boy?'

'No, my lord,' Enrique placed his buckets down and waited for Dom Jaime to continue. Dom Jaime paused, eyes narrowed, the way he looked at Enrique was the way one looked at a roach that was about to be stomped. He decided to tell the slave boy, hoping that by telling him his tale the boy might give him more respect.

He sighed, scoffed at the slave boy yet was eager to tell it to him, hoping to impress someone he thought of as having a much lower station than him.

Enrique could sense the disdain, and the thinly veiled vanity in his tone, as Dom Jaime began; 'When I was a child, I witnessed my father and uncle being executed for treason by the Crown. After my father's death, my family, the House of Braganza, were banished to Castile and all our properties were seized.

'After King João II's death in 1495, the throne passed on to my father's cousin Manuel. He forgave the House of Braganza and welcomed us back to Portugal with all our wealth returned, on the condition that I devoted absolute loyalty to King Manuel.'

Enrique nodded and didn't know where to place his head. He wondered if he would look at the Duke's eyes and be wowed or to simply know his place and remain quiet, but recognized a smirk carved out of the Duke's pride.

The other thing Enrique noticed was how young the Duke was. Enrique nodded at this young Duke, and left him to go about his business. He reckoned the Duke was in his mid-twenties, while his master was in his early thirties. Enrique was not used to the concept of a younger person having greater authority than an older person.

As an older brother to two younger siblings, he felt authority was handed by age, and as their older brother he held more power over them. Now a Duke younger than his master was leading this ship, and soon, the battle that was to come. Dom Jaime was leaner than Magellan, but there was an air of authority to him that spread throughout the ship.

As the days passed, Enrique had the nagging feeling that something was amiss. He still had to avoid the demands of the other sailors asking him to do things for them, but Magellan kept him away from these menial tasks.

This did not escape the notice of Dom Jaime, who noticed that Enrique was as a bird free to come and go around the ship, always close, hovering around Ferdinand Magellan.

When they bumped shoulders again, Enrique was quick to bow before the Duke and tell him, 'Greetings, my Lord,' in perfect Portuguese.

'Where did they find you?' Dom Jaime wondered.

'In the far, far east,' Magellan replied from the shadows, stepping out from the odd angles that candlelit ships gave, the dark shapes his own shadow cast loomed over the Duke.

'Señor Magellan. I believe I was speaking to this slave.'

'Brought from the other side of the world.'

'And is he a good slave?' Dom Jaime wondered, stroking his beard, teasing it with the tips of his fingers.

After a moment's pause, for good effect, so that the Duke would have to wait, Magellan said, 'He does well enough.'

The Duke scoffed, and left the deck. 'One day, he will fetch my slippers, more like.'

'Gracias, Señor, and may we have a good journey ahead,' Enrique told Dom Jaime, bowing his head low enough that his hair draped over his forehead. It shielded his eyes from the Duke's piercing glance.

Dom Jaime paused to think of his words. 'Your boy has . . . interesting manners. Best you watch his tongue.'

'We shall all watch our tongues, Duke,' Magellan ended the meeting, and for the first time since the ship sailed, Enrique felt the thick air of authority thin out.

The days before the landing Enrique filled his time doing chores for his master, and later, chores for the ship, with Magellan finally relenting and allowing Enrique to work at other tasks, scrubbing floors, tying masts, lifting crates and barrels.

When they were almost nearing Azemmour, his new clothes seemed years old. He slept in these same clothes, and perhaps stank more of himself than saltwater, a splash of which might have done him good. Tonight in this ship he dreamt of something that he thought he had forgotten, it was a dream he thought he would never wake up from.

He dreamt again of his capture, the Portuguese soldiers that grabbed him, the stink of their armour and the force from which he was taken away, in sight of his father, who ran toward his son, only to be shot dead. This scene repeated itself again and again, at different angles, and in this dream he screamed so loud that he woke up sweating, thinking someone in the ship was screaming but it was only him.

He looked around, glad no one was awake. Leaving his hammock, he stood on tiptoes so he wouldn't wake those below deck.

He slinked to his master's quarters and stood by the doorway. His master seemed to be sleeping peacefully, his beard vibrating along with his snoring. Enrique wondered what it would take to motion to his sleeping master and perhaps just strangle him? Or if he had a knife, could he kill this man that now owned him?

Enrique clenched his fingers, imagined a knife in his palm. He took a deep breath. He wondered if he were to be better owned by Magellan or the Duke? He knew the answer, and it made him want to drive that imaginary knife straight through his own heart. He banged his fist against the wall, and headed above deck.

For a moment the sky seemed darker than below deck until his eyes got used to the stars and moonlight. He looked around for the deck hands that would be here, but found only the wind howling at him. He felt its chill, tasted the salty mist it brought to his tongue. The sky was clear tonight and even in the darkness he could make out the horizon every which way he turned.

He walked along the deck, balancing himself ably. He had grown a good pair of sea legs, and soon heard someone call him. 'Oi, Garoto!'

Enrique turned to find the voice, groaning at the fact that the last time he heard someone call him Garoto was not too long ago, in a ship much like the one he was in now. The other half of him was glad because he had someone to talk to.

'Hey you deaf, kid?' the voice asked, a tad impatient. Enrique finally saw a lean shape no larger than himself crouched and leaning against the mast, smoking a rolled cigarette.

'Hold it, hold it, I'm coming just give me a second.' Enrique said. He motioned toward the shape barely illuminated by the volcanic glow of the cigarette's tail end. He grabbed the cigarette from the voice and added, 'I'm not deaf,' and bummed a smoke from him before returning it.

Enrique coughed a little and to save himself from further embarrassment he looked out at the sea and let its breeze calm him. There was nothing out at sea, and beneath nothing lurked leviathans and dark, sunken secrets.

When Enrique talked to people, he looked beneath their own oceans, their sunken secrets. His knack for language was a beast unearthing sunken ships and their treasures.

'What brings you up here?' Enrique asked his companion. He knew the other person should have asked this question, but Enrique wanted to gain the upper hand in the conversation.

'Couldn't sleep,' the young man said.

Enrique reckoned the man was barely eighteen, but had the life beaten out of him, and wondered in a few years' time would he himself be this emaciated and hopeless?

'Same here,' Enrique said.

'I sometimes come out here to clear my head. When everyone is asleep, I feel as if I can find myself, you know?' the young man said, the tail end of his sentence imploring, reaching out to a kindred soul.

Enrique took the bait but took his time to answer. He wondered who or what was his version of self? 'At least you have a self. I lost what I am. I am just a slave.'

'You are your own man. Don't let anyone tell you different. Me? I'm just a deck hand. Been so for years. My mates call me by name, but it took years before they would. Before that they just called me names. All kinds of names. But listen,' the young man paused, trying his best to articulate his next string of words. 'Listen, you are a man, you are your own heartbeat, your own soul. Your own eyes and ears. Serve your master well, yes, but don't forget that you are more than what people make you. Make yourself useful. Make them wish they can't survive without you. Give yourself value.'

Enrique scoffed and snatched the cigarette again.

'Hey!' The young man resisted.

'I'll start by finishing this cigarette you started, eh?' And he dragged in and tried not to cough this time.

Both of them laughed, and Enrique felt something roll down his eyes, something he had not felt touching his cheek in a long time. He wiped those wet things off his cheeks and laughed. He liked to be free, even if it was from stolen moments like these. At these moments, he did not feel the inevitability of time. Soon the ship would rouse to waking life, and he would return to his role as slave, but with a renewed and more determined energy, armed with the knowledge he was as much of himself as he wished to be.

But not just yet. He was laughing so hard his stomach hurt. Today, the sunlight hurt him even more. The young man and Enrique had these nightly smoking sessions, until the day they arrived in Azemmour proper.

On the day they docked outside the city they were greeted with dry, warm weather. For weeks their only knowledge of the world was the wide-open sea. The city was as full of sand as the ocean was full of blue. The buildings were different, and even the animals the men rode were unique. They were not horses, but donkeys.

As their ship docked in, Enrique noticed the buildings were close to the shoreline, as though they could slide off the shore and sink into the waters just a step ahead. Enrique thought it was nothing but the tobacco that nourished him, this strange nourishment that gave him the energy to fetch his master's boots, and prepare his master's sword and musket.

Enrique did not know how a musket worked just yet, but he knew it was a dangerous weapon he had seen being fired into his father's chest, and now it was his job to polish it, and his master's sword. But there was one implement that he was unable to touch, a weapon that his master that kept safe and away from him, and he was only able to steal glances of it. Today he saw that sheath in his master's chest, a wavy sheath that kept the keris his father died holding.

On top of acquiring Enrique, Magellan also acquired this keris. But it was a keepsake for his master for now and not for him. He longed to grab that wavy blade and hold it, wishing the blade could somehow call forth his father's spirit, and if not that, at least his father's memory.

Regardless, Enrique was only now beginning to process the enormity of this endeavour, the fact that King Manuel has sent five hundred ships with fifteen thousand soldiers, all of them docking now, by the thousands.

'What am I to do, master?' Enrique asked Magellan.

'You'll stay close to me,' Magellan told him.

'Even into battle,' Enrique implored.

'Close enough,' Magellan said.

If he were any other type of father, he may have asked Enrique to stay in the ship while he and the other troops began to do battle, but he did not bring his slave boy here just to protect and mollycoddle him. He brought the boy along as reinforcement. As the others began disembarking, Enrique heeded his master's advice to stay close, though he never realized how close he had to be.

He stumbled as he tried to keep pace with the other soldiers, and in the most inopportune of instances his memories would flash back to his old life in his village, where disputes with neighbours were settled with barely three men as a show of force.

But when it came to the might of kings, three men became fifteen thousand. It made Enrique wonder how many men had Moulay Zayam mustered?

As more and more Portuguese troops amassed onto the shore, Enrique had lost count. 'Don't I at least get to wield a sword, Master?'

Magellan paused for a brief moment before he carried on marching. 'Here. Pray you know how to use it.'

Enrique tucked the short sword contained in its leather sheath to his side. 'Pray I don't need to, Master.'

This amused Magellan, who quickly slapped the side of the boy's scruffy head, then he chuckled. 'This is war, son. May the Lord bless us, the victors.'

This was the last thing Enrique heard from his master, before his master's voice was overpowered by the Duke's. Dom Jaime was all silent power and authority in their ship, as though he were reserving all his energy for the battle. Dom Jaime belted out his orders with the buttery smoothness of a seasoned professional.

Enrique recalled a very similar charisma back in Malacca, and the memory made his heart sink into a dark hole he seemed to keep aside in his heart in times like these. He remembered Alfonso Albuquerque.

Dome Jaime was still a couple decades younger than Albuquerque, but from the way he ran this operation he was going to turn into him very soon.

They had already set up camps before sunset. The air turned colder as the sun shied away from them. Enrique felt sand within his hands and within his boots, and he felt it in his lungs, breathing it in as he craved for another cigarette from his friend on the ship.

The young man smiled and nodded to Enrique before falling in for orders. Enrique wondered if he would see him again. Would he have conversations with him, or anyone again, for that matter?

Every minute alive was precious to him, and he wondered if he would survive this coming battle.

Night fell, and Dom Jaime gave a speech to those who could hear him, knowing his voice would not reach fifteen thousand but he could reach a few hundred. Enrique and Magellan listened to the Duke's more refined form of Portuguese, not the Portuguese Enrique was used to, the Portuguese of pirates and prisoners.

After the speech there was a weapons inspection in which Magellan brought Enrique along. He showed him the types of muskets and swords which they would be using. Enrique kept silent, until Magellan couldn't stand it anymore.

'What's going on in your mind?'

'I still remember everything,' Enrique lamented, his shoulders hunched low as he exhaled. 'This all reminds me of the last time I saw my home.'

Magellan could hear nothing except their breathing. He had never considered a slave's thoughts and feelings, and the boy's remark left him wanting to say a soothing word. He tried to think of a word or a phrase to make Enrique feel better, and he even caught himself uttering half of a syllable before catching himself short when he concluded he still had not found the right thing to say.

Enrique darted his eyes away, felt sorry for bringing this up. 'I'm sorry to upset you, Master.'

Magellan wished he could find the right way to say sorry, but what flashed in his mind, was the sight of Enrique's father being shot, of Magellan himself having to bury the man. All he could do was grunt, turn away and leave the boy alone with his thoughts. He decided to talk to the Duke.

Enrique looked on as his master talked to Dom Jaime, guessing they must be talking about battle tactics or something similar. He saw Magellan holding the hilt of the sword tightly, clenching it as if his life depended on it. Enrique realized he was also clenching his own smaller sword by the hilt. No one wanted to die. But he knew many of the men here would have to.

There were no signs of the Moroccan army. Enrique figured they were doing what they did, gathering troops and having speeches and preparing weapons. He wondered if fighting was the right thing to do. He thought of Sultan Mahmud Shah of Malacca, and knew he wasn't the best ruler, but many would die for the Sultan, because it was loyalty to the ruler, and not to your own thoughts.

Was that what these fifteen thousand men were doing? Were they doing this just because Manuel was King? Were they all slaves in some ways? Was the King or Sultan slave then to his own whims and fancies?

The young Enrique felt a stirring within him, an anger heating up his entire body. His skin turned red and he tightened the grip on his sword with the inescapable inevitability of a hangman's noose around a prisoner's neck. There was no way out for him, a boy thousands of miles away from home, caught in a battle within himself he cannot win, caught in a battle that was soon to come, a battle in which he knew many would die.

We are all slaves, he decided at last.

He waited for everyone to sleep, but that was a hard thing to wait for. Out here in the open, there were sentries pacing along the camps, and the wideness of space did not feel as safe as the confines of a ship. He was frustrated he could not have some peace to himself. He held on to his sword tightly and imagined what he could do with it. He imagined this for a long time until he couldn't stand it. He left his camp after making sure his master was asleep. He paced along until a sentry told him, 'Go to sleep, garoto.'

Enrique looked up, glad it was that buddy of his from the ship. 'Can't sleep,' Enrique told his buddy, whose name he still did not know.

'Excited about going to war?' the young man asked. As if out of thin air, a cigarillo appeared in his hand, already rolled. He placed it to his lips and struck a match to it, savouring it as though it were his last. 'That's the trick, kid, you have to take each one of these things as though it were your last. That's why they taste so good.'

Enrique eyed the cigarillos and wondered if he would have any more of that. They breathed in the night air, and the clear sky revealed the stars above them.

'The night is honest, and it does not lie,' the young man said. 'Look above. Each star tells a different story. I want to be one of those stars when I die. I want the world to hear my story.'

'I am a star,' Enrique muttered.

'What's that?' His friend asked.

'Nothing, my friend,' Enrique paused. 'Do you think this battle will end badly?'

'All battles have bad endings, even for those who win,' the young man told him. 'Now go to sleep,' he offered Enrique the last bit of the cigarillos.

Enrique took and inhaled it, as though it were his last. He wanted to give it back to his friend, but the young man implied that he should finish it. Enrique threw the stub once he was done, and both of them left each other's company.

'Sweet dreams. Dream of stars. And happy endings, eh?'

Enrique nodded, and only part of that was true as he dreamt.

He awakened at dawn with a sudden jerk, as if he had lost his sense of self. The night's taste of fresh air and the twinkle of honest stars gave way to the day's deceptions.

He went about getting things for his master, and once both of them were dressed, they entered the formation of fifteen thousand soldiers.

Magellan placed a hand on his shoulder and asked, 'How goes your Arabic, Enrique?'

'Better than yours, master,' Enrique told him in Arabic. 'We shall win this battle,' he said now in Portuguese.

'Well then, we may have use of you after all,' Magellan told him.

'I am glad to hear that, master.'

As the Portuguese army gathered and marched on, Enrique followed, looking back and regarding the remnants of the tents they had built, leaving behind unwanted tarps and wooden frames, and thousands of footsteps carved into the sand, marching forward to meet Moulay Zayam's army. Enrique couldn't find his friend. At this point, he may never.

The sun rose high and scorching above them, the heat closer to the climes of his own Malacca, a dishonest heat that seared his skin. He wondered how the soldiers in the armour stood the heat.

By the time they were anything remotely close to civilization, he saw the city's buildings grow out of the horizon, like plants blooming along with their march. He saw something familiar, but couldn't decide if the structure was what he thought it was. He looked up at the sun, gauging the time. Had they been marching for so long?

He heard the *adhan*, the call to prayer, a faint call in the distance, wondering if it was either in his head or in his heart, the call so great, it shifted the movement of the Portuguese soldiers sideways, the way a hurricane changes the flow of the tide.

It was *zohor*, the early afternoon prayer, and it soothed him, though the call that came after brought within him nothing but dread.

Horses galloped up ahead in the distance, and he could only hear them before he could see them, thunder before the lightning. After the cavalry came the troops, and they were as far different from the Portuguese as the Portuguese were to them.

The Moroccans had no armour, their swords were curved along its top half, reminding him of a much larger keris, and he could also see the unshakeable resolve in their countenances.

Enrique recalled the last time he was in war, and the resolve on all the faces of his Malaccan brothers. It matched the faces of the Moroccans he saw ahead of him. The call to prayer grew stronger, and he knew he was not far away from a mosque, which meant he was probably not too far from the city. He whispered to himself, hoping that God would help them all. But in war he had learnt that God watched and lead only in silent prayer.

Who would win depended solely on the whims of man, and not upon the whims of God, who worked in great, mysterious ways, and it was these mysterious ways that had lead him here, from Malacca to Portugal, to Morocco. Maybe God had a plan for him, but he did not yet know what it was.

Moulay Zayam was at the forefront on his steed, and he spoke first. Enrique stepped forward, snaking past the other soldiers without permission, and began to translate what Moulay was saying back to Dom Jaime, both of them a little more than surprised that this mulatto could translate for them.

The Moroccan army raised their swords high in the air, on steeds that were bought from the Portuguese, yelling a victory yell.

'They shouldn't be yelling too soon,' Magellan scoffed.

Enrique wondered why they had not yet started fighting, not that he was anxious for it. The air turned quiet, and he noticed the call to prayer had stopped. The Moroccan army lowered their swords and bowed their heads, whispering a shared prayer led by Moulay Zayam, who then lowered his cupped hands to his thighs, the spread of his arms wide and confident.

Enrique took a quick look at the man, guessing Moulay was in his forties, his face as hirsute as his master's, shades of grey peppered evenly throughout. The prayer had calmed them and suddenly Moulay snapped, his index finger pointed forward sharply. 'They will not take us!'

The Moroccan army, though lesser in number than the Portuguese, charged with the might of an army twice its size.

Behind him he could hear the Portuguese army scream, and their combined cries of battle almost burst his eardrums. His shoulders hunched in reflex, and he saw his master on horseback leading a platoon of forty men that diverged from the main wave of soldiers.

Enrique heard the gallop of cavalry from both sides, the drum of hooves against the sandy ground below became war drums, the hooves stirring sand in their wake, forming a dust storm, and his heart raced and his breath held within his throat afraid for release, and when it finally escaped, he could only breathe in dust and his own false convictions, wondering if the Moroccans would lose——his pondering smacked out of him when he heard the muskets firing, a sound more fearsome to him than thunder.

He ran at odd angles, scrambling to find a safe spot, only to realize seconds later, there was no such thing in the chaos of battle. The other soldiers ran past him, into the melee with swords raised, and he had no other choice but to raise his own short sword, and join them.

With their swords raised, there was only the inevitability of battle, and soon swords clashed, armours and shields collapsed upon one another, a thousand separate thunders coalescing under the report of Portuguese muskets.

The Moroccan soldiers fell, their bodies trampled underfoot and haloed in clouds of blood. Enrique couldn't find his master and had no time to even contemplate his allegiances. He only knew of what was happening now, and the fact that the Moroccan army would come after him even if he was just a boy, for the simple fact that he wore Portuguese clothes.

He ran forward with sword raised overhead, looking for the closest thigh he could find—he couldn't stand the idea of stabbing someone in the chest or gut just yet. The first thigh he pierced belonged to a soldier barely a few years older than he was, a face young and fresh and not yet hardened by war, the face screamed, clutching his thigh at an obtuse angle.

Enrique ran forward and dodged the soldier awkwardly as the soldier slashed his sword at him.

His goal now was to survive long enough to find his master. He finally spotted Magellan, fighting with an efficiency that matched his ferocious temperament.

Blows were given with maximum force and registered with equal measure with some soldiers falling to the ground bruised and bloodied, while some fell dead from direct stab wounds.

His master was in the thick of battle, his face showed the fighting confidence of a man who was determined he was going to win. This made Enrique smile, and he was proud that his master fought well, though that pride lasted a mere second before he was lifted off the ground by a Moroccan soldier just a few years older than he was, a soldier no longer a boy, not yet a man. Enrique, inspired by his master's prowess, was determined not to be stomped upon the ground like a bug, and being held by a soldier against his will reminded him too much of being caught in Malacca; it made him angry enough to clench his sword's handle, smacking the hilt against the soldier's neck. He yelled out, '*Puta!*' and the grip loosened causing Enrique to drop badly.

He lost orientation, shaking his head before he saw that soldier again, his view askew, as if the world was curved like he was looking at it through a rounded drop of water.

He felt tears welling in his eyes. He blinked, and when the soldier tried to grab him again, almost by reflex he swung his sword in a wide arc that cut the soldier's arm. The soldier was stunned that this little *sabbi* was able to cut him.

The soldier charged ahead, pride clouding his common sense, he should have covered his vulnerable spots. This gave the little sabbi the perfect chance to dash ahead and stab the soldier in the gut, where his sword stayed.

Enrique could not believe he had done this. For a moment, this felt as illusory as a dream, until the warmness of the soldier's blood flowed onto his arm, staining it red. He tried to find an expression to describe the blood, it was not grotesque, but unbelievable that someone else's blood was flowing onto his hand, and he was certain the blood's temperature rose from mere warmth to a painful boil.

This was the heat of death, and this being his first time, he was so trapped in its moment that he did not know how to remove the sword from the soldier's body. The soldier did it for him, forcing the blade out, and took two steps back, but that only made the blood gush out with nothing to hold it in. The soldier fell back, the back of his skull knocking hard against the desert ground.

Enrique looked at his once silver blade that had turned crimson, not knowing what to feel, if he should feel pride or guilt. He looked on as the muskets and cannons fired, and the other Moroccan soldiers were shot down.

He found his master fighting like tomorrow did not exist for him, as he swung and slashed with the full knowledge that he had a whole army with him. He saw Dom Jaime lead the troops expertly, knowing when to direct and redirect his troops to gain greater advantage, and the way Enrique saw it, the Portuguese army was trampling the Moroccans the way a mad bull stampeded and crushed bugs.

What bulls forgot though, was that bugs bite back. A shield struck Magellan's thigh, and he got punched in the face. A sword then struck his thigh, and he yelled loud enough for Enrique to hear, dropped to one knee, but gathered enough strength and leverage to leap with the force of his good knee to strike against his assailant. He revelled in the feel of warm blood against his hand, he was intimately familiar with death, they were close friends, closer to him than family.

Magellan landed above his attacker and felt his knee crack against the ground, certain he heard something pop, yelling again and hiding his pain by focusing on his kill.

He removed his sword and looked on at his attacker's face, blood gurgling from his lips, blood masking the olive skin, but did nothing to hide his honest eyes that wondered, *why, why did I have to die for this,* before the light within them faded into the horizon of his inner mind.

Magellan was out of breath. This was a victory that felt less than victorious. He noticed the attacker was just a boy. He raised his head, and from hearing the last reports of muskets ringing through the air, knew that victory was inevitable.

He lamented that the Moroccan soldiers were just boys turning into men, and never would they know the joy of a woman's company; even the joys of having children and old age were robbed from them. He was a robber of lives that would never be.

Magellan tried to stand, but a pain shot through his knee. Enrique saw this and ran to his master. He placed his master's arm over his small shoulder and tried to make his master stand. Both of them stumbled. Magellan clutched his knee.

Time seemed to slow down, and it was at this juncture that Enrique was of two hearts, the darker heart imagined killing his master, but then where would he go? The Moroccans, who might do worse against him? Ahead of him was a sea of sand, and behind him a sea of blue, both large expanses he could get lost in.

He looked at his master's knee and called for help, but the soldiers did not care much for him. Enrique asked for a medic, though no such healer came. He set his master down and his master clutched Enrique's head, and thanked him.

Enrique nodded and called again for help, but as the battle quieted down, all he could hear was the voice of Dom Jaime growing ever louder as he led his most dedicated troops and cavalrymen as they flanked him, and surrounded Moulay Zayam.

Enrique saw Moulay Zayam raise his arms in defeat as a cavalryman alighted his steed and pulled Moulay's arms back to bind him. The sight of Moulay's face was ever-defiant, and though they tried to hold him, he struggled and did not make it easy for them, until the cavalryman kicked his knee to shove him off balance, and tied the binding proper, all the while with Moulay screaming this was injustice. The cavalryman dragged and then threw Moulay up the steed and they rode from the scene of battle. This was the last Enrique saw of the Moroccan.

Time seemed to slow down for Enrique and all sound lost its meaning. He kept calling for help for his master, all the while witnessing the same kind of death and violence he saw in his old land of Malacca.

Were all the Portuguese this violent, he wondered in the back of his mind, or was this propensity for plunder the same for all peoples of all races of all the known lands of this world? He had to avert his eyes, and he did close them for a second but those lifeless bodies had their eyes perpetually wide open, and they stared back at him. He yelped, coughed, gagged and cried at the same time.

Enrique turned and looked in the distance to find his friend, hoping they would congratulate each other for a job well done, but his heart sank when he saw a body, bloodied, face permanently petrified, a few feet away. He knew who it was, and he whimpered a quiet 'No'. He had just met the young man, and the young man's body had no life left in him. It was his friend. He never even knew the young man's name, and it was a strange sort of hurt, to know he was mourning for a man whose name he did not know. He wiped away a tear, but he didn't know if this tear was for his unnamed friend or for the other corpses surrounding him.

The next thing he saw was his master wincing, then he felt himself being yanked aside. Two medics tied a tourniquet above Magellan's wound and added wooden splints to Magellan's injured knee, securing those splints with slim strings that reminded Enrique of nooses.

He could not believe the battle was over. The intensity he felt in battle gave way to a thing that was the opposite of a celebration or the thrill of victory. All he saw was an aftermath, and was reminded of the end of a wedding celebration, where he had to participate in its cleaning, where he had to assist in clearing tables, pulling aside tablecloths dirty with gravy and leftover rice, pulling down tents, scrubbing cauldrons of soot and hardened curry, but he had never seen a cleanup where men had to drag the bodies of other men.

He turned away from that sight and focused on his master, who was dragged along the ground as though he were already a corpse. Enrique was relieved when he heard Magellan moaning and writhing.

His master was dragged to their ship while Enrique ran alongside, assisting the medics that did not welcome him. He knew he was a large pest to them, but he couldn't stay and do nothing. He then noticed a disquiet within him. He felt something that had been long gone since the beginning of battle. He did not hear the *adhan*, the call to prayer anymore, it was not in the air, or in his heart or mind.

Tears filled his eyes, though he did not know why they appeared. The world around him had been changed, it was not a fact he was willing to accept, but he had to grasp this cruel, harsh reality. He was taken away from his home and family, robbed of his name, and now, with the absence of the *adhan*, he had lost his faith. He was no longer the boy from Malacca. He was now Enrique, slave and servant.

7

Night fell and Magellan closed his eyes, resting his head against old pillows that made him itch more than he cared to admit, but he was too exhausted to worry. The pain in his knee was excruciating and he drowned the pain with alcohol to his wounds and through his lips.

He had drunk enough to numb his mind, and all he waited for was sleep. He wished to be alone but he sensed someone beside him.

'Will that be all, Master?' Enrique asked, prying the bottle away from his master's stubborn fingers. It was hard for Magellan to relinquish, but his resistance was weak. Enrique had the bottle firm in his hand while he waited for his master.

Magellan closed his eyes, not even acknowledging his servant, breathing harder than necessary to block out the other sounds, and to numb his pain, struggling at first, but soon all the forced shutting out worked in his favour, and it was only his snoring that filled the bunk.

Enrique lowered his head and took a couple steps back and left the room, making his way to the main deck to let the cool evening breeze caress his face. He ran his fingers through his hair to hold it in place against the breeze, his eyes looking far into the city of Azemmour only to be saddened by its deathly quiet, as though the battle had never happened.

He came to understand that battles were won and acknowledged by the quiet that came after, it was the quiet of victory, the same quiet that occurred as Malacca fell. He reckoned Magellan was intimately familiar with this unnerving silence, and Enrique wished for any other sound but this silence. He returned to his master's bunk, just to listen to him snore. For some reason, its regular rhythm comforted him.

There were spoils with every battle won. For the Portuguese, they won Moroccan slaves. Enrique thought that was the norm anywhere in the world. The soldiers they captured were bound and only the strongest were chosen to be taken to the ships where they were made to be sold.

For Enrique, it was perhaps his youth or spunk or talent for languages that drew Ferdinand Magellan to him. He knew he was no soldier, and being dragged into battle did not make him one.

He dared not look into the captured slaves' eyes, yet their shadows and silhouettes haunted his periphery. There were so many of them down here, and he could not help but feel he had a small part to play in their capture, if not by his own hand then definitely by proxy via his master.

These slaves were bound in the cargo hold, though Enrique did not know how many were captured in total. But eavesdropping on gossip for all these nights told him that these slaves were to be sold in Cairo, Egypt.

These slaves reminded him of himself not too long ago, shackled and brought to places far from their homes. Enrique felt the guilt of being free to roam while these slaves were bound, yet he did not want to be in their position ever again.

The slaves did not sleep but did their best to simulate something akin to it. Being tied and bound were not the best conditions to churn out sweet dreams. His ship moved languidly across the sea and Enrique ambulated through the dark halls of the ship, shoulders hitting the ship's walls in time with the waves crashing against the hull.

He wished his nameless friend was here with him, but admonished himself for thinking it. His friend was dead, and he knew his friend's ghost would never be so courteous as to haunt him.

In the weeks that he had been in the ship, he made nightly sojourns around its dark corners, and he knew where the food was stored, how much of it was left in storage, and figured that there was enough food to feed the slaves. They would be hungry, for sure. This fact saddened him, and he realized he had to be grateful that he was never hungry on his journey to Portugal, thanks to his master, he was only tired and sad, but never was he wanting for food.

He found himself in the food storage, and decided to feed the slaves. He still had the sword his master had given him, with it he cut open a sack and stole some bread. He smelt it to determine its freshness. It had gone a little stale, but he reckoned it was edible enough. He brought the bread in a bag to the slaves, fully aware of what others might do to him if he were caught, and he thought, 'let them catch me, I am only doing what's right'.

He entered the bowels of the ship, breaking the ice by muttering in broken Arabic, 'I am come here to help you. Peace be upon you.'

'Peace be upon you too, young man,' one of the slaves strained those words out of his parched throat. He said this weakly but sincerely.

Enrique said nothing as he motioned forward, tearing off a pinch of bread, feeding the slave that greeted him first, then moving on to the next slave and the next, until the bread was nothing but crumbs flaking against the floorboards. He dusted the remaining crumbs off his palms, until what was left was just its scent.

Feeding the ravenous slaves reminded Enrique of feeding pigeons, and his soul was relieved he was doing something good, though he could not ignore the fearful beating of his heart. He almost jumped when he heard the floor creak somewhere around him.

He crouched low and waited for the creaking to subside, but the creaking grew louder as it circled around him before silence once again crept in.

Enrique finally exhaled, nodded to the slaves, almost crawling out the dungeon, making his way to Magellan's bunk, thinking no one was the wiser, and laid down on the cold, moist wooden floor without so much as a sheet to cover him. He closed his eyes, glad that he had fed the slaves and had done something good for a change, and in spite of the damp floor and cold air, went to sleep dreaming of a time not too long ago.

He dreamt of a childhood lost.

He dreamt of running across the plains that lead out from the forest in his bare feet, panting and breathing harder than he had ever done in his young life.

The calloused soles of his feet dug into pebbles and twigs with barely a split second's relief as they rubbed against grass, wincing when something sharp poked into his foot.

He lost his balance with one foot traipsing over the other before he fell. But the thing about Enrique was that he had a resilience and an ability to get back up when other boys fell.

In dreams, he could remember his real name but when he awoke, that name was a pyramid of sand on a shore stolen away by a Portuguese tide.

When he awoke, he was in a ship that rode on a turbulent tide which rocked and swayed and shuddered against the waves. The ship could not still the sound of thunder nor the threat of lightning.

He awoke next to his master and wondered if the slaves were all right. He went to the cargo hold and took a peek at the slaves, who could not sleep, and he regarded them with equal parts pity and disdain.

Through that thick mess of hair that fell over his eyes, he saw them not as they were but as what they could have been. What he could have been, if he were not kidnapped and taken away from his home.

As the slaves moaned, his first instinct was to hush them, but he had no rank on this ship. He was just like them, except that he had shackles of a different kind. He heard his master calling out to him. He searched for the steps that lead to the bridge.

The storm had cleared and the sun had dawned upon them as Enrique boarded the bridge. He felt a man's hand on his shoulder. The man gave Enrique a long hard stare while he stayed his hand.

'You do grant your slave way too much clemency, Ferdinand,' Dom Jaime said.

Enrique's eyes searched for his master as Dom Jaime raised his hand away, and the boy went toward his master. The ship had stopped rocking and the waves were calmer, though the rain still drizzled against the boy's burgeoning teenage frame.

'You called, Master?' Enrique asked, his head bowed down.

'I need you to speak to the Egyptians when we land,' Magellan told Enrique.

Enrique did nothing more but nod. He contemplated the slaves, some of whom looked weak while others remained strong in bearing, though their malnourished bodies had become thin and wrecked.

Their faces made no attempt to show their weakness, and if they were unshackled, would they strike Enrique through the heart like his father had once said?

Their ship was close to reaching port. Enrique heard from his father that the Arabs dealt in slaves, though their prejudice did not include colour as they welcomed slaves of all races and creeds, including European and African slaves.

Magellan ran his fingers through the curly mass of hair beneath his chin, and looked upon Enrique with a father's realization that his son was growing up before his eyes. He could see the boy growing a hint of a mustache, and his hair had grown below shoulders broad and carved by working on ships.

Both master and slave felt the wind smack their faces. Enrique felt the salty wind against his tongue. The air was fresher than he had hoped, but he was disheartened as he knew now was the time. He looked up at the mast while Magellan commanded the sails to be raised.

When Magellan turned, he found his boy already gone. He found the growing boy on bare feet; his limber frame climbed the sails faster than the others, and soon he disentangled the ropes, to let the sails drape downward to catch the wind's advantage. One hand held the rope and he swung down like an agile monkey leaping off coconut trees and landed perfectly on deck.

He spun his elbow and wrist counter-clockwise to release the rope while the wind blew against his hair. He breathed hard, sweat glistening on the sinews of his chest.

'Again, he is too free to do as he pleases, Ferdinand.' Dom Jaime remarked.

Enrique stepped toward his master, head bowed, and Dom Jaime presumed the boy was being subservient to him, until the boy spoke, 'I am only free to do what my master commands.'

Magellan raised Enrique's head and shoulders, brushing the boy's shoulders as though he were grooming a prized stallion. The ship swayed and Enrique stood firm.

'You have good sea legs,' Dom Jaime noted.

'Only from all this time at sea,' Enrique said.

'So you have been taught to have a smart mouth? The slave, the black, the blasphemer, the apostate.'

'That's enough, Jaime,' Magellan interjected.

'Of course,' Dom Jaime bowed, 'perhaps I have overstepped my bounds.'

'No, your lordship, it is I, the bastard slave, that has overstepped mine,' Enrique lowered his chin.

Dom Jaime took great pleasure in this, smirking, 'I shall be at my quarters. We should be arriving soon, until then, I shall not be disturbed.'

Enrique took a step forward, his heel punctuating the deck, a hammer and nail and exclamation point rolled into one. Magellan held him back.

Enrique exhaled and clenched his fist. 'If he continues this way, Master, I may insult more than just his ears.'

Magellan chuckled, then caught himself and prepared to sound slightly more serious. He lay a hand on his slave's shoulder, and said as seriously as he could, 'That may be, but please, stay that hand until after the sale is done?'

Soft, cool air billowed against the ship's sails. The sky shifted from black to grey, then bled red before turning into a pale dead blue. Magellan was already on deck as the crew raised the sails and prepared to drop anchor.

Below deck, Dom Jaime and his assistants began unshackling the slaves while Enrique watched to make sure they did not escape. Enrique soon felt the air shift, it got warmer by the minute, it made him shift and fidget. Though he had fed them in the dark, he still dared not look at them in the day, when their faces were much clearer for him to see. He averted his eyes to make sure they didn't burn into his directly. Even as he stood at attention like a guard, he shifted his body to ensure they did not get a good look at his face.

He felt the heat of the sun stream through the deck entrance, and the dead blue shifted to a warm hue.

He heard one of them mutter for him, but Enrique snapped his head quick and lead his finger to his nose. He didn't want him or any slave to get caught and be found out that Enrique and them were getting too familiar. He pretended to scratch his nose to mask his gesture and heard the Duke call him.

'Boy!' Dom Jaime exclaimed, though the Duke was unaware of his exchange with the slave. 'Don't just stand there. Your favour with Magellan does not extend to me, do you understand? Show these men the way to freedom.'

Enrique wondered what the Duke meant, he stood still waiting until Dom Jaime said, 'Freedom away from the shackles of this ship,' the Duke concluded.

Enrique sighed as he climbed up the steps to the main deck and the Duke's assistants followed. He felt the warmth of the air and felt the first rays of sun against his face. He saw the docks clear and rife with activity before him.

He always thought Egypt was an endless sea of sand but ahead of him was an endless sea of people in all manner of colour, shape and size. The traders he could tell by their bearing and disposition, they stood alone while others fidgeted around them, helpers lifting crates and barrels while the traders watched and gave orders.

The sight of them pointing their arms and waving fingers was a sight that Enrique knew. He had been the subject of nothing but orders for most of his life, from his parents, to his captors, and now, from his master.

The sea breeze left a salty taste in his mouth, but as the ships got closer he noticed the city's smells, the scents of spices unique and different from Portugal and Spain, it smelled wet and dry at the same time, and he wished he could take the time to taste and learn what foods the Arabs and Egyptians had to offer.

The only Arabic thing his memory could conjure were the dates that the Arab traders brought to Malacca. It was chewy and sweet, a food of divine origin, and this was what Enrique's nose caught now, a memory of dates, wondering if he could steal one from the open markets.

The slaves went to the main deck, their captivity punctuated by the clink of chains with each step they took, their calloused feet dragging against the weathered wooden deck.

The crew dropped anchor as the ship got closer to the ballasts, hoisting their thick ropes around them to hold the ship in place, and the anchor took a good two seconds to hit the sea floor, a sign of deep water. Soon the plank was laid out and Enrique was given the signal by his master to lead the slaves, much to Dom Jaime's chagrin.

'They trust him,' Magellan justified this to Dom Jaime.

'Sending a groomed sheep to lead the other sheep to slaughter, then,' Dom Jaime said with glee.

Enrique moved first and the slaves followed him down the plank while Dom Jaime and Magellan followed behind. The Duke fingered the whip looped into his belt, and waiting for them on land was a man in white robes and a hirsute countenance.

The man in white did not once look at Enrique, he had no concern with some boy leading slaves, his eyes focused instead at the Duke, a smile creeping from beneath the man's beard. Both of them spoke, and Enrique listened. What Enrique knew of Arabic was from his Quranic recitals, he knew bits and pieces of Arabic, learning by rote, and he had been trying to listen to this language again as best he could.

The boy had an innate understanding of languages, and what took others years to learn or master, took him barely months. As the Duke and the man in white spoke, he tried to discern the differences in cadence between Dom Jaime and the man, whom he noted called himself Idris. The Duke spoke in a low drawl, while Idris spoke in a deeper register.

Enrique noticed as well that Idris's dialect used different words for the same things, though those meanings remained the same, different accents for different regions, Enrique reckoned. The only similar situation he could imagine was his time at the docks listening to the Indonesian sailors by the docks, similar to Malay, but Bahasa Indonesia was far thicker and far more melodic and polite in its intonations.

The more Enrique saw the world it was the similarities, rather than the differences, that attracted him. He heard Dom Jaime closing a deal with Idris.

'A new batch, Idrissi, courtesy of our friends from Portugal,' Dom Jaime pointed out to the shackled slaves, and Enrique translated.

Magellan stood a respectable distance from Idris, bowed and spoke and gestured, not caring but confident Enrique could translate, 'My master says it's a pleasure to meet you. These men are strong, and will serve you well, a gift to you from the Portuguese kingdom.'

Idris looked on at the slaves, studied their bodies. Though their bodies were malnourished, the shape of their muscles still remained, and he knew with enough prodding he could get some good work out of them. 'And is this interpreter also a gift from King Manuel?' he gestured a steady hand at Enrique, and he felt strange translating about himself.

Magellan knew what the Egyptian was trying to say, and spoke via Enrique, 'No, my good sir. This captive is from Malacca. I've had him for a good while now, he is one of my most valued assets.'

Idris chuckled, 'I see you are a fair master, possibly even fairer than I am.'

'Perhaps, but I am also a fair trader. The Duke tells me you will be using these slaves for your plantations. I only pray you have them well-fed and drinking well enough against the desert heat. Your kind are after all the slave masters. Builders of pyramids.'

After he translated that last bit, Enrique perked up, this was the first time he was told about Egyptian history.

Idris's eyes turned darker shades of grey, as though he controlled the amount of light that fell against his face. 'That may be true, Master Magellan, but we built out of a desert that had nothing. Ours was the last great ancient empire, and you should do well to acknowledge that.'

'You'd still have nothing, were it not for the slaves that built those pyramids for you. No man needs nothing, and you need my slaves,' Magellan told Idris.

'And you need, no, want. You want our spices, from the Moluccas Islands,' Idris conjectured.

'As per the agreement,' Magellan reiterated, his tone curt, impatient that their verbal dalliance was taking too long.

Idris fidgeted, his fingers rapping against a handle from an older world. 'I have been thinking, that perhaps the markets fluctuate, and my price has changed from what we had initially agreed upon. Tell your master, *al as-wad,*' Idris pressed for the boy slave to translate as quickly as he could catch up.

Enrique made sure his master understood what Idris was saying. Magellan and the others paused, and rather than replying back with signs of anger, Magellan smiled, a taunting sort of laughter, one that showed that he wasn't fazed by such amateurish demands. He had dealt with worse scum than these.

'You wish to recalculate prices? Is there a new exchange rate for slaves that I am not aware of? Give me an offer, then.'

Idris thought about this, told Enrique who in turn told his master, 'Perhaps four slaves per barrel of spice?'

Magellan chuckled. 'Surely that is too little, it strays too far from what we had agreed upon, Lord Idris?'

'Look at the slaves you have given us, Master Magellan. They are weak, malnourished, they can hardly stand on their own two feet!' Idris complained.

Magellan closed his eyes to gather his thoughts. 'Tell him this, Enrique. Tell him and his people that the slaves will be strong enough once they are fed well, and do not skimp out on the feeding, either. If they are fed well enough, they will be strong enough to rake in say, a slave per barrel?'

'Surely you jest, Magellan? No, no more than three slaves per barrel,' Idris told them firmly.

There was a silence long enough for Enrique to think about the conditions of these slaves. Had they become nothing more than commodity to be traded and sold? He wondered about their lives back home, of their families and perhaps wives and children, of them being displaced. He wondered where his mother and siblings were, if they had remained the same as they grew up. He thought of his village and of Sultan Mahmud, and all these thoughts sunk into his heart as though it were a great physical weight massive enough to sink through even the bottoms of oceans, a painful weight that would never be excavated. He wanted to welcome this pain, and let it hide in the abyss where his heart lay, for without this treasured pain, he knew he was nothing more than just a commodity, an unfeeling device to be used in eternal servitude.

Magellan raised a hand and showed his first two fingers. 'Two slaves,' he told Idris, and there was a nervous calm in the air.

Idris kept silent, and Magellan chose to exploit this and cut in again. 'Your silence is telling. Let me tell you what you're thinking. You know that my deal is a fair trade, but someone is holding your tongue. Agree to my new terms, and I shall speak to the man who holds it in check.' Idris stepped forward, sword in hand, raising it toward Magellan. Enrique stepped back, fingers rapped along the sheath of his own blade.

'No discounts, Idris,' Magellan was confident of his safety, as one would be when he had a dozen soldiers flanking him with their swords pointed at Idris.

'I highly disagree,' Idris too had his own dastardly dozen who flanked him, pointing curved scimitars at the Portuguese.

Dom Jaime gulped and pulled at his collar. He would rather be home, or in bed with a woman.

Enrique though always enjoyed these moments between life and death, these calms before storms, he liked to escape with these little stolen moments, for these were when he felt truly free and alive. It made his heart beat faster, it made his life feel more precious, and that his life had worth beyond shackles both real and metaphorical.

These stolen moments though, were short and fleeting. He knew the most likely resolution to this standoff was violence, after the calm was the storm itself. Soon he would be an eye of this storm, observing the true effects of its devastation.

He looked at the slaves, these stolen soldiers from Azemmour, weakened by the trip, huddled together now helpless to witness an ordeal that was about to take place on their account. Enrique motioned a couple steps closer to them, his free hand gently hinting at them to step back. Part of him wanted to protect them, while another part of him hated himself. If he were to admit it, he wanted to make sure these slaves were not damaged in the tussle that was about to happen. The last thing he figured was that if the merchandise were damaged then this whole trip would be for nothing.

'Pray for mercy, my friends,' Magellan said to Idris's bunch.

A Portuguese soldier charged forth.

'Wait! I did not ask you to!' Magellan ordered him to halt, and for once, Dom Jaime agreed with him on something. The other Portuguese soldiers, loaded with the fervour of victory from their time in Azemmour, charged ahead as well, and having lost control of so many of them despite his insistent screaming, Dom Jaime and Magellan had no choice but to continue.

'Remind me to keep this idiot alive if he survives this,' Magellan told this aloud, hoping Dom Jaime and Enrique heard it clear.

Enrique ushered the slaves to safety and seconds later, swords clashed and rang iron thunder, and the slave boy hoped his master would remain unharmed. This was not the first tussle his master had been through but each fight presented new dangers, and it was only a matter of time before Magellan's luck ran out.

Enrique's eyes darted searching for his master, but could not find him. Magellan though was a thinker and not a brute, he would never charge headlong into a melee unless he had to.

Magellan liked to think he was close to the ideals of the generals of ancient Rome who stood wisely at the tail-end of the cavalry leading the men from a safe distance, and Magellan knew that a leader was nothing if he was dead, for no one would lead.

Enrique found his master trying his best to contain the entire fight, trying to pick up the pieces before they would suffer further losses, screaming out orders before more blood was shed, and this predicament reminded Enrique of his own life where he was always in the middle of things, between his father and the Portuguese when he was captured, between two armies, between the captured slaves.

In the chaos, a lone straggler sneaked his way into the fight the way a snake wraps itself around large prey, and the young slave boy's sharp eyes saw this snake. He bolted and coughed out all the air in his lungs as he twisted arms and kicked people out of his way as he dashed toward his master, but the damned snake had one curved and sharp fang that it chose now to raise and reveal to Magellan.

'Master!' Magellan heard Enrique call him, his head raised and eyes widened as he saw the blade cast its shadow over him.

Enrique grabbed the snake and twisted it, his short stature making it hard for him to gain leverage, and both of them rolled back at obtuse angles, and the slave boy grabbed the sword handle that was poking his side, it was random and the length of even a short sword such as his gave him certain advantage, the snake was certain he would overpower the boy although his sword was not yet raised.

Enrique thanked that sword and drew it out clumsily as he charged toward the snake, swinging it in a wide arc that threw him off balance, but close enough for its tip to cut the snake's neck. The snake held it to stop that geyser of hot blood from spurting, not believing a stupid, mere slave boy had done him in the end. He dropped on one knee before his eyes rolled back into his head and he fell backward onto the ground, knees twisted in opposite directions.

Enrique gasped and caught his breath. 'Are you all right, Master?'

Magellan held his own neck, thinking about the snake his slave had just killed. 'Yes, Enrique. Yes, I think I am now.'

They rested in his master's bunk, nursing their wounds. Enrique knelt before his master wrapping his hand in a clean white strip of cloth, though in such ships, no white was truly pure white, cloth strips recycled so many times it was off-white by at least twenty shades of red, with cloth sterilized by immersion in boiling water, wounds baptised clean by the sting of alcohol.

Enrique knotted the dressing tight, and his master brought his hand closer to inspect the dressing. He nodded and grunted a low purr like that of an old, tired cat.

Enrique stood but Magellan stayed in his seat, contemplating his slave. It had been less than a year since he took Enrique, and he felt like he did not recognize the boy anymore. The boy was growing and soon would be a young man, and reckoned this was how fathers felt as they saw their sons grow up, proud to see them reach their full potential in strange and unexpected ways. He thanked Enrique and stood up. He placed a hand on his slave boy, and contemplated what would happen if he died, and where Enrique would go, if he would continue to be a slave, or be set free.

'Is there anything more I can do for you tonight, Master?'

'I am fine,' he told Enrique simply.

The next day, Magellan had to help Dom Jaime settle matters with Idris, and Enrique followed. This time Idris and Magellan had sealed an unspoken agreement not to draw swords or draw blood.

Enrique strengthened his resolve and now looked at the slaves with more confidence. As they walked past him, he took a deep breath and exhaled and looked them in the eyes, though he knew for certain this bravado was more of an act than actual bravery. He knew he had to act the part or be shackled again.

He nodded his head almost imperceptibly at the slave who recognized him. It took a long time before all of them were handed off and when they were gone, Enrique could finally heave a sigh. He closed his eyes and it hit him all at once how sorry he felt for them, and how close he was to being just like them.

Enrique glanced at his master and wondered if he should thank him, though his gratefulness was laced with an excessive amount of caution. He was seeing a side of the world he had never known before, but it took being an indentured slave to do this. He still could not fathom this dichotomy.

His master shook hands with Idris, and the slaves were sold. With nothing left to be said, the Portuguese sailed away from Cairo, leaving nothing but windswept dunes of memory, forever shifting with each new dawn.

Interlude

Valladolid, Spain, September 1522

Transylvanus did not face Antonio Pigafetta but was buried in deep in a tomb in the shape of a journal, digging and shovelling into the words with his pen, excavating information.

There was a gulf between continents but none in memory, especially the traumatic one Pigafetta and the surviving crew had had to face. Pigafetta thought hard over this simple question. 'What did they do to me?' He couldn't decide if he was going to tell the whole truth or a partial lie. The pain in him was broken crystal, shards and fragments of it still sharp and clear in his mind.

'They did terrible things to us all,' Pigafetta finally said. He would keep his answers short and brief.

'Let us assure you, Señor Pigafetta, that we here at the council are glad for your safe return,' Transylvanus leaned back against his chair, his posture firm.

Formal chairs made for the courts were crafted for regal posturing. His fingers, tainted with ink at its tips, diddled against each other, as though playing a musical instrument. He thought about their account, not knowing if he wanted to believe its veracity.

To his right was one of the many journals Pigafetta had written. Transylvanus flipped the journal to the end pages, to the page where Pigafetta had chronicled the return journey to Spain. It was written in a thin hand, one shaken by the ordeal, not the same hands that were anticipating adventure. They were worn-out hands that couldn't wait to go home.

Now Pigafetta couldn't wait to leave this inquisition. He was a man always looking forward to the next adventure, but his drive to escape was equal to his absolute resignation. He eyed the inquisitor's hands.

'This is informative, to be sure,' Transylvanus had the tone of a principal overseeing detention. There was a silence in the court, which made the autumn air more obvious to Pigafetta, who felt his lips turn dry. He ran his tongue across his lips to wet them, yet felt perpetually dry. This must be what hell might be like, an eternal repetition of irritation.

They had been here for almost an hour, and the interview with the survivors of the Armada de Molucca had been slow and deliberate, with most of the questions arrowed toward Antonio Pigafetta.

The others in the courtroom included the survivors, Juan Sebastian Elcano, Francisco Albo, and Hernando de Bustamante and João Carvalho.

'From what I am able to gather thus far, it would seem Juan Serrano might be the one who caused the slave interpreter to revolt and plot with this Rajah Charles against the Armada,' Transylvanus noted without timbre or fluctuation, a flat tone he had perfected for conducting interviews.

'I think you may have misread my accounts, Mr Transylvanus. I think it is clearly stated in my journals that it was Duarte Barbosa who had mistreated Enrique, not Juan Serrano,' Pigafetta surprised himself when he leapt to the interpreter's defense.

'Barbosa may have mistreated the slave, but he did not drive him to breaking point,' Transylvanus said without a hint of passion.

PART THREE

1518-1521 A.D.
(SAUDADE)

8

Even after coming back from Cairo, Ferdinand Magellan was still determined to carry on with his plans to find a shorter passage to the Moluccas Islands, on the ostensible condition of getting the spices before the Spanish did, and in order to achieve this, he found a pair of mutual partners in the Faleiro brothers Rui and Francisco. Magellan had met Rui over a period of time during his visits to King Manuel, whom Rui had served already as cosmographer for the better part of almost two decades. In spite of his long servitude, he was rejected by King Manuel when he applied for the position of royal astronomer. This mutual rejection by the King was what eventually drew Magellan and the Faleiro brothers, especially Rui, together.

The spices he attained from Idris, and the letters he received from his cousin Francisco Serrano about the majesty and abundance of the spices there, and the potential riches he would attain if he did discover the shortest route, convinced Magellan his plans were not crazy.

After all the pain suffered in battle, there was little doubt part of him had changed, and part of Enrique had changed as well. His bloodlust, his desire to strangle his master had been satiated by his killing of the soldier in Azemmour and the lone straggler in Cairo. He had also gained a new respect for Magellan, though these feelings were something he was unable to express, not because he was not able to tell it fittingly in Portuguese, but because there was something sunken within him, and he sensed something sunken within Magellan as well—an old dead wooden ship, vacant with no treasures to be found.

They had gone to war for Magellan's king, and limping back to Portugal, Magellan had hoped King Manuel would now listen in on his plans to sail westward on the opposite route to the Spice Islands, rich with nutmeg, mace, cloves and other varied spices.

Magellan spent many nights home drawing up his plans, while Enrique looked on from his barn, his master's office glowing within from dim candlelight. Enrique noticed his master's eyes had grown darker from lack of sleep, and he had drank more and spoken less and less to his sister Isabel.

He knew his master was angry, angry enough to bring him along to meet King Manuel again, and on the day they went to the king's court, Magellan brought with him stands and rolls for a presentation.

'Are you going to ask him again? It's been two years, Master,' Enrique asked Magellan in the carriage. Magellan was on the way now to meet Rui Faleiro at the King's court.

Magellan's palm rubbed his bad knee, that pain would haunt him for the rest of his days. He wished for a cigarillo, grimacing when there was none to be had in the carriage. 'He fills my mind with a hatred, a dread that I cannot describe, but I have to talk to him. I have met some people who have told me of a faster way to the Spice Islands, we call it *el paso*, a passage, a shortcut from here to the east. We can make it to the Spice Islands in no time, but I need funding for this expedition.'

'Do you think the King will fund you this time?'

Ferdinand Magellan remained silent until they arrived in the king's court, where he made his presentation, limping from point to point as he and Enrique raised the drawings and maps that showed his proposed route to the Spice Islands, while Rui Faleiro seemed to be pointing along with his pronounced chin that seemed to jut out an inch further than most men. It gave him an arrogant air that was only multiplied with Magellan's fervour.

'Now if we sailed westward instead of the usual eastern route, we can get there faster, though the path might be more treacherous. We can also avoid the Spanish if we take this route,' Magellan and Faleiro went on, both of them completing each other's sentences.

This combination irked Manuel even further. He was fidgeting, upset by any number of things at present. He did not like Faleiro or Magellan; both persistent pests to him, he reckoned met in the same hive of alcohol-filled rotting garbage and became fast friends. Both of them had made requests to him on various occasions that he had always rejected. Now they were here again, and he only found the strength to entertain them with goblet upon goblet of liquid courage, or, as he called it, his royal patience.

He was also weary thinking about his age. He was almost two years past the half-century mark, knowing well enough that he had known men that died at this age, and that he was lucky if he made it past fifty-five. He also felt like he was a new man in an old man's body. His new wife sat beside him, more than half his age, he worked twice as hard to keep up with her.

Queen Leonor leaned forward; bosom high and mighty, they seemed to undulate with the motions of Magellan and Faleiro's presentation. She sat still though, when her husband spoke.

'I appreciate your enthusiasm, Ferdinand, but you should have known what my answer would be, shouldn't you,' King Manuel stood up, waiting, stringing Magellan like a horse with a carrot. The other court officials waited and seemed to contain their laughter.

Enrique rolled the maps and charts aside, while Magellan took a deep breath. 'And what would your answer be, my King?'

'This plan is outrageous and expensive. Guess then my verdict.'

Faleiro interjected, 'My King! This is outrageous! My plans and charts are accurate, my astronomical work flawless!' He thought about the time King Manuel rejected his application to be a Judiciary Astronomer at the University of Coimbra, only for his scholarly rival to gain that same post, but even in his outrage, he knew well enough to hold back his rant.

'Commander Magellan's plan should not be rejected, it should be commended!' Faleiro gesticulated, arms snapping and twisting as though he were fighting an invisible specter of the King.

'I have fought wars for you on distant lands, my lord. Here I am on wounded knee, and was only paid a pittance for my services in Azemmour when you consider my rank,' Magellan seethed. He sucked air through his teeth and he made it a point that King Manuel looked him straight in the eyes.

'And you seem to have forgotten the incident with the slaves you sold from Azemmour to Cairo,' King Manuel lashed out a finger at Magellan. Rui fell back, as though Manuel's voice were a physical presence that had kicked him side.

'Charges that have been cleared' Magellan reiterated, not moving, his resolve rooted deeper than Rui's was.

'You left for a time without official leave,' Manuel withdrew his finger, turned his head away, knowing well enough he would not give Magellan the satisfaction of looking him in the eye.

Magellan stood up and limped toward Rui Faleiro. He waved his arm, but Rui did not gather if it was for him or for the King. Magellan closed his eyes, and smirked when he sighed, 'Old stories, my king. And we did profit from that endeavour, did we not? But how goes the marriage with your new wife? Strange then I find, that she was almost your daughter-in-law instead? Rumours persist that your son Prince João still has relations with her,' Magellan moved out of the throne room trying as best he could to hide his limp and project an air of dignity as he left. Rui Faleiro dashed to walk alongside him.

The courtiers and officials gasped while Enrique hurried behind his master, holding the scrolls, chuckling as he did, hoping that they did not hear him.

Without a second's thought, King Manuel called out for his guards, who quickly turned and were ready to act.

King Manuel darted up on both feet, his fury held in check by Leonor's arms, she calmed him and implored him to cool down. He relented and told the guards to stand down and let Magellan and his posse leave. A moment later, Leonor lowered her head, a mind overflowing with guilt. She hoped that her new husband did not notice this.

Before he tried for the third time, Magellan had taken a conscious effort to spend time in sailors' bars and hideouts, watering holes in which he could listen in on any new developments in the world, and especially of any rival sojourns to the Spice Islands.

When he had a few too many to drink, he placed his arm on Enrique's shoulder, the teenager nodding nervously to Rui Faleiro as he continued to drink from his own cup.

Enrique could smell the stink of alcohol on his master's breath. Without looking directly at his slave, Magellan tried his best to keep his head upright and slurred, 'You're not really a boy anymore, your shoulders are wider, your voice sounds like a man's.'

'Thank you, Master,' Enrique shrugged, and wondered what to do with the hand on his shoulder.

Faleiro and Magellan had been eavesdropping on the sailors that had come and gone, and instead of talk of the Spice Islands, there was now talk of Portuguese sailors wishing to leave for Spain brewing, with many sailors attesting to the rigidity of the King. Seville was the Spanish city that kept popping up in these sailors' conversations, and Magellan kept that city in mind.

He had to do it one more time, because it had killed him inside that he would not see the glory of the Spice Islands.

On the third try, it was just him and Manuel. Enrique was told to wait outside while Ferdinand Magellan was alone in the court with the King—here was no scandalous young Queen, nor courtiers, or advisors and ministers.

Magellan brought nothing but himself, there were no scrolls; there were only words, quiet and restrained. He only wished there were cushions for his knees crushed against the cold floor.

'I have overstepped my bounds, Your Highness. That was only in anger and spite. I know, perhaps I have been a rebel in your eyes, and Faleiro a temperamental fool, but I beg of you, on my knees, if you would be wise and kind enough to fund this expedition.'

King Manuel scratched a tangle of beard that knotted beneath his chin. He thought of the possibility of funding this expedition, and mainly, of funding Magellan. The fact this proud soldier was on his knees was a boost to Manuel's ego. He wanted to see Magellan grovel.

'You are if anything, persistent, Ferdinand. I remember years ago, when you made claim that the Spice Islands did not fall into Portuguese territory. That was silly, stupid. We make anything ours.'

'Then lay claim to the other side of the world. Don't go east the way the Spaniards do. We sail west, past el paso, I am sure we can get there at the same time, and without Spanish interference.'

Manuel leapt off his throne, his hand a bow, index finger a burning, pointed arrow shooting right at Magellan's last morsel of hope. 'Let me tell you something, Commander Magellan! Your temperament is well-known here. That is an issue to consider. There is also the matter of your so-called partner, Faleiro. I don't know which honey-laden garbage heap you found him in, but you must have smelt the honey instead of the garbage. The journey west is too far, and this *el paso* that you speak of is untested territory. Both risky propositions, and the cost is too much for the crown.'

Magellan raised his head. 'I presumed a man like you was very adept at taking risks,' not regretting at all saying those words. He hoped the King knew what he meant.

Manuel eyed the empty throne beside him, and thought of his new wife, suddenly worried she was in bed with his son. 'Some risks are too great,' Manuel told Magellan. 'You will live to regret it.'

'If that is the case, then perhaps I can offer my services elsewhere, ' Magellan told King Manuel.

'You are free to do as you please,' Manuel told Magellan.

Magellan rose up, wincing at the pain of his bad knee just so he could approach the King. He went down to rest on his good knee, and took his King's hand, to kiss it. In that transient moment, he thought his king was fair and kind enough to let him go and find another investor with his royal blessing.

As Magellan bowed to kiss the King's hand, something inside Manuel snapped. Maybe it was the words Magellan kept harping on to him about his wedding scandal, or the guilt that hit too close to home for him. Or the fact a man he did not admire was about to kiss his hand. Perhaps it was all these combined that made him reel his hand away before Magellan could place his lips on the King's hand. Manuel pulled and hid the hand behind his cloak. Both men felt the awkwardness, an invisible wall of ice between them.

Manuel turned away and Magellan took this slight as a major insult.

Once he was at the door, he pulled Enrique harsh against his arm. *Hey! What did I do!* Enrique wondered as they kept on walking.

The weeks after that Magellan met Faleiro frequently, sometimes at Magellan's home, at other times at a tavern or bar. Most of these talks were of moving to Spain and of polishing their plans for their expedition. At times, Faleiro would burst at the smallest slights. If they got his food or drink wrong, he would snap and scare away the waitress, and Magellan had to calm her so she would serve them the rest of their order.

Faleiro's head was filled with ideas and charts and calculations, his mind was dark but sparkled ever brighter like stars in the night, because of it. He would twinkle with random bits of genius and when the clouds of doubt filled his head, he would lash out with his own strange thunder.

After a month of meetings, they finally decided to leave for Seville, Spain, and Magellan embraced Isabel, and she in turn wished her brother good luck, and to write to him as soon as he could.

Enrique nodded kindly to her, if he had to admit, he would miss her. 'I hope to see you again, Lady Isabel.'

'Take good care of my brother, Enrique. He's all I have.'

'I will.'

The carriage left her and they took a ship to Seville with Faleiro in tow.

When they arrived in Seville, Magellan placed his hand on Enrique's shoulder and told him, 'Once you deposit the luggage, meet me tonight.'

Enrique nodded in agreement, and smiled, because this was a signal that he was free to roam this new city until nightfall. Though his master never explained these terms explicitly, Enrique was always aware of the implicit terms his master suggested.

His ears were open to listen to the language of Seville. He noted how Spanish sounded similar but totally different from Portuguese, and decided for his master's sake that he should capture the flavour of the Spanish language, and soon he wandered into a marketplace, colourful with food, fruit and character.

Hunger took over his senses, and he found a fruit stand. His hand hovered over a large, red, juicy apple and he asked, '*Cuanto cuesta?*'

The old woman behind the counter gave him a quick glance. She noticed his tan first, then studied his odd face, his larger, more rounded nose, before telling him the price, and he paid for the apple, biting into it and letting his teeth crunch into its thin skin the second he left the stall.

He savoured the fruit's sweetness as he chewed, but that sweetness turned sour after he was done eating the apple. Though he was free now to roam, he felt eyes watching him. This was almost like being chained.

Those eyes knew he was not of this land, he heard them whispering the words 'mulatto' and 'negro', 'brown' and 'black', in Portuguese and Spanish, they made no difference to him.

The only thing different was him.

He finished the fruit quickly and wiped his hands off his shirt, snaked into an alley and hid, leaned against a wall and slid down until he was almost at a squat, relieved the way a snake trying to hide from the searing eyes of the sun would be. As he calmed down, he began to observe the people around him, and he did his favourite thing. He began to listen for the rest of the afternoon, standing, finding other spots to hide, until he lost track of time.

He meandered through other streets and alleys, making sometimes three left turns and after that, three right turns, before he found his way back to his master's lodgings, sweating, puffing, afraid his master might reprimand him, but his master had other concerns in mind.

'Where did you go?'

'I got slightly lost,' Enrique told him as he closed the door of the inn.

Magellan pointed to a table too crammed for his usual work of maps. 'Get these plans laid out,' he told Enrique.

Enrique unrolled the scrolls on the table and struggled with the space he was given. Faleiro stood by the window, drinking a goblet of diluted red wine.

'Should he be allowed to listen?' Faleiro asked Magellan, fidgeting as he looked to close the curtains.

'If he leaks any of these plans out, I'll slit his throat myself,' Magellan winked at Enrique knowingly, knowing this was just to appease Faleiro.

They talked into the night, and even if Enrique wanted to leak such secrets, he knew no one would listen to a slave boy. He stood by the window, hoping Faleiro would leave soon, but as night wore on, as sunlight was substituted with candlelight, he still sat by the table, sat by the beds, drank more, threw his arms up in excitement.

Magellan might have as well, if his knee was as good as it were before Azemmour. They spoke of star charts and territories and treaties, things Enrique did not like to get lost in. He was already lost, and his eyes grew heavier. The night grew darker, and Magellan had the sense to end the meeting, and save the candlelight. 'Candles don't come cheap,' he told Faleiro.

Faleiro left, and Magellan soon went to sleep on his bed while Enrique slept on the floor.

It was in a sailor's bar that his master met again an old sailing mate. They locked eyes, Magellan always on the lookout for people, things, clues, a sign that his coming to Seville was of value. What Magellan didn't count on was meeting an old friend.

Duarte Barbosa approached first, gave a grin that showed that he wasn't high on ale, but high on the meeting of an old friend.

Magellan was weary, his tired eyes not even caring that the ladies who served him his beer had shapes that caused waves of desire in the sailors in the bar. Magellan was more interested in the tides that would bring him to an investor, and to the other side of the world.

'Ferdinand?' Duarte Barbosa called to him.

'Duarte?' Magellan wondered. Enrique looked up, eyes squinting to get a good measure of this stranger.

'Praise the lord, it is you!'

Duarte gave Magellan a bear hug, two old bears stepping out their caves seeking a thing they thought they had lost. Duarte noticed Magellan limping back to his seat and took moment before he could find the right words. 'The world has not been kind to you, old friend.'

Magellan rubbed his bad knee. 'A permanent reminder of battle.'

'Azemmour,' Enrique said proudly, but was silenced by Duarte's glance. What disturbed Enrique about that glance was not that Duarte was looking at him, but through him. Like he were a specter whispering at the table but could not see it.

'Aye. I have been through my fair share as well. But we, as Portuguese brothers, we should stick together, eh?'

'Yes, we should. But the tragedy is that our bonds are not forged in Lisbon itself, but in another country. I barely speak Spanish,' Magellan said.

'And why is that, you wonder,' Duarte said, his hand empty, waiting for a glass that was soon to come.

'Let me tell you why,' an older, more gruff voice weathered by the march of decades of alcohol and barbiturates said from a few feet across. He stumbled along the floor holding two large glasses in either hand, crashing them and allowing the foam at the tip to erupt and spill over, many heavy drops of which absorbed themselves into Enrique's shirt and lap.

Enrique placed his own drink back on the table and wiped what he could as the three men spoke with loud enthusiasm. This older man was no better than Duarte, and he noted how similar they looked.

'My father, Diogo Barbosa,' Duarte began, 'has been living here for almost fifteen years.'

'Fourteen,' Diogo corrected his son.

'Bah, what difference does a year make?'

'What does it, indeed? But let me tell you why we are all here.' He paused to make sure his son and Magellan were listening, not caring that Enrique was still wiping his shirt. 'We are all here because we are angry. We have had enough of Portugal. It has grown rich on the backs of people like us but we have no rewards for our toil. Others profit while we suffer still, in bars, nursing wounds in our bleeding hearts with alcohol down our throats.'

'He sent all of us here, I reckon,' Magellan said.

'And what brings you here then, Ferdinand?' Duarte asked.

'Hope when there is none left.'

They next met in restaurants instead of bars, and the Barbosa family increased exactly to one with these restaurant meetings. She was a perfect rhyme in name, her full name rolled off Ferdinand Magellan's tongue like a good song, or an enchantment. Maria Caldera Beatriz Barbosa. Beatriz for short.

She was there for these lunches with her father, and Magellan took a liking to Beatriz's radiant, fair skin. She was also fair of hair, and fair of heart, and she brought out a kindness others hardly saw in Magellan.

While others might shy away from the sight of a man with a limp, Beatriz showered him with a concern and affection he had not yet known in his harsh life. She was also the only one of the Barbosas to even acknowledge Enrique, but she treated him more like an odd cat than an actual person, but she was still kind enough to share leftovers with Enrique.

Magellan later asked Enrique to leave during these lunches, and for many months, he was free to roam the streets of Seville, sometimes under his master's pretense of running some errand that did not need running.

They even graduated to dinners by themselves, she walking with the grace fit for a queen and he limping alongside her to restaurants and waterfronts. They talked of the future and the crunch of time.

They spoke of their difference in age, and most of all, they spoke of Magellan's plans.

'You intend to do something most normal people would not fathom,' Beatriz told him.

'Then either I am not normal, or I am less than a man,' Magellan told her as the wind caressed their faces. Barges floated past them returning from voyages out at sea.

'No, Ferdinand. You are more than just an ordinary man, and if you come back, you will be remembered as a great one,' she kissed his hirsute cheek.

She asked then where his slave was.

'Out on an errand,' he told her.

'You treat him like your own. Most men won't treat their slaves like a beloved pet,' she chuckled, 'and there's no other errand to run except fetch.'

'He fetches well.'

'He'll fetch my slippers, but I won't let him, that's beneath even him,' Beatriz said.

'He's a good boy,' Magellan told her, and he grazed his fingers along hers.

For the better part of a year, Magellan, Duarte, Diogo and Faleiro made plans and socialized with Spanish high society through the Barbosa's connections, and for many of these occasions, Beatriz followed, sometimes invited by her father and at other times by her own volition.

Enrique watched as she hovered through Dukes and Duchesses and lords and merchants and farmers grown rich through good seasons of harvest, an angel that if she wanted, could capture the hearts of many a man, a secret, angelic weapon Magellan and Diogo Barbosa used to gain favour, more so than influence, among the rich and famous of Spain; her Spanish was impeccable and it was through listening to her that he learned much of his Spanish.

He was trying to master now the art of not being seen, and he figured it suited him quite well, liking the anonymity of it. It was better than being seen and called names and insults. Sometimes he would notice Dom Jaime, and even the new young King Charles I of Spain at these parties, and he came to conclude that rich people spent most of their money on parties to make more money. He found attending these exhausting, though for the most part his master seemed to have forgotten all about him at these events, his focus on other things.

One night after such a party, Enrique was about to retire, when Magellan landed a hand on his shoulder. 'I want to show you something,' He reached out with his free hand and showed Enrique a ring.

'Have you asked her?' Enrique wondered.

'I haven't found the right words, my boy,' Magellan said, and in his heart, he knew things were amiss. But he was patient, and he had other matters weighing over him, it felt to him the world was on one side of him and it caused him to limp under its weight.

He stood firm on both feet, each time talk of his expedition came about. What Magellan liked about the Spanish were their openness, and their willingness to explore and share their knowledge.

With these connections he had made with the Barbosas, he was able, along with Faleiro, to gain access to the court of King Charles I, the first of many to come amongst ministers and investors.

'I have read your letters with great interest, Captain,' the young King said.

'Please, your Majesty, I have been stripped of my captaincy by King Manuel. I am merely your servant, if you would have me serve you.'

The young king scratched his smooth chin while Rui Faleiro scoffed at this posturing, his jaw a cannon ready to fire his tirade against young monarchs, if he was given the chance.

Enrique could tell from the cleanliness of the King's face that he was no older than Enrique was. At eighteen, King Charles I already had more ambition and rank than any slave boy could hope to achieve. Charles had a country under his command, while Enrique had a man that commanded his every waking hour.

This young king was tall and buff. He had shoulders of enormous leverage that he tried to make smaller by draping his cloak.

'It is such an exciting honour to meet you finally, Your Highness. I hope the letters we had sent had reached you well and in good order,' Magellan bowed and introduced Faleiro, who still managed to bow with his chin up. Enrique figured that chin had been the cause of plenty an eclipse.

'Yes, Captain Magellan, I have read them,' King Charles eyed his ministers, who nodded and agreed. They had read bits and pieces and doubted the King had read even a line. Faleiro thought he noticed this, but knew that telling Magellan would only stoke his anger.

'Let's not speak here,' Charles continued. 'Show our guests the drawing room.'

Charles wasted no time when all of them were in the room, and he led the conversation, eyes sharp and curious, behind which was a yearning to prove himself. 'So you say you plan to sail the westward route to the Spice Islands? The Moluccas?'

'Yes,' Magellan said. He raised his chin and waited for the silence in the room to shatter.

'It is a dangerous route,' Charles firmly said. 'Why do it then?'

Faleiro stepped forward to explain, but Magellan cut him off before even a syllable left his partner's lips. 'The eastern route is a trusted route, but many have sailed east. I proposed the westward route, because for one thing, no one has ever gone there. The other thing is that the route west is faster. Our world is getting smaller and if we don't act, we lose.' Magellan waved a hand, beckoning Enrique to step forward.

Enrique reached his fingers into a pouch and showed the audience in the room the spices now laid in his palm. A cinnamon stick. Nutmeg. A clove. And ungrounded black pepper. The smell of these combined spices filled the room. Sharp, sweet and more precious than gold. 'You can't taste gold,' Enrique began in Spanish. 'But even if you were to lick gold, it would not taste as sweet and as significant as these spices.' He spread his open hand and let the scent of those spices waft across the room. It reminded Charles of a dangerous woman. Forbidden, spicy. He had to have her.

Enrique could hear nostrils flaring and sniffling. A minister spoke, 'What about the Treaty of Tordesillas?'

'What about it?' Faleiro spoke quickly before Magellan could cut him off again. He could see Magellan pound his fist against his end of the table, but he didn't care. He wanted this moment to be his. 'The treaty divides the lands of the new world in essence between the east and west. Portugal owns the eastern territories. And the western territories belong to Castile. To the Spanish.

By sailing west, you avoid Portuguese encroachment,' Magellan said this fast and without stopping. He stood and with Enrique's help, they unrolled a map that showed these territories.

'And the best part, my King, is that the Moluccas islands are firmly on Castilian territory.'

The ministers studied the map and the lines and demarcations. As they discussed this, Magellan continued to gather King Charles's attention, exalting and impressing upon the king the beauty and legends of these islands, even going as far to paraphrase the letters Francisco Serrano described the islands in, 'he survived shipwrecks and pirates, and found riches beyond compare. And by sailing west, we are not violating the Treaty'.

Before Charles could think, Magellan presented him Enrique, 'Even my slave here is from these islands. He is good with languages, having mastered Portuguese and Arabic in a very short time, and is even becoming fluent with Spanish by the influence of his time spent here. And he can speak with the locals of the islands. They speak the same language as he does.' Magellan knew he had lied plenty in that statement.

Charles regarded Enrique as though he were a device, a piece of machinery that had the potential to fail. After some thought, King Charles told Magellan, 'He will have his work cut out for him. I wish all three of you luck,' he told them, though for all of them, luck was in short supply.

Months passed, and King Charles, after many meetings, finally agreed to fund the expedition. The young king was supposed to pay for the expedition, but debt had led him to the House of Fugger, a prominent German family of bankers; having held a near-complete monopoly of the European copper market, they took over the de Medici family's assets and political influence.

King Charles' accountants had tallied the costs of the expedition of the Armada de Moluccas, amounting to 8,751,125 maravedis, which included the ships, provisions and salaries of the sailors.

Food itself had cost the expedition 1,252,909 maravedis, that amounted to about two years' supply of wine, hardtack (these rations amounted to almost four-fifths the food on the ship), flour, salted meat and even livestock.

Delicacies for the captains had included Carne de Membrillo, made from the golden-green fruit known as quince, and almonds, cheese, mustard and figs were also loaded onto the ships.

Enrique saw the men laughing, while he stood at the other end of the room, not even daring to lean against the wall. He saw the young King Charles of Spain exclaiming, 'We shall go west, Ferdinand,' toasting the newly appointed Captain, all of them sipping red wine in the drawing room. 'There are rumours of rumblings about me being unfaithful to Spain,' King Charles placed his shoulder over Magellan's and left it hanging there like a dead log, 'because I hired you and Faleiro for this expedition westward. I even authorized the conversion of your nationalities and made you all Spanish citizens. I may be young, but that does not mean I do not have royal wisdom. We are the same, you know? We are both traitors of a sort. You're my kind of traitor, and I reckon I am your kind as well.'

Enrique still could not get over how much power a young man such as King Charles had, and how much his master was sucking up to this new King's every whim, almost just because he had given his master money.

'Indeed you are, my King,' Magellan took a sip of his wine, and regarded the ring on his left hand.

Magellan's mind was now elsewhere, in a restaurant on his good knee showing Beatriz a ring. He had been reliving this moment again and again for days, and couldn't believe that she had said yes.

Magellan found it ironic that life was a bore until it wasn't anymore. All the waiting that seemed to be taking forever, now felt like there was no more time left in the world. He had to marry Beatriz before they set sail. The expedition would almost be a year later, but that was still too short a time to plan a good wedding. He had plans of both the marital and maritime kind to consider.

The hiring of a large sailing expedition required many hands, from barbers to men skilled enough to fix ships. Magellan needed operators, oarsmen, and pages, teenage boys who would work on minimum wage for the promise of adventure. Many of these pages were called nephews, a kind euphemism for sailors' children borne out of wedlock.

'You should go to him,' Beatriz told Magellan grimly as she set the letter down. She spoke as though she had had to swallow an entire ocean of salt. She had agreed to accept that she was marrying an older sailor with personal baggage.

'I am glad you understand.'

'This was you before me. But don't expect me to like it,' she told him, that last sentence a determined punctuation of finality on her opinion on this matter.

Magellan knew about his 'nephew' from letters the kid's mother had sent years ago, while he was sailing to India with Diogo Lopes de Sequeira and Francisco Serrano, and now he had been sent a letter from her family that she had taken ill and passed away.

He decided to hire the son he had never met, whose mother was Spanish, and as fate would have it, the nephew was found to be in Seville, working in a smithing shop.

When Magellan stood outside the smithing shop, he saw the boy walking across the shop alone, carrying a box of tools. He tried not to move, didn't want to show his son an old man with a limp, not just yet, anyway. He wanted to present the boy the image of a fit father.

When his lingering presence became uncomfortable for the boy to bear, he asked, 'What you want?'

'Haven't you heard?' Magellan began baiting the boy.

'Heard?'

'There's a major expedition happening in the next few months. Funded by King Charles himself,' Magellan said.

'What's it gotta do with me?' the boy asked.

'We need someone of your skills. Doing ship maintenance. Sailing around the world. You'll get paid more than what you get paid here.'

The boy put the tools aside. 'Where we going?'

'The Spice Islands,' Magellan said proudly.

'Hasn't it been done before?' the boy wondered.

'Not the way I want to do it. We're sailing on the other side of the trade routes, to avoid the Portuguese,' Magellan said, feeling weird that he was referring to himself as an outsider.

'I'll think about it.'

'Good, son, good,' Magellan extended his hand, hoping the boy would catch the word 'son' as just a figure of speech. 'They call me Ferdinand Magellan. Formerly of Portugal.'

The boy smiled. 'Cristovão Rebelo. Currently of Spain.'

9

The Italian walked along the streets of Seville, streets very much like his own back in Italy. In one hand, he had a journal and a pencil which made the other hand free to touch the city's walls. Touching these walls made him feel that the dream was real. He was truly in Spain. Slung around his shoulder was a small leather bag that held more papers and another journal.

His eyes were like an artist's, in the sense that he loved the beauty of the smallest things, even the cracks on walls and especially the cracks and ruins of people's faces, and he longed to capture and express all these details in some shape or form, but alas, he couldn't draw to save his life, hence he painted with words. He crossed the market and picked up a peach, bringing it close enough to his face to smell and savour its sweetness before he placed it back. He was not here to buy provisions today.

When he had first heard of Magellan's ambitions, he had been in Seville for three months, awaiting the true commencement of the long voyage to circle the Moluccas Islands on an unusual western route. The audacity of such an idea excited Antonio Pigafetta no end. He considered himself a learned man and a man of religious conviction, but was yearning for adventure, and the scholar had left his usual circle of diplomats and learned people to find Magellan.

Pigafetta made his way past the market street, through the entrance of Santa Maria de la Victoria, where he greeted the emissary of Pope Leo X, Andrea Chiericati, at first absorbing the scene and gathering crowd, with priests then asking the guests to gather while they said their prayers to christen the Armada de Molucca's voyage.

Pigafetta looked out for the man who masterminded the expedition, but could only find the other four captains of the five ships. He had not yet seen this last captain in person, but that was soon about to change.

Finally, after the prayers had finished, he saw a man limping and wielding a large cross, raising it high to signify the beginning of this voyage. Despite the limp, the man bore a charisma like that of a wounded general that had seen many battles. He cheered the captains and the crew on, and with this fervour, Antonio Pigafetta knew this dream could be real if he joined their voyage. He left the christening but met Magellan days later, after pulling little stray threads together.

'So you tell me you're here under the auspices of your Emperor and Lord Francis Cheregato, and that you wish to be a supernumerary on my voyage?'

'That is the gist of it, Lord Magellan,' Pigafetta said.

'Then I might have a job for you, scholar.' Magellan looked at the papers that came straight from Rome, papers as official as the ordinances he himself had prepared to be read by the captains of the other four ships. 'You will receive just a bare stipend,' Magellan sipped his wine. The day was cool and the drink tasted all the better warm, and these two men seemed unremarkable next to the journey they were about to embark upon.

'Yes, but the stipend of a nobleman, and from these papers, I believe I do not have much to prove to you, Captain, of my own personal rank and standing in Italy.'

'In Italy, perhaps,' Magellan scoffed, 'but here, in Seville, there is much left to prove. I myself, as a Portuguese, have much to prove against the Spaniards and Castilians of my crew. And you are the only Italian on this voyage.'

'Fluent in all those tongues,' Pigafetta added.

'Regardless,' Magellan paused, distracted by the Italian's interjection, 'prepare yourself for prejudice when you board my ship. But I still need a chronicler for this journey, Italian. What do you say to that?'

Pigafetta looked around the emptiness of the Trinidad, but there was no one save for a couple of footsteps. 'For the chance of a lifetime, I will follow you to the ends of the earth, and back again. And the world will know our glory through my chronicles of us.'

'Then you have earned a place in my ship,' Magellan nodded.

'Master,' those footsteps said.

Pigafetta eyed Enrique and wondered what he was. He tried to figure out his race, and presumed he was Indian. 'You keep interesting company,' Pigafetta remarked to Magellan.

'This is my slave, Enrique,' Magellan told Pigafetta.

Enrique bowed slowly, and eyed Pigafetta. There was a palpable urge between the two of them to say something. Emboldened by his master's encouragement, Enrique said softly, 'Prejudice and me are close friends, Sir.' He then turned to Magellan. 'I have delivered the copies of the ordinances to the various captains. They will be honour-bound to follow your instructions to the very last detail.'

'Excellent,' Magellan scratched his chin.

'So, when do we leave?' Pigafetta asked.

Magellan gestured for them to step to the main deck of the ship. The bunks below were dank and dark, but the deck was blinding from the glare of the sun. As Pigafetta adjusted his eyes, he began to understand that the silence was just temporary.

Men had begun lifting crates and shifting around supplies. Magellan placed his hand on Pigafetta's shoulder. The Italian hunched nervously then shivered. He was excited.

'Once the men have completed loading, we set sail.' Magellan pulled Pigafetta aside and their backs were turned from the men. 'Watch your back, I only have enough eyes to watch my own.'

'Don't worry, I will watch yours. I've had a lifetime of people looking at me strange. You'll learn the ways of the sea and the storms that guide it. We'll be good friends, Señor Pigafetta,' Enrique told the Italian.

Rui Faleiro fidgeted at his desk, then stood, then sat, then looked at the window and was only consoled in that half-second glance before he finally decided to scrape his feet toward the door. Even then, he opened it and was not convinced. The door was held halfway while he stared at the desk smothered with papers and scrolls and drawings on top of other drawings. He looked at the empty beds that once hosted Magellan and his slave. Magellan had moved to live with the Barbosa family with his slave and Faleiro had taken this room at the inn. Part of him convinced himself this was nonsense, part of him was also convinced that it was fact.

He had to do this while the sun was still out. He decided to look away and lock the door. He ran to the docks to find the captain of the Trinidad.

Friend was a term that Antonio Pigafetta regarded loosely. He knew the mulatto slave calling him one was a taunt. He had never made friends with a slave. When he thought about it, he didn't befriend too many people in his life, one led mainly in scholarly pursuits, and friends seemed secondary to that. Now those pursuits had turned into business ones.

Today was the day, finally, after waiting for three long months— his excitement was a lurking dark cloud, waiting for rain. In his bunk was a set of blank journals waiting to be filled. The first thing he wrote in a brand new one was the date, September 20th, in the year 1519. He closed the book and stood on deck. He waited for the now-declared Captain-General Ferdinand Magellan to give orders and commands.

The Trinidad was alive with the motions of men moving crates and supplies, shuddering with the weight of one man's worries. Faleiro called for Magellan, panting and sweating in the autumn air. Instead of the sweat keeping him warm, it only made him colder when a breeze blew over him. 'Ferdinand!' Faleiro called.

The other workers wondered who this madman was, failing to realize he was instrumental in their employment. 'Hey, hey, you looking for him, he's below deck, or in his bunk,' one of them said.

Faleiro thanked him, not knowing if he should bow or smile and in his own confusion, contorted his body into the shape of exactly what he was making himself into. An ass. He ran into the Trinidad and found a slim Italian holding a pencil and a notebook the way an archer held a bow and arrow.

'You must be looking for Captain Magellan,' Pigafetta said calmly.

Faleiro ignored him, and bumped his shoulder against Enrique. 'Where is he?'

'Call me three times and I'll appear,' Magellan said. He eyed the workers ambling around him, taking crucial estimates of embarrassment and its accompanying compensation to his stature.

'I've been measuring the stars, Ferdinand. I have a bad feeling about this expedition,' Faleiro panted and hoped Magellan would agree.

'Did you consult a gypsy woman with a magic ball?' Magellan asked, with insult more than irony. He took notice of Rui Faleiro's stance, of his sudden change of heart, and with each passing second, felt more at a remove from Faleiro, the man fading in Magellan's eyes as though Magellan had never known him.

'What? No, I just have this, feeling. I can't put into words but if you go, terrible things might,' he paused, corrected himself, 'will, happen.' Still, Rui Faleiro, fading, kept searching Magellan's eyes to anchor him to sanity.

Antonio Pigafetta wished he could write this scene down right this moment, and reckoned this was great material, one captain-general ready to sail on the greatest adventure of a lifetime, another vehemently against going, although he was instrumental in plotting its navigation. Part of Pigafetta wondered if Faleiro was right.

Magellan caught Pigafetta's curiosity, which caused the Italian to shrug it off, his pride an armoured wall, guarding himself from embarrassment. He did not want to project any weakness, and Faleiro was not helping. He furrowed his brows, gritted his teeth and spat out, 'And you want to tell me all this now, when we're so close to leaving?'

'Better late than never, Ferdinand,' Rui Faleiro implored, his eyes still locked with Magellan's, but instead of hope staring down into Magellan's eyes, it was utter despair. Faleiro knew there was no hope, but that didn't stop him from trying.

'Captain!' Magellan corrected him. Faleiro stood still, half-convinced he was being ridiculous but the other half that wasn't, won him over.

Enrique cocked his head this instant, almost jumping at Magellan's thunderous tone. His eyes met Pigafetta's, and for a moment, the Italian's eyes blinked as though agreeing with Enrique.

'Don't go,' Faleiro said.

'I am Captain-General of the Trinidad. On the most adventurous voyage this world will ever know. Nothing will stop me from going.'

'Nothing will stop me from not,' Faleiro said, resolute.

'Why, Faleiro?' Magellan asked.

Faleiro said nothing. He clenched his fist, ready to box his own rage. He turned and walked out of the Trinidad, descended the plank that connected the ship to the dock and faded into the crowd.

Magellan felt many pairs of eyes around him. 'Write this incident down, scribe, and I'll burn that book of yours,' he told Pigafetta. Then he turned his attention to his crew, who turned away to pretend as if nothing had happened. He scoffed and stood to watch one of his most important allies leave him.

Nodding, Pigafetta sheathed his pencil within the folds of his notebook and went into his bunk.

Enrique watched as his master watched Faleiro walk away. Could Rui Faleiro be right that the voyage would end badly? It would've been easy to label Faleiro as a madman, but he was an astronomer and cartographer. But, he did spend more than a decade hoping for a promotion but got sidelined. Maybe this was what made him snap? Could his master snap at any time? Enrique himself had seen time after time how audacious, how ambitious and how explosive his master could be. But he knew, at the very least, his master was never cruel toward him, though he could vouch for his master's behaviour among other people that got in his way.

Soon, Faleiro was in his room at the inn, packing up his things in a hurry. He stopped at the table and took a long, hard look at all the scribblings. He thought of whether he should keep these scribblings for posterity, or discard them, and these options were one too many for him. He smacked his temples with each hand and whimpered and closed the door, running down the steps and onto the streets, muttering over and over that they were all doomed.

Pigafetta hid partly in shadow. He tried to forget the portends of that madman, and made sure the sailors did not call him out to work. For now they were still docked, and he was still a scholar.

He could hear the chatter of these Spanish sailors hating the idea that a Portuguese captain was about to lead them, though the sight of Ferdinand Magellan along with Cristovão Rebelo lifting crates and boxes and rolling barrels up the ships alongside the other sailors, inspired Pigafetta.

Pigafetta noticed Magellan stuck close to the new hire, Cristovão Rebelo, he seemed closer to Rebelo than even his slave. Pigafetta furrowed his brows. He knew what Rebelo was, and that he was no 'nephew'. The Italian watched Enrique as the slave folded his arms. The slave was smiling at the sight of his master spending time with the 'nephew'. Pigafetta wondered why, expecting some jealousy from the slave, though it would have been impossible for him to know the fact that when Enrique saw this sight, it reminded him of times spent with his family, especially his father. Enrique never forgot them. They were vivid in his mind's eye.

Pigafetta decided to pay Enrique no mind and turned his gaze away, and scoped in the distance a parallel line of five other ships docked at Port Sanlucar De Barrameda. He heard the Trinidad was always to sail ahead, a stipulation too many, and one he was sure would be the cause of many a grudge from all the other ships.

Within the hour, the Armada de Molucca, with strong winds in their favour, were far enough away from sight of land; five ships lead by Magellan that were enveloped by murky blue beneath them and sunny blue above.

Magellan then made a mental note of the men in charge of the ships. The roll call included himself, commanding the Trinidad, with a crew of fifty-five; the San Antonio, commanded by Juan de Cartagena held sixty men; while the Conception held a crew of forty-five, commanded by Gaspar de Quesada; the Santiago (the only caravel, while the others were classified as carracks, or large merchant ships) held a crew of thirty-two, commanded by Juan Rodríguez Serrano; and finally, with a crew of forty-three was the Victoria, which carried the supplies and provisions, was commanded by Luiz Mendoza.

Antonio Pigafetta noticed that the hiring of ships was not just hiring based on paper qualifications, but on connections, who you knew. The sailors seemed to know each other before they had even come onboard. He had no true friends on this journey, save for the pen, his truest companion. He did not want to include the mulatto slave. It was not on his list of priorities to make friends with him.

Ferdinand Magellan looked wistfully in the distance. In his eyes, he could still see her, his Beatriz, his Mrs Magellan.

Within the year, he had married her, and by the time they had set sail on 10 August 1519, Mrs Magellan had given birth to a sweet boy named Rodrigo.

A man has many regrets in his life, and at many a time, he wishes for how things might have been. He wished Rebelo could have played the part of a joyful and protective big brother to Rodrigo, and he wished he could have been with Rebelo and seen him grow up. Perhaps he would have this opportunity with his newborn son.

Magellan said goodbye to Mrs Magellan with a passionate embrace before he boarded his ship. He kissed his baby goodbye and promised them he would see them all soon, when he came back. They left each other with tears in their eyes.

Saying goodbye to his new wife and newborn must have been hard. But at least for him, he had family on board. He had his brother-in-law, and, unbeknownst to Duarte, he also had another blood-kin on board.

As the days went by, Pigafetta spent his free time roaming the ship and began to know its dark corners intimately. He was a man of journals, and his room seemed to have more blank journals than clothes. He always carried a small notebook as he roamed around the ship, pencil in the other hand, ready to write.

On most nights, he situated himself at the tail end of the ship, looking up at the poop of the ship, where he saw the fire made of reeds leading the way for the other ships to follow. From where Pigafetta stood, he reckoned the fire burned all night. Looking at the water, he felt he was an upside-down constellation, a lone star burning in a black and blue sky.

Sometimes it rained, and he felt brought down to earth. On these rainy nights, he hid in his bunk while the other crew worked to keep the ship on course. He knew they wondered where he was and knew the answer. He reckoned they knew he would be useless above deck. After he justified his own reasons for hiding, he transferred his pencil notes into his larger journal using the most precious of writing commodities, ink.

The hardest part of any writing task was organizing thoughts into something a reader understood, and he found the rewriting made his writing better. Though he was encouraged to write in the day, he chose to write at night, when most of the men, and especially Magellan, were asleep. The burning of precious candles at night was frowned upon. To console himself, he imagined that Magellan secretly wrote at night as well.

There were nights the storm raged fierce enough to tilt the ship at impossible angles. On those nights, Pigafetta made sure his books and journals didn't fall out of place. Above him, he heard the stomping of hurried boots, winced at the grind of hands blistering against ropes, hoisting and adjusting masts. After the storm calmed, he went to the cargo hold, glad that the ship was not the worse for wear, but the supplies were a wet mess, they looked like healed scars that had been whipped open again. Raw, fresh wounds.

'A little help, Italian?' Enrique implored, while Rebelo stood a few steps behind, wondering what the slave might do next.

Pigafetta rushed to the closest sack and hoisted it off the floor. The sack was wet and he knew that if it didn't get dried out, the food would spoil and they would have nothing to eat.

'This would never have happened if we had gotten a Spanish captain instead of a Portuguese one', he heard people mutter around him. He paused but could not detect the source, those words were a phantom haunting him, goading a monster he hoped had not heard it. He decided whatever hearsay or heresy was spoken was nothing but nonsense.

Storms formed when clouds gathered. Prejudice had no ready schedule on which to predict. *Borders made hate,* Pigafetta figured. Though many of them spoke a similar language, and were comprised of many different nationals, they created their hate based on nationality. If they weren't from the other's homeland, they were instant enemies. Cats and dogs. Separate strays that barked at the other on sight.

Pigafetta was glad the hatred was thinned out and separated among five ships.

Among the Trinidad itself, the men were directing their hatred toward their captain-general. Today, post-storm, they all worked to dry out the food on deck. Pigafetta was close and sharp enough to listen to them whisper against Magellan while they carried and placed the supplies. These phantom voices now had form, dense enough to wrestle with.

The Conception's ship master Juan Sebastián Elcano was a soldier fighting with the Spanish army in Italy and Algiers, until he reached a certain age where he felt he was old enough to stop fighting. In time, he settled down as a captain and owner of his own merchant ship, but fell victim to the biggest demon a man of the civilized world had to face. Debt. He owed money to Italian financiers and when he couldn't pay up, he had to surrender his beloved ship to the Italians. He had broken Spanish law in doing so, and this expedition with the Armada was part of the conditions for his pardon; King Charles had agreed to pardon him, on condition he served this expedition which he was funding.

For days now, Elcano had listened to the rumblings of mutiny with deliberate consideration. He was always within spitting distance of Quesada, one of the only men in this expedition who not only had thoughts about committing mutiny, but one of the few who actually made plans to carry it out.

In the meantime, the sailors did plenty of fishing to pass the time, and squid was a prized item.

An open secret that all sailors and captains had to contend with was not just food and drink but lust. Magellan could see their eyes light up whenever they heard there were squids about. He knew the squids were not for eating. He could not stand the sight of them now. The ship reeked of squid.

'How long do we have, Master?' Enrique asked. He was looking at the distance.

'I'm afraid we've done nothing for too long,' Magellan said.

'What do you need me to do, Master?'

Magellan looked at that same distance Enrique was squinting at. He estimated two fleets. He wondered how they had gotten so close. 'They are still too far away for effective cannon fire, though I reckon with these winds, that won't hold true for long.'

Enrique fidgeted with his hair and swallowed hard. 'A week, maybe?'

'Sooner, perhaps,' Magellan said. He wondered what extent King Manuel went to, to get back at him. He heard that Manuel in his spite had done terrible things to his relatives back in Portugal. He was glad to have married Beatriz in Spain, but some days he worried about her safety.

'We need to outmanoeuvre them,' Cristovão Rebelo said. He stood in between his father and the slave.

'I reckon two fleets,' Enrique squinted. The caravels were light and he prayed the winds would change direction.

Magellan said nothing. Enrique knew this was a sign he was thinking hard. Magellan thought about maps of the known world, lamented how incomplete maps were, and what regions had yet to be discovered. He pictured the world in dimensions. Below was water filled with beasts, above were the sun and the stars. And to the east, land. He knew they were not far enough away from land to make any difference or to proclaim they had gone further than any man. Magellan needed to be close to land to divert these two fleets.

To the west was nothing but an endless blue, and he feared if the fleets were to flank him there, then there would be nowhere to escape, save for the sharks below beckoning them, the way one might lure a roach only to stomp on it.

He left his slave and his son, not acknowledging either of them.

Those on deck saw their captain-general but continued working, tending to sails. Pigafetta rose from below deck and felt Magellan brush against his shoulder without so much as an apology.

The Italian stood on deck and saw the sails of the Armada's other four ships at the rear, tailing them, then noticed the other Portuguese caravels bearing Portuguese flags. He sighed, then eyed the other men, too busy manning the sails to bother about him. He saw the page and the slave chatting, the son and the surrogate, both of them laughing at some joke he could not even begin to imagine. The Italian felt the seas were slowly drowning his sense of humour.

The page and the slave then busied themselves with work, and Pigafetta had to admit that at least they knew how to make themselves useful.

He descended below deck, one of the few men allowed his own room, before they would force him to do menial labour he felt was still beneath his stature as a man of words.

He decided to peek into Magellan's room, knocking with a confidence that surprised even him.

Magellan opened the door, his frown tumbling into a smile. He was glad it wasn't any one of the men. 'Pigafetta, come in,' he offered, and the Italian entered, journal in hand.

'Do you worry, Captain,' Pigafetta began. He tried to find a place to sit on, but save for the bed and Magellan's chair, there was nowhere he could sit. He leaned against the wall at an awkward angle, not totally giving up on the idea of sitting.

'Always, scholar,' Magellan said. He limped back to the chair at his desk. 'Always.' He regarded the maps on his desk, then rubbed his bad knee. 'If we flank east, hug along the African coast, we can lose them.'

'How?'

'Islands, Italian. Like playing catch, hiding behind walls. Diversions. The Portuguese do not have knowledge of these areas. Not like I have. A few years ago, Enrique and I sailed these parts, transporting slaves from a battle in Azemmour.' Magellan looked at the map on his desk again. 'Call them in,' he told Pigafetta.

'Who?'

Magellan sighed, and wondered how smart scholars truly were. 'The pilots and the boys, scholar! Now!'

The two pilots Estevao and Francisco entered the room, followed by Cristovão and Enrique. They listened in with Pigafetta as Magellan explained his plan to sail through the African coast.

'And my slave knows the route quite well,' Magellan concluded.

'You expect us to trust this slave of yours?' Estevao said. Francisco added fuel to this doubt. 'He's just a boy.'

'A young man, who traveled these waters before,' Magellan told the pilots. 'If you doubt him then you are doubting me.'

Both pilots eyed each other, then noticed their own boots shuffling.

'And what about the rest of the fleet?' Pigafetta wondered.

'If they are as good as they claim to be, the pilots of the other ships will be able to follow my lead,' Magellan addressed the room.

'You sure you know the way, Enrique of Malacca?' Cristovão Rebelo ribbed him, then punched his shoulder.

'Trust me, trust your Captain, Cristovão Rebelo of Spain,' Enrique told him. He pictured the Portuguese fleets in his mind as two giant hands beneath the water, and the caravels were fingers that at any moment, might clench into fists and drag them all back to Portugal.

Enrique stood at the sails, arms wrapped around the ropes, ready to release them. It was getting dark, and seafarers knew better than to gain speed after sunset. Magellan had banked on the hopes that the caravels would slow down after dark, where he would take the chance to gain speed. Even with the beacons burning, it was still hard to see.

'You going to be sailing blind,' a crewman said. Enrique wondered who it was, but decided to pay it no mind. He looked up at the stars and in the dark night, the stars burned his eyes and he had to close them. He reckoned his master was not sailing blind, but sailing bright. As the night wore on, the stars shone brighter, and Magellan lead them away, but they were by no means safer.

For weeks, the Portuguese haunted them, but were never close enough to cause a true threat.

Even as far as he had imagined, he never thought the distance between lands were so vast, and even at less than halfway along their journey, they were already starving.

10

As they were crossing the Atlantic at the tail end of 1519, Enrique was told to tally the supplies they had in the various docked ships and one night, in the cargo hold of the Victoria, there were grunts and the pounding of flesh against flesh, their silhouettes shaped like a two-back beast in the dark, a hard beast pounding with passionate purpose. Enrique heard these sounds. At other times, hearing this kind of moaning might have excited him, but these moans sounded wrong. It dawned upon Enrique that this was an all-male ship. 'Salamon?' Enrique said curiously when he began to realize who it was in the dark.

Antonio Salamon was in the throes of passion, the recipient of his ministrations, Ginoves, was moaning as Salamon finished himself inside the cabin boy, both of them ending their lovemaking thoroughly and utterly spent. Enrique stood there, mouth agape. 'Ginoves? Salamon? What in God's name are you?' Even as he said this, he knew all of them in the room could not deny the throbbing in the sailor's loins.

Salamon scrambled to put on his clothes. Ginoves, on his knees, back facing Enrique, did nothing but scowl at Enrique. Salamon stood with pants on but shirt loose, blood rushing to his head. Part of him felt he did nothing wrong, as there were no women aboard expeditions such as these, and his lust had to be fulfilled, but part of him knew, from Magellan's no-nonsense demeanour, that if this slave told his master, he would be in big trouble. 'Don't tell,' Salamon whispered, pleading.

Enrique considered this. He turned his head away, then pivoted on one heel. If he didn't say a thing and turned a blind eye, it would have been wrong. But if he didn't tell his master, and if Magellan did find out, then Magellan might have Enrique's head.

'Don't,' Ginoves now stood, shivering and naked, back still toward Enrique.

But it was too late. Enrique left the cargo hold, knowing full well he'd have to tell his master, and seal the deathly fates of Salamon and Ginoves.

Magellan stood in the main cabin of the Trinidad with his fingers stroking his chin, back away from Enrique. 'And you did indeed see them in this unholy act?' he asked his slave.

'Yes,' Enrique said simply. To elaborate this act further would seem to make what he saw more real than he wanted it to be.

'This is not the first time this has happened at sea, Master. Don't sailors always turn a blind eye?' Enrique asked.

'Don't be a fool, Enrique. Those ships were not run by me. This now is my expedition, and they have to be punished. I have to show them who is in charge.'

Enrique bowed his head, and only now did he feel the heat of the other men in the cabin. Today was a grand day, with all the other captains of the other ships in attendance as well.

'Or do you just want to use this incident as an opportunity to exert your power, Captain?' Juan de Cartagena asked.

'It's Captain-General,' Magellan corrected Cartagena. Quesada, Mendoza and Serrano stood watch, waiting to see how this was going to play out.

Magellan turned to Enrique. 'We will deal with Salamon and Ginoves later. Now, there are other matters I need to address. Matters of mutiny.' He paused, then spoke directly to Cartagena. 'And of insubordination. For many a time, you have referred to me only as Captain, and not my full rank, Juan de Cartagena. I hope this does not happen again.'

On 20 December 1519, Antonio Salomon received his punishment while the expedition was in layover in Rio de Janeiro. A sailor in a black hood approached him, and the last thing Salamon saw were two large hands around his neck. He could still feel the other sailors looking on as his breath was slowly taken from him and his vision turned cloudy. His eyes saw only the release of darkness.

There were whispers amongst Salamon's friends, who didn't approve of this punishment, and approved even less of the captain-general.

Antonio Ginoves, on the other hand, was thrown overboard, left to drown in the open sea.

'I want them all to remember, this act against God shall not be tolerated,' Magellan told Pigafetta and Enrique soon after the deaths of the cabin boys.

Pigafetta only listened. He was quieter now. The man that he had painted in such a great light was not the man he thought he knew. As the days raged on, there was a shroud of darkness hovering over Magellan. Pigafetta knew as well as anyone that love between the sailors continued, this time more in secret than ever before, as they did not want to get caught and killed and made further examples of.

What troubled Pigafetta for many nights after the two cabin boys died, was the fact that he shared their first names.

Antonio.

He could not sleep at all on those dim and chilly nights.

11

At the end of March 1520, they had created a makeshift port that Magellan named St Julian, during which time they were experiencing a hunger that verged on madness. The man walking in the hold of the Conception saw a large blank space full of boxes and bales overturned in an attempt to seek out the last morsels of food.

The ship stank with the funk of bodies that had not had a proper bath in months. Gaspar De Quesada felt something had to be done fast, and they all had to deal with Ferdinand Magellan, and Quesada's ship master Elcano, trailing behind him, had to agree.

The clouds grew darker, and there was only thunder that would come next. The grim facades of the sailors grew darker. Prejudice filled their minds, it had been festering within them for months. The air grew colder. Winter was fast approaching.

There had been a chill of personal discontent among the other captains; Juan de Cartagena, conductor of the San Antonio, and Louis Mendoza of the Victoria, all felt that a Portuguese captain should not be leading a Spanish fleet.

In the San Antonio, Cartagena had reiterated this sentiment many a time through tense whispers, his countenance grim and sour, marred in shadows cast by large shoulders. From the beginning of the expedition, he was soured by King Charles' preference toward Magellan, a Portuguese and a stranger, always enquiring why their king would favour Magellan to lead such an expedition, though Cartagena should have known better. Juan de Cartagena had little to no seafaring experience, not like Magellan did.

From the perspective of languages, Spanish and Portuguese were not that far off, and so too were their lands, and it was only the division and demarcation of lands by royalty that made these two peoples hate each other. People defined themselves by creating lines of difference in an effort to make themselves unique.

Enrique followed Magellan as they roamed the countryside surrounding St Julian, while Pigafetta witnessed the rumblings of these disgruntled men and crew. They talked and he listened to the captains, while the other crew stocked up on supplies provided by hunting and foraging. Sometimes they would shoot daggers at the Italian, especially when they were huddled during deep, hushed whispers. Pigafetta learned to leave them alone, and they did likewise. This scholar would not be much of a threat.

As the days wore on, these clandestine meetings were becoming an open secret. Now more and more crewmen joined in, all of them unhappy with the conditions on their respective ships.

This journey already had many meandering false starts. Winter was soon coming and they knew they had to endure many months in the cold.

Pigafetta knew mutiny was a foregone conclusion. Should he tell Magellan, or let this play out its natural course? The guilt was an invisible dagger, stabbing his heart. He bled, blood unseen.

One cold afternoon, Enrique stood, one foot twisted as though about to leave. He wasn't sure who's wrath was worse, his master's or Juan Cartagena's, the man who was in mid-rant: 'Well, Captain, you have lead us into storms, and now you want to subvert this fleet, this entire expedition, because no matter how loyal you claim to be to our king, your loyalties still lie with King Manuel,' Cartagena cast a sharp, accusatory glare at Magellan.

'The reason I chose this course, was to shake off the Portuguese caravels,' Magellan sighed, exasperated that the other captains still thought he had ulterior motives, even though he had denounced his own country of Portugal to be with this Spanish expedition. He only had three goals to accomplish; to find the shortest route to the

Spice Islands, to claim it for Spain before the Portuguese do, and to bring these said spices back to Spain. These goals sounded simple but seemed impossible to achieve.

Enrique stood behind his master Magellan cautiously. If need be, he would fight for his master, remembering how as a boy, he fought in Azemmour with his master in a battle of thousands. What then was punching one jealous Cartagena?

'That's what you would like us to believe,' Cartagena said, 'But I am the fleet's inspector general, and have been appointed persona conjunta. For all intents and purposes, I am this expedition's co-admiral. And I don't need to take orders from you, Captain.'

With the slight flick of Magellan's raised arm, the Trinidad's master-at-arms Gonzalo Gomez de Espinosa stormed the cabin along with Magellan's brother-in-law Duarte Barbosa and his 'nephew' Cristovão Rebelo, with swords drawn.

Magellan leapt at Cartagena, pulling him by the ruff of his shirt, shoving him onto a chair. 'This is mutiny, rebel! In King Charles' name, you are now my prisoner.'

Cartagena spat from where he sat, commanding the other captains to, 'Stab him now!'

Enrique looked on at Duarte Barbosa and Rebelo, and wished he had a sword. He felt when he wasn't in a battlefield with a chance he might die, that he wasn't allowed a weapon in enclosed spaces. He hoped he wouldn't get stabbed.

But the captains only rushed barely two steps before the sight of the swords loosened their resolve. Quesada and Mendoza let their daggers hang loosely in their hands, and for that, Enrique felt relief wash over his skin, erasing away his goosebumps.

Gonzalo Gomez grabbed Cartagena and shoved him out of the captain's cabin and out onto the main deck, securing him to the stocks intended for common seamen who had committed minor offences. Quesada looked on at his fellow Castilian officer, knowing this was a grave indignity. 'My lord, please free Cartagena. Or at least release him into our custody. We have proven loyal to you by ignoring Cartagena,' he and Mendoza pleaded.

'Why should I release someone such as this? He deserves nothing more than a proper death,' Magellan walked toward them, taunting them while Enrique paced alongside his master.

'You have nothing to fear from us, Captain-General. Please.' Mendoza implored.

Magellan thought about this. He wondered how much mercy was left in him. Then he remembered the kindness of his late mother, and his dear sister, and most important of all, he remembered Beatriz. 'He will be confined to the Victoria, relieved of all duties,' Magellan told Mendoza. Flanking Magellan were Barbosa and Rebelo, swords still ready at a moment's notice. Enrique took a step forward to be shoulder-to-shoulder with his master and knew it was not his place to say a thing. He did, however, see Magellan praise Rebelo.

'Good job,' Magellan smiled, and Rebelo gushed, smiled back at him. It felt good to be acknowledged by a man who had been absent all his life.

The second time, though, Pigafetta could not ignore it. There were still plans for a mutiny. He had heard even more rumblings:

He's taking too much of a gamble.

He's been lying to us about his plans so that we'd be fools enough to follow him.

Now we're cold and hungry and angry.

Pigafetta wondered what they thought of him, the only Italian in the entire expedition. Something caught his attention, and reckoned the moons with its one bright silvery eye, was witnessing a boat of twenty men rowing in darkest night to board Quesada's ship, the Conception.

The men seized Quesada in his sleep, struggling as he was dragged out onto the main deck, surrounded by a circle of candle and torch flames. He felt as though he were in a ring of hell.

'Why?' Quesada asked as he saw Cartagena encircling him.

'Magellan shouldn't have been so merciful to me,' Cartagena began. 'You'll make a good hostage.'

Magellan opened his eyes.

Innately, he knew the motions and sounds of his Trinidad, every rock it made under waves, every creak that footsteps made, down to the footsteps of the men who worked on the Trinidad.

On this cold night on the first of April 1520, what woke him were not the creaks, but the way the creaks formed a different kind of music in his ears. It was the disharmony of strangers.

'Enrique!' Magellan called for his slave, and the slave sat up. Magellan gave him some hand signals to say they were in danger, and Enrique knew immediately what he needed to do; he ran across the ship and roared for his sailors to awaken immediately, some of them startled, rolled and leapt off the floors where they slept. It was close to dawn now, the sun rising to replace the moon, a new witness to this mutiny.

'Get boats to the San Antonio and the Conception now!' Enrique commanded.

Around them, the awakened sailors grabbed and held their intruders, tying and binding them. 'What's going on, Captain-General?' Rebelo wiped sweat off his brow, panting.

'Good, I need you two to get on the boats,' Magellan said.

Rebelo shared a look with Enrique. He could have been wrong, but he reckoned he saw a smile.

Their boats arrived between the San Antonio and Conception, and one of the lieutenants from the San Antonio asked, 'What do you all want?'

'My master wants you to beach your ships!' Enrique raised his voice, making sure they would hear him clear.

'We take orders from no one but the true admiral of this fleet, Juan de Cartagena!' the lieutenant replied.

Enrique and Rebelo tried again, but they were obstinate. They were firm in their decision. Magellan's men rowed back to the Trinidad, and soon enough, he saw the boats. He turned and demanded, 'Fernandes! Where the hell are you? Fernandes! Fernandes!'

'Yes, my lord,' the chief constable answered.

Magellan held his breath, unsure if he should let his temper flare, or dissipate. A few deep breaths later gave him the peace of mind to choose the latter. He began to give Fernandes instructions.

Six armed men rowed toward the Victoria, the other ship in the fleet they still had a chance of stopping. When they were just below the Victoria, Fernandes made a concerted effort to keep himself unarmed. He walked toward the bow and placed a foot forward. The breeze gently blew his straight locks and tickled his mustache, which was by now, weeks untrimmed. He stuck out his chest, calling for Louis Mendoza, the Victoria's captain. 'May we board your ship, Captain Mendoza?'

'I will not allow it,' Mendoza told him.

Fernandes expected this, and pulled from behind his belt, a rolled letter. He held it high as though holding a torch in the night. 'Surely, you are not afraid, Captain, of just one letter?'

Mendoza took a step back to confer with his officers.

'It's a trick, or perhaps a parlay,' one officer said.

'There's no other reason for the constable to be here but to barter peace. And even if this was a trick, we will kill him soon enough.'

'Die if this is a deception?' This answer satisfied Mendoza.

Mendoza told them that only Fernandes was to come up, and it was only him that climbed aboard the Victoria.

'The letter might be a letter of surrender,' an officer reckoned.

Fernandes held out the letter, and Mendoza reached out his hand for it. Before he could hold on to it, Fernandes leapt and locked Mendoza's arm across his back. 'In the name of the King! You are under arrest!'

The officers were shaking. They were learned men and not warriors. When they came to their senses, they drew out their swords but Fernandes' party of six rushed on deck with swords drawn, and the officers, not knowing what else to do, looked at one another for confirmation before agreeing to charge at Fernandes's men. They fought wild and unsteady, arms trembling, hearts pumping.

It was a quick melee, where the six men slew the officers, their blood hot and bursting thick from the pressure. The other sailors from the Victoria stepped back. They did not want to be the next to die.

Fernandes held Mendoza by the throat. 'You shall die, traitor,' he whispered in his ear as he threw Mendoza on the deck, holding him down with his knees.

'Please, please, I beg of you, mercy,' Mendoza pleaded. 'How, how did Magellan know?'

'The real admiral of this expedition has eyes and ears everywhere. And it was simple for Magellan to deduce that if Cartagena and Quesada were conspirators, you would be forced into this as well.'

'Yes, please, forced. I had no choice.'

'You always have a choice,' Fernandes drew out his dagger and pierced it past Mendoza's arms, into his neck. Mendoza writhed while using both hands to try and stop the flow of blood spraying out his neck, and his legs were a wriggling pair of serpents, struggling for but a moment before fading into dead silence.

Fernandes got off Mendoza's corpse and looked on around him. The deck of the Victoria was a deck shining with blood.

The scent of blood wafted and rode over the breeze and into the Trinidad itself. Magellan told his men to drop down alongside the Victoria, 'And load and aim the cannons.'

Soon, the Trinidad was close enough that Magellan was able to cross the ad hoc plank from one deck to the other. He was glad to see that Fernandes had bound the sailors.

'Find me six of these offenders. I want them punished,' he instructed Fernandes.

Soon, Magellan's faithful hoisted Mendoza's corpse by the feet onto one of the masts, while the six offenders were hung by the yard-arms for all to see.

'There's still the matter of Cartagena,' Fernandes reminded Magellan.

'He's never left my mind. Just be careful. He'll be surrounded by his Spanish faithful. He'll be too strong to take on directly,' Magellan advised.

'What should we do next?'

'Rebelo! We have a task of you,' Magellan ordered the cabin boy, his 'nephew'.

Rebelo sailed out of the Victoria in a skiff, and soon clambered up to the San Antonio.

'Who are you?' Juan Sebastián Elcano, now commander of the San Antonio, asked Rebelo.

'I need help,' Rebelo implored. He had blood on his clothes and his hair was in a wet mess. A constable pointed a pistol at him and he raised his hands up willingly.

'Ferdinand Magellan has taken the Victoria,' Rebelo told the constable, panting for good effect. 'I barely escaped. The deck is soaked with blood. But I survived. Please, please help me. As one compadre to another. We can't let the Portuguese lead us any longer.'

The firing end of the pistol taunted him like a dangerous woman's lips. He felt alone, and the shroud of night gave way to the streaks of dawn, as if the sun drew these other shapes on the San Antonio's deck into being. Rebelo gulped and prayed that he would not get shot.

Rebelo had his eyes closed, and heard the pistol's hammer click to safety and the constable lowered it and laughed, 'Of course, even with the Victoria fallen,' he paused.

'We have enough men to complete the fall of Magellan,' Juan de Cartagena interrupted the constable, walking into Rebelo's line of sight. If the other sailors appeared drawn by sunlight, Cartagena seemed to be drawn from deep darkness.

Rebelo felt his heart, and other parts of his anatomy, drop. He sighed, and the corners of his lips curved into a nervous smile.

He was taken to a bunk to be given clean, bloodless clothes. He didn't expect much in the way of food, but he was given biscuits. He thanked his benefactors, trying to hide the guilt he felt inside him. He just had to wait for nightfall.

The waiting was the easy part. He now had to wait further for the sailors to sleep, and when they did, there were still sentries patrolling the deck. Knowing stealth was necessary, he took steps to avoid those five sentries. He approached a cable and cut it with his knife, fast enough to be effective, but slow enough not to make too much noise.

Once the cable was cut, he leapt over a crate and hid behind it and waited as the San Antonio drifted toward the Victoria.

The collision of these two ships seemed like divine coincidence, and Magellan immediately called out the words, 'Treason! Treason!' as he leapt on board the San Antonio with his men and began attacking Cartagena and the mutineers.

Cartagena faced Magellan without compunction, but in Magellan's rage, he overpowered Cartagena, their swords parting and parrying, the captain-general raising and slashing as he got closer to Cartagena, his experience as a soldier clearly overshadowing Cartagena's swordplay antics. Cartagena, an accountant, was but an office boy to Magellan, and as Magellan raged on, he recalled the meetings when Cartagena called him merely a captain. He pushed the office boy to the ground and limped toward him, pointing his sword to Cartagena's chin.

Magellan's men tied up the crew of the San Antonio, and in this rising dawn all the five ships of the Armada de Molucca knew who was their true leader.

As for Mendoza, Magellan made Enrique read out an indictment to state that Mendoza was a traitor, and his corpse was tied to the Trinidad's deck. The next sight made Enrique retch.

The appointed executioner pulled Mendoza back and made an incision on his abdomen, a sharp, clean slice that caused his intestines to spill out on their own volition.

The executioner lit a flame, and threw it at those spilled guts. Soon Mendoza passed out, and the scent of those burnt guts smelled almost appetizing if not for the sight of the dead man.

Mendoza's wrists and ankles were tied to the capstans, where sailors the then rotated the cables and pulled apart his limbs, and bit by bit pressure was applied until his lifeless body was ripped to pieces.

Quesada too was made to watch this. He eyed Magellan's slave wiping the vomit off the corners of his mouth. Quesada held his puke in his throat.

'Display him. Let them all see what happens to traitors in my fleet,' Magellan told all the men.

As for the rest of the body parts, they were parboiled with herbs to keep them from birds. Enrique and Rebelo helped with some of the organs, Enrique was in charge of boiling the lungs, and Rebelo, the heart, and though they had now seen their fair share of violence and bloodshed, they had never seen organs on display, let alone never in their life would they imagine having been tasked to parboil organs. Rebelo retched and coughed and when Enrique first saw the lungs he puked and calmed himself. Minutes later he had to reassert his thinking. The lungs were just meat. He'd seen sheep being slaughtered at the mosque during Eid ul-Adha, back when he was still Muslim, and chose to focus on that memory instead.

After the organs were boiled sufficiently the herbal smell seemed almost delicious, though Rebelo's and Enrique's faces were still pale from this task.

The two young men were also tasked with displaying those parts for everyone to see, though they were not proud of this fact.

In the days that followed the mutineers were kept in irons, but many, including Juan Sebastián Elcano, were made to be workers forced to do daily menial tasks.

He released them on land and said, 'Go now, before I change my mind.'

At that, many of them stumbled, wondered if those words were true, then, as if to confirm their suspicions, Enrique stepped forward, 'Go! Before my master changes his mind.'

The freed slaves strode across the shore, past grassy hills, fading into lush forests, spreading and fading into the distance.

Enrique saw Magellan smirk, and figured his master knew something no one else did.

Days passed before Enrique saw those freed sailors. When they left Magellan, they strode with hopes of freedom but now they came limping back to the shore, their feet sore, bodies tired and weary.

In St Julian they died a little each time they tasted what they perceived was freedom, though this was but an illusion. There was nowhere to go around the verdant hills and forests of this island, and Magellan knew this, laughing as he saw them groveling back to him.

'Join us, back to your respective ships. Order has been restored, and we can all come back to the mission at hand, to travel westward to the Spice Islands,' Magellan told them somberly, the tone of a father teaching a young son a moral lesson. Cristovão Rebelo listened on as he pretended to do chores on the Trinidad. This lesson resonated within him.

For the sailors, this point struck home, strengthening their resolve that Magellan's mercy was to be respected, but it was a tenuous mercy.

Juan Elcano, partly complicit in the San Antonio mutiny, was among the men who ran too far in the wilds of the island. As the new commander of the San Antonio, he had to lead them by example, he was the first to hold a rag or broom or volunteer for some shit chore.

The trials for the captains who headed the mutiny took weeks, and in that time Quesada was found guilty and sentenced to be quartered. Magellan looked to Quesada's servant Luis de Molino, and gave him an ultimatum.

'You can either die alongside your master, or be the one who takes the first step to your own freedom,' Magellan told Molino while Enrique stood behind his master, head bowed low. He knew the violence of what was to come next.

Molino knew which option he would choose. He reckoned any sane man would make the same choice.

Quesada, tied to a chair on the shore, could only droop his lips in a resignation of his own fate as an audience gathered around the main deck of the Trinidad. Quesada was on his knees, awaiting his fate. Molino had a sword in hand, and tried to meet eyes with the sailors around the deck, as if to gain approval. The sailors averted their eyes from Molino. His eyes looked to Magellan, and that was the final seal of approval, though meeting eyes with the Captain-General reminded him this was the only way to prolong his own life.

'Forgive me,' Molino said to his master Quesada.

Quesada said nothing. He closed his eyes, bowed his head low, and waited.

Molino raised his sword and in one quick and powerful strike, his master's head left its body. Enrique closed his eyes, wondered if he could ever get used to this brutality.

'I want his body drawn and quartered and displayed,' Magellan told a detail he had already planned for this occasion.

The severed bodies of Mendoza and Quesada were later placed on full gory display in St Julian with the aid of Rebelo and Enrique. Birds came, and were repelled not by the gruesome sight, but by the scent of herbs.

12

'Could it be a more perfect day,' Magellan wondered to Enrique. It had already been a few months since the quartering of both Mendoza and Quesada, and the July sun warmed the port of St Julian, but ever so slightly. The winds along the coast still carried with them a chill capable of stirring shivering bones.

'I guess not, master,' Enrique said, not knowing if he was being honest or ironic.

'It's times like these that I miss my Beatriz the most. When the world is calm like today it reminds me of all the good things in life I have forgone to make this journey. I wish to spend more time with my family when I return.'

'And what of Cristovão Rebelo, master? What will become of him once this expedition is over?'

Magellan pondered this, and his answer was simple. 'He will do as he pleases,' he said in the tone of a proud father setting his child off into adulthood.

Enrique paused, satisfied with the answer.

The breeze straddled the fine line between gentle and harsh, and both slave and master walked along the shore toward their anchored ship, but they had to stop when they saw something that defied their sense of scale.

The giant danced along the coast, breeze tickling his hair into tangled wisps, hands gesticulating in a manner that Enrique had only seen in children. The giant's singing was dissonant but happy, a rusted nail against wet board, though they knew not what language the giant was singing, it brought out in Enrique something he had not felt in a long time, a sense of carefree abandon.

When the giant saw these two strangers he was enveloped in awe that was soon overtaken by fear, two corners of the world, one primitive and one modern, meeting for the first time.

The giant stopped dancing, began screaming in his own dialect, 'The Angels are here!'

'How about you dance with him,' Magellan suggested to Enrique. Magellan figured, I will have broken new ground if I have found this primitive. I can come back to Spain and circle back to the Spice Islands.

'You want me to dance?' Enrique pointed his finger that may as well have been a dagger to his chest. He also wanted to scream, to ask if his master was crazy for suggesting this or if he was crazy for not following orders.

'Follow me,' Magellan said, placing a hand on Enrique's shoulder. They walked to the Trinidad, and Enrique couldn't help but feel relieved he didn't have to dance. Not yet, anyway.

As they walked away they heard the giant screaming, feet planted in the ground as though his thighs were the trunks of ancient trees. He saw the Trinidad and screamed something in his language, something that later on Pigafetta was able to understand after spending some time with the giant and his people. The giant screamed, 'The Angels are here!'

Magellan and Enrique could hear the giant screaming those words over and over again as they boarded the Trinidad.

'I can't believe we have not seen him or his kind before,' Pigafetta said. He looked around him, and he looked up, at the verdant summits and undulating valleys of this land.

'We have not been out that far. We've been mostly here, we haven't explored that deeply yet,' Rebelo offered.

Not that we want to, Enrique thought. Magellan whispered something in his ear and Enrique nodded, though by the squint in his eyes and pursing of his lips Magellan knew his slave did not agree to this.

'What strange plan have you cooked up this time, Ferdinand?' Duarte Barbosa asked. Duarte stood on the deck that regarded him as a ghost. Sometimes he knew the Italian Pigafetta's purpose on the ship was a better and more useful one. Duarte on the other hand felt like he was only here to keep his brother-in-law company.

Magellan paused, a habit he knew would always keep people on edge. He knew they would listen to him if he did. 'Rebelo!' Magellan called out.

Cristovão Rebelo stepped forward cautiously. 'Me, Captain-General?'

'You remember the plan I told you about?' Magellan let those words hang over Enrique like a knife.

Enrique gave two quick nods. 'You're going to dance along with him, and then we'll take a boat to the next nearby island. We're going to make friends with him, Rebelo.'

By the time Rebelo and Enrique lowered their boat they sun had grown dimmer. Both young men rowed, each holding a paddle, taking turns so the boat did not spin or tilt, but went in a straight line.

The dancing giant saw the two men, wondering who they were, He stopped dancing as they approached the shore.

'So this your master's bright idea, Mulatto?'

'Guess so,' Enrique said, and before he knew it, his arms and feet gesticulated into odd angles that Rebelo laughed at. He joined Enrique and the giant laughed too, and all of them began dancing.

'Speak Spanish, friend?' Enrique began looking up and up at the giant, whom he reckoned was about two and a half heads taller than he was.

'Or maybe Portuguese? Italiano?' Rebelo added.

The giant slowed down to consider what the two men were saying, but understood exactly none of it, nothing they spoke was of any dialect he had known, but he replied in his own tongue, knowing the men would not understand him. 'You are emissaries from the heavens, I reckon.'

Both emissaries from heaven faced the other, stifling their laughter.

'This your master's plan? Dancing like idiots?'

'Just be quiet and lead him to the boat,' Enrique said.

The two men and the giant danced their way in a circuitous path that lead to the boat. Rebelo entered then Enrique followed, to make sure the giant was doing the same, but when the giant did get in he almost shot the two men off the boat.

Rebelo and Enrique held on to the boat, and grabbed their oars to paddle once the boat was in balance. They exchanged a brief glance before Enrique calmed the giant.

'We are taking you to a special place,' Enrique said this slow and loud, looking at the giant right in the eyes.

The giant had his knees tucked into his chest, shoulders slumped, looking like a kid who signed up for an adventure that was too large for him to handle. He constantly looked down at the water below him. His large index finger poked through the water's surface but he quickly retracted as though it were fire before even the first digit fully entered the water.

The boat rocked now in sync with the waves below them, and that meant the giant was calm, calm enough for Enrique to introduce himself, 'Meu nome é Enrique, que é seu?'

The giant grunted something, most likely his name, something neither Enrique nor Rebelo could pronounce.

'Obrigado,' he thanked the giant.

The air wafted between tufts of warm and cold as they approached the island, where Magellan and crew greeted the giant, trying as best they could to fake smiles imagined to be pristine white but were in truth laden with grime, with faces lined with scars and scabs.

'Greetings, my friend,' the Captain-General told the giant, spreading his arm, revealing, like a magic trick, a table spread that began to fill the giant's head with wonder. The jagged bangs on his forehead ruffled against his thick brows furrowed together in curiosity, while the corners of his lips, blunt with doubt, sharpened into the points of a wide smile.

'Come, come, these are for you,' Magellan offered as the giant walked to the food like a curious beast, tongue already wagging while he picked a loaf of bread to his large nostrils, shoving it instantly into its mouth instead of trying just a pinch of it.

'He's almost twice as tall as the rest of us,' Pigafetta remarked.

Next, the giant attacked a piece of preserved meat, munching on it with his hands, tearing it apart the way predator eats prey.

Magellan wanted to offer the giant a goblet, but it seemed so tiny in the giant's hand that he decided to give it an entire bottle of wine, a decision he knew would not be popular with the men.

The giant snatched the bottle, drinking half of it before the wine's potency kicked in. His cheeks flushed red and his eyes began to tear, he felt his heart race before he began to emit a deep bass of laughter.

'What say we join the giant,' Magellan suggested, hoping this might gain him favours with the crew. With their minds filled with alcohol they might think better of him. He awaited their reaction, felt the doubt in their eyes. Everyone waited for a long moment before one and then another sailor motioned toward the makeshift table and handed another bottle to the giant, and passed around goblets and another bottle to distribute and drink.

They sang a harmonious 'salute' and made sure they got the giant's attention. He indeed had their attention, tilting his head up, and pointed to the sky. 'Are you from heaven?' the giant asked.

Pigafetta stepped in when he saw this, smiled, laughed and spoke in his native Italian, 'We are but mere mortals, my friend.'

The giant smiled, mumbling words only he understood. He finished the last drop of his second bottle and threw it away, but not before looking at it and through it. He reckoned he could see the heavens through the small end of the bottle, and he was partly right, if one were inebriated enough.

The sailors proceeded to entice the giant further, like salesmen, showing the giant their wares, and it was brutal calculation that they did not line the table with anything sharp. The last thing their

Captain-General wanted was some brute poking at them with a sharp object.

The giant seemed happy, accepting of his new friends from the heavens. Their words were music to his ears, and the thing that caught his eye, a shining silver pool that reflected the outside world. It lay framed on the table and it drew darkness and light in before casting it back out at you.

The giant dared glance into the silver pool, and he saw a tall, grotesque thing with squinted eyes, coarse hair, thick brows, a wide, misshapen nose, and lips that were no different than whatever beasts he might hunt. The sight of himself made him squeal loud enough that it deafened his friends from the heavens. The visage he saw in the mirror scared him, and he did as dogs did when they saw their reflections in a mirror. He barked at it, himself, grunting, and doing one better than dogs, acting against his reflection with his fist.

The mirror shattered, its shards clinging into his skin so deep that he was unable to open his fists. Blood tainted the shards a deep red and though he was in pain what worried him even more was the worry that he had likely broken a thing from heaven, and in his confusion he raged ahead at the closest sailor, then another, lifting them in his arms only to slam them down seconds later.

Enrique ran ahead before Pigafetta, Magellan, Rebelo and Barbosa, panting to catch his breath while they ran to catch up to him.

'Hey! Tranquilo, acalmar meu amigo,' hey calm down friend, Enrique began. He knew he might get reprimanded by his master, but he carried on, 'Come my friend,' his voice warbling, he had begun to dance the same way Rebelo and him were dancing when they first met the giant.

'Remember, we were dancing, like this,' he leapt and slapped Rebelo on the shoulder, urging his comrade to dance. Enrique also implored Magellan, Barbosa and Pigafetta to dance along, but they felt they still had their pride and dignity and stood aside.

Rebelo danced along, his brows feigned reluctance, but his feet proved otherwise. 'This plan had better work, Mulatto,' he grinned through his teeth.

The giant calmed down at the sight of these two tiny men gesticulating wildly. This isn't dancing, the giant thought, and he coughed out his first gasp of laughter, followed by another booming gasp, before falling to his knees, almost out of breath.

Rebelo tried to get Enrique's attention, waiting for a signal to stop. Their dancing slowed down, until they were only jogging on the spot.

Magellan signalled for Enrique and Rebelo to go to the giant, who was now wheezing out his final gasps of laughter. Enrique reached out his tiny hand as a gesture of friendship. 'Amigos,' he told the giant, pointing to himself and the others.

The giant looked at the men he lifted and threw like paper, and felt a pang of guilt. He extended his large hand that made Enrique's look like a child's hand, imitating the sentiment. 'Amigos,' the giant said in a rough, booming voice, the pain in his hand seemed to have faded for now. With his other hand he slapped his chest.

'Si, amigos,' Enrique told the giant, and handed him a sheet of cloth for the wound.

The day was cold even with the sun streaking high above them, the heat even baking the well-sewn fur pelts the giants wore to keep themselves warm. They were armed with spears that were taller and larger than the Spaniards, and it surprised the Spaniards to notice the giants had yet to invent something as advanced as a bow and arrow, or even boats, for that matter.

It was a week now that the Spaniards had been together with the giants that called themselves the Tehuelche, or Fierce People, in their language, tagging along on their hunts with animals as strange to the Spaniards as the giants were, a totally different world that might as well have been on a distant star.

When the Spaniards saw the giants launch their spears, they came to understand why they did not need to ever have invented the bow and arrow, as they saw the giants launch the spears with their well-muscled arms as far as any bow could launch an arrow, hitting their targets with an uncanny pinpoint accuracy, and chasing after their dead prey wearing their large guanaco leather boots.

When the Spaniards first came to this land the giants gestured and wondered if the Europeans came from above, pointing their fingers up to the heavens.

At this, Enrique gestured a no, and tried to imply they were mere mortals. But now, during the hunt, they felt like they had fallen into a backward time and place. Enrique followed them on this hunt, crouching along with the Spanish sailors and the Tehuelche, low among the plains, and Enrique was amazed at how something so large could make themselves invisible amongst the tall grass.

The animal they were after was something that looked like a sheep, but with an angry disposition and a neck as long as a giant's shin. This was the creature that fed them and kept them warm.

One of the Tehuelche signalled for all of them to lay low, and wait for the right time.

So Enrique waited.

And waited.

The cold wind blew in their faces, a biting wind unencumbered by the shelter of buildings, made worse by the fact they were staying still. The wind enveloped their shoulders and sometimes tickled their feet.

Enrique so desperately wanted to move so that he could keep warm. What he couldn't bear was the cold in his fingers, and wondered why the giants did not wear gloves when he himself could not feel the tips of his fingers. He tucked his hands under the warmth of his armpits and felt his blood ebb away, it forced him to squeeze the digits of his fingers in order to keep his blood pumping.

Just when he felt he would be frozen in place, the giants began to make the first move. They stood faster than anything of their size had any right to be, and, with one foot ahead of the other, leapt into a sprint, leaving Enrique and Rebelo panting as they tried to catch up.

He heard their prey of long-necked sheep running before he could see them, but he could see the giant ahead of him, the first giant they met lifting his spear and cocking back his arm before springing the spear high into the air. It shuttled down in a precise arc, its sharp end landing precisely against its prey's long, easy to target neck.

Another one of the giants gave the Spaniards the signal to flank the dead animal while the other long-necked sheep galloped away. The Spaniards surrounded the fresh corpse, and dragged the carcass aside. The first giant gave Enrique a large, skinning knife, which he stabbed into the animal's belly while the giant, which Enrique had decided to name Uno, number one, removed his spear and took over from Enrique.

Uno sliced the blade horizontally to let the blood and guts and intestines pour out onto the verdant ground, and with methodical precision pulled out the internal organs.

Magellan saw this, and stepped inside his tent. In his journal he wrote down the word pata which meant large, animal foot, then Pigafetta, who had been in the tent, saw the word.

'I'll call this land Patagon, and the people the Patagão,' he told Pigafetta.

'Patagoni,' Pigafetta said in Italian plural.

Magellan smiled. 'I'll call this place Patagonia,' he finally decided.

Antonio Pigafetta left the tent, and was soon on his haunches, struggling to keep the pages of his journal from flipping away. He had been writing down all he had seen here, and he knew the interpreter was watching him.

Pigafetta was a learned man, while Enrique was a man struggling to learn.

Enrique wondered what the Italian was writing in one of his many journals. It was a skill he was not accustomed to. Reading in Portuguese had been hard enough for him. He was better at remembering words by how they sounded, not how they looked, their intricate shapes and patterns did not concern him as much as what saying those words invoked in another person.

Slaves like Enrique were not privy to the private words of a scholar. In time, he knew someone would be reading those journals, someone perhaps higher in status than Magellan and Pigafetta, who would judge those words the way someone might judge a slave. He knew his autonomy was only illusory.

Everywhere he went, he knew eyes were always upon him. After all these years he was used to being the bearer of suspicion, though he ignored it. Today it was too cold to be worrying about such insecurities.

Pigafetta watched from the distance, following them from afar, choosing not to partake in the menial and dirty work, deciding he would need to keep his hands clean in order to do his writing.

They placed the meat on a plateau of rock to cut and hang it to dry. The firewood was brought and a campfire was made, and the entire village of giants gathered toward its warmth.

The meat fed plenty of them, and this was to be the first of many hunts.

Magellan and Duarte Barbosa kept to themselves in their tent, planning and plotting their next course of action.

'I reckon once were get out of here, we can cut through these straits,' he showed his brother-in-law a drawing he had made. 'And once there, it should be a matter of days before we're on the other side of the world.'

Duarte listened, almost convinced of his in-law's plans. 'I just hope your plan works. The expedition, the men, they are getting impatient,' he told Magellan, then eyed his slave. 'He haunts you like a hawk, brother.'

'My slave, at my beck and call.' Magellan said. 'Go make yourself useful.'

Enrique nodded, and left the tent. He found the scribe and scholar busy writing in his journal by the campfire. He motioned toward the scribe and asked what he had been writing.

'Nothing much,' Pigafetta closed his journal and tucked it under his arm, his wrist turned inward at an awkward angle.

'Your book's almost full,' Enrique remarked. He could feel this conversation grow colder in spite of the campfire.

'So what have you learnt here?' Pigafetta took on the tone of a schoolmaster.

'I've learnt scholars write in books, while slaves do all the dirty work,' Enrique left the scholar, and wandered around the fields. As the wind bit at him he could only thank God they had become friends with these giants, who had provided him with the fur pelt around his shoulder.

This was the first time he had been left alone in a long while, and he was glad for it, it gave him time to think, but he also dreaded it, because sometimes thinking lead to worry. His master and Barbosa were busy talking. He reckoned Rebelo was on the ship tending to chores while Pigafetta busied himself in his journal.

He had reached the apex of a cliff high enough to overlook the wide ocean, an endless blue where sailors were left to the tantrums of tides. It made him realize how small man was, and how large the world might be.

The sun kissed the tip of the horizon, and he had to leave now. When he entered his master's tent it was already lit with candles. He was afraid his master might wonder where he was. He found him buried in a Bible, a journal on the side, his head bobbing in tandem with the flicker of the candle flames as he moved between both books, his erratic motions creating the most curious of shadows.

'Master.' Enrique nodded, and waited.

Magellan was busy casting disagreeing shadows to care. Enrique waited. He would wait all night if he had to.

'These savages,' Magellan started, closing his journal, 'do not have the grace of the Lord to guide them. They worship things made of stones, sticks and mud, Enrique. And yet, there is something about them that is as pure as when Adam and Eve first roamed Eden. If I could just guide them, show them a better path, I could show them a path closer to God.'

Enrique nodded. 'Yes, master. If that is what they wish.'

'What they wish? They will be begging for me to know more about the word of Christ our Lord and the Holy Spirit, my boy! I want all of them to believe.'

'Like the Spaniards believe in you?' Enrique threw this question knowing well enough that it was a question without armour.

'Be careful where you tread your words, Enrique.'

'I am careful, but I do not tread lightly.'

A light gust of wind shook the candlelight and in turn both men's shadows danced as phantoms across the tent.

'They still plot to kill me, don't they?' Magellan said, his voice an octave lower. He stood up to graze his fingers against the pages of his Bible.

Enrique gave an imperceptible nod. After a long moment, he felt the air turn colder, as if all the heat in the tent were escaping from the solid form of Magellan's anger, which was only pacified when his fingers stopped upon a passage which he began to read aloud.

'James 1:19-20. Know this, my beloved brothers: let every person be quick to hear, slow to speak, slow to anger; for the anger of man does not produce the righteousness of God.'

'You should do well to remember that, master,' Enrique said before leaving the tent.

'Wait,' Magellan stopped him.

Enrique's feet anchored an inch into the ground. He pivoted and waited for what his master wanted to say.

In the swaying candlelight of the dark tent Enrique's face looked older, more matured. The shifting shadows cut and accentuated his features. Not too long ago, Enrique was short and all bone but in a short span of half a decade he had filled out and grown many inches taller. Aside from his voice which had gone deeper, Magellan noticed how Enrique, who was a scared child when he first acquired him, had come into his own, confident enough to talk back to his master, and though that defiance could have been punished, Magellan sometimes felt in some ways it could be rewarded.

Magellan had raised the boy from the point Enrique left Malacca. He had shaped the boy, better or worse, into what he had become. He only wished he could have made the same claim with Rebelo.

'I want to bring one of the giants back with us,' Magellan said to Enrique after a moment's pause to consider all those thoughts.

'And how do you intend to do that?'

'I have a plan,' Magellan told Enrique confidently.

In the passing days Magellan went about with renewed vigour, as if he had removed an arrow embedded deep in his body. The wound caused by the removal of this arrow was free to bleed and heal.

He took this time to give the ships a thorough cleaning, emptying the ships, removing the provisions from their stores, and gave the ships a cleansing bath of seawater, and though Pigafetta fancied himself a learned man he began to learn that out here in the middle of nowhere even scholars did the hard work of hauling provisions. During the evening, exhausted, Pigafetta took to his journals and wrote down what he was experiencing, for posterity.

Apart from the cleaning the sailors had taken to killing the seals among the shore and breakwater and preserving their meat. Rebelo and Enrique joined them, on account of their experience with bodily organs and herbs.

The most gruelling tasks were assigned to Elcano and the forty mutineers, who performed these duties bound in chains, while Cartagena, the last to be put on trial, waited, bound, was caught again attempting a third mutiny, this time conspiring with a priest.

But Magellan had a dilemma. He couldn't draw and quarter Cartagena as he had with Mendoza and Quesada. Cartagena had royal Castilian lineage, and furthermore, he felt guilty for punishing the priest.

At dawn one day they were at the shoreline, with Cartagena and the priest bound, surrounded by guards. The morning was cold and windy, and Antonio Pigafetta jogged toward this scene, curious as to what Magellan had to say about these two.

Magellan's piercing stare caused Pigafetta to stand silent. The Italian bowed his head, and let Magellan carry on. Enrique stood beside his master, listening.

'This might have been the fate that would have awaited you both,' Magellan pointed to the remains of Quesada and Mendoza on display. 'But I am not a man without mercy. You will live, but only here, in St Julian. When we leave, you both do not.'

Magellan nodded, glanced at Enrique for a split moment as though admonishing him. Magellan walked past them, looked at the deck, at their anchored ships, smelt the air, raised a hand with a finger extended. He felt the winds and licked his tongue.

He smiled. He knew they were now ready to finally leave Port St Julian.

The next day, the crew of the Armada were busy preparing the sails in the morning, and by midday Magellan had them all gathered by the shore, including those who conspired against him the third time.

Juan Cartagena and the priest were brought to shore, shackled and held by two of the crew.

With a nod from Magellan the shackles were unleashed and Cartagena and the priest shook their wrists. He trusted they would not try to retaliate or escape.

'The day has finally come for us to leave St Julian,' Magellan addressed the two mutineers. 'As I promised months ago, once we leave, you two do not.'

Cartagena and the priest hung their heads low, sobbing.

Father Valderrama stepped forward and began, 'Today, we are soon to leave again for our journey. Our Captain-General has ordered for us to have a final confession. For those of you who are willing, come forward, and I will hear all your sins. Do not worry, for only I alone shall know your burdens.'

The sailors paused, some looking at each other, before they stepped forward, each whispering to Father Valderrama their sins.

'I stole a loaf of bread,' one sailor said.

'I have a son from a woman whose name I do not know,' said another.

Enrique was standing behind Magellan, afraid his master might ask him for a confession. He would have liked to have confessed to anything, but felt his list of sins too many to start with, though to any one of these men they might have seemed like petty grievances, not worthy of an audience. What he would have wanted to say, most of all, was that he let his father die. He turned his head away, felt a tear escape him, but said nothing.

'I killed a man once,' someone else said.

'I loved a man once,' this sailor said quietly. Even after all these months the memory of the two Antonios being slaughtered on the shore lingered in his mind.

Father Valderrama, dressed still in his priestly robes, listened with a burden as wide and as deep as the ocean. He felt sorry for the priest about to be abandoned, but could not object the Captain-General. After what seemed to be an hour, he performed sacrament and he implored all of them to raise their hands and begin praying to their Lord and to Christ for a safe journey ahead.

Amen, Magellan finally said after an hour of silence.

The sailors dispersed, and Cartagena and the rebellious priest tried to follow.

Magellan gave Rebelo and Enrique a nod, and they held back those two.

'You're not going anywhere,' Rebelo said, almost leaping at them.

'You were on a skiff,' Magellan began. 'There was a storm. You both were trying to look out for other islands. You drowned out at sea. You died bravely.'

Enrique saw the tears in their eyes as they fell to their knees.

Magellan and everyone else left the shore, and both mutineers were left to ponder their fate.

The rest of the Armada raised anchor, and soon they left the shores of St Julian.

'Come back! Please! Don't leave us here!' Cartagena and his priest pleaded as the Armada faded into the distance.

'I couldn't bring myself to kill the priest,' Magellan told Enrique as they were out at sea.

13

The way Magellan regarded the giant Uno walking among the plains was the same way a fox regarded a rabbit before hunting it.

Over the last few days the giant had grown accustomed, even friendly with them. Magellan had explained to the men about his plan to lure them Uno, hopefully, using metal goods, and the man assigned for the task was once again Enrique.

Enrique approached Pigafetta in the Trinidad and asked what the Italian knew about the giants.

'Scholars do have their uses,' Pigafetta remarked.

'Next time you'll be the one on the front lines,' Enrique told the Italian.

Pigafetta kept silent, until he opened a journal of notes, explaining to Enrique what the giants liked, their gestures of communication, and the things that they worshipped. When he was done the sun had risen, and Enrique went to his master's quarters.

'Don't give them our guns or swords,' Magellan warned. 'That would be dangerous. 'This, however, would be a good start. Make them think this is jewelry,' he raised a pair of shackles.

'Do you think this will work, master?' Enrique picked the shackles off his master's hands.

'We must endeavour to try,' Magellan told Enrique with an optimism that seemed out of place.

'You might mean, *I* must endeavour to try.'

'Careful where you place your words. Or you might be the one that ends up shackled,' Magellan warned.

Enrique said nothing, his throat anchored by anger like a bucket of iron falling in a well.

'You are not doing this alone. You will have help,' Magellan reassured him.

'These are all the things we need?' Rebelo asked Enrique later as they stood in the lower deck of the Trinidad.

'We'll take as much as we can to the giants. I promise you, no dancing this time,' Enrique said.

'These biscuits are turning to powder. Good that the Captain-General is giving this shit out.'

'Better biscuits than raw meat, eh?' Enrique remarked.

'It's so odd they know how to make fire but don't know how to put meat in it,' Rebelo said, but there was no pleasure in his remark.

Outside the Trinidad the other men were ready. They had learnt much from Pigafetta, who also tagged along, and this posse walked to the giant's camp and led them back to their makeshift tent, where Uno walked first in line.

Two other giants followed Uno, all of them looking at the wares Magellan tried to push them, circular pieces of dull iron that were bright to the giant's eyes. They took those irons linked with chains but did not yet know what to do with them.

The young giants had silverware almost spilling out their hands, and Rebelo and Enrique suggested, at Magellan's behest that the best place would be, 'Wrapped around your feet.' Enrique said with a straight face, even kneeling down to point to his ankles for effect.

Uno and the other two grunted and nodded in agreement. Magellan snapped his fingers and his men placed the irons around all the giants' feet, bolting the shackles with hammers and rivets.

Enrique looked away. This kind of scene was all too familiar to him, and his pain almost felt like a bruise to his heart, a tangible physical ache.

Magellan pointed a finger to the giants while they grunted, nostrils flaring, like bulls, screaming for their lord Setebos, 'Setebos! Setebos!'

'Your devil won't be able to help you.' Magellan spat back at them.

Nine other men began to bind the other two giants, and all of them would later compare bruises as they dragged the giants to the shoreline, but one of the younger ones got away, and in spite of his size he was but a feather whose feet did not touch the ground, or make any indent in the grass.

'We lost him,' Pigafetta said.

'It's too quiet now,' Rebelo said.

'This is not a good sign,' Enrique said.

Uno stood still, and smirked. Good giant, Uno thought.

The giants came back with reinforcements, but were soon quelled and outgunned. Magellan gave an order to fire and the cannons boomed high in the air.

'Don't kill them!' Magellan warned.

The reinforcements ran away, and the two giants were brought inside the Trinidad. Uno, who felt he had a rapport with them because he was the first one they met, began raising his voice, and his buddy soon followed.

'Shut it,' the men kept warning the giants.

'Let me talk to them,' Enrique told the men. Rebelo and Pigafetta stood behind him.

At the sight of Enrique the giants quieted down. Their eyes met and were filled with a mutual understanding.

I so want to release you all, but I can't, Enrique thought. He knelt down, hoping his subservience would make them empathize. *I have to do the bidding of my masters. Of my betters.*

'I'm so sorry, my friends,' Enrique said softly, in Malay, a language he had not spoken in years. Speaking his true tongue was the only way he could express what he truly felt. He knew the giants wouldn't understand his speech, but he hoped they would under how he truly felt.

Enrique nevertheless knew this feeling, this burden washing over him. He felt it in Cairo. He felt it now, this overbearing need to release their shackles. He turned away, breathing hard between his teeth. He left the cargo hold, and felt a hand on his shoulder.

'Master,' he said softly, then went above deck.

He wondered whether life in his world would be an ongoing series of real and imagined shackles. He also wondered, in spite of his autonomy, how free was he, really?

14

Estevao Gomes wished he wasn't so much a mirror of his Captain-General. He saw so many similarities within himself he wished weren't true. At times he saw himself as the good version of the reflection while Magellan was the darkness within.

At other times, he saw himself a failure. He was a reflection rippling in a storm, his success fragmented along with his visage in the water, spread out and scattered and sunken like so many ancient ships.

He came to Seville the same time as Magellan, forming part of a circle of tightly-knit sailors that Magellan was also a part of. Within a few months in Seville, he received a pilot's commission, and had plans to raise his own Armada de Molucca. He too heard from Magellan and other sailors of these lucrative Spice Islands.

He took very similar steps to Magellan, raising maps, drafting out proposals, imagining his presentation before the young King Charles, whom he thought he could convince because of his youth.

When he did meet King Charles the king was interested, but Charles thought something was amiss, and the king found that missing thing when Magellan came, with a more detailed, passionate, and well-connected network of sailors and acquaintances, especially of Duarte Barbosa, marrying Beatriz Barbosa, and Gomes had learnt that young kings also had short memories. He forgot all about Gomes.

He settled for a commission as Magellan's pilot major, but he still seethed. He was promised by King Charles some caravels with which to discover lands, but again, the deal was cut when Magellan came into the picture.

When they had finally come to the straits, Gomes knew he would have to make things difficult for his Captain-General.

'Was that really how you found it?' Pigafetta asked.

They stood over a table, looking at a journal Magellan had drawn of his plan across the straits.

'One of many maps, Italian. There were many maps, and I noticed a pattern amongst all these maps. My suspicions were confirmed when I saw a map in the Portuguese treasury, the clearest one of a strait, if you look at it, that cuts through lands. It would save us the time of circling those lands.'

Pigafetta nodded. He was certain of his leader, but he still harboured doubts like a small child hiding in a corner. He felt like he trusted Ferdinand Magellan the man, but did not trust the world he saw before him. For the first time in his life he began to feel how large the expanse of the seas truly were, and wondered if Magellan himself had come to this same realization.

Magellan left his bunk, he had many things to think about. He called on Rebelo and Enrique, and they reported to him that the giants in the San Antonio and their own ship the Trinidad were doing fine.

'They are a little hungry, though,' Enrique remarked. He wished he hadn't. Earlier, he took some salted fish and fed it to their giant Uno. Now he hoped his guilt did not seethe through and show on his face.

'This doesn't bode well,' Francisco Albo said as he looked skyward. He held the steer of the Trinidad, felt the waters too calm, before drops of rain as sharp as pins pierced against his cheeks.

'Can't we sail through?' Magellan sighed. He did not want to waste any more time.

'Not like this. Storm's going to come when we least expect it and then we'll be in trouble again.'

The rain got heavier just then, and kept drenching whoever was on deck.

'There!' Albo said, pointing to the mouth of a river.

'We'll waste valuable time,' Magellan lamented.

'Time we can waste. It's lives we can't,' Duarte Barbosa laid his hand on Magellan's shoulder. 'For the fleet, Ferdinand.'

Even the will of Ferdinand Magellan was not strong enough to will against a storm.

They spent weeks along the river while the storm raged on. The river provided better cover than the turbulent, open sea, and the sailors took this downtime to catch fish and dry and salt them. They stocked the ship with these fish.

On some days, they went ashore to chop wood and haul it back to the ships.

With this downtime, Enrique spent some time with the giant Uno, feeding him their salted fish, which Uno ate raw, while outside it poured like it would never end.

Their time together was quiet, and the two souls bonded together so well that they did not require words to speak, though sometimes Enrique spoke.

'I sometimes feel as you do,' he said in his native Malay. He could feel and smell Malacca when he spoke in his own tongue. The sand that filled his nostrils. The rustic scent of coconut leaves. He could even remember the sweat on his body in the tropical air, so much warmer than these cold climes he found himself in now.

Uno grunted, and thought of dancing as he did when he first met Enrique. He was free to dance then and free to dance now, but only in his mind.

Enrique stood and felt that memory in the giant's eyes. He began to dance as he did before, but that contrast of freedom then and his confinement now, only made him long for life to be as simple as it was before.

Uno's eyes began to well up, and he began to bawl, an ugly, painful, sad sound that escaped from a well of infinite loneliness.

Enrique left the giant alone, choosing to make himself seen and useful on the main deck, where above him the mid-day sun was covered by the moon. It felt like a cloudy day and it felt like the day was being robbed. He could imagine the giant in the lowest part of the ship, his wail still haunting Enrique's ears.

Magellan waited in his bunk for news. Even in the relative safety of an oblong box that was the Trinidad he could hear the wind and the constant pelting of a thousand raindrops per second, soft and pattering and incessant.

He wished for some reason to have Duarte Barbosa by his side, he needed something close to family, and Duarte was the closest blood to Beatriz. He wondered if Duarte missed his little sister, but Magellan knew he missed Beatriz even more.

He missed the smell of her hair that smelt of rose gardens. He missed tracing her shape with his fingers as they lay in bed, her every curve to him a divine revelation, and he missed making love. He buried these longings with the work at hand.

Duarte followed along behind now captaining the Victoria, and the next best thing to family he had was Rebelo and Enrique, though he would never admit it to the mulatto.

Rebelo ran in to report. 'There's no channels that lead inland, fa—, Captain-General,' he said awkwardly.

Magellan nodded, the magnitude of his silence equal to the immensity of his disappointment.

It was three days before he had any progress. After Rebelo's report, he spoke to Father Valderrama of his doubts in his own bunk.

With the rain still droning outside Magellan began to speak. It was not easy for him, with each word coming out his mouth as though he were gasping. He sighed, 'Am I cruel, Father? Have I gone too far? Or, Lord help me, have I not gone far enough?'

Father Valderrama gasped at this. Had he gone too far? He thought the answer was obvious. He restrained himself from saying out loud the first thing to come to his mind. He paused, bought time, before he answered. 'Have you gone too far? Only you yourself know the answer to that.'

Perhaps he did know the answer to his doubts, but still felt hollow. Three days later, that emptiness came to him as divine revelation. The scattered skeletons were his hollowness turned inside out for the world to see.

Long-dead whales, their remains haunting a sandbank, rib cages acting like gates that welcomed them into the mouth of a big gulf that was discharging the river.

Out here the drizzle washed out the sun. Magellan consulted his compass and looked at the cloudless sky. He sighed and told Albo, 'This way leads west.'

'You reckon this is the strait?' the pilot asked.

'I know it is, Albo. I know it is. Go west,' Magellan commanded.

Francisco Albo, pilot of the San Antonio, went west, into the strait. As the hours went by the temperature got colder.

The bare bones of whales were nothing, while this strait, seemed to be filled with everything, all the things a crew did not want. Albo complained of the currents, 'they're strong, and the waters are deep.'

'Then we can't lay anchor,' Magellan lamented. He looked out at this strait ahead of him, gave the meandering view some thought, before he called upon his two boys. 'Rebelo! Enrique!'

They were manning the sails, tying up the ropes, holding them in place, before they dashed to Magellan.

'Yes, Master?' Enrique asked.

'I want Carvalho to find an opening,' Magellan said in a tone deep and flat.

Rebelo ran first to the Trinidad's stern and shouted to the San Antonio, just behind him, this message. He repeated the message, while a crewman of the San Antonio passed on the message to San Antonio's pilot. João Lopes Carvalho nodded, wondering why didn't the boy Rebelo just do it. He had no say in any matter, this far out in the world.

Within the hour, Carvalho was already at the poop of the ship, its highest point, resisting the drizzle, it felt like flies smashing against his face, flies he had no luxury of swatting away. Carvalho squinted his eyes, unable to discern an opening. It felt to him as though the islands ahead of him were interlinked like loose webs, preventing them from escaping.

When Magellan got back this news from Carvalho, from a series of passing shouts from one man to another, he lamented, but knew this was the right way.

'Albo, take note of all the turns and twists,' Magellan ordered.

Every few hours saw Albo noting in the log the nautical distance, latitude and longitude of this journey into the strait. His eyes felt tired, the lack of night, only three hours a day, made him feel like the days never ended.

One night, the Armada caught glimpses of distant fires threatening to turn the verdant shores into ash. The fire turned the air foul, permeating it with an acrid odour.

'There might be tribes lurking here,' Magellan said to Albo of these fires. 'I want everyone to remain onboard.'

As they passed through this land of fire, the clouds above collided, scraping against one another, the result of their collision striking down into the land in the distance. The crew heard the rumble of thunder afterward.

'We can't see where we're going,' Albo sighed.

The crew looked up at a sky without a sun. It was cloudy and rainy in the day, and the night sky offered no stars. Miles away, snow landed atop glaciers while closer still the Armada got closer to giant glaciers that seemed to grow larger the further in the strait they went.

Magellan heard these glaciers speaking to him, grunting, cracking, groaning, telling him in the language of glaciers that he was not welcome here. Their warnings were punctuated by the whistling of the winds, guiding the ice into the waters, threatening to collapse on the Armada at any moment.

Magellan also noticed how blue these glaciers were.

'It's like how water gets a deeper shade of blue the deeper we go into the sea,' Pigafetta suggested. Though he acted calm this was the first time he had ever gazed upon glaciers so large it seemed to be a world unto itself.

'No, I think it's because of the ancient age of these glaciers,' Magellan retorted.

Not wanting to agitate the Captain-General, Pigafetta simply nodded. He felt a cold gust of wind against his head. He had kept his hair short and he had begun to regret it. Pigafetta began to come to the realisation his heroes were just men, just as fallible as anyone else. Though he admired Magellan, the Captain-General was getting on his nerves with his obstinacy.

He began to notice strong, katabatic winds descending from high among the glaciers. When the winds hit them, it was as though there were being approached by a storm.

The chill Pigafetta felt also served to preserve his anger. With a hand on his shoulder, Pigfetta looked up and saw Magellan smiling. 'Come inside,' he said to the freezing Italian.

Inside Magellan's bunk it was slightly warmer, and Pigafetta didn't know why the Captain-General wanted him here. He could only reckon it was due to him being their chronicler, and major events were now taking place that needed to be recorded.

'The San Antonio is now technically without a captain, now that Cartagena is no longer with us,' Magellan began.

In his mind's eye he could see Cartagena and the priest pleading for their lives on the shores of St Julian as the Armada slowly moved away from them.

Pigafetta's only response was a nod, imploring Magellan to continue.

'I need to appoint a new captain. I have thought about it, and I have a new candidate.'

'Whatever you decide, Captain-General, you know I will support it,' Pigafetta said.

'Good,' Magellan smiled.

By daybreak, Alvaro de Mesquita stood on the deck of the Trinidad, his shirt dusted, his posture straight, his back a mast, awaiting a good wind to tide him.

'You know what you must do?' Magellan asked Mesquita.

'Yes,' was all he could think to say without sounding stupid in front of his Captain-General.

Mesquita was younger, and looked up to Magellan, he even looked up now to meet eyes with him now.

'Does the family speak often about me?' Magellan asked.

'Always,' Mesquita said.

'When we were children, we played pretend ships. Funny how we're this far out in the world,' Magellan told Mesquita.

Mesquita paddled a skiff to the San Antonio. Earlier on, orders were passed down and the crew was waiting for him. As Mesquita rose to the San Antonio, Estevao Gomes stood last among the crew that greeted him. Around the San Antonio, there were already whispers against Mesquita.

Why was he appointed captain?

Why was Gomes not elected?

Why didn't the Captain-General choose Gomes?

Mesquita was all too aware of these whispers. He kept his resolve firm. But inside, he felt sometimes like a teenager pretending to be an adult.

The sailors had complained about the cold but today Mesquita welcomed it. It kept him calm and focused. After the crew of the San Antonio greeted him, they dispersed and did their various chores. Only Gomes stood on deck. 'Captain Mesquita.'

'Gomes.'

'What are your orders,' Gomes spoke not with lips but with grinding teeth.

'We have to enter the mouth of this strait for reconnaissance. Then report what we find back to the Captain-General.'

'And you decided this order?'

Mesquita kept quiet. He knew Gomes was dying to undermine him. 'Ready the sails. The Trinidad and Victoria will wait while we seek the curves of the straits.' The winds blew colder, stronger, stirring the waters below them. Mesquita saw the air swirl in gusts which crackled in his ears.

Mesquita went to the next logical place on the ship, that of Cartagena's quarters.

Entering these empty quarters, he could only recall the sight of Cartagena being stranded with the priest on St Julian, calling, pleading, begging for forgiveness. It had been months. They were either dying or already dead. Mesquita might as well now be walking in the room that belonged to a dead man. He had to sit down, his legs felt weak as though the burden of his responsibilities was weighing down on him. Outside, a storm was brewing and he wondered what to do next. Asking Gomes so early on might be one step closer to walking off a loose plank.

He knew the broad strokes. Navigate the strait. Come back and report to Magellan. The sun was setting outside. He felt the air grow colder.

'It's growing dark,' Gomes said. He stood at the doorway, his silhouette a specter looming over Mesquita.

'We should sail into the night,' Mesquita said, his voice low, tired.

'We should sail back to Spain to get more provisions, and a better equipped fleet,' Gomes said.

Mesquita stood, his knees trembling, fighting the weight off his shoulders. 'No. We should press on, use the short nights to keep going.'

'And these are your words?' Gomes challenged him.

There was silence, then there was the voice of a child trying to be a man. 'Daylight is in two hours. Get the ship ready by then'.

'You're making a big mistake,' Gomes slammed his fist against the wall.

Gomes left Mesquita to his own devices, warned him that he had better prepare himself.

As Gomes walked away, he thought again about how close he was to leading his own armada to the Spice Islands. Now he was just a stooge, just a man at a wheel while this insect of a man with a similar namesake was assigned to be captain. Mesquita. Mosquito. That's what he was to Gomes.

Days broke easily at the strait, while shadows struggled to catch up. Gomes was ahead, cautious, arms holding the wheel as though he were holding a shield.

Mesquita appeared on deck, languid, a revenant rising from the depths of the San Antonio. The cold was bitter and he felt his teeth chatter. 'Why aren't we speeding ahead?'

'A captain,' Gomes began, 'doesn't need to ask. He commands.'

'Well, then. Raise the sails. The wind is good on our side. Speed on ahead, pilot,' Mesquita commanded.

'The strait is full of tidal mouths where the tides meet streams,' Gomes drawled.

'Estuaries. I know that much, Gomes.'

'Meaning we can't raise the sails or we'll go too fast. We're going as fast as we're going to go now,' Gomes said.

Mesquita fidgeted with the shroud over his shoulder. No matter where he pulled the cold came to him at all angles.

It had been days since the San Antonio came to make any report. 'Both my ships have yet to return,' Magellan lamented to Enrique.

'The Conception is safe I feel, master,' Enrique assured Magellan.

'Aye. And what about the San Antonio, you think?'

'You're worried for Mesquita.'

'And Gomes. He'll do anything to spite me.'

The Trinidad had slowed by a river full of sardines. The crew had taken this chance to net them, and prepare and preserve them. For days Enrique and Rebelo had assisted in the catching and salting of these fish.

Today, the boys were beside Magellan. As much as the Captain-General failed to admit, he needed someone to talk to, and Enrique and Rebelo were the easiest to talk to. Their presence calmed him, and calm was something that didn't show itself much on this voyage. There was now the heavy burden of waiting. Time had hardened into a sculpture. If he could see it, Magellan would have seen the sculpture show the face of boredom, and perhaps a face of heavy worry.

'Andres,' Magellan called out.

The astronomer came on deck after a minute of crew men calling out his name in a daisy chain, all in all six men called out his name before he came running. 'Yes, my Captain-General,' the meek man said.

'Do you think they will come back? It's been days since the San Antonio has been seen. Almost a week, by my reckoning.'

'Don't hope for them to come back,' Andres de San Martin sighed, his breath hardened blocks of air, waiting to be severed by Magellan's displeasure.

'Is that what you really think?' Magellan's voice was not displeased, but rather worried. His voice was heavy with the weight of trapped air that forced itself out his throat.

'They are nowhere in sight. If they did come back, we would have seen them by now. I think something has happened.' Andres paused. 'They're either dead, or they're on the way to Spain.'

Mesquita stood by the cannons and gave the order. The crew of the San Antonio lit the cannons with their torches, and fired. Mesquita closed his ears with the palms of both hands, after firing afterwards his arms were tentative. There was still the ringing in his ears to consider.

'We are lost, don't keep trying,' Gomes had a finger in his ear, trying to dig out the ringing inside.

Mesquita sighed, then let his arms lower. 'And you are just going to give up?'

'I am going to do the right thing.'

'The right thing is to rendezvous with the fleet and then continue on the journey through the strait,' Mesquita looked at the cannons. They felt like the only way home now.

'It's been six days, and even you, this ship's captain, can't find a way out,' Gomes taunted. 'And now you come crawling like a little boy to papa when you can't solve your own problems. I think, you're not grown yet. It's time for the adults to take over.'

'Take over? I have been appointed by the Captain-General himself,' Mesquita squeaked.

Mesquita felt the world closing in on him, but in truth it was the gathering of five men like a fist that will soon clench and squeeze him.

Mesquita tried to move, but he was well-cornered. 'You are all making a big mistake. You can be tried for insubordination. Executed, at best,' he cackled nervously, his mouth sneering, his eyes indignant, not believing this was happening.

By the time he screamed it was too late, the fist had clenched around him, his struggle was brief, and the crew, strong and hardened, held Mesquita by his arms and legs.

Gomes stepped forward, brandishing a dagger. 'I have thought for many a night about this moment. This blade has carved up so many of my dreams about how I would stop you. Now, in person, victory will taste so sweet.' Gomes knelt hard as the knife followed, piercing into Mesquita's thigh.

Mesquita screamed, the pain finally giving him strength to break free. He leapt, or at least tried to, before falling on his chin, elbows and knees. He grimaced and removed the blade.

'Hold him!' Gomes commanded.

Mesquita swung the blade madly, and that stopped the sailors from coming closer. Seeing no other recourse, Gomes himself tried to stop Mesquita. He tried to get the blade off his hand, but in the mad swing of his arms, Mesquita landed the blade into Gomes' hand.

'Fuck!' Gomes yelled.

Mesquita's lips raised to a faint smile, but a second later that was knocked out of him with a fist to his lower jaw. The other sailors leapt at Mesquita and held him again.

'Put him in my cabin,' Gomes ordered. He looked at the dagger still lodged in his bleeding hand. It was worth it.

'If the San Antonio is truly lost, then I have other problems to worry about,' Magellan confided to Pigafetta in his cabin. Circling them were Andres de San Martin, Enrique, and Rebelo. 'San Antonio was the largest ship we have. Now that it's gone most of our supplies will run out. And soon.'

'And the other giant along with it. Either that giant might die, or Gomes will get famous before you do,' Enrique said.

Magellan gave a silent nod.

For a few days after, Magellan followed protocol to the letter. They stopped on an island surrounded by penguins. Enrique lead first, younger and stronger and fitter now than his master was, up a small hill. He held an earthen pot in his hand. Inside the pot was a letter addressed to the crew of the San Antonio, in case they found the Armada, written by Magellan himself. Enrique reckoned it was more addressed to Mesquita alone.

Magellan limped on up the hill holding a pole with a cloth banner attached, bearing the arms of the Kingdom of Spain. When he arrived at the summit of the hill, he was sweating. He planted the banner, while Enrique planted the pot into the earth beside the banner with his bare hands.

Enrique leaned back, comforted with the knowledge he was safe for now. The ships were ashore on the island. The penguins were curious things that he had never seen before. They reminded him of birds. He smiled. The way they waddled reminded him of Magellan.

The Armada waited for a few days more, days in which Magellan spent most hours of the day at that hill, arms taking turns to hold the banner. There was no sign of the San Antonio. Sometimes, he saw a ship, but it receded into view, into the back of his overactive mind. Sometimes, Enrique would stand beside his master, laying a hand on the Captain-General's shoulder.

At the foot of the hill Rebelo would stand looking up. He would smile at Enrique and feel a tinge of jealousy. He felt more distant to his absent father than ever. He heard cackling behind him.

Rebelo turned and saw a school of dolphins leaping out and into the water, their sheens pink and glistening, their smiles happy as they splashed back into the water.

Even up on the hill, Magellan smiled at those dolphins. It brought him some respite from his sorrow. 'They're never coming back, Enrique.'

'They're not coming here, that's for sure,' Enrique said.

'I wonder if it's a good idea to go back to Spain. What if all this was for nothing, Enrique?'

'Are you joking, master?' Enrique got down on his knees and now laid both hands on Magellan's shoulders. 'We made it this far, with your guidance. I've seen you survive battles against thousands, master. What is the sea to a man who has fought thousands? Nothing. It is an endless nothing for you to conquer.'

'The nothing is what frightens me, Enrique.'

A few days later, when Magellan had determined that the winds would not grow any calmer, he gave the order to weigh anchor.

Magellan and the captains and Andres de San Martin the astronomer stood by the foot of the hill.

'We should at least continue until mid-January. We'll have longer days until then. The shorter days in January would slow us down,' Andres advised Magellan.

Magellan nodded, and patted the astronomer on his back. Everyone dispersed leaving only Duarte Barbosa, Magellan and Enrique on the shore.

'Duarte,' Magellan began. 'Here. Read it when we're out at sea.'

Duarte took the letter and pocketed it, looked at Enrique and without good reason scoffed at the slave.

He walked away, and Enrique sighed, knowing Duarte Barbosa had never given him any respect.

Once everyone entered in their respective ships they pointed their cannons to the sky, firing a salvo that told the world they were going ahead. In the cloudy skies it felt as though men were capable of bringing their own thunder.

The ships weighed anchor afterwards, and began to sail west, cautiously, slowly, and even now Magellan wished for the specter of San Antonio. After a cautious few days, they had reached the end of the strait.

The sailors of the entire Armada were ecstatic, leaping on deck and embracing one another.

But escaping the strait was only the beginning. Now the Armada faced a wide-open sea, hundreds of miles of nothing but blue, the nothing Magellan feared the most.

On the Victoria, Duarte Barbosa sat in his cabin. He considered the folded letter, with its wax seal, at how fragile wax was. He broke the seal, and he began reading.

Nov. 18th, 15–
Duarte,

I am writing to you in the hopes this letter may convey the feelings I cannot express in person.

The men are restless, and it is only by showing a face of firm resolve I am able to keep the Armada in check.

It is only a matter of time before we find the route to the Spice Islands via these straits, though I do not know at what cost. With the San Antonio missing we have lost half the fleet's supplies, and from this point forward, things will get worse. I pray to our Lord and Saviour we may find a way, perhaps even a miracle to get us through this.

I am constantly watching my back. A second's lapse may lead to another mutiny. In the event of my death, my slave Enrique is to be set free, and I have assigned a certain amount of maravedis to him. The details of his release are in a separate letter in my bunk, and I implore you to follow it to the letter.

This expedition was created with the best intentions, but I feel as though all great things are met with doubt, and people do not celebrate greatness but challenge it at every turn. Jesus died on the cross because he believed. I am challenged out at sea because I believe.

All this time I have tried my best to be a good man, and If I have wronged or angered you, I am sorry. I hope you accept my apology.

Sincerely,
Ferdinand.

Duarte placed the letter down, and wiped the tears from his eyes. After a moment's thought he motioned toward the candle, and considered its languid flame. He brought the letter to the flame as though it were a moth awaiting immolation. The fire ate the letter, swallowing its words, leaving nothing but ashen remains.

For almost a week after they were in nothing but an endless blue, without any land to give them bearings. The pilots of the Armada looked up at the night sky, at the stars, to guide them.

Magellan trusted them enough to navigate, but he was still haunted by the San Antonio's absence.

He was with Enrique in the Trinidad's cargo hold. Enrique, along with Rebelo, had been tasked with counting the food supplies of the Trinidad. Magellan had to make an estimate of how much food they had left.

'Not much, by any measure, master,' Enrique said rolling up the inventory list.

'It's time to ration the supplies,' Magellan told the young men.

15

Antonio Pigafetta pulled his pants up. It was getting harder to keep his dignity on, literally. He had been eating less and less as the year came to an end. Even the giant in front of him now, Uno, seemed to be getting smaller.

Pigafetta imagined Uno's ankles getting smaller until they were small enough to wiggle out of his shackles. The later part of the year meant shorter days, which brought his task further urgency. With his pen and his bottle of ink he wrote down his encounters with Uno, and he began writing down the words that Uno spoke, as best he could, kneeling, sometimes even sitting on his ass when it got too long.

Hanging in between them was a specter that emerged from the dead space within their bellies. That specter sometimes growled and groaned, waiting to be fed. Ever since the disappearance of the San Antonio their food supplies were getting scarce, and the signs of malnutrition were beginning to show.

Many of the sailors' gums were beginning to swell, and Pigafetta had even stepped on some loose, bloody teeth onboard. Uno always smiled with blood-stained teeth at the sight of the tiny Italian man.

Regardless, in spite of the hunger and of the scurvy the Armada was experiencing, Pigafetta kept his days filled with communication, him showing Uno his words, while Uno taught him his. It began with simple things, like eyes, ears, nose, mouth, and then leading to almost-conversations.

Pigafetta would come down during the morning, after sunrise, after Uno would hear the murmurs of men above, in waves of deep, silent contemplation followed by hushed chants and murmurs. It reminded him of something he had done sometimes, but to a much lesser degree.

Uno pointed up, wondering what it was they always did in the morning.

Pigafetta held the cross around his neck the same way one held a roll of tobacco during smoking, like a habit he couldn't break.

'We are always praying,' Pigafetta explained. 'The Captain-General always holds prayers in the mornings and the evenings. We ask for guidance. For a safe journey.'

Uno pointed to the cross. In the darkness of the cargo hold it seemed to gleam, though it was a simple thing made of dull silver.

'You want this?' Pigafetta offered the cross, and the giant held it, and felt calmer. Pigafetta came closer to Uno, and explained with many hand signals while he talked. 'Jesus Christ,' he began. 'He died on the cross for our sins. If we pray to him and his father, and if we are good people, hopefully, we can find a passage to heaven.'

'Heaven?' Uno repeated.

'Only the faithful, those who believe in Christ and the Holy Spirit, may be allowed to set foot into heaven,' Pigafetta explained, not believing his own words, or the fact he was actually saying them.

He was soon interrupted, by the chirp of a rat, and by the sound of air escaping from the rat. He heard bones crunch. Uno grabbed the rat by the tail, and threw it aside. At one corner was a collection of five rats, seemingly fresh kill.

'Oh,' Pigafetta gasped.

Enrique closed his mouth with a piece of old cloth, while Rebelo retched at a corner. After he was done retching he pulled his hair back, trying for some semblance of dignity.

'The seals have gone bad,' Enrique said.

'No kidding,' Rebelo went on. 'Where do the maggots come from?'

'From the bad meat of seals, of course,' Enrique rolled his eyes.

'Just like that? They appear out of nowhere?'

Enrique didn't want to admit that line of thought never did cross his mind. 'Get more men in here. We're going to throw these seals off the ship.'

'Damn it,' Rebelo cursed.

The crew came in soon, and began hauling the seal meat from St Julian in Patagonia off the boat and into the sea. All of them took turns retching at different corners of the main deck.

Rebelo stood by the sails, noticing that the sails and rigging were being eaten away by, 'Maggots,' he lamented to Magellan.

Magellan looked at his crew. At their bloody gums. They were barely able to stand now. 'We have no meat now,' he told Rebelo.

Days later, they had begun the work of throwing off dead bodies. The scurvy had killed some of them. Father Valderrama held prayers for them. For those who were still alive, albeit barely, hunger had taken over their minds.

They were without fresh food, fish were hard to come by at this part of the sea, and all they could eat were biscuits that had turned into powder and were infested with worms.

Magellan kept to himself, worried about what he should be doing to keep the men alive. He sat in his cabin and ate his Carne de Membrillo. He consulted his maps, and his own knowledge of the stars. He began to feel so small in this world, and he wondered how large the world actually was, and how little he knew of it, how little anyone knew of the world.

As he finished his quince, he could hear commotion through the walls. He went to the cargo hold, and there he saw Uno growling, like an ugly child whose things have been robbed.

Pigafetta and Enrique and Rebelo stood beside the giant, trying to keep him from doing anything stupid.

'Look at this giant! His gums are clean compared to the rest of us!' one of the sailors said.

'It must be the rats,' another suggested.

'How did you guess that?' Enrique asked, curious that the sailors knew.

'Stupid giant smiles all the time when he grabs a rat. His teeth are white, means no gums are bleeding, see,' another sailor pointed out.

'Well that still doesn't account for why you guessed it was the rats,' Pigafetta noted.

'Because the giant's been eating rats and has nicer teeth than the rest of us. If you're so learned, why didn't you figure that out,' the sailor said.

Pigafetta was taken aback. He felt blood flush his cheeks and his skull, either ashamed or embarrassed or wounded that his standing and pride were insulted. 'Listen, you . . .'

'All right! All right!' Enrique held his arms up. 'How about we make a deal,' he implored Uno. 'There's five rats. Uno takes two. You take three for now.'

The sailors thought about it. They thought about the bodies of friends they had already thrown overboard. They nodded, while Uno sighed.

'We'll get more,' Enrique laid his hand on the giant's shoulder.

'What do you reckon they're suffering from?' Rebelo asked Magellan.

'Bad air, I suppose.'

Those who ate the rats and the quince had better chances of survival, their gums did not bleed. Those rats were of great use to them. While the sailors kept healthy with rat meat and fruits, Uno himself was not doing so good.

Uno slumped against the wall in his shackles. Enrique placed his palm on the giant's forehead. 'He's burning.'

'And getting sicker by the day,' Pigafetta said.

Uno beckoned Pigafetta to come closer. The Italian leaned in and Uno gestured, brought his hands to his chest, closed his eyes, and pointe toward the sky, and if he could speak in coherent sentences he might have said, *If I die, will Heaven my spirit go?*

'Only if you truly believe in Christ Jesus, our Lord,' Pigafetta whispered.

Uno raised a shackled hand weakly, a hand large enough to crush the Italian's skull. It found purchase on Pigafetta's shoulder. 'I believe,' he told Pigafetta faintly.

Pigafetta nodded.

Enrique's palm left Uno's forehead. He sighed and stared at the floor, then back at the giant. Uno at least had the choice for conversion, while Enrique himself did not. Even an imprisoned giant seemed to have more autonomy than he did.

After evening prayers Father Valderrama came down to the cargo hold. 'In these conditions I can't perform the full rites and observe the scrutinies.'

'Can you at least perform the baptism, Father?' Pigafetta offered.

Father Valderrama thought about it. 'Where can we get a bucket of water?'

'The one in charge of the supplies would know,' Pigafetta said.

Moments later Paul, the Trinidad's boatswain came below deck with the bucket, but the water was not fresh.

Father Valderrama said his prayers, and held the back of Uno's head. Pigafetta held the bucket, and Uno's head was lowered into it. 'He is cleansed, of all his past sins, born anew,' Father Valderrama explained, and chanted further, his hand still holding the giant's head in the water.

Uno choked and the water bubbled out the bucket. Father Valderrama released his head and Uno gasped and coughed out the water in his mouth and nose.

'From today onwards, you are known as Paul,' the priest said.

'Paul,' the giant gasped his new name, and the boatswain could only commend the priest on his startling originality.

After the giant's conversion the Armada's fates seemed to have turned, as though his new found belief in the cross had been the good tide of luck they needed.

The waters now had fish for them to take in for salting. They also caught something much larger. The smaller fish they had just caught provided the perfect bait for the sharks. Fishing could have been done alone, but shark fishing was a different art altogether. It was an art of teamwork. There was the use of sharpened spears, and sometimes nets and hooks.

The more experienced sailors whispered, if anyone were interested, that the days around a new moon were when they were most likely to see sharks. Younger ones claimed sharks were always hungry, and the idea of waiting for a full moon was ludicrous.

They had caught mostly smaller sharks the size of their torsos or smaller. Paul, the giant, could only smile faintly. He wished he could revel in their excitement. He wished he could dance along like he did so long ago. He had been coughing blood. It was not blood from his gums, but from deeper within his body.

It had taken some convincing on the part of Enrique and Pigafetta, but Magellan had finally allowed Paul to be unshackled. Even then, free to move, he was too weak to even try.

Enrique and Pigafetta tended to Paul, feeding him their freshly caught fish that he ate raw like the sharks did. He could not stand cooked or salted anything. Even the fish could not ease his ailments.

'He's homesick,' Enrique told Pigafetta.

Pigafetta gave a resigned glance. He did not want to admit that the slave was right. Enrique knew the feeling of being taken away from everyone and everything he ever knew.

Within the week Enrique's worst fears had come to pass. For each day since Paul had gotten sick, he worried if this day was going to be the last before Paul expired.

The day came when Enrique tried to wake Paul up, but he did not move. Enrique had seen dead things before. His grandmother. The cows in the field in his village. Some slaughtered, some dead from exhaustion.

The dead cattle in his memories were vague things that clung to the walls of his mind like black stains grown from years of neglect. His grandmother, he remembered well as though he were able to paint the scene if he had a brush and all the time in the world. He must have been five, and his mother tried to wake his grandmother

up. His mother tried a few times before she got worried, noticed
nenek wasn't breathing, and ran to his father.

After a few minutes of trying to rouse her, they were resigned to
the hard facts. She had passed on. Her body was cold, but still pliant.
It was a cold he did not understand when he felt her feet, which had
yellowed. Her lips had turned pale. But her face. It seemed content.

Paul had the same look on his face. Why would he have this face,
one who was captured, kept cold and hungry in a dungeon?

'When I die, do you think I'll have this same look on my face?'
Enrique wondered to Pigafetta and Rebelo.

'Perhaps he saw heaven just before he died,' Pigafetta remarked.
'The Christian heaven.'

'Dead is dead no matter how you want to sweeten it,' Rebelo
said bluntly.

'I'll call Father Valderrama,' Enrique said.

The crew of the Trinidad dragged Paul's corpse up from the
cargo hold to the main deck, the dead weight of the giant resisting
as though it did not want to leave its little corner at the bottom of
the ship. Dragging Paul was made harder by their hungry, weakened
bodies, and painful, swollen gums.

Seeing how the crew were struggling to drag Paul up, Magellan
sent another man to assist: himself.

He came and held one arm, in spite of his bad knee. He began to
sweat, his bad knee trembling, but he had no regret.

Magellan would have preferred a proper coffin, but resources
being as limited as they were, he could only hope for the power of
ingenuity to help him.

Once he and his men dragged Paul to the main deck, they rolled
his body on a plank. Enrique tied Paul's feet and torso with ropes
around the plank, making the body straight and proper.

Using another set of planks as leverage, they slid the corpse up.

Father Valderrama said his prayers, planted a rosary and cross
around Paul's wrist. Enrique wiped a tear, so did Pigafetta, the men
closest to Paul in the end.

When Father Valderrama was done the crew lifted and slid Paul's body up the board. At Magellan's count, they heaved the body, high up enough until the body slid down in the opposite direction, splashing down into the waters below them, the giant now a small speck swallowed in an infinite sea.

16

They were even out of rats, their gums bled, their lips swelled, and even worse, circling their ships now were sharks. The Armada, a hungry fleet, did not care for the fins of sharks cutting through the water around them. They were just wilder, more ferocious fish, ready to be eaten.

Many of them, Magellan could remember had meat on their bones. Now the meat had gone and he could only see bones wielding harpoons. They were determined to have shark for breakfast.

Enrique crouched low to observe the more experienced sailors, studying how they harpooned and hauled shark on the deck, it took almost ten men to steady the writhing shark, but with the determination of starvation driving them, they held it, avoiding the mouth, with its rows upon rows of blade-sharp teeth, cutting it open, to let it bleed and die before they cut the meat itself. Some of the crew even drank of its blood, anything better than sawdust and rat piss.

There were times when Enrique would puke and retch at the thought of drinking blood of any kind. He had grown thinner and paler, but he was lucky as he consumed the quince his master had kept for himself, from time to time. When that ran low, he joined the other sailors in the hauling of shark and drank its blood.

When he looked into the waters he thought of the sunken giant, and lamented, felt how tragic it was to be like Paul, taken from his home, then to have died. Enrique considered himself lucky, and did not dare do anything to irk the people around him and twist his luck lest he too was thrown off the ship to die and be forever forgotten.

He felt he was a different person from the young man he was back in Seville. He was now more than youth could contain, but he still had to sail entire oceans to discover the man he could yet become.

It had been almost two months since Paul died, and life carried on, languid as ocean waves. They fed on shark meat and blood, until they finally found two landmasses, two lush green forms shaped to their eyes like two curvaceous women, with a hundred guardians surrounding them.

These guardians came on small, swift boats, by the hundreds, surrounding the remaining four ships of the Armada, but it soon turned out they were not guardians.

They were taller and larger than the Spaniards and Portuguese on the ships, not even half but three quarters naked, even. Their small boats leaned against the ships. They climbed into the ships, their intrusion only faintly protested by the scurvy-weakened sailors.

The gasps of the weakened sailors were almost unheard by these natives. Some of the sailors stumbled as they stood up to raise a hand, to say no, or don't, but the natives did not notice them; the sailors had become ghosts of their former selves.

There was one man still with enough energy to retaliate. Paul the boatswain, in charge of the Trinidad's supplies, felt his heart beat rising, the blood rushing to his head and arms. They were not taking away all the things he had painstakingly stockpiled.

'Get off my ship,' he muttered, raising his good arm and landing it into the native beside him. He was just a ghost to him, but the ghost had bite.

The native screamed as he saw the knife in his thigh. The other natives began hollering, a high-pitched series of sounds that reminded the Armada of bats in caves. At the sight of their comrade's blood they jumped overboard.

'Open fire,' the boatswain yelled.

All four ships of the Armada began to shoot arrows from their crossbows at these native thieves, but none of them connected, the sailors still too weak to aim straight.

'Stop firing, all of you,' Magellan commanded.

The natives swam, some rowed away, those that managed to get back into their boats. Magellan stood to see them move away, and he took note of their size.

'What is that?' Rebelo wondered. His eyes couldn't make sense of what he was seeing.

A second group of natives glided back toward the Armada's ships, their boats now bearing fruits and foods the Spaniards, Castilians, and Portuguese of the armada had never seen before.

'Are they offering us something to eat,' Enrique wondered.

'*Makan*,' one of them on the boats said.

Sure enough, the natives were offering the sailors food. It had been so long since he heard anyone else besides himself use any Malay words. A smile, joyous and ecstatic, filled his cheeks. He chuckled, and asked them to come on up.

'*Naik*,' Enrique said, gesturing them repeatedly with his arms, as though they were old friends. It was not the seas that bound the world together, Enrique thought. It was language.

'We must be close,' Magellan smiled, thinking about the Spice Islands.

Seeing that his master had offered no resistance, Enrique let them come up with food, an assortment of fish and fruits and bread, wrapped in banana leaves. They distributed the food to the sailors of the Armada, and the weakened sailors at first grabbed it without a thought or hesitation.

Only after a few bites did the incredulity of the situation give rise in their hungry minds. The natives stood and waited while the sailors fed themselves. Once they had satiated their appetites, and had gathered their strength, they turned trying to find their friends, fellow sailors, thanking the natives for their good fortune, but at the same time remaining wary.

The food was free, and as much as they knew, all things free came at a price. It was as if this realization sunk into them like a ship dropping anchor, and their minds found purchase at last.

The natives loomed closer now, with their weapons drawn, and the sailors' suspicions were validated.

The natives had been fattening up the sailors for the slaughter. They charged at the sailors and the fighting began again, more vicious, blows struck harder, the motions and swings of clubs and sticks and blades more passionate.

When it seemed the natives of this island had outnumbered the sailors, they in their desperation began to arm themselves with crossbows, the next best thing, and faster, than muskets and rifles. Some arrows were launched, and many missed, but the few that hit their mark hit hard, as luck would have it, those arrows pierced thighs and arms and not hearts or necks.

'I think that's enough for today!' Magellan ordered. He was not really in the mood for fighting, at least not today.

The injured natives escaped on their boats. The boats that stayed, were filled with coconuts, and fish. 'We have these for you,' one of the natives in the boats said to Enrique.

'You promise not to fight?' Enrique asked.

'But if you want these,' the native referred to the coconuts and fish, 'then we want something in exchange.'

'A sale?'

'What is that?'

Enrique looked to his master for approval.

'Tell them to meet on the shore,' Magellan said.

While Enrique told the natives the order, Magellan told his crew to lower the sails, the orders of which were yelled at across the other three ships.

What they didn't notice yet, were some of the natives circling around the Trinidad, their boats swift enough to catch up to the ship, latching on, climbing up, hiding, then unleashing the knots at the poop of the ship, the knots that held Magellan's dinghy, his personal little boat.

He only heard the dinghy splash in the water, a gentle splash made by men who knew how to keep a boat quiet, men with experience in the water.

Magellan was a man who trusted his senses. He turned and he limped toward the poop of the Trinidad, and saw the empty space where his dinghy should have been.

'Enrique!'

Enrique knew the tone of that voice, one that meant his master wanted something done, and nothing was going to stop him. 'Master?'

'These pagans are thieves,' Magellan said.

'What do you want to do, Master?'

'We'll trade with them. We need the food they're offering. But tomorrow, we reign fire.'

'All this just for a boat?' One of the Trinidad's crew lamented.

'The Captain-General sees this as an affront to his dignity,' Rebelo tried to offer.

'The sooner we get out the better,' another sailor said. He was inspecting a crossbow, imagining an arrow in it, shooting it in a native's heart. 'Having forty men in either case to avenge one man's dignity is a bit much, eh?'

'Just come back with some native spleen and liver, eh,' a crewman smiled with bloodied teeth and swollen gums. He coughed and leaned against the sails, spat out blood. He was speaking for all of those affected with scurvy. 'Maybe their blood can cure my bleeding gums.'

The Armada docked against the shore at dawn, boots caked against the wet sand, arms holding lit torches, dozens of tiny suns, infernos waiting to happen.

It didn't take long for the forty men to find the village. What Magellan found strange was how the natives said nothing at the sight of them armed with torches, as though they came with glowing jewels. 'Burn the houses,' Magellan said.

Rebelo ran along with his torch and began burning the first hut.

Enrique held his torch steady, but did not yet want to burn anything just yet. He found Rebelo's glee disturbing. He searched his master's visage, and saw a shadow of remorse on his face. That shadow soon was cast away by the brilliance of the inferno, and all that was left on his master's visage was the brilliance of his rage.

He could also hear them screaming, but they were unusually calm, and they yelled in a dialect of a language he understood: Malay.

The women, naked, only covering their shame with thin bark, bodies adorned with beads, hair down to their waists like loose, dark dresses, and children, ran while some of the crew fired crossbows. There were no clear instructions to kill, but the shots were random, and only seven arrows landed into the natives, seven arrows that pierced either hearts or lungs or necks.

Those that had less severe arrow shots knelt, their pain not yet registering even as they removed the arrows. Some of them bled before they died.

It was only a miracle that Magellan's dinghy was not engulfed by the flames, but there it was, for Enrique to see. He ran to it, and with Rebelo's help they dragged the dinghy away, back to the shore while behind them the village burned.

'All this for one boat,' Rebelo remarked, smiling.

The stench of burnt ash and sand wafted as far out as the shore. Enrique tied the dinghy back to its designated spot, with extra dead knots this time to make sure it wouldn't be stolen again.

Daybreak.

Magellan had come to his senses for the most part. He knew it would be a tactical error to just leave the island. He was sure he could get some supplies, food for the Armada, as the natives were kind enough to offer them fish and coconuts the day before. These were the most generous of thieves.

'You said they spoke Malay?' Magellan asked Enrique.

'Some form of it. It's a different inflection, master, but I know what I heard.'

Magellan had ordered the healthier of the crew to help clean up the aftermath of last night's inferno. He noticed the natives did not seem angry, even at the deaths of the seven men who were shot by the crossbows. He searched for the oldest of the natives, reckoning the oldest-looking one might be the village elder.

'*Kamu adalah penghulu*,' Enrique kept asking the senior natives. But they didn't seem to understand what that meant. The concept of a village elder seemed foreign to them.

The crew were partly now motivated to work, shoving burnt logs out of the way. In the daylight, the women, with their tanned olive skin and bare chests were a sight. The men didn't even mind their red teeth when they smiled, red, they were soon to notice, from the constant chewing of betel nut and betel leaves.

Pigafetta trailed along behind the men, careful to hide the stirring in his loins. He knew studying and recording them was a once in a lifetime opportunity.

'We need no one to show us the way,' one of the natives told Enrique, implying their culture did not need a leader, or had no leaders at all.

'We have come from afar. Our journey has been many moons long,' Enrique explained.

'We Chamorros had always thought we were the only ones in this world.'

'So did we,' Enrique said.

In Pigafetta's hand was a notebook and a pencil. He crouched by a tree and began drawing the women, taking down notes. One of the first words he jotted down on this island was the word Chamorros. He also noted what Enrique then told him. That there were no leaders in the usual sense. These people had no defined social order. Their weapons were sparse.

'What's mine is yours and what's yours is mine, my friends,' one of the Chamorros said to Enrique.

'We do apologize for the fire,' Enrique told him, his tone sincere and apologetic. 'The boat you stole belonged to my master. He was upset.'

'Don't all things belong to everybody else? What's mine is yours, what's yours is mine?'

'We don't see it that way, I'm afraid.'

'Aye. Much to learn today. Much to learn. But we still mean peace and togetherness. If we give you the bounty of our land, promise not to burn or shoot us?'

Enrique patted him on the shoulder. 'I promise, no more of that my friend.'

By the evening the crew of the Armada were hauling fruits and fish on their ships, and Enrique was given a good pat on his shoulder by Magellan. In the distance Duarte Barbosa could do nothing but scowl.

'It's amazing how you bartered peace with them with not a single drop of blood being shed,' Magellan told Enrique.

'Sometimes words are better than arrows, master.'

'Perhaps you are right,' Magellan had to agree, albeit begrudgingly.

Over the coming days fruits such as mangoes and coconuts were taken, and Magellan saw a marked improvement over those affected with scurvy. The gums stopped bleeding, their swelling reduced.

In gratitude he arranged to give some of the Armada's wares. Silver spoons and blades were given in exchange for more food.

Pigafetta took the time to study their swift boats, their proas. He remarked their slim design and how sleek its shape was. It was meant to cut into water the way a knife glides through butter.

Everyone was happy, but in Enrique's heart something loomed, a fear he could not name, but knew was lurking. He did not tell the Chamorros how long they were staying. They were not even meant to encounter all these islanders, these tribes and the people. He felt bad the Armada was leaving them, that they were not friends by choice but passing friends and only by coincidence. It was like a big brother leaving a younger sibling behind, and knowing the little sibling would cry when the big brother went away. Did Jali and Suri cry when *Abang* was gone?

Some of the sailors were getting accustomed and intimate with the women, some doing it behind trees, some bringing the women on to their ships.

Magellan did know of these, he could do nothing but feel guilty. These things were common amongst sailors. He knew deep inside it might not have been fair to have quartered Quesada for buggery but do nothing when the sailors were with women. They were still committing sin, this much Magellan knew, though at the same time he had to let this go, because selfishly, he wanted to gain favour with his Armada again.

Andres de San Martin advised Magellan the weather was good, and that it was the best time to leave the island.

At dawn on March the 9th, 1521, the Armada raised anchor and left the island.

One of the Chamorros, the one Enrique spoke to, spotted the ships receding into the water. He told the other men, who prepared over one hundred proas to slice into the water.

'Where are you going!'

'We gave you food! You can't leave and not tell us!'

They chanted these words as they slid into the water, some even presenting fish raised high above their heads to entice the Armada back.

Enrique turned his head as he saw this sight, thinking, what simple, innocent men. He admired and envied their innocence, understood even when they began to throw stones at the Armada from their proas.

Soon they gave up, and the sight of the one hundred proas faded into distance, black marks on the sea receding into blue and the twinkle of sunlight against the water's surface, like stars in the ocean.

The Armada sailed westward, and it was week later that a lookout saw the mountains of a large island rising from the sea. 'Over there,' the lookout yelled from the mast.

17

'We must be close to the Spice Islands,' Magellan confided in Enrique.

His optimism was short-lived. After two miles of shore they began to realize the island was bracketed by unforgiving cliffs. There was no safe harbour. Magellan changed course and found an island where they dropped anchor to rest.

After a few hours they went to another island, one filled with lush palm trees and filled with abundant water. They erected two sheltering tents. The fresh air was beautiful, next to the stench of unwashed sailors on their ships.

The island was filled with wild boars, one of which they shot and slaughtered, roasting it and passing the meat. It was a little feast amongst the men. Once their bellies were content they continued sailing, hoping to find other people.

They did, two days after they left the Chamorros they noticed a boat bearing nine men approaching them. 'Get the arms ready,' Magellan instructed the gunners. 'No one move or say anything without my command.'

The boat touched the shore of an island, and five of the most ornately dressed of them gestured they were pleased with the Armada's presence.

'Give them food and drink,' Magellan advised his sailors.

Magellan and Enrique and Rebelo took the time to bring down combs, caps, mirrors and other trinkets, things he figured the natives might find odd or strange and perhaps valuable, but were common things for the Europeans.

The five men nodded, speaking in their own dialect. They seemed small next to Magellan, speaking and moving with an intelligence and grace that seemed far more advanced than the giants of Patagonia or the Chamorros.

The five men gave Magellan some fish, and a jar of what they said was 'vraca'.

'They don't speak any language we know of, master,' Enrique said to Magellan. He smelt what was inside the jar. 'Palm wine, master.'

Later, they gave the Armada some bananas of various sizes, and two coconuts. The five men raised their fingers minus their thumbs, then showed the sun, and then they showed examples of rice, coconuts and other assorted foods.

'I reckon they mean they'll bring us other foods in the next say, four days, master.'

'Tell them thank you,' Magellan bowed to them.

The sailors were fed the rice and coconuts, which they ate ravenously. 'Tastes better than rats and sawdust,' one of the sailors lamented.

Pigafetta took the four days to observe how these islanders made the palm wine. He noticed how it could be distilled from the sap of an unopened coconut flower, with the sap harvested into bamboo receptacles by cutting small lines into the coconut flower, tapping out the sap. Exposure to the air ferments it quickly in a matter of hours, the end result having a viscosity as thick as goat's milk.

'Why, two of these palm trees could sustain a family of ten for a hundred years,' he proudly proclaimed to Magellan.

Pigafetta used the time on this island to write down the basics of the islanders' dialects, and the names of the neighbouring islands.

'They speak a form of something I recognize, but it's a dialect that escapes me, master,' Enrique told Magellan.

'But enough for them to understand you,' Magellan tasked him.

'Barely.'

Magellan smiled at the party of nine who had come on board the Trinidad, showing them the ship's supplies of cloves, cinnamon, pepper, walnut, nutmeg, ginger, mace and gold.

Their guests gave gestures, then specific directions of where they could find these spices, on other islands.

'These spices are all around us,' Rebelo concurred.

Pigafetta nodded, understanding. Magellan whispered, 'We may be very close to the Spice Islands.'

'Indeed, master,' Enrique agreed.

'Tell them, this is the end of the tour. Ready the artillery,' Magellan waved his hand as Enrique stumbled with the telling.

The gunners prepped their arquebuses that were supported on a forked rest. Discharging these arms was always done at great risk. The discharge when fired could spread everywhere and if the gunner was too close he might injure or burn himself.

The nine islanders on the Trinidad wondered what this was, and their curiosity was rewarded mere seconds later. The discharge of the arquebuses rang and reverberated amongst the distant hills of Homonhon.

They leapt and ran to the edges of the Trinidad, almost ready to leap into the sea.

'Hold them back,' Magellan instructed Enrique and Pigafetta along with Rebelo. The three of them removed their hands off their ears, the sound of gunfire still reverberating in their ears.

Enrique motioned to them, reaching out his hand. 'Come my friends, there is nothing to fear.'

Magellan bowed to apologize and once they approached, he patted them on the shoulders. Those shoulders shivered before calming down. 'On this side of the world, gunfire is thunder,' he told Enrique.

Enrique nodded, sighed, knowing what his master meant, the power of one man over another.

The men rested in Homonhon for about a week before they sailed southwest.

Pigafetta was every bit the pampered scholar, taking the spoils of the sailors' hard work. But he had been observing them enough over these months to know how these men fished, and decided to do it for himself. The sea was tranquil save for the drizzle that multiplied and merged into hard rain. The Italian had his feet propped upon the yard that lead down into the storeroom, his ass loose at the edge of the Trinidad. He didn't know how the sides of ships were slippery when it rained, on account of their polish when being made. Peering over the edge when he felt a tug on his fishing line, the weight of his upper body provided enough leverage for him to slip off the ship, his yelp swallowed quickly by his body splashing into the sea.

He rose out the water, gasping for air. He swam back to the side of the Trinidad, caught hold of the mainsail's clew garnet dangling in the water. 'Help!' The Italian called out a few times, before a small boat rowed alongside him.

A hand reached into the water, 'Fool Italian. Are you the fisherman or the bait?' the sailor asked.

Ashamed, the Italian did nothing to alleviate his loss of face. Grabbing the sailor's arm he pulled into the small boat.

'You might have drowned if it weren't for us,' the sailor said. Rowing the boat was Enrique, who kept silent and rowed back to the Trinidad.

'Don't tell your master,' Pigafetta told Enrique.

'I won't,' Enrique said as he kept on rowing. While Pigafetta wiped the water off his face, Enrique took this stolen moment to let out a quick chuckle.

'Eh,' Pigafetta grunted.

'What,' Enrique rowed the oars against the water, moved forward, and pretended nothing happened.

The next night there was a dull, red glow emanating from a nearby island.

'Campfires,' Rebelo reckoned.

'Set course for an approach in the morning,' Magellan instructed his pilot Francisco Albo.

In the morning party of eight men approached the Trinidad, but they were wise to keep a safe distance from the Trinidad in the water.

Enrique stepped forward on the main deck and began, 'Good morning,' he began.

'You Malay speak?' the men in the boat asked.

'Yes, I Malay speak. I speak Malay,' Enrique corrected his syntax.

'You with them?'

Enrique looked at his companions, 'Yes. I am afraid so,' he smiled back at the men in the boat.

They laughed at his secret jab. 'What brings your party here?'

'We are explorers. We have come from very far away, and are in need of supplies. Your kind assistance would be much appreciated.'

'What can you offer us?' they asked after conferring with each other.

Magellan sent a plank with a red cap, and other gifts. The plank reached the boat, and the men seized the gifts.

They paddled back to the shore and came back two hours later in two balanghai, larger boats, one of which stood a man with regal bearing seated under an awning of mats.

'Forgive me my lord, a thousand apologies, my lord,' Enrique began. 'We are but humble sailors come from far away. We seek your kindness, for we have been at sea for months without a friend in sight. If my lord could extend your graciousness to us, we will be most grateful.'

The man in the boat considered those words. 'You are most kind in your greetings. My men will come aboard, if that is no intrusion?'

'What is he saying, Enrique?' Magellan asked.

'He wants his men to come aboard, master.'

'Let them,' Magellan said.

'Your men may enter, my lord. I am glad we speak the same language.'

'Kings here know more languages than the common folk,' the man in the boat said.

Enrique nodded with the utmost respect. The men entered, but the king remained in his balanghai. They explored the ship, eight pairs of eyes for this king.

Enrique tailed them, explaining what the ship was.

'Our king offers a large bar of gold, a basketful of ginger,' one of them said.

'Tell them I refuse the offer, but that I am glad for it,' Magellan told Enrique.

The men understood, and rejoined their king on the balanghai.

The Trinidad soon dropped anchor near the king's hut for the night, though Magellan accepted their hospitality with caution.

'If they are willing to give us gold and ginger, they might have other resources. Women, even. But mind yourself. We have to maintain caution and distance. Trust and open gestures can be dangerous things,' he advised Enrique.

Enrique nodded, understanding.

When they reached the shore, they walked along sands so clean it seemed luminous in the sunlight. They met the king, whose ornaments around his neck, wrists and waist rattled as he walked, each ornament tasked with accentuating the sinews of his body.

'They call me Kolambu,' the king began.

Enrique bowed and addressed him proper, 'Rajah Kolambu. We appreciate your hospitality.'

'You are not the first outsiders to come here,' Kolambu told Enrique. 'For centuries, we have traded with the Chinese in porcelain and silk. They give us their wares, and we offer them ours. Cotton, pearls, shells, coconuts, things like these. There are also men dressed like you, but they speak a different language. We are honest, and we hope you extend the same level of honesty.'

Portuguese, Enrique knew his master best avoid them. 'We are true to our words, your highness. We do need things of you, if you may be so kind. We need food for our Armada. We will render payment. I assure you, your kind highness, that you will all be well satisfied, for my master has come to this side of the world as friends, not enemies.'

The men and even Kolambu himself boarded the Trinidad, and began trading their goods, porcelain jars filled with rice and leaves and two large fish called dorados. In exchange, Magellan gave Kolambu a garment of Turkish red and yellow cloth and a red cap.

Magellan had prepared a spread for the visitors, and as they ate Enrique leaned in and heard Kolambu speak the words *casicasi,* then demonstrated by imitating an imaginary blade across his chest.

'He wants to be *casicasi* with you, master,' Enrique explained.

'I then wish for the same thing,' Magellan agreed.

'Are you sure about this, master. That means to become blood brothers. To literally exchange each other's blood.'

'Give me a cup,' he told Enrique.

Someone fetched a cup while Enrique stepped back, not believing the lengths his master was willing to go through. Kolambu passed a knife to Magellan. Magellan cut his chest, letting the blood drip into the cup, and Kolambu did likewise. The blood was then mixed with wine and both men drank half each of that concoction.

'We are brothers now,' Kolambu smiled.

After dinner they adjourned to the deck above the stern. Enrique brought a sea chart and compass.

Pointing to the chart, Magellan explained, 'See here, this was where we were, a vast sea of blue and nothingness. We have not seen land for many, many moons. We are grateful for your kindness, your highness,' Magellan told Kolambu sincerely.

Kolambu nodded to both Enrique and Magellan. 'Amazing,' he remarked. 'All this time alone. You have ventured even further than the Chinese have.'

'We have suffered much. So many men dead. So many others killed,' Magellan chose not to mention the men he had to kill himself, the likes of Quesada and Mendoza and the Antonios he had to kill for sodomy. 'I have something else to show you, my lord.

Magellan should have known better not to use the arquebuses, the prelude to their discharge was met with curiosity by Kolambu and his men.

'What are these?' Kolambu asked.

Magellan didn't need any translation. He understood Kolambu's curiosity. Magellan's own pride would help alleviate Kolambu's curiosity, of this he was certain.

The gunners loaded the arquebuses, waiting for their Captain General's instructions.

For Kolambu's benefit, however, Enrique leaned in to whisper, 'Those are fire sticks. I recommend closing your ears.'

The arquebuses were aimed high at sea, away from anyone. The gunners waited for a few long seconds before Magellan graced them with the order to fire.

Not really understanding Enrique's warning, when the arquebuses fired Kolambu's men leapt, splaying their bodies against the sides of the ship.

Kolambu stood firm, though the distance between his shoulders and his neck had shortened considerably. 'Impressive,' he remarked, his neck stretching back to its original length.

The next hour lead Magellan to another display of his suggested power.

One of his men came on the deck dressed in armour from the neck down to his knees. Another three men came charging at the armoured man with swords and daggers, striking him on all parts of his body. The armoured man winced but the swords and daggers glided off the armour, metal clanking off the metal but doing him no harm.

'Your man has . . . special powers?' Kolambu wondered after a moment's pause.

Magellan whispered to Enrique, a long moment that detailed everything important that he needed to say.

Enrique took all this in before turning to Kolambu. He smiled and said it slowly to ensure there was no room for error. 'With all due respect, my master says that one of these armed men is worth a thousand of your own men, my lord. This armada has two hundred warriors and weapons of all sorts.'

Kolambu looked at the armoured man, and at the weapons the other three held. 'Indeed, it seems a single warrior is truly worth a hundred of us.'

'I mean this with the utmost respect of course, your highness, but my master also requests permission to inspect your food stores?'

Kolambu laughed and signaled his agreement.

When they reached the shore Kolambu raised his hands in the air and turned toward them. In the daylight sun the long black hair hanging on his shoulders glistened along with the gold that adorned his teeth. The cotton cloth around his waist did nothing to hide the tattoos that covered every part of his body.

Pigafetta later took the time to observe the women. They were fair of shape but had only tree cloth covering them from the waist down. Their dark hair touched the ground, brushing the sand as they walked.

Their smile though, was blood-red like the Chamorro women. They chewed the same betel leaves as the Chamorro women did.

'Come,' Kolambu grabbed Pigafetta by the arm, leading the Italian to a bamboo covering, beneath which was a long balanghai about the size of eighty adult sized palms.

Enrique and Pigafetta, along with Rebelo sat on the stern of that balanghai. Kolambu's men stood about them in a circle with their swords, daggers and spears.

'Bring the food in,' Kolambu ordered. A plate of pork was brought in, along with a jar of wine. Enrique flinched at the sight of pork still, old customs dying hard, old customs that would never leave him. They drank a cup of wine with each mouthful of pork, but Enrique held his greed, and only had his way with the wine.

But before Kolambu drank, he extended the fist of his left hand toward Pigafetta, who flinched, but soon realized it was just the signs they made when they drank.

'Isn't this Holy Friday, today,' Enrique whispered to Pigafetta. 'You're not supposed to take meat.'

'I'm afraid so,' Pigafetta lamented. He couldn't help himself.

As they ate Pigafetta wowed his hosts with the power of the written word. He wondered if they even had a literary culture, or if they were even literate.

'*Apa itu?*' he asked Kolambu.

Kolambu explained each item on the table while Pigafetta wrote it all down in his journal, then read the words aloud afterward. Pigafetta's audience cheered him on as though he were a conjurer.

After this demonstration they went to Kolambu's palace, a hay loft made of banana and palm leaves.

In the palace the night wore on, with more pork and wine and fish. Kolambu's eldest son joined them. Besotted with wine, Kolambu retired for the night while Pigafetta, Rebelo and Enrique and the prince slumbered in the palace on bamboo mats with pillows made of leaves.

The morning was alive with promise, for Kolambu lead Pigafetta by the hand with an offer of another lavish meal, but as soon as Pigafetta stood up he saw a boat filled with Magellan's crew come ashore.

It was time to return to the Trinidad.

On the last day of March, on a Sunday, Easter Day, Magellan sent Father Valderrama ashore to celebrate mass while the islanders and Rajah Kolambu, along with his brother observed. The brother had come from another island, and like Kolambu he was a king of his own island.

Both brothers kissed the cross that was erected on the shore.

Soon the Armada's ships fired all their artillery at once when the cross, adorned with the body of Christ, was erected.

After this solemn ceremony Magellan organized a fencing tournament. There were murmurs about the cross and Magellan told the two kings to 'display it on the summit of the highest mountain, then neither thunder, nor lightning, nor storms would harm you in the least.'

Kolambu, who had yet to know the full meaning of this cross, but knew enough from suggestion that the cross had some kind of holy power over these foreigners, agreed to say, 'We shall accept this cross and place it on the highest mountain.'

'What do you believe in,' Magellan wondered.

'We worship nothing, except Abba,' Kolambu raised his hands to the sky.

'Well then,' Magellan turned to Enrique to translate. 'Our beliefs are similar after all. Do you have any enemies, my lord? If you do have enemies, I would destroy them with my ships and render them obedient.'

'It is most opportune that you mention this. There are two islands that are hostile to me. But now is not the right time to go there,' Kolambu said.

'They are definitely not the Chamorros then,' Magellan was confident in this.

'Who are they?' Kolambu wondered.

'If God would allow me, I would make your enemies bow before me by the force of my weapons.'

Kolambu nodded, certain of Magellan's conviction.

A day later, the Armada's ships returned to formation, firing their guns skyward as a sign of goodbye.

Magellan embraced the kings, while the sailors ascended the summit of the island's highest mountain to erect the cross as he had promised.

He also requested for more food, and both Kolambu and his brother told him to go to the island of Sugbu. It was close by and convenient, and Kolambu chose to follow them.

'Two more days is enough time for us to harvest the rice for you,' Kolambu said.

Magellan took this agreed-upon time to trade with locals, who cared not for coins. They placed their value in knives and the iron from which they made these knives. Magellan also knew the gold Kolambu had was abundant, so he traded pound for pound his iron against their gold.

'Treat the gold as though it were of little value,' he advised Enrique, and in turn he expected the advice to be passed down to the other crew members. 'They can't know how precious the gold is to us.' Magellan reckoned the value of the spices in the Moluccas islands would out-value the gold in either case.

After the trade in iron and gold they left Limasawan, and made a pit stop at the island Pigafetta named Gatigan, where the flying foxes outnumbered the people. Some of the hungrier sailors caught and ate the bats, claiming it tasted like fowl.

After leaving Gatigan the Armada pressed on, peacefully, with there being no talk of mutiny. Kolambu's hospitality sated their rage, the way a good woman cools a man's temper.

But a shadow still hung over Magellan. He knew if he returned to Spain, he would have to face punishment for marooning Cartagena and the priest at Patagonia. He chose not to dwell on that, and thought of only the spices he came halfway around the world for, pressing on until they arrived at the next island.

18

The Armada saw village after village emerging, built on stilts above the water, almost appearing magically and at random, with the tall palm trees above providing ample wide expanses of shade.

'Ready the arquebuses,' Magellan ordered across his four ships.

'You will only scare the locals again, master,' Enrique lamented.

'I mean only peace and friendship,' Magellan ignored his slave's warning, and ordered the artillery to be fired.

The villagers cowered at the sound of gunfire and children jumped in the water while women screamed, just as Enrique had expected. The Trinidad and the other three ships dropped anchor.

'Tell them you serve as ambassador,' Magellan placed his hand on Rebelo's shoulder. 'Bring along Enrique.'

'Yes, Señor,' Rebelo said. His shoulders stiffened, and his eyes met Magellan's. Both of them exchanged knowing looks and nodded to each other.

The two of them set foot on the shore and Rebelo felt now Enrique's hand on his shoulder.

Rebelo slid the hand away. 'The Captain General wishes us to speak to the locals. Let's do what we were asked, eh?'

Surrounding them on the shore were a crowd of villagers lead by this island's king, cautious of the new arrivals.

The king of this island was the total opposite of Kolambu. While Kolambu had broad shoulders this king was older, shorter, more stout in bearing. Beneath the thickness of his skin were old muscles withered away with age, pounded upon by years of pork and wine.

'Good day,' Enrique bowed before the king and Rebelo followed suit. 'A thousand apologies, my lord, but I am Enrique and this is your appointed ambassador, Cristováo Rebelo. I must immediately seek your forgiveness if I have startled you and your people, but the discharge of weapons from our ship is a sign of peace and friendship when greeting others. We mean to be friends, in the best way possible.'

The king thought hard about this, though from the way he moved it seemed he thought with his stomach more than his head. At least their manners, and the sound of their weapons, impressed him. 'What can we do for you?'

'You can perhaps thank Rajah Kolambu for us finding you here. My Captain General decided to pass this way because of Rajah Kolambu's recommendation. We also wish, if you are so kind to allow us, to purchase your food, my good Rajah.'

The king stepped forward. He gathered his thoughts the way his belly gathered food, quick and decisive. 'You are welcome to stay here, but it is customary for all ships that enter here to pay tribute. Only a few days ago a Siamese junk laden with gold and slaves had come here and paid tribute in exchange for safe passage.'

'This is a strange thing that you request of us, your highness. Rajah Kolambu did not ask us of such tributes,' Enrique told this Rajah, cautiously.

'Come, Idris, show these people that I am no liar.'

Idris stepped forward. 'On the other side of the world and yet we meet again, boy,' Idris remarked to Enrique in Arabic, taking notice of how much the boy soldier from so many years ago had grown. 'Tribute to Rajah Humabon in exchange for safe passage. I implore that your master follow suit.'

'Did you hear all that, master?' Magellan had just stepped onto the shore. And he did not look the least bit pleased.

'These lands I shall claim for Spain, and these souls I will claim for Church. Idris' lackadaisical approach is a foolish one. Tell him, and tell this Rajah that King Charles of Spain is the greatest king in this world, and that the Armada de Molucca would never pay tribute to a lesser ruler. If this Rajah wishes for peace then he will have peace. But if he wishes for a war, then he shall have a war.'

Idris regarded these ships before him, the stern visage of the Captain General searing through his eyes. He rose to a panic, turning to the Rajah, 'Have good care, my Rajah, with what you do or say, for their leader's people, they have conquered Calicut, Malacca and most of India. If you treat them well then you will be treated well in kind. Otherwise, it will not end well, for all of us.'

'If your highness refuses to yield, then with all due respect, my master would send a thousand men to descend upon you,' Enrique added.

'I will seek council from my chieftains. And I shall return tomorrow. But in the meantime, let us not talk of war. Wait and give us some time. Before the sun sets you shall all be fed,' Rajah Humabon promised.

'So, this is what your neighbours define as hospitality,' Magellan told Kolambu, who had secretly followed them, and hid below deck. 'I hope you will put in some good words for me to Humabon.'

Enrique translated, and Kolambu took his time to respond. He had hidden because he needed to see what Humabon might say to these foreigners without Kolambu's words to influence his judgement. 'Rajah Humabon will hear of your good deeds, and your kindness to me, Magellan.'

Monday morning came, and the Armada's notary met Rajah Humabon under a hut. Humabon spoke while Enrique translated the Rajah's offer. 'If what you say is true, then it is I who shall pay tribute to the most powerful Rajah in the world.'

'King,' Enrique corrected Humabon.

'You both should become of one blood,' Kolambu suggested to Humabon and Magellan.

Both of them drained a drop of blood from their right arms, and shook hands, their union now sealed.

The next few days happened rapidly; Magellan had meetings and feasts with Humabon as well as his other nephews, and he demonstrated again his armour-clad warrior, whose indestructibility scared the local Sugbuans. The armoured man seemed a beast made of iron, a beast that would haunt their dreams.

'What is the meaning of peace?' Magellan asked one of Humabon's nephews when he came aboard the Trinidad. Magellan sat in a red velvet chair, leaning forward with the bearing of a false king. 'In fact, do you pray to someone, asking for it? And what of your heirs, Rajah?'

Enrique stood calmly while he translated to the nephew.

'My uncle has no sons but many daughters. When our mothers and fathers are old, we will rule over them,' the nephew said.

'Is this true, Rajah?' That the young ones would cast you aside?'

'Such is life,' Humabon lamented.

Magellan leapt off his chair. 'This is not what our Lord hath taught us,' striking his chest with his fist. Passionately, he continued, 'God made the sky, the earth, the sea, the air we breathe, the sand beneath our feet. He commands us to honour our fathers and mothers, and that whoever does otherwise will be condemned to the eternal fire. All of us, we are descended from Adam and Eve, the first parents, and we all have an immortal spirit that lives on when we die.'

'And if we were all to believe in this God of yours,' the nephew and Humabon wondered.

'Do not turn just to win my favour. If those among you choose not to believe, it will cause me no displeasure.'

'We swear to believe not out of fear, but on our own free will,' Humabon professed.

'Then I will honour all of you with this one suit of armour. But there is another matter,' Magellan said this gravely, scaring Humabon and his nephew. After a long pause he carried on, 'My men, as you can imagine after months out at sea, are hungry for intimacy. This hunger is more overpowering than their hunger for food. They have sometimes even paid the price, for being intimate with other men in my fleet,' Magellan let that fact hang in the air like a dark cloud, hoping Enrique's translation carried the same weight, and they understood his insinuation.

'If they are intimate with your women who have not converted, it would be a great sin. But if your women start to believe in our God, then it would be no sin at all.'

'You wish to make love to our women according to your own customs?' the nephew asked.

'My satisfaction is of a more spiritual nature. But I have to give my men their due. This is for peace with the king of Spain. I only wish for all of us to be happy,' Magellan clasped hands with Humabon, the nephew and Kolambu. 'What do you say? If you believe in my God, you will help us?' Magellan eyed everyone in his presence, and glanced at Enrique, to make sure his words were well translated and spoken, 'Again, I urge all of you not to convert just to win my favour, but, Christians will get better treatment, and eternal peace with the King of Spain,' he raised his hands high in the air, as though he were a preacher doing the work of the Lord.

Humabon shed a tear and wiped his eyes with his free hand. 'Yes. We believe. We believe!' He embraced Magellan, and their deal was sealed.

The evening became an ad hoc feast where many swine and goats were gloriously slaughtered, along with the fowl, to be feasted upon and washed down with rice and alcohol.

Beautiful, bare breasted women beat on the gongs while other women danced with the men of the Armada.

'This feels like as though it were all for me, Enrique,' Magellan laughed as he drank a cup of rice wine.

'My master says he thanks you for all this,' Enrique told Humabon, not wanting the Rajah to hear Magellan's exact words.

The night was just beginning, as the nephew brought Pigafetta, Enrique and Rebelo and some others to a raised hut, climbing up the ladder they soon found many young girls playing drums and gongs with a graceful and practiced melody, though this was the last thing they actually noticed.

The girls were fair, had long black hair and were bare-breasted save for the palm cloth that hung from their waists down to their knees. The men in the hut were mesmerized and wished the girls would play their own erect instruments and drum their lusts even further. The effects of the music and wine lead to less and less music being played, and more and more moans echoing off the thin palm-covered roof.

The noise and merrymaking of the early night gave way to the quiet of the early morning. It was still dark, and the men in the huts were awoken by the soft moans of the women laying on them, their soft, delicate arms wrapped across the men's chests. The men slid off the women and escaped laughing back to the ships, Enrique kept punching Rebelo's shoulder happy with their night's conquests.

'What are you laughing about,' Magellan stopped them as they boarded the Trinidad.

Enrique slid his hand off Rebelo's shoulder while Rebelo punched Pigafetta's arm. They looked sober but were still drunk on the high of being around those women the night before. 'Master?' Enrique implored.

'We would need to give these men a proper Christian burial, Lord Humabon, one that would require erecting a cross here after burial,' Enrique explained.

'Yes,' Humabon wiped his eyes. 'And I shall be the first to worship the cross as soon as it is erected.'

The men began to make space in the centre of the village square for the cemetery. Martin Barreta and Juan de Areche had breathed their last the night before. Martin was a passenger on board and Juan was a sailor. Both had succumbed to the effects of scurvy.

'They were good men,' Magellan proclaimed grandly at the eulogy, but Enrique doubted how much his master knew them, 'they suffered the long journey here, fell victim to the sickness. Let the Lord God grant them a better life in heaven than they had here on

this harsh earth,' Enrique tried as fast as he could to translate while
Father Valderrama said his prayers as loud as he could, the priest
perhaps hungry for an audience on land after all these months out
at sea. The sailors raised their hands in the air, something familiar to
Enrique from his childhood prayers in Malacca. He encouraged the
islanders to do likewise, while Father Valderrama culminated the end
of the prayer with a word that all of them, Christian and yet-to-be
Christians alike could say with ease: Amen.

Pigafetta had gained much insight into the Sugbuanos and
their customs. He knew of their burial customs while observing the
funeral, but could still not fathom their sexual practices. They had
explained to him *palang* was in essence genital stretching.

The males, no matter how large or small, had their penises
pierced from one side to the other near the head, with a gold or
tin bolt as large as a goose quill. Both ends of the same bolt had
something resembling a spur with points upon the ends. In the
last few days Pigafetta saw many penises, both young and old. He
found the piercings endlessly fascinating and well-engineered. In the
middle of the bolt is a hole through which they urinate, yet the bolts
and spurs always held firm.

'Does it hurt when you make love?' Pigafetta asked through
Enrique.

'No, not at all. Our women wish it so. If we didn't have this
palang the women wouldn't want us.' Palang in fact, enhanced the
sexual pleasure of both men and women.

Enrique and Rebelo leaned forward, fascinated. Pigafetta was
sure they were thinking the same things as he was. On the night of
they made love to the women they felt something in them, though
they didn't think much of it in their drunken state.

When the Sugbuano men were about to do it they introduced
the palang very gently into a woman's vagina with the spur on top
first, then the other part. Women also had their version of genital
stretching. From the age of six their vaginas are gradually opened
to accommodate the men's penises. Having sexual intercourse with

the palang prolonged the act of lovemaking. The bolts and spurs did not encourage sudden movements, intensifying the pleasure of both sexes.

'I reckon they used the palang because they are of a weak nature. Their weakness is pleasure, it seems. They can't get enough of it. They also told me they can have as many wives as they wish, though there is a principal wife,' Pigafetta explained careful not to add the detail of his and Enrique's indiscretion with the women.

'These savages. So un-Catholic,' Magellan lamented.

'There's so much more to their ways. The ruling class sometimes buried their infants or hurled them into the sea. In fact, unmarried women regularly undergo abortions to make it easier to find a husband. Being a virgin can be such a liability to them that they engage what they call professional deflowers to take care of the problem, though they do care about the females' sexual pleasure.'

'*Jesus Maryo Sep,* the women sound more vile than the men,' Magellan's heart sank. He uttered in heavy whispers, as though the air around his breath was struggling to escape the weight of guilt sinking from above him.

'Perhaps they are,' Pigafetta added. 'There are even artificial penises made of wood to satiate their lust when they are alone, or when their men are not around.'

'Thank you for telling me all this, Pigafetta. A clarity has washed over me. God has made me come all this way to cleanse these people. I am now an instrument of the Lord. Providence has sent me here to shepherd the Lord's faith to these heathens. In order to rid them of these vile customs, of their centuries of weakness, only the Lord's touch can cure them!'

And with that proclamation Magellan and his crew made the preparations for baptism, in which Magellan had a very intimate hand in organizing.

19

According to their calendars it was April the fourteenth. It was a Sunday, and the day before, the crew of the Armada constructed a platform in the village square, decorated it with palm branches, coconut leaves and other vegetation for ornamentation.

'Now, my Rajah Humabon, I shall discharge our weapons. I implore you not to be frightened as it is our custom to discharge them at our greatest feasts,' Magellan said.

Humabon nodded to Enrique. Now the entire village waited for the inevitable volley of gunpowder discharge, giving a sign to his guards who in turn gave the signal to attendees in the village square. They hunched their shoulders and waited.

The crew fired their weapons into the air, it was thunder on a sunny day.

Once that was done Magellan entered the stage and embraced Humabon. 'My friend,' he showed the royal banner that displayed the eagle of St. John with inverted wings, arrows and a scroll. 'I am breaking the rules of the Spanish Kingdom's protocols. The Royal Banner is not to taken ashore except with fifty armed men, with fifty musketeers, but my love for your people is great enough to break these little rules.'

'Even on these distant shores, you seem devoted to your Spanish Rajah,' Humabon remarked.

'Faith is all we have when we are so far away,' Magellan concluded.

Father Valderrama appeared on stage as if no one saw him walking the steps, as though he were a holy thing made of ash and fire. He said a prayer and splashed water from a jar in his hand over Humabon's forehead.

'You are now Rajah Charles, after my own Spanish King,' Father Valderrama proclaimed. Humabon beamed with gushing pride.

Kolambu was baptised after that, and took John as his new name. Magellan and Rajah Charles and John sat on red velvet chairs, while their subjects sat on other cushions and mats. 'I thank the Lord that you have been inspired to become Christian, Rajah Charles. Now you can conquer your enemies more readily than before.'

Rajah Charles whispered to Enrique and Magellan the way a child was about to tell a father something that might deserve the back of a gristled fist. 'Though I have made my choice, others still resist this idea.'

'Do they now? I will have these men killed,' Magellan proclaimed.

This pride worried Enrique. 'Be careful your words, master,' he whispered, like a child who knows he is about to be smacked.

Magellan later changed into white robes and walked along the middle of the square. 'If you indeed wish to become Christian as you all have declared, you have to ignore and burn all your old idols. Set up a cross for each idol you burn. Worship the cross on your knees, hands up, toward the heavens,' he demonstrated, though some were concerned and whispered among themselves about the burning of their old idols.

When the morning was over five hundred men had been baptized, though at the end of it Rebelo whispered, 'You really think they will remain faithful?'

'As faithful as I want them to be,' Magellan shifted in his chair, biting on a piece of fruit.

'Doesn't the Lord want us to be faithful on our own volition, my master?' Enrique wondered, waiting for his reprisal.

'You do seem to test me more often these days. Does being so close to home bring out something inside you,' Magellan sighed deeply.

'On the contrary master, seeing them so readily accept your faith, has been most inspiring. Even the other chieftains seemed to accept conversion readily after you told them they might be killed otherwise,' Enrique said.

The rest of the dinner went by in silence. After dinner, Father Valderrama along with Pigafetta and the other crew members returned to the island to baptize Hara Humamay, Rajah Charles' wife. She brought along with her a retinue of forty women. As they came to the stage square, Pigafetta whispered to Magellan of how beautiful Hara and the women were.

Hara was covered in white and black cloth. Her lips and nails were painted red and adorning her head was a large crown of palm leaves. She approached the platform, and sat down on a cushion with the other women surrounding her. Enrique brought a painting of Mary, while another sailor brought a wooden child Jesus and a cross.

Tears rolled down Hara's soft cheeks as she saw these. 'I am sorry for not believing. I had my doubts. But seeing the cross, it compels me to beg forgiveness.'

'All sins shall be forgiven. You will be born anew,' Father Valderrama told her through Enrique. 'Henceforth, you are Joanna, after the mother of our King.'

Names though, brought along a history, one Hara would not ever know. Their King's mother was infamously known as Joanna the Mad. She suffered for years after her marriage, succumbing to mental illness and the pain of an unrequited love. She also suffered from the indignity of one of her sons confining her in a room in a convent in Castile. Father Valderrama hoped this new Joanna would turn out better.

In the week ahead, the entire island of Sugbu had converted to Christianity. Word spread to other nearby islands, and Father Valderrama converted over two thousand souls.

'One who so quickly accepts conversion might readily accept another religion to suit them once we're gone. Or they might become heathens again,' Enrique observed over dinner in the Trinidad.

Rebelo stopped chewing. He was waiting for a reprisal, but there was none.

There was just the containment of silence waiting to ignite. 'You may be right. But that is up to them. If that is what they do when we leave, then the Lord shall punish them all.'

The rest of the dinner was quick but silent. Magellan left them alone. 'You always question him, yet you do not get punished,' Rebelo wondered.

'The master has treated me well. He is kinder to me than I deserve. But I am right, aren't I?'

There was a brief moment of silence, which only served to magnify both Rebelo's and Enrique's breathing. Rebelo's eyes glanced quickly to make sure Magellan wasn't within earshot. All this while Rebelo had felt abandoned, as a boy without a father, and though he was wont to admit it, he felt strange that his biological father seemed more fatherly to the slave than to his own son. Tears rolled down Rebelo's eyes. 'I know exactly who Magellan is, but I don't yet know what he means to me.'

Enrique was taken aback by those tears. He recognized those quivering eyes as tears borne of abandonment. He knew what it was like to lose a father, but maybe he had yet to know the feeling of never having had a father.

'You and me both, my friend,' Enrique laid a hand on Rebelo's shoulder.

The newly-converted women seemed to be a kind of license for the sailors. They had their squid, and were tired of fucking grey skins that bled in black, and wanted to fuck fair flesh that bled red. Drunk on the rice wine that Rajah Charles was courteous enough to provide, the sailors spent these halcyon days grabbing the youngest girls they could find, girls who had barely blossomed, deflowered them under the bushes, on the sand, behind rocks, inside huts.

'I heard the tribe has professional deflowerers? We taking their jobs, eh,' one of the sailors laughed.

One girl, strewn alongside a bush, burgeoning breasts bare, got on her feet and tried to run, only to be grabbed by Rebelo.

'Where you going, *mi amor,*' Rebelo told her in as soft and sweet a tone as he could muster. He kissed her on the forehead, then lead her to a tree, where he entered her from the back, while she moaned her disagreement.

'You're getting sloppy seconds, Rebelo,' another sailor remarked, only to be given Rebelo's middle finger.

For those girls that did manage to run, they ran to Joanna's hut, crying, but Joanna told them to remain silent, 'For I have a plan for these savages, and in time, they will pay,' she promised them.

'Who else are not with the cross, Rajah Charles? You did mention some who weren't with me,' Magellan began.

'There are a few,' Rajah Charles contemplated the names, but dared not say them.

Magellan moved around in the hut, one a size too small for his frame. Enrique sat in the centre watching his master keep pace while he refrained and contained his silence.

Was Rebelo right? Would Enrique soon receive a reprisal? 'Isn't the purpose of the Armada de Moluccas to get to the Moluccas?'

'We are on course,' Magellan stopped pacing, and the temperature in the room seemed to get warmer. 'Soon, we will be as rich as we want to be, but not before I punish these disbelievers.' Magellan swept his arm in one large arc. All that was missing was a cape to complete his theatrics.

'Well, there is one,' Rajah Charles said. The theatrics and temper of Ferdinand Magellan were getting to him.

Joanna of Sugbu entered the hut. 'So they say my new name means madness.' She met eyes with her husband. 'Tell him. Tell him who refuses Magellan's offer.'

Rajah Charles sighed. 'There is word among the chieftains of the other islands. There is one who is strong. He is stubborn, and does not follow anyone's orders but his own.'

'Who is this disbeliever? Who!'

Rajah Charles didn't need the translator for this gesture. He knew what the question was. 'His name is Sri Lapu-Lapu Dimantag, of Mactan. He came here years ago from Borneo. He asked me for a place to settle. I gave him and his people his new land. His people have cultivated it well. We are prosperous in trading crops because of his efforts. But when he turned to piracy, raiding merchant ships, I fell out of favour with him. It affected trade in the ports. His island then earned the nickname Mangatang, or those who lie in wait. Then it was shortened to Mactan,' Rajah Charles confessed with a heavy sigh. 'What will you do to him?'

'I shall let God decide their fates,' Magellan told Charles and Joanna.

20

'Is it true what the foreigner says?' Reyna asked her husband. 'That he would kill us if we do not follow their worship and bow before their king?'

Lapu-Lapu turned away from Reyna, his hand still holding her waist. They caressed in their bed on the wooden floor of his hut and he thought about it. If he acceded to bowing to some king on the other side of the world and start worshipping a giant cross, he would be submitting before something he didn't believe in.

If he didn't relinquish to their demands, his people might suffer and die, and it would be all his fault. He straddled between these two thoughts, his mind drifting. He would rather be straddling Reyna.

'Why should we bow before some king we have never seen and two pieces of wood tied together?'

'It's either that or we all die,' Reyna sidled closer to her husband, her chest pressed against his back.

Lapu turned around to face her. Their lips met. 'Then we die fighting.' Their fingers intertwined, and their tongues began to tangle, so did their bodies, merging into a two-backed beast, motioning in a swirl of moans and screams, their bodies enjoying the act, their faces betraying a worry they could not hide. Their brows were furrowed tight, jaws slackening from pleasure.

They worried this might be their last night together, they dug into each other, never wanting to let the other go, their motions were of desperate love. Tonight was the night that would change everything.

By the shore there were three hundred of Rajah Charles' warriors streaming on their war boats. Accompanying them were sixty

Spaniards who would commend on the remarkable craftsmanship of these balangay, surprised that these savages could craft such refined boats.

'My ancient ancestors,' Rajah Charles told Magellan earlier, 'brought slaves to and from here. We built temples for other kingdoms.'

Magellan limped alongside the half-naked Rajah, each limping step reminding him of that javelin in his thigh from the battle in Azemmour. 'My men still can't believe you made these boats. I've seen your wooden dowels. We use iron.'

Rajah Charles smiled proudly at this.

Enrique followed along, found their slow pace excruciating. For a younger man this was way too slow, but he had no place or position to express his discontent. He limped along, more in his mind than for real, to keep with his master's pace. Keeping up with conversations had been hard enough, but keeping up with these two older men made him feel he had aged along with them.

He could hardly see, in spite of the flaming torches. He registered their heat more than he recognized their luminance.

Above him, the moon was three quarters full, in its waxing gibbous phase. While the moon waxed gibbous, Rajah Charles waxed lyrical about the might of his people, and from where Enrique stood he found it harder to understand what Charles was saying. Though their languages were compatible not all of their words were the same. Rajah Charles talked fast and Enrique was just winging it. He had been lucky that his translations had proved beneficial enough that their heads have not been lopped off just yet.

But now the Rajah was talking about a war he would rather prevent.

Enrique knew enough about the world to know of its invisible borders, and of man's penchant for blood. He worried this was the only legacy mankind had to offer itself.

The night wore on. The waves rolled turbulently, showing its discontent. Rajah Charles boasted about his concubines waiting for him back home.

Enrique reckoned Rajah Charles' boasts were as large as his belly. He imagined the body had grown stout not from food but from feeding his own ego. He gave a courteous smile to the Rajah.

A few hours later they were approaching Lapu's village. The night air was cool but humid. The tropical air suited Enrique. This was the kind of air he was born in, the air his mother breathed into him in the womb, it was the air he came home to after a decade of slavery.

This air did not do the Spaniards well. Magellan winced at the pain in his thigh. The air turned warm. It was almost sunrise. All these hours to think on the boat, brutally cut off by the impending dawn.

Enrique took a drink from a wooden cup. His eyes were wide open, his ears sharp, he was the razor thin bridge between two cultures, and each step they took only served to slice open old wounds.

They found they were not alone as they approached the shore.

Enrique looked at the sky. The dark of night had turned a shade of violet, then a shade of red he had no words for.

The Mactan people were waiting for them. The sun would soon rise. Eyes acclimated to the night made out the shapes of the welcoming party. It was not bright enough to for their eyes to define faces and details just yet.

The Mactanese oohed and awed at the Spaniards and their supporters, those Lapu-Lapu had decided were turncoats.

Pigafetta had a sword in hand. His heart was racing, timed to the beat of the Mactan's taunting. He wanted to write this down. He caressed his sword and stroked his beard, dipping his thumb into it until he could feel the skin on his chin. 'It's time, isn't it?' he asked Enrique.

'*Si*,' he told the Italian chronicler. Enrique ran his fingers through his hair. He stepped forward, preparing to listen to a conversation he knew would end in crimson ink, if the Italian was alive at the end to tell it.

'I have never been into battle. Not even a fight in school,' Pigafetta confessed, trying to get Cristovāo Rebelo's attention. Rebelo seemed more ready, more eager to fight in his armour.

'Never been one for school. Beaten kids for money, though,' Rebelo smirked.

'Your Captain-General would be proud,' Enrique said.

'Aye,' Rebelo remarked, knowing full well Enrique meant for a more paternal word.

'Why fight now, when dawn is the best time for battle. We can see you die clearer when the sun rises,' Lapu taunted along with all fifteen hundred of his men wailing along in support along the bank, some in the water, some with moist sand caked at their feet. Lapu-Lapu wiggled his toes in the sand.

A man hobbled alongside Rebelo, Pigafetta and Enrique. Ferdinand Magellan took stock of the three of them. The chronicler Antonio Pigafetta. His out-of-wedlock son Cristovão Rebelo. And the boy with no last name. Enrique the Black.

Death and mutiny had faced Magellan at every turn, but yet here they were, their lives on a precarious periphery. They were sailors, walking planks, straddling the boundary between wood and water, a misstep, a slight imbalance of footing, and they were overboard.

Behind Magellan his own men were ready. The captains of the other ships had already prepared their artillery.

Magellan thought about Juan Serrano, and his brother-in-law Duarte Barbosa. He hardly spent time with Duarte, barely speaking to him since they landed in Humabon's island. He spent so much time working he ignored those closest to him. He then thought of Beatriz. He wanted to see her again. When he fought, the fight would be for her and his children.

'This will be easy enough,' Magellan whispered to Pigafetta and Enrique. 'Just like the taking of Mal—' he cut himself short. 'It will be fast. They will run at the sight of our firepower.'

'Perhaps they might. Or they might fight, like my people did,' Enrique said, pretending not to notice.

Magellan sighed. 'Tell him, that he has one last chance to accede to our demands. Pledge allegiance to the King of Spain.'

Those words bore a weight when tipped favoured only one party. Enrique told Lapu what he was instructed to say, then thought about how the wind moved in circles, like cyclones do.

Lapu laughed as he boarded his boat as two Spanish boats came to converge with him, from a distance forming a triangle.

Magellan was anxious while Enrique rowed their boat, struggling to keep pace. The winds had grown stronger, the tides agitated. Enrique wished the Italian did some rowing, but the Italian was not a slave. Being a slave was hard and unrewarding. Surviving his master's kindness was harder.

Lapu noticed Enrique struggling. 'You are a man of many talents and skills. All your hard work, yet they reward you with nothing.'

'They let me live,' Enrique stopped rowing, and considered Lapu's physical appearance. He was a man whose body seemed to be carved out of marble his veins taut like ancient roots held deep within the earth. There was much to fear in just Lapu's physical presence alone, but Enrique's time serving on ships and getting entangled in battles himself had caused him to shed his fear of men like Lapu. If he were ever in a fight with Lapu he might lose, but he would never have been afraid to be in a fight with him.

'But is it enough, just to live,' Lapu wondered, the sight of this young man with the same skin tone and facial features sparked within him an inchoate curiosity of how someone so young could ever be so subservient.

'I am a slave without chains,' Enrique remarked.

'Ties that bind,' Lapu said. 'Break free from those bonds, boy. How can you be so willing to serve these foreigners? They must have taken you from your home but it must have been so long ago you've forgotten what it was like to be free.'

'Do you see any chains, Si Lapu-Lapu?' Enrique raised his right arm, showing off his free wrist.

'Stupid. But brave,' Lapu laughed.

'This is a one-time offer my master is giving. Do you wish to accept this offer,' Enrique let those words hang, hoping the words might sway Lapu toward the Spaniards.

'Who are you to make offers, slave?' Enrique knew this was just a delaying tactic from Lapu.

He felt the tedium in this banter. He exhaled with deep resolve. 'I speak on behalf of my master, for he does not know the language that we speak.'

'Then he will learn my lesson quickly. I will never bow down to a foreign power. We bow to no one. Humabon has grown fat and lazy, and will roll over to anyone who feeds him. But not me.' Lapu's boat turned away, the water around it rippling into the shape of an arrow in the wake of his exit, fading into the darkness, along with his men.

Enrique saw his master's grave face, that determined resolve of it, the resolve that struck thousands in Azemmour, the same face Alfonso Albuquerque had in Malacca. There would be death next, and maybe children taken, like he was. He knew the fiery temperament in his master's visage and knew what his master wanted:

He wanted to watch their world burn.

The sun rose in the sky. The clouds were now a misty shade of pink. Crickets were silenced by the crow of cockerels in the distance. The gentle waves rolling along the shore provided a calming, regular rhythm.

In the Trinidad, Enrique observed his master. He had grown thinner, his cheekbones more prominent, his face skeletal. His aura had the prescient air of death. He had become death incarnate in Enrique's eyes, the eyes of a man he used to know.

'Are you sure about this?' he asked his master.

Magellan did not answer. Above deck, he heard the motion of his men, who swore their allegiance to him as far as they could spit.

Enrique imagined the brutal inferno that was to come. He searched his master's face for some kind of answer, finding none. In his mind's eye he saw his burning village, and the burning of Mactan. Lapu's words, even if he chose to deny it, had got to him. He wondered how right it was to burn the villages, and how un-Christian it was to torment the innocent. He wondered too if he was able to escape all this, the madness of having to follow orders he knew was wrong. Part of his conditioning had made him always indebted to his master, but this burning urge inside him to know if what he was doing was right, burned the blood within his veins, made him growl, 'Answer me, master!'

'Yes it is necessary!' Magellan lost all restraint. Then he held back. 'We have to. For Spain.'

'For Spain? Or for yourself? I was taken from my family in such a fire like the one you're about to cause. Are you hoping for more slaves? Or are you hoping for death?'

Magellan held his silence.

Less than an hour later Enrique sat in the dark of the Trinidad's cargo hold staring into the deep shadows that knew no end. Magellan called him and Enrique went into the bunk, reluctantly.

Enrique was still sore for their argument earlier, and was in no mood to be talking to Magellan so soon. He saw a chest at the corner of the bunk, and presumed it held nothing of any importance.

Magellan opened the chest, pulling out a weapon with intricate patterns. He turned to Enrique, who turned his head away. Magellan mustered as much of a smile as he could and said, 'Before we go, I want you to have this,' and handed Enrique a short-sheathed blade. 'Your father's keris. I have held it for too long. It's now yours to keep. A boy deserves to be close to his father.'

Enrique took the keris carefully, with considered motion, and he recognized it. The keris his father held when he died. Enrique trembled. He couldn't believe it as he began fighting back tears, he could not stop from falling. He thought of his father's death, a memory he had shut out for a decade. He suspected Magellan's gesture involved motives other than altruistic, but he was too moved to point that out. 'I don't know what to say'.

Magellan nodded, patting Enrique on the shoulder. He had bought back part of his slave's loyalty with sentimentality and nostalgia.

The boat he was in later held Rebelo and Pigafetta. The younger Rebelo brandished a flaming torch in one hand, eager to set the world on fire. Pigafetta though seemed more pensive, afraid to fight.

'Heathens, all of them,' Enrique heard someone from another boat proclaim. He couldn't see who it was, but he could see the other boat harbouring a cross. Above them, the cloud-covered moon seemed half-full, and Enrique was half-hearted.

'I can't wait to start,' Rebelo said to no one in particular, but loud enough to let his older shipmates know he was doing a man's work.

Enrique had no one to argue against tonight. His master had turned mastermind, waiting in the Trinidad, no longer doing the dirty work.

The boat cut swathes into the sand while the villagers in Mactan slept. The Spaniards' feet shuffled swiftly, with determination. A fervour had swept over them, and midnight had brought with it fire.

Rebelo threw Enrique a torch, urging him on. 'Let's start the burning,' he coaxed.

Enrique contemplated the fire in his hand, while Pigafetta remained in their boat, eyes soaking in each detail. He did not want to miss a thing.

The Spaniards came along flanking and met in the centre, burning the houses in that order.

Enrique threw the torch in the sand, where the sand swallowed it and exhaled black smoke.

The sleeping villagers smelt the fire and felt its heat, woke fast to rush the children and find a safe way out. There was none. Children screamed and women panicked. The men tried to douse the fires with little success.

The Spaniards rushed to erect the cross they had brought, then ran back to their boats, paddling away as the fires swallowed the village.

Pigafetta sat in his boat, enraptured by the power of Magellan's words, by the power of that man's will, watched as this little part of the heathen world turned to ash.

'We showed them!' Rebelo exclaimed, joyful for all the wrong reasons.

'Yes, we did, didn't we?' Enrique shot back at Rebelo. The irony of that statement silenced Rebelo.

Stepping out his own home, Lapu-Lapu saw his village burning. He could discern the screams of men, women and children, running across the village like flaming apparitions. Lapu felt immobile and helpless.

There was a rage inside of him trying to make sense of this madness. Had he done something so cruel that he was being punished? He felt Reyna, holding onto his arm. It shook him back to sanity, and all he could think of was the night before this, when they were blissful and making love. That passion now had turned to rage. He screamed with that rage still burning, and grabbed his machete.

He shoved past Reyna and looked for his men. Reyna called out to him, but he did not answer.

So this is what the foreigners truly are,' Lapu thought. He had never known someone as zealous as Ferdinand Magellan, a man who claimed to be doing this for God. *Does any God condone violence in his name,'* Lapu wondered. What gods had he worshipped and what wars have legends told him of? Did not all legends have heroes and villains? And angry gods? If a monster came to his shores burning his village, did that not make Magellan the villain?

Am I a hero, then?

No time for such pondering. If he lived and survived this day, he would let the people decide what he was. For now, he had a duty to save his world.

He ordered the survivors to extinguish the flames, pulling water from buckets along the shore, but their efforts seemed futile.

The fire burned for most of the night, smouldering ashes rising and sending dark plumes into the night sky, a colour darker than black.

As his village burned, Sri Lapu-Lapu Dimantag looked at the boats rowing away in the distance.

For a brief second, Lapu-Lapu met eyes with the darker-skinned one. He dressed like the Spaniards did, but did not look anything like them. Enrique averted his eyes, in guilt.

'Send a message,' he told his chief Sula. 'We will kill all of them.'

21

'Was that all really necessary,' some of the sailors were saying. The joy of seeing a village go up in flames was slowly being replaced by the smoke of doubt in the Trinidad.

'Yes it was!' Magellan rose to the main deck. 'Right now we have fifty armoured men going to Mactan, and we will win! No heathen is going to defy God or me ever again. I would have the next man hung and quartered if he doubts me again.'

The Trinidad remained silent as the sun rose, and it floated ever closer to Mactan. That was until the ship shook. It had hit something. Magellan limped toward his pilot. 'Albo! What in the heavens is happening?'

'We must have hit the rocks below,' Albo said matter-of-factly.

Magellan huffed and shouted to the other ships, 'Lay anchor! We're going to walk the distance.'

He heard the men groan and knew he had to rally these men by example.

Soon the fifty armoured Spaniards followed him in the water, all of them armed with swords and muskets.

'There's no way they can win against gunpowder,' Magellan said aloud.

He looked up, and saw the sky darken with rain drops laced with feathers. The men blocked the arrows with their shields, but the shower of arrows from fifteen hundred men were more than enough to overwhelm a mere fifty Spaniards, some of whom got cut on their thighs and arms.

Enrique ran out the Trinidad, wading into the water, armed with only his father's keris sheathed to his side. He was worried that in his master's fervour his master had become reckless, and he had no true idea what he was capable of.

Just before this battle, Magellan had urged Rajah Charles not to interfere, that their armour and cannons, along with a few of the Rajah's men, were all he needed to defeat Lapu and his men, a decision Enrique reckoned his master would now regret.

He approached his master and pulled him aside. 'Trust me, my lord!'

Magellan spun around to look for Rebelo and Pigafetta and he did glimpse them fighting bravely, Rebelo with the bravado and recklessness of youth, Pigafetta with the concerned doubt of a learned scholar.

Lapu's men had their arms cocked way back, launching those thick spears farther than humanly possible. Enrique soon heard the wet, firm thuds against bone and hearts and lungs, punctuated with the clang of armour against jagged rocks below.

What unnerved Enrique more was the alarming regularity in which the bodies fell.

Now it was Magellan's turn to pull Enrique aside. The arrows and spears had longer range than Spanish muskets and gunpowders, with range enough to kill the gunners and cannon loaders before they could reload.

Magellan tried now to find Rebelo, but could not see him in the increasing melee. Now his own concerns as a father began to sink in. *Why did I let Rebelo join the fight?*

An arrow grazed Enrique's shoulder and between screaming and whimpering he looked at his shoulder, noticing a clear gash of red against his white shirt. The wound would have been worse if it weren't for the armour he was wearing.

'I'm fine,' Magellan answered without the question being asked.

'Don't speak too soon, master.'

Lapu's people began charging barefoot in the water, and among them was Lapu-Lapu himself. He stopped and locked eyes with Enrique before he continued charging again, disappearing among his horde.

That brief moment was time enough for Enrique to figure what kind of man Lapu was, a man with a goal, an undeterred ambition that would not break no matter what came his way.

In the Trinidad, Duarte Barbosa held back the second wave of armoured sailors, now turned soldiers. He found this battle unnecessary, until he saw how many men had already fallen. The other captains stayed in their respective ships, uncertain of this endeavour, Duarte Barbosa thought of Beatriz, and he worried he might have to tell his sister her husband had died here. He couldn't bear to see her sad. He belted out the order.

As the warriors charged in the water, a bang punctuated the world in blood. An iron pellet had pierced through a Mactan warrior's chest.

Enrique had ducked and glanced to see who fired. The Spanish soldiers charged proudly, this time better armed with muskets and rifles that continued firing, but that did not stop the native warriors from charging.

Theirs was the cry of a thousand warriors, loud enough to make even the thunder afraid. The air grew louder, and the waters once blue were turning crimson.

A short distance away, bets were being placed. The spectators were mostly sitting in their own well-made floating sampans. There was the slight risk of them getting entangled in the upcoming melee, but they knew at least that neither Rajah Charles nor Lapu Lapu's men would cause them harm.

Magellan had boasted to Rajah Charles and his cohorts that he could win. Now he might have to swallow his words.

Those who voted for Magellan were getting nervous while the ones that had bet against him were already planning on what to do with their winnings. Both parties winced and roared as though this were a cockfight, a spectator sport.

In a larger boat than the others Rajah Charles sat in his wooden throne at the back of that boat. His wrinkled features crusted even further as he squinted to see the battle raging ahead of him in the harsh sunlight. Truth be told most of what he saw were blobs of red and green and brown. His eyes were giving way. A man of his position could not reveal his own affiliations or his own preferences. He would cheer for the victor, whomsoever that might be at the end.

'Let's be fair,' he told the two young men rowing his boat, hinting his indifference. He set his narrow eyes on the blob of red that was the Spaniards, and cursed his old eyes. When he was of rowing age he could see distant islands with crystal clarity. But now all he could do was depend on his hearing.

He thanked the old gods he worshipped that he could still hear as well as he used to see. No, the one true God, he corrected himself. He shook his head for a second and felt his heart tense. *The one true God might be angry I have neglected him,* he thought. Forgive me, he prayed. It had barely been a few days since he had converted.

He was now Rajah Charles. He had to get used to it.

With his good ears he heard Lapu's men scream in confidence, while it sounded like the Spaniards were screaming out their impending loss. He could hear the piercing of spears and arrows into flesh crunching bone, of armour smacking against the coral-filled waters below them.

Lapu took his turn now to wade into the water. Fish departed in his stead, hurriedly avoiding him.

'Jesus, Maryo, Sep,' many of the Spaniards uttered. They saw the Mactan warriors retrieve and throw the spears left in the water again and again.

Rebelo stood among the dead bodies of his fellow Spaniards. He found Pigafetta crouched low next to one.

Enrique noticed the archers too were recycling their arrows. These were not savages as his master had called them. Just because they were practically naked, or ate animals that seemed strange to Magellan, did not make them monsters. Their battle tactics were not borne of savage minds. Theirs was a tactical intelligence, a working knowledge of numbers and scare tactics and clever recycling of weapons to whittle their enemies down.

Magellan limped on beside Enrique. He saw Lapu-Lapu wade through the water in reptilian, alligator-like precision. Lapu raised his bow high.

The Mactan chief pulled the arrow taut before letting it go, it waded among the other arrows as if it had its own authority.

The arrows came raining back down and from where he stood Rebelo realized he might be too slow to raise his shield.

'Cristovão!' Pigafetta called out for him. He stole the closest shield to try protect Rebelo but the arrows rained through Rebelo's body. Pigafetta hid under the stolen shield, screaming, waiting for the volley to end.

Magellan gasped as his son bled, the body splashing into the water while the face met the coral below. He still wanted to believe he could save his son, and dashed toward Rebelo's body, but a pain shot though his knees. He screamed, frustrated beyond all belief at how an injury was keeping him away from his son.

Enrique could hear the air escape his throat, the sound of speech lost. He almost couldn't believe it. During his time with his master he had seen plenty of death, and the death of Cristovão Rebelo invoked the same feelings he had when he saw his nameless young friend die at the battle of Azemmour.

Enrique saw Rebelo's body, and for a moment considered forgetting his master and running toward his friend, but Magellan limped on and found Erique's shoulder and held himself there for balance. 'In case I do not survive, Enrique, remember that no matter what, you shall be set free.'

'Don't worry about that now, Master,' Enrique held Magellan as an arrow pierced his master's thigh. A moment later, a spear did something far worse to his master's face. The body twisted and snapped away, landing in the water. The water hid the damaged face but Enrique saw the armour, the helmet blanketed by crimson that spread around Magellan's head as a blood-red halo, expanding into what looked like angel wings.

Enrique couldn't believe how fast things were changing. His master and his master's son both dead within minutes, and at any moment he could suffer the same fate. He looked on at Pigafetta, crouching low with shield high, and cursed about how lucky this scholar was, a man untrained in the fighting arts to still be surviving this melee. He scoffed and screamed and let it all out, until his voice turned hoarse.

Forget this Italian, Enrique thought, and searched his own torso for something to fight with. It was on his waist all along. His father's keris. The one made all those years ago. He felt connected to his father in this moment, and felt charged enough to continue fighting against the ones who killed his second father, the only man in his new life that treated him like a human being.

Part of him felt anger still at Magellan for all the things his master had done and and ordered him to do, like the brutal quartering of Quesada and having to boil the body parts with herbs to prevent the birds from eating them, and more recently the burning of Lapu's village, yet part of him was so blinded with the rage of his master's death he felt he was avenging his master's death with the spirit of his real father via the keris.

He ran toward the water, the wavy blade of the keris making its first stab into one of the Mactan warriors, digging deep into the stomach, screaming and crying as he did. He cried contemplating who was he was killing for? His master, or himself, for pursuing vengeance due to some imagined slight?

The motion of waves caused ships to move across the world. The rusted waves of the keris moved the warrior to a world of pain.

The warrior slid, knees smacking against coral, hands grasping for purchase against Enrique's shoulders. He fell face first into the water with a crack and a rush air rocketing out the water where the face was, his last breath before dying.

Enrique held his shirt stained with the man's blood. He would never know his name. War felt to Enrique like the most intimate of encounters, so close you could kill your enemies with blades or fists, yet it had the most disconnect, was the most dispassionate, anonymous form of contact. He felt mankind bred only soldiers that killed one another. The most ruthless of all killers claimed the right of king.

Did Lapu-Lapu earn this right? He had already killed the man that mattered most to Enrique. In order to get to his master's killer, he had to wade through a throng of warriors all ready to kill. He did not care if it was a wise decision, or if he died before he could reach the Mactanese leader.

His eyes locked against Lapu-Lapu. His decision was swift.

Lapu stifled a laugh when he saw the old Rajah Charles sit in the throne of his boat. He laughed at the old rajah's audacity, and at that new name of his. No way was he going to call him Charles.

What stopped Lapu from laughing then was the man darker than the Spaniards, the same skin tone as him, but dressed in the trappings of these foreigners. Lapu knew he was not a warrior, just a boy pretending to be one. He saw the boy dodge a machete, then pierce his own wavy blade into his enemy's neck, blood gushing out onto his white sleeve and splashing against his own face, panting and breathing hard as his opponent fell into the water.

Lapu-Lapu waded into the water, machete in hand, making no sound, hair halfway down his back flowing along the breeze, bangs grown so long they covered his eyebrows. Muscles still tense enough that with one swift motion they could swing into murder. The machete swung upward, cleaving into a Spanish soldier's armpit. The Spaniard fell, but he wasn't dead yet. Lapu stepped back with an urgency suggesting he found the Spaniard utterly disgusting.

He walked on, callused feet stepping against coral and jagged rock, ignoring cuts under his toes and soles. A lesser man might wince at the pain, though for Lapu it was just another day.

He aimed low, striking in sweeping motions against exposed thighs. Spanish bodies knelt against the water, he bled them out to make them suffer.

For instant death, he set his sights on the ones that turned traitor, the ones that sided with Rajah Charles and Magellan, the ones now charging against Lapu's men. For them Lapu lunged his machete straight, aiming for the cage of bones that sheltered their hearts.

His men still outnumbered the turncoats ten to one. The battle cries had subsided, but the fighting still went on. Cannons meant for the battle could not be mounted due to the shallow water, forcing the Spaniards resort to only their swords and armor and guns. Guns were loud and deadly but slow to load.

But before the Spaniards could carry on fighting, the boats were already retreating on orders from their various captains. Lapu saw the surviving Spaniards wading toward the boats, screaming for rescue, not wanting to be left behind.

While the Spaniards retreated, one of them stayed behind. The loyal slave. He was tired but he was relentless, he could not stop. His fire was the fury of a newborn sun.

Lapu motioned forward, killing those Spaniards that were still halfway toward death, while Enrique made a beeline toward Lapu.

Enrique motioned through the water, felt the water in his boots itching his toes. Lapu stood and waited until Enrique was a few paces away. By standing firm, he caused his enemies to do a double take, though Enrique took a few steps too close. Lapu had to give the boy that. The boy was determined.

'The slave avenges his master,' Lapu began.

'He was like a father to me,' Enrique choked those words out, felt his own lips quiver and his eyes water. Even as recent as now his mind raced, wondering what would indeed happen to him now. Was Magellan's death truly going to set him free, but all the same, he felt afraid of being set free, and he wondered what a freed slave's life would be like?

'Too long under the chain of one master, boy. I have had many young ones under me. All like children and sometimes they tried to call me father. You, I hear spent ten years under your new father's wings.'

'When everyone else hated me, he treated me like an equal,' Enrique wiped the tears out his eyes with one hand, and raised his keris with the other. 'I should kill you!'

'What would killing me accomplish? I have set you free, and now, you have no one. What is your place in this world, now that you're free?'

Enrique thought hard. His fantasy of killing Lapu cut short by this question. Where does a slave go, once released from bondage? What life could he lead? What money was he allowed to have? Lapu's words, no matter how much he chose to deny it, had tainted Enrique with an infectious desire to be truly free, in spite of all his fears and doubts if he were to do so. Enrique sheathed his keris, sighed, calmed himself down and chose his next few words carefully. 'I have nothing in this world, and therefore I am free to roam it, wherever I want to go.'

Lapu nodded, satisfied with the slave's reply.

Rajah Charles raised his hand in the distance and in a nearby boat Datu Sula did the same. Their men rushed to retrieve the bodies of the fallen warriors, choosing carefully not to take the bodies of Lapu's men, discerning one from the other by the tattoos and decorations on the corpses, different insignias for different tribes.

Another group was in charge of retrieving the bodies of the dead Spaniards, and Enrique stood and watched, helpless, and cautious of how Lapu left him alone after their exchange. He was left alone and wished the retreating Spaniards were dead in this water instead.

Lapu raised his machete-wielding arm high enough to let the blade glint in the sun. The battle was over. His men dispersed, as silent in their exit as they were cacophonous at the start of the battle.

The removal of the bodies went on for many quiet minutes, silent save for the waves cutting through coral and jagged rock. The blood-red water turned grey then shaded itself back to its usual blue. The water was resilient that way. In time, if left alone, the bodies would have met the same fate, dragged without mercy or thought, across sharp rock into the sea, fresh enough for the predatory fish to eat, until they were nothing but bone and memory.

Rajah Charles' men approached one body that was stopped by Lapu's firm proclamation. 'His body stays here. The fool Magellan will not be touched.'

'You can't be serious,' Rajah Charles declared.

'Humabon,' Lapu said flatly, with utter disgust.

'He gave me a new name,' Rajah Charles told Lapu.

'Charles,' Lapu stretched out each syllable.

'We are helping you clear out this mess,' Rajah Charles noted, fat pride and fat behind still floating on his sinking throne.

'We don't need your help. My men will clear what we can,' Lapu said.

'And leave the sea to do the rest,' Rajah Charles lamented, realizing this as he stepped down from his throne, while his rowers struggled to balance the boat. The stout Rajah stepped into the water, and any doubts from his men were silenced by a wave of his hand. The water touched his stomach while the water seemed to barely touch Lapu's ankle.

'The sea will wash away the plague of these foreign invaders,' Lapu corrected the Rajah. 'It washes away everything, making the world pure again.'

'The sea brings good tidings as well. It brought us their new teachings,' Rajah Charles explained.

'Stupid,' Lapu spat out the word. 'I'll believe what I want to believe.'

'And I believe what I choose to believe,' Rajah Charles pronounced confidently.

'Go, before we turn the sea red again,' Lapu raised his machete, pointing it at Rajah Charles, then motioning the blade to the Rajah's men. 'And you better leave, before you suffer your master's fate.'

Enrique stepped away from Magellan's body, his hand snapping to the sheathed keris, breathing hard, wondering if removing his keris would be a good idea.

Interlude

Valladolid, Spain, September 1522

Juan Elcano gently rubbed his stubble. He was a man who sought recognition for the ordeal he had to go through.

He was not interested in the fact that he had survived the massacre in Mactan, for him the greater challenge was the six months they undertook to get back to Sanlucar de Barrameda, Spain, finally finding the Spice Islands and facing further dangers and temporary imprisonment along the way. This inquiry was nothing to him compared to the meandering journey João Lopes de Carvalho took them through the archipelago, forcing him to take over from Carvalho due to his weak leadership.

Elcano felt he had not been given the proper thanks or reward, though he knew this inquiry was not the place for recognition or reward. He saw fire in Transylvanus' eyes. The inquisitor wanted to be famous and this was the story that would bring him fame.

Elcano was no fool. He knew their expedition was the stuff of sensation. Battles against savages. Death, mutiny, insubordination, and a missing slave.

There was glee in Transylvanus' eyes as he asked Elcano the next question, though it was not the question he was expecting.

'Now, about the supplies of the ship,' Transylvanus began.

'Why would the supplies in the ships be of any interest to you?' Elcano snapped.

This pleased Carvalho, who did nothing but smile.

'I am just getting the facts straight,' Transylvanus replied without any hint of emotion.

'*And this is because he needs to rally these details to us,*' *an official who stood at the doorway said, waiting for his small audience to face him while he motioned into the room and walked in an arc, drawing as much attention to himself as possible, and Elcano wished he could have made such an entrance, envious and jealous this fool had stolen his thunder.*

Elcano could stand this no longer. '*You speak for the courts, I presume?*'

'*I speak for Spain itself, Señor Elcano. As the court-appointed official I am authorized to gather all facts of this expedition, and every detail, every grain of sand, every splinter in the surviving ships is to be accounted for.*'

'*So you are taking over this interview from Transylvanus, I presume?*' *Elcano was bold and direct, and losing his patience.*

'*No, but Mr Transylvanus has a vested interest in your adventure, and he works not for the court, but with it,*' *the diminutive official said.*

The room remained silent enough for them to hear each other's breathing.

Elcano broke this silence. '*Coming back here was a difficult time for all of us. This much everyone in the room knows. I had to wrest control of the ship to rescue it from Carvalho's incompetence. His poor navigation guided us way off course, and he even used three female slaves we acquired on the journey back as his own personal harem! In any case, I am willing to lend you my journal.*'

'*It is not only our pleasure, Señor Elcano, it is your duty to do so,*' *the official smirked.*

'*I will pore through any writings you may give me, gentlemen. But I have to wonder the fate of the slave interpreter*', *Transylvanus' eagerness betrayed any pretense of objectivity he portrayed earlier.*

Antonio Pigafetta wrapped his arms around his body, able to do this due to his bone-thin frame. '*No one knows what really happened to him. When we escaped, we did not see him.*

'*We only saw the visage of death looming upon us. A sharp, dark visage launching spears at us. He could have been killed by them, or become one of them. Who knows? We can only make wild guesses.*'

'*Perhaps he made his way back home to Malacca,*' Transylvanus added. '*But if he did find his way home, would he be truly at home? He has the scent of Spain and Portugal on him, even his own people may not welcome him. What would he be coming home to?*'

The official interjected curtly, '*Bah! Enough of your poetic ramblings, Transylvanus. Who cares about what happened to some slave.*'

'*He was no ordinary slave,*' Pigafetta chimed in. '*He was more than a slave or an interpreter. He was everything to Ferdinand Magellan, yet he meant nothing to us. He survived the fall of Malacca. Survived a decade alongside Magellan, even survived the battles he fought with him, while Magellan himself perished.*

'*When he comes home, he won't have much of a home to come back to. Malacca is still under Portuguese rule, and when he returns he will have risked capture all over again. He might know this already. He might decide to travel the region and never lay his eyes on his homeland ever again. He has no ties to anyone now. He is a rover, a wanderer, a nomad. He is a free man, while all of us in this room are slaves to a royal inquiry.*'

Everyone in the room lowered their heads, looking upon each other with accusing stares. The air grew thick with desperation.

They couldn't wait to leave each other's company.

PART FOUR

APRIL - MAY
1521 A.D.

(LAST SUPPER)

22

Life was fragile. Human lives were suspended like glass high above, waiting to be dropped. Some broke in minor ways, while some shattered into infinite pieces, and spread across like sharp, fine sand.

Enrique did not know what he was right now, except for the fact he was bleeding. His wounds hurt, his arms and torso were wrapped in white cloth to hold the blood. His body burned but he felt he was freezing, his forehead matted in sweat.

The Trinidad was a dead ship without the presence of his master. In all their time at sea Ferdinand Magellan's movements seemed to give the Trinidad life.

Now that he was gone, all Enrique could hear was the sea, calling out to him. The waves faintly caressed the hull the way a mother might caress a child's forehead when he was ill.

Enrique wiped the memory of his mother off his brow, shivering as he walked to his bed. Before this he made sure the door of his master's bunk was locked. He grabbed a blanket, wrapped it around himself and lay down.

His shivering created a rhythm that calmed him enough to close his eyes. He saw not darkness but memories, dreams, imaginings, a whirlwind of images that solidified into the face of his real father, fading into distance as a soldier grabbed his father from behind with so much force his father faded away. Enrique called for him then saw his new master.

Young Enrique looked up to be met with a bearded man kneeling down in front of him, and felt the man's hand against his cheek, his fingers felt like waves rolling against a ship's hull. The boy wept a little less, and a calm and gravelly voice spoke to him in a language he did not yet understand. It calmed him. He felt the shackles being unchained then those hands were on the boy's shoulder. With his free hands he wiped his tears and looked up, into Magellan's hard eyes that belied a passion and caring that hid beneath his pain.

Today, there was nothing to calm Enrique. Both his fathers were gone. According to Magellan's will, he was free, but there was still much to consider after his death. Who would take over, and what would the Armada do now?

There was a knock on the door of Magellan's bunk, they were calling out Enrique's name, but he chose to ignore it. But the door kept on banging so loud as though it were banging against his skull. He finally stood up to open the door, if only just to make the banging in his skull go away.

'We need you, boy,' it was Barbosa, bitter from too many things. He had lost a brother-in-law, and needed something to hit.

'I am no longer bonded to any of you,' Enrique told Barbosa.

'No longer bonded?' Barbosa scoffed. 'You are still slave to this expedition.'

'Not according to my master's will. It clearly states that I am a free man upon his death.'

'You think you are bonded by the words of a dead man? We still need you to speak to the locals, to talk our way out these lands and continue to the Moluccas islands.'

'I am no longer a slave,' Enrique reiterated. His blanket dropped to the floor.

'You are still a slave to me! As the closest relative of Magellan on this side of the world I speak for him upon death. Although your master is dead, you will still be bonded to us. When we return to Spain you will continue to serve my sister. And if you do not go ashore, we will drive you out of this Armada, and you'll suffer the same fate as Cartagena,' Barbosa spat out this rant.

Yet, Enrique still said nothing, both men now at a stalemate. Enrique turned his back, about to close the door but Barbosa's hand held it.

'Who do you think you are,' Barbosa said.

'A free man! I am a free man! I am no longer bonded to anyone. Not you, not any man in this fleet. I am slave no more!'

Pigafetta sneaked in a peek, and Juan Serrano joined him a second later.

'Oi! Garoto. Know your place,' Serrano stepped in. 'You are still a slave, and if you do not obey us, you will be whipped, you stupid, idiotic, fucking slave.'

'Fuck this,' Enrique shoved his shoulders against both men, exiting the ship.

Barely twenty steps out, Serrano placed his hand on Enrique's shoulder. 'Where do you think you're going?'

'Where I go is not up to you anymore,' Enrique kept walking.

'Oh but it is, Garoto, it is,' Barbosa had caught up with him, placing his hand on Enrique's shoulder.

'This conversation is getting old. I am a free man,' Enrique slapped Barbosa's hand off his shoulder, but Serrano pulled him from behind. Enrique countered this, twisting away and pinning Serrano to the floor. 'I am free!' Enrique kept yelling, his forearm leveraged against Serrano's neck. 'None of you helped and offered aid when Magellan was outnumbered. All of you just hiding in your ships as they slaughtered him. I reckon you wanted him dead!'

Enrique was caught unawares when something knocked him on the back of his head.

He awoke to discover himself tied to a chair in the cargo hold, footsteps circled around him, then he felt a fist against his cheek.

'Freedom,' Serrano said as his knuckles cracked against Enrique's cheekbone. 'Fool,' Serrano smiled at the bloodied nose. 'There have been meetings, and they have decided to appoint me as the new commander of the Armada. You're under me now, *puta*.'

Enrique spat out blood, but he felt no pain. He saw only darkness in his future, because he had none. Barbosa untied him, his rancid breath whispering in Enrique's ear, 'Can't damage the merchandise too much. Beatriz would be displeased.'

Barbosa pulled him up, while Enrique spat more blood. 'You are making a mess of this ship. Clean that off the floor. I'll speak to you in the morning.'

Less than an hour later Enrique had caught himself with a bucket and wet rag in his hands, wondering how he got this low. He wiped his own blood off the floor, recalling Barbosa's instructions to carry supplies in and out the store bunk while they planned their new leadership, the best way out of here, and the new routes that would lead them to the Moluccas spice islands. The chores provided a perfect opportunity to find some ample time to slip out and speak to Rajah Charles.

23

Rajah Charles wiped his tears while his wife consoled him. 'I was willing to offer him reinforcements. Maybe then he might still be alive.'

'My master made his choice,' Enrique lamented. 'Now that he's gone, I seem to be less free. He was a good man, in spite of all his flaws. I hope people see that about him.'

'I do,' Rajah Charles said, rising up from the floor on wobbly feet, almost losing balance before Joanna caught him. He took a step forward and placed a hand on Enrique's shoulder. 'I have seen your master's greatness first hand. And I can see your plight now, Enrique. They wish to keep you in their service, even if you are no longer bound to them.'

'They are greedy. I reckon they will not stop until they take your riches. On the other hand, Lapu-Lapu will soon come for you. Now that my master is dead, he will want to take his revenge on you for siding with my master.'

'All this talk has done nothing but increase my appetite. Join us,' Rajah Charles said, catching Enrique off guard.

'No, my lord, I can't be away from the ship for too long.'

'Invite your crew to dinner two nights from now. A farewell before they leave. I shall present your people a gift for your King. And perhaps I can discuss with your new leaders a safe way to navigate to the Spice Islands,' Rajah Charles paused, thought hard about something. 'When they are gone, I will deal with Lapu.'

'Don't forget, though, of the things your Spanish sailors have done against our girls,' Joanna said.

'They are the daughters of many of my men. Your people violated them in ways we do not accept. They were girls, not yet women. You think us savages, but even we have our limits. Perhaps you are guilty too, but for you I'll turn the other cheek,' Rajah Charles said, his tone final.

Enrique understood, nodding as he turned to leave, but not before saying, 'I will try my best convince them.'

'Good,' Rajah Charles nodded. 'Come with me.'

Enrique walked along the shore with Rajah Charles, his head low, constantly bowing to hear what the old ruler was saying. They stopped and the Rajah looked up at the young man, then averted his gaze to the wide sea.

'If I could cry an ocean for him, I would,' Rajah Charles said, thinking about Magellan.

'All the seas cannot contain my tears,' Enrique told him. He wondered how long it would be before they would look for him. The expedition seemed to have done exploring, they were in a nothing place in a nothing land with nothing left to invigorate their spirits.

'I appreciate these stories you have been telling me, Enrique. About your fleet's journey here. But you have told me nothing about yourself. How did a boy from Malacca come to be with the Spanish?'

Enrique sighed and took a deep breath. The breeze grew colder, and he reckoned it dried the tears forming in his eyes.

'I was just a boy when they took me,' he began.

'One last farewell, before we voyage to the Spice Islands,' Enrique paused for effect, his lips broadened to a smile. 'There will be women.'

'And more of that rice wine,' Pigafetta presumed.

'You will be drowning in it, Italian,' Enrique remarked.

'When you get older, you might learn the value of restraint,' Pigafetta warned him, thought of the women on the various islands, their nude bodies, the strange ways the islanders mated, and of the recent battle, of blood and death, the memories enough to compel him to say, 'No, I shall restrain myself from this invitation. I shall have better use of my time in this ship.'

'If you insist,' Enrique nodded, turning away from the Italian's bunk. The next steps he took were heavy, though with guilt or regret he wasn't sure.

'You don't think you're leaving this ship again without an explanation?' Barbosa stood in his way, demanding an immediate answer.

'All of us are invited. I am simply relaying a message sent by the new Christian King,' Enrique looked at Barbosa in his eye, a tactic he knew to use when telling a lie to make it more convincing.

'I find it rather curious that you had the time to speak with this Rajah Charles,' Barbosa circled Enrique, but the interpreter stood his ground.

'I am fulfilling my duties as you and our new commander Captain Serrano have asked. I am still the liaison between the tribesmen and us, am I not? My chores on the ship are done. I am making myself useful, and chose to ask the Rajah what he might need. He wants to congratulate us, and gift us with things we can present to our King when we return.'

'If there is deception at hand, you will suffer the same fate as Quesada and Mendoza,' Barbosa warned him.

'Don't kill the messenger, my lord,' Enrique snapped, wanting mostly to hide the gruesome images of the aforementioned men being drawn and quartered back in Patagonia. 'Rajah Charles' motives are pure. And he sincerely expressed great regret over the death of my master Magellan. This is the least he can offer. If there is nothing else my lord, may I continue inviting the others to dinner?'

The banquet house reminded Enrique of something his old *kampung* used to have, a wooden structure with dried coconut leaves as its roof. He almost felt like he was back home. The table was long enough to hold a considerable feast, one that was already laid out before them.

Laying plates on the table were the Rajah's handmaidens, dressed in tops that revealed their bare shoulders. From the way the men at the table eyed them, it seemed they wished the ladies would bare more than just that.

The maidens circled the table with their bodies growing more luminous as the sun set, they lit candles that hovered around the house, their streaks of light reminding the men of beautiful fireflies in a faraway Eden.

They wondered if the women tasted as good as the food, but the sight of women seemed more familiar than the food laid out before them. Some of them took the chance to touch the maidens, their hands landing on whichever curve they could land on.

Rajah Charles sat at the head of the table with pride, and close to his side was Enrique, who had been asked personally by the Rajah to sit beside him, away from the twenty-seven Spanish guests in attendance.

This did not sit well with Duarte Barbosa and Serrano, and even Carvalho, who whispered his doubts with the other men. Everyone at the table seemed to be skulking, enjoying the sight of the maidens but not the air of festivity itself.

The candlelight cast but the best kind of shadows that highlighted the maidens' best features, making the length of their eyelashes seem longer than they were, their noses sharper in sculpted shadow, its glow radiating against their skin. It was hard to tell if it was the candlelight or the maidens' own skins that illuminated the dinner hall.

Enrique could not deny the maidens were beautiful, but he was not in the mood to enjoy them. He was still weak from the battle, he had too many thoughts fighting for attention. His eyes reeled and caught sight of Barbosa and Serrano. What did he know of them? Of anyone? Does anyone know the depths or heights in each person's soul? Everyone seemed to be a world unto himself, with their own horizons and sunken treasures to be unearthed.

For Enrique, reading Magellan's journals were archaeology. He had been reading them since he was a boy. He knew would no longer be able read them. The pain of his master's death was still raw, an open wound yet to heal. He ran his fingers along the stubble beneath his chin. He had not shaved since his master died, and contemplated growing it into a goatee.

The hall was rising in chatter, with the foreigners speaking amongst themselves while Rajah Charles' people were more cautious in their presence. Carvalho decided to slip out of the dinner, and a few others followed, returning to their respective ships. Rajah Charles' men noticed this, but the Rajah gestured them to ignore it. He had to look the part of the jovial host. The chatter in the hall was punctuated by the clinking of wooden cups filled with rice wine.

After a sip, Rajah Charles stood, a giant turtle rising after a long slumber, awoken with alcohol in his veins, hands on his hips, his dark tattoos sinuous in candlelight, coming to life as only dark things in dark places did, snaking across his shoulders with sinister intentions.

Enrique took this as his cue to start paying attention. Joanna implored Enrique to follow her husband's lead, and he did, listening intently to the Rajah's speech.

'Fellow friends,' the Rajah began, and Enrique limped forward, resisting the fever and the sweat matting his forehead. He finally caught up, and began translating, though he felt his allegiance to Barbosa and the Spaniards diminishing. 'I am glad that you have come here to this banquet hall tonight. I am honoured by your presence. I know that this gathering tonight is not one without consequence.' Rajah Charles paused. 'Many have died on both sides, and I only have myself to blame,' he said contemplatively, with barely a hint of regret in his voice.

'But this dinner is not one of mourning, and neither is this dinner one for consolation. No, my friends, this dinner is one for celebration. To the ones who fought. To the ones who died,' Rajah Charles raised his wooden goblet as high as his short stature would allow.

The guests raised their goblets and drank their wine, aromatic and strong, and intoxicating. Enrique drank along with them. He glanced at the corner of his eye and caught Rajah Charles and Joanna whispering to each other. There was a glint in Joanna's eyes.

The guests slammed their goblets, then held on to their necks. Instead of revelry there was a cacophony of gurgles before falling to the ground and Enrique threw his own goblet, knowing they only had seconds left at best.

'What did you do,' Enrique took a step forward toward the Rajah and his wife.

'This is for my girls,' Joanna told Enrique. 'This way they will never lay a hand on any of them again,' she said with utmost satisfaction as the other bodies fell to the ground.

Enrique couldn't believe he was defending the Spaniards and Magellan right this moment, but he remembered, 'Magellan told you that the men making love to newly-converted Christian women was a lesser sin for them. I thought you agreed.'

'They were just girls,' Joanna seethed.

'Didn't you yourself say your people planned to take over my kingdom, much as they did your homeland?' Rajah Charles cut Enrique and Joanna off.

Enrique could do nothing as the other guests writhed on the floor, gasping their final breaths. 'That was merely hearsay! I only said if! If they were going to take over the kingdom it would be bad for you, but they have no plans for this, not this time. They just want to get out of this place.'

'But I cannot take your word for it, even if there is the faintest chance they might take over us, we have to act on it. Your men may leave, but in the future others might come and do the same thing. I have to show the world we will not tolerate losing our freedom. This is but the first act, Enrique of Malacca. When the time comes, we all, myself and Lapu-Lapu included, shall act.' Rajah Charles raised a hand and pointed it at the other Spaniards still standing.

Enrique saw the men looming from the corners of his eyes, stepping forward, machetes raised. There was the ring of iron chiming in the air.

Duarte Barbosa stood and threw his cup away, and pulled Serrano aside, almost not believing their luck they were still alive for now.

Enrique yelled for the soldiers to stop.

Barbosa ran from the banquet, and Enrique leapt onto one of the Rajah's men that tried to chase after Barbosa.

'Traitor!' Serrano yelled as he ran out the banquet hall. He was relieved to find the ships there by the shore, and called for the men to get the ships ready.

Enrique was this close to having the business end of a blade gut him, when suddenly a knife landed in the man's back. The man fell and Enrique stepped back, and tried to process what was happening. He still couldn't believe the dead bodies, sailors he once knew seconds ago now covered in blood and decorated with half-twisted faces frozen in horror. The floor of the hall was red where light could catch it, fading to black in the darker corners of the hall.

The smell of blood outside was masked by the salt-tinged sea air, but inside, the odour of blood was magnified by the stale air. Barbosa stood rasping at the end of the hall, cursing the bastard Serrano who ran ahead of him.

'I am sorry,' Enrique told Barbosa.

'You're welcome,' Barbosa snapped, itching for another knife to throw. Another man with a machete ran toward him and he raised a forearm to protect himself, but soon his arms got cut, and he felt the broad blade enter his kidney. His eyes were wide as he looked upon the man who had become the death of him. The blade slid against bone, and there was a minor hiss of air as the blade exited Barbosa's body.

Enrique could hear those not yet dead by the poison being cut down, an equation of blade and bone that equaled blood, and final rest.

Juan Serrano ran to the Victoria. The moon above him was high and the wind whipped against his face, tearing at the tips of his shirt and collar. Arrows whistled in the air and hissed upon piercing the sand. Serrano dodged the arrows, he was lucky for only this brief moment, until—

An arrow grazed against his thigh, dropping him on one knee.

'How many,' Enrique wondered. 'How many must you slaughter until your taste for blood is satisfied?'

Rajah Charles and Joanna did not answer, as though they were savouring the carnage. Enrique then heard Serrano screaming. The ships, still anchored began to roar back to life, a mad scramble of sailors loading cannons and lighting them, cannonballs booming into the sand spreading it in all directions, Serrano saved by the cannons, and his pursuers, not so lucky, blown off the ground, not all of them with limbs intact.

Once the cloud of sand cleared the men from the Victoria and Trinidad appeared with muskets.

'Hold your fire,' let me on the ship, Serrano looked back, and saw two more of the Rajah's men slowly flanking him in the distance.

'What happened to everyone,' Pigafetta cupped his hands around his mouth so he could be heard all the way from the Trinidad's main deck.

'They're all dead,' Serrano yelled.

'And of the interpreter,' Pigafetta wondered.

'He's inside. I reckon he conspired with the Rajah,' Serrano told Pigafetta.

Carvalho pulled Pigafetta aside, and gave his own orders. 'Do not take any boats ashore. I want us to remain masters of our own ships.'

'*Bastardo,*' Serrano shot at Carvalho. 'If you leave me here, I will be killed! May the Lord God bear witness to your deception Juan Carvalho!'

There was the slash of a blade against neck, cracking like tidal waves smashing against breakwater. Serrano's blood receded into the sand, and the wind howled to announce his death.

Carvalho gave the order to release anchor, and Juan Elcano reiterated the order to the Victoria's crew, and the Armada de Molucca left the shore, leaving behind Juan Serrano, the man that was to have taken command after Magellan's death, and Duarte Barbosa, and, though they would not admit it on any records, they had also left behind their most valuable asset.

Antonio Pigafetta was loath to admit in Enrique's absence communicating with any islanders henceforth would be a challenge. In his bunk he pulled out one of his journals, filled with detailed summaries of his personal translations of the Sugbuano and Malay languages. He hoped it was enough for all of them. Pigafetta once only thought of Enrique as a slave, but now had begun to see him as more. Enrique had earned Pigafetta's respect. He had spent plenty of time with Enrique over this entire voyage, months starving and working together, especially together caring for the late giant Paul, and spending time drunk and merry together with the tribal women, and he would be lying to himself if he said he didn't feel betrayed by the slave, and did not want to believe Enrique had any part to play in the slaughter.

In the banquet hall the bright candle lights dimmed. The thick air stank of blood, and Enrique breathed in the last breaths of the dead men for them. He looked around the room for a blade of any kind, concluding they were all out of reach. He resorted to his only weapon, opening his mouth, hoping his words would cut deep. 'So you plan to kill me last,' Enrique sought both the Rajah and Joanna's eyes.

'Both of us should thank you,' Raja Charles told Enrique in deliberate, measured breaths.

'I don't need your thanks,' Enrique made a beeline for the door, grabbing a Spanish sword that lay on the ground. He noticed a man guarding the exit. He kept going, keeping his sword guarded until the last minute, springing it out in a circular arc.

The guard tried but was too slow to block the larger sword. Enrique swore he could hear the blade crack into the bones of the guard's chest. The guard must have thought this to be a dishonorable death, one not worthy of his skills.

Enrique pulled out the blade, and without it as leverage the guard fell face smacking against the wooden floorboards. He faced Rajah Charles and Joanna and charged at them, the pointed tip of his sword accusing them like a large metallic finger. 'Maybe the Spaniards were right. You are savages.'

'We all are,' Joanna told Enrique.

Enrique didn't want to accept this statement as fact. He turned away, disheartened for the human race. Duarte Barbosa's body lay before him just a few steps away, the body twisted enough to reveal a wavy wooden sheath that held a wavy blade. Enrique ripped the sheath off Barbosa's belt before leaving the hall for good.

He ran to the beach, his boots digging deep into the darkened sand. The waves rumbled from deep beneath the sea as though the sea was angry. Serrano's body greeted him. He couldn't escape the crimson sand surrounding Serrano's body, and he knew he couldn't escape the men who had killed Serrano.

Enrique raised his sword, watching as the wind pulled at the killers' long hair and loin cloths, revealing their palang-enhanced genitals beneath. He breathed in the air, felt cleansed and reborn by it. He waited for Serrano's killers to come.

They flanked him from both sides. He dug his sword into the sand, twisted it so the blade's broad side could act as a scoop. The killer on his left rushed toward him. If he planned this right . . .

One step, two steps, and by the third step Enrique raised his sword out of the sand, splashing sand into the attacker's face.

His fatal flaw was trying to wipe the sand off his eyes. Enrique had been in many battles, but he was no great fighter. Even then he knew when was a good time to go for it.

Enrique's sword entered the killer's gut, and out through the spine. The other killer ran toward Enrique. He had no time to pull out the long sword, but felt a wavy wooden sheath tempt his thigh. He relinquished his grip on the long sword, pulling out the keris.

It swiped at and sawed the other killer's chest, rising until it stopped at the neck. Enrique pulled out his keris, and the man before him could only hold his neck, unable to stave the blood gushing through his fingers. He dropped onto the sand.

Enrique took a few steps back, gasping and regaining control of his breathing. With the wind and the waves his only company tonight, he ran to find a boat.

24

Enrique ran through the night, leather boots sinking into the soft sand with each step. His soles began to tire and hurt, and he decided the boots were holding him back. He threw them aside and ran along without them, feet touching the sand, toes caressing the fair grains.

The sand comforted and calmed him. He thought about everything streaming in his head. He had no ship to go to, no masters to tie him down. The cool breeze enveloped him while he checked his belt, searching for the keris.

He removed his blood-stained shirt, and the cool breeze gave way to the sun. The sun's light revealed an overturned balanghay, a small islander's boat. He checked its condition, reckoning it to be sea-worthy, meaning to him that it would not sink. He turned the boat right-side up, the effort made difficult without the aid of other men, leaping into the boat once it began floating on the water. With the oars on the boat he started rowing.

When he was far enough away from the shore he felt for his keris again, unsheathing it, recalled how his real father said, 'When you stab an enemy in the heart, you have to make sure he stays dead.' He thought of the Spaniards as well, and of their crossbows, and of Lapu's arrows. He threw his keris, imagining it was an arrow. It landed ringing against the boat's bow, but didn't land where he wanted it to. He tried a few more times, once almost falling off the boat to catch the keris. Finally, it landed where he wanted it to. He grinned, holding back a laugh. Good enough for today, he reckoned. He kept his keris and carried on rowing.

It was hours later when he arrived in Mactan, where his master Magellan had died. The sun was riding higher now, casting the first shadows of doubt beneath his eyes. He reckoned he was not alone.

In the dark of night they were almost invisible, though in the rising light of day he began to hear them, the rowing of their oars, the determined way the oars acted like blades cutting into the water.

Rajah Charles and Joanna did not want him alive. He wondered if Rajah Charles would keep Joanna as his sole wife as the Rajah's new religion only allowed for monogamy. He knew Magellan had made many concessions to convince Rajah Charles's entire tribe to convert, but he figured these things had become inconsequential. He would never see these people again. He didn't even know if he might survive this day. He dared not look back, knowing the oncoming boats were lurking close by.

He made sure again that his keris was on his belt, though knowing it was there only made him more anxious. How many more people would come and hunt him? How many inner demons would haunt him for the rest of his life?

He set his boat on the far side of the island, away from civilization, intending to make his entry quiet. He ran to the village, and sensed his stalkers the way an insect might be buzzing in his ears. He couldn't see them clearly, yet he knew they were so very close. He stopped and turned to face them. They flanked him on opposite sides.

'Our Rajah has an offer,' the one on the right began. 'Come back to us. Be one of us. You can show us the foreigners' ways, and there is so much we can learn from you.'

'And if I refuse?'

'Our Rajah did think you might say that,' the stalker said. 'And he prepared an answer.'

The other one motioned toward Enrique, machete held high, and he knew his keris, short, wavy, was no match against something as broad as a machete.

Timing was everything, and to buy time he leapt forward, sidestepping to confuse the stalker, hiding his keris. Timing, he reminded himself, revealing the keris at the right moment, on the edge of a split second.

When the second stalker saw it, his eyes widened. He knew it was too late to stop it. The wavy blade sawed into his gut, the entrance inelegant, blood flowed thick, a red deluge parting from the wound. He stumbled back, but Enrique held him, remorseful he had to kill this man.

Enrique let him fall after a moment, the man screaming as the wavy blade exited his body. The sand absorbed his fall, as if ready to accept his death.

The first stalker, now wiser, began running in a strange loop, a seemingly awkward stagger, muscles of thighs and calves taut as he paced two steps forward for each step that Enrique took back. If this is how I die, then so be it, he thought.

Enrique yelled a battle cry, sweat running cold down his brow. He raised his keris, resigned to a painful death. He ran forward, but the stalker stopped dead in his tracks, wincing in pain, tried to grab the thing stuck to his back, fingers desperate to pull it out. Within seconds his faculties began to fail him.

He took his last breath, the light in his eyes fading as his knees gave way, his face splashing into the sand, a ceremony of embarrassment.

Enrique faced his saviour, tall, lean, wind sweeping his black locks aside before circling to caress his face, muscles twitching like living marble, developed from years of battle and hard labour. 'I guess I should thank you.'

'You are almost good in a fight.'

'I have left Humabon,' Enrique said, eyes darting again to his rescuer.

'And your friends?'

'They have left me,' Enrique said this eager and loud.

'You are free now. Free to roam the world, but yet you have chosen to come here.'

'Perhaps you might ask me to join you, like Humabon did.'

'I have no need for deserters, and I have no need for any more slaves,' the man told Enrique.

Enrique wiped the blood off his keris before sheathing it. After a brief moment both men locked eyes. Since Enrique left Rajah Charles, he had done nothing but fight. He wasn't sure if he needed to anymore. 'Si Lapu-Lapu, Chief of Mactan, apologies are in order, my lord. Since they are going to kill me in Sugbu, and since I am not needed here, perhaps we can help each other out. If you help me leave these islands, you will never have to see me again.'

'If you are asking for my help, you will have to earn it,' Lapu warned Enrique.

Enrique lowered his head, knowing the gravity of that statement. He wondered if this was worth fighting over, and decided, yes, it was. 'I've been thinking,' he began.

Lapu motioned forward, inching closer.

'About what you told me at the battle where my master died.'

'A slave has no allegiance to anyone,' Lapu said, feet firmly planted in the sand.

'Once my master died, I wanted to kill you. But now I see no point in violence, in death. I have seen so many die in my life. My father, my village. Yours. My adopted people. One day we are friends, the next we are enemies. But today? Our value to one another has yet to be decided.'

'Perhaps you want to thank me? Or just want my ships? There are traders on the other side of the island. But you'll have to get through me first.'

'So, fight you to get to the traders? I guess I have no choice.' Enrique raised his keris, tightening his grip around the handle.

Three men appeared behind Lapu-Lapu. He raised his hand to stay them. 'There is fear in your eyes. Do me a favour, and let me kill you before breakfast.'

'Come lunch, I'll be far from here,' Enrique stepped forward. The moment he did, his chest felt heavy, his head felt light and he reckoned Lapu-Lapu felt no such conflict, just a surety of self.

The experienced warrior knew the value of patience, of how the split seconds in a fight were all it took to tip the outcome of battle. True enough, Enrique rushed in first, his pretend patience worn off, snapping like brittle bones. Lapu dodged his three strikes with ease, without fear.

Enrique turned impatient, afraid, angry, all at once. In his mind he imagined clashing blades, but he really had been reduced to a game of tag, one in which he was about to be 'it.'

He tried all he could, but Lapu just took a few steps back.

'The problem is,' Lapu kicked to Enrique's gut as precursor, 'that you fight with your hands and mouth, not your entire body. Your shoulders, your hips, even a twist of your own neck can help do wonders in surviving a fight.'

Enrique's feet slid along the side, stumbling like a crab against the sand with a lot of fight left in him. 'You should listen to your own advice about not using your mouth.'

'Come then, what are you waiting for,' Lapu-Lapu laughed, taunting Enrique.

Enrique gained his second wind now, striking forward with his keris. Lapu dodged to the side and with his free hand Enrique smacked his open palm to Lapu's face, moist sand and a gust of wind enveloping itself into Lapu's eyes.

Lapu almost clawed his eyes out. Enrique tried to get closer, but even now, Lapu's senses were honed, blocking each strike Enrique tried to take. The last strike slashed at Lapu's forearm, but it was seconds before he even bled, and the warrior showed no signs of pain.

Both of them paused to regard the next step in this fight. Enrique continued attacking Lapu on his weakened and bleeding forearm, and Lapu couldn't stand any more of this.

With his good arm, he struck, like a swinging log, at Enrique's neck, fingers and thumb tightening against his throat. Enrique had to think quick. He threw his keris weakly in Lapu's direction.

Lapu caught it with his bleeding arm and it distracted him enough to loosen his grip around Enrique's neck. With both hands free, Enrique struggled to free himself off Lapu's fingers. The fingernails had serrated his throat as it loosened. Enrique fell sideways stumbling, gasping for air.

Lapu, instead of continuing the fight, stood there, laughing. He eyed his hands now devoid of a neck to choke. He smiled as Enrique held his keris in a way that was as languid as the ebb and flow of the ocean's waves.

Enrique's brows remained firm, narrowed and pointed, his eyes tinged with curiosity. 'What are you doing? We going to fight or what?'

'Not unless I want the rest of my arm cut off,' Lapu raised his bleeding arm, fingers trembling from the loss of blood.

'So,' Enrique dragged the word a tad too long for effect, 'when do I get my ship?'

25

The port was shitty and makeshift next to the ones he had seen in Portugal and Spain, but it would have to do. He knew he had to be grateful for this chance, glad that he had help.

The fact he almost died to be face to face with this ship wasn't lost on him. The man who brought him to this ship, he now had a complicated relationship with.

The way life turned out, one day someone might be an enemy, the next an ally.

'This ship, good as new, Sri Lapu-Lapu, just for you,' Idris told Lapu in makeshift rhyme.

'And how many heads will roll for this ship,' Lapu wondered.

'As many heads as you wish,' the Arab trader said.

'Sula still thinks you cheated at that gamble you made with him.'

'You travel around, I see,' Enrique said to Idris. Enrique did not care how Lapu acquired this ship. It was not important now.

Enrique was adorned in a crimson vest, and a pair of loose slacks. Draped over his shoulders was a fur coat, another import from an eastern trader.

He nodded toward Idris, then at Lapu.

'The food is in the bunk. Enough to last you a week. Two, if you ration. There are a few villages a few days out if you need supplies,' Lapu told Enrique.

'I'll keep that in mind. But it may be best to avoid the routes the Spaniards may be taking. I don't wish to meet them along the way,' Enrique said.

'Where will you go,' Idris wondered.

That was a good question, Enrique thought. He eyed the ship before regarding Idris. He gave a nod to Lapu-Lapu, with the same kind of respectful glance one might give to a wounded tiger.

There was a wrap of white cloth around Lapu's forearm, hiding the long cut Enrique gave him, with hints of a brown-red scab near the elbow. The healing itched madly, and at times Lapu felt it was easier to bleed than to heal.

Enrique just smiled at both his companions. He boarded his ship, too large for one man. Its sails functioned the same as a European ship, but they seemed sturdier with battens running from left to right all the way up to the mast's highest point.

The Chinese called it *zhoū,* or sailing vessel. Enrique walked along the ship and studied it.

Flashes of his life spent on boats, which he reckoned he spent half his life on, flooded his mind. He recalled being forced to learn how to man the sails, pointless at first though it would prove invaluable now.

He set the sails down and felt for wind direction. He waved goodbye to the last two friends he would ever meet for a long time to come.

Lapu waved at him with his good arm, running his fingers across the scabs of his other arm, resisting the urge to scratch.

Enrique turned away as the wind caught the sails. He pulled the lashings away from the ballasts, and moments later the *zhoū* sailed the open sea.

> 'When he comes home, he won't have much of a home to come back to. Malacca is still under Portuguese rule, and when he returns he will have risked capture all over again. He might know this already.'

Mactan receded from view. Up ahead was the open sky, the wind beckoning him ever forward, the sun bringing rays full of hope, the sea wide and endless, an infinite blue world full of possibility.

The future was his. He felt the wind caress him, long hair billowing in all directions, each chaotic strand whipping against the other.

'He might decide to travel the region and never lay his eyes on his homeland ever again. He has no ties to anyone now.'

He thought back on his life, of all the things that happened to him the past decade. The fall of Malacca, wondering where Sultan Mahmud Shah was now. He thought of Albuquerque, of his mother and siblings and bowed for a moment to offer his father a silent prayer, and did the same for his master Magellan. He raised his head, his belief in God's greatness validated by the expanse of the open sea.

He ran his fingers through his hair to pull it all together, gathering it into a knot.

'He is a rover, a wanderer, a nomad. He is a free man . . .'

He laughed, because he was finally free of bondage, of the past, free to create his own future.

It had taken a decade, but he finally chose to acknowledge his real name, not Enrique the Black, but the name his real parents had given him.

The name tasted strange and foreign on his tongue. He mouthed it gently to get used to saying and hearing it again after all these years.

Saying it built up something within him. He wanted to scream it out, and ran to the *zhoŭ's* bow, perching himself loosely, almost losing balance, though his sea legs kept him from falling.

He called out his true name, and it echoed forward in time, into distance, into history.

FINIS

Glossary of Terms

Keris	Malay dagger with a curved, or wavy blade.
Panjak	Assistant who assists in the making of a keris.
Supit	Clamp to hold a hot keris during its making.
Bendahara	Admiral, at times a Sultan's advisor.
Balasan	Retribution.
Retribuicao	Retribution. See balasan.
Mahout	Elephant tamer.
Fidalgo	Nobleman.
Retiro	To retire.
Garoto	Young boy.
Mulatto	Someone with white and black ancestry, or a brown skinned person.
Saudade	Melancholy, longing.

Afterword

The more I write, the more I come to discover that writing is indeed, literary archaeology.

Characters exist in your mind long before you come to recognize and get familiar with them. All a writer has to do, is dig up the layers of the character, and find out who they are.

They are alive. They are part of you. They are living, breathing people, with their own lives, and they have given you the opportunity to look deeper into their lives, to let you tell their story as best as possible.

In the case of Enrique, he is for the most part a real, historical figure, and the people around him were filled with all their flaws and faults and idiosyncrasies.

The good thing about writing historical fiction based on real people is that the facts are right there, in many, many reference books, and by the people themselves, through their journals.

The bad thing, however, is that history doesn't always give you the drama you want. I have taken the liberty to change things here and there, but I have kept up with the spirit of people like Enrique, Ferdinand Magellan, Antonio Pigafetta, Cristováo Rebelo and all the rest.

I would like to thank Antonio Pigafetta, for his adventurous spirit, for chronicling this great adventure, for letting history know the pains he and the Armada de Molucca went through, and for surviving to tell the tale.

I would also like to extend my thanks for Mr Harun Aminurrashid for writing *Panglima Awang*, for being an inspiration, for inspiring me to do better.

Also not forgetting Hidayah Amin for writing *Malay Weddings Don't Cost $50*, the book that had just one mention of Enrique the Black, that lead me to the journey of writing this book you now hold in your hands.

Writing this book was hard, in that I did not have the free will to write what I liked, that I had to verify my fiction against fact, and that ultimately, I had to decide what to include and what not to include.

For this matter of inclusion, I would like the extend my greatest thanks to Laurence Bergreen, sir, with your book *Over The Edge of the World* being the most detailed account of Magellan's voyage. I took a lot of detail from your work, and I would like to simultaneously thank you for your research, and to apologize if I took too much detail from it. Either way, many thanks for your work, Mr Bergreen, this book would not have been completed for a long time if not for your research, and I hope you like the fiction I have to offer.

I also hope you, dear reader, enjoyed reading Enrique as much as I have enjoyed the labour of writing, and re-writing it.

Keep reading, keep supporting the arts and literature!

Sincerely,
The Author
April 2020